Chronicles of Sophron Book Two: TheSaviour Squad

Written by Martin Poirier and Alibast Page

© 2025 Sophron Arts Productions www.sophron.art

Martin Poirier

Born in 1974, Martin Poirier is a professional screenwriter and author based in Quebec. He began developing the fantasy world of Sophron in 1996, as both a personal mythos and a creative playground merging philosophy, metaphysics, and narrative experimentation. After years of world-building and narrative refinement, he established a definitive model for the universe in 2012.

This novel, Chronicles of Sophron: Book One – Seamus Chron, is the first installment of the Babel War trilogy, a sprawling metaphysical epic where ancient truths, cosmic forces, and the fate of souls converge.

Alibast Page

The approximate time of Alibast Page's emergence into our world would place his birth around 356 BC. His essence first revealed itself to Martin in a series of vivid dreams between 1996 and 1999. Troubled by the wars, greed, and injustices ravaging Earth, Alibast took it upon himself to awaken Martin's inner vision — guiding him toward the hidden structures of reality.

Together, they began shaping the world of Sophron — a mirror, a warning, a sanctuary. Yet both remain bound by the subtle pull of the Greater Councils of Zendoria, whose designs may stretch far beyond their own awareness.

It remains uncertain whether Martin and Alibast are the true authors of these chronicles or simply characters in a story that was already unfolding before them.

For Cognitia

Presenting the Singularities

Seventy-two layers form the foundation of the pluriverse — inner universes inhabited by existential beings: Dreamers, Authors, echoes of soul and self. Each layer, shaped through axioms, weaves the tapestry of Sophron.

At the heart of this grand design stand Four True Layers — the Four Singularities.

A soul traverses these Singularities before the Great Entities open a gate for it to incarnate anew.

Matter, under the Ocorsur Barbelo. These realms give rise to solidity: rock, ice, bone. Existence unfolds through intricate neural depths. Quantum laws entangle realities into blooming certainties.

Life, under Archeus. Beyond matter, consciousness awakens. Biology becomes architecture. Life dreams itself into being, lifts its gaze to the stars, and dares to wonder.

Thought, under Logos. In these realms, perception stretches across twelve dimensions. Matter becomes mist, life a memory. Pure thought remains — forming cities, beings, and civilizations spun from reflection. Certainty sharpens into the edge of knowing.

Void, under its eponymous Ocorsur. Here, all is absence. Inhabitants — hollows — breathe blankness. Thought dissolves into silent echoes. Yet through that blankness, quantum stirrings begin anew. And matter returns — birthing again the seventy-two domains of Sophron.

Consciousness emerges from a constant flow of information, reflecting as it is reflected. Where consciousness arises, a soul is born.

Singularities serve as thresholds — liminal borders between states of awareness. The Great Entities of Zendoria watch over the flow of axioms as they shape realities and dreams. To guide this flow, they bestowed gifts upon the enlightened, known as Walkers.

– **Glancers** manipulate axioms within the essence of consciousness. They walk among souls.

– **Mancers** manipulate axioms within the world and its illusions. They walk among matter.

– **Dancers** manipulate axioms within the Veil that separates beings and worlds. They walk among borders.

– **Fencers** manipulate axioms within the vast field of possibility — the multiverse of *what if*. They walk the walk.

And you, reader, will follow the stories — told by both Authors and characters. You, too, will walk among the Great Entities, their wonders, and their choices.

Prologue:
Kitana hates her job

Nempty died? What about his beloved daughter? Kitana kicked
the small wall that blocked her feet. She felt this close from exiting
ultimate hell! Bummer! Stuck in here for another hundred
thousand years. She sighed, just as a new call came in. She quickly
flushed it and walked away. If her coach hears that, she'll pretend
that some technical issue occurred. For the caller, at the end of the
line, that's no big deal! Just a hundred years' worth of waiting to be
serviced, right?

Like she cares. the dwarf presented her only way out! It's not
as if she could find another dumb client with all the resources that
she needs to escape this lousy job. She looked at the photo pinned
to her cabinet, and she sighed. Will she visit her friends again?
Jamieson Fairfield, that clumsy bird. Nathan Lord, the handsome
pirate, and Alicia Light. she misses them. She grabbed a picture
that showed her aging mother, a week before Kitana's abduction.
Tears filled her eyes, knowing very well that her beloved matriarch
now belongs to a forgotten past. If she escaped, however, she
might wander around the worlds, across the possibilities between
the Below and the Beyond.

Discouraged, she summoned a game of Sennet from her orb computer. She concealed her head under a cap that showed an Ultra Police logo, and she tried to avoid interacting with a bear-shark humanoid who doubled as her supervisor. He walked down her aisle, ensuring that everyone worked diligently. Could she have saved the merchant? Perhaps Nunc, the impaired personality that Jamieson shares, rescued Nempty's soul. She could contact her buddy, but the thought of him, probably, saying: He's dead,

Mr. Kennedy. terrorized her. Maybe she did this. The blood is on her hand. She pushed his android daughter to her oblivion as well. Double homicide. "No way!" she shouted.

"Angel Kitana? Is everything pristine, angel Kitana?" The bear-shark inquired.

"Of course, nymph-chimera Damloot. sir. sorry, I just had a difficult call."

"Would you want me to sign you on a break?"

"No, no. I'll take the next one, thanks."

The annoying manager walked past her. She sighed and put the picture away. How can she escape from this hell? "Welcome to the Mancening Network, my name is Claudio, how can I be of assistance, today?" That voice got to her nerves every time. How can he enjoy slavery like that? "Sure, my lady, I can visualize your essence, as we speak." he added. "If I understand you correctly, you tried to visit a limbo produced by your ex-boyfriend. It wouldn't be polite of me to ask why, so I will just give you instructions to exit his new wife's basement."

Why is he so good at his job? Damn. Claudio annoyed her! Oh well. let' take another call. "Welcome to the Mancening Network, my name is Kitana, how can I help you?" She sighed, before miming a gun shooting at her head.

Journey into the Hourglass: **Thirteen**

After Martin and I published the first book in our initial Sophron trilogy, I stopped hearing from my co-author friend. On Avalon, Seamus Chron became a phenomenal sensation. We sold over three million copies, and I gave half of my share to charities. Martin bought himself a mansion, and he burned half of his wealth on alcohol and prostitutes. He even fell in love with a fairy escort who never reciprocated his affection, but she gladly accepted his gold coins. When I confronted him with his self-destructive behaviour, my friend turned evasive and changed the topic.

"I'm happy that we're a success in your home world, Alibast.

"He would confide in me, before tears would struggle to leave his eyes. "But on Gaia, I'm still an unknown, failing author."

"Don't rush your luck, Martin." I comforted him. "You'll get there in time."

It appears that editors in his home world couldn't understand our concept of a pluriverse, with characters breaking the fifth, sixth and seventh walls. Avalon, on the other hand, shelters quite a vast population of awakened souls.

Three years had passed since our success story smashed the news. I never enjoyed the spotlight, so I offered it to my dear friend. He went to every interview, smiling on various photoshoots, appreciating his Avalon-based celebrity. I stayed home, exploring my adopted domain of Alibastat to care after the life, over there. I would often visit my cottage to sit down and brainstorm ideas for our second book: The Saviour Squad. When the spotlight faded, Martin returned to his apocalyptic New York residence. How should we start the sequel? He texted me, one morning.

Let's write Erato's story. I replied.

Come on, Alibast! Romance? No way!

I felt his disillusioned wounds, but I knew I was right. Yes, way! I retorted. Give it a chance, Martin. We need a strong character to lead our heroes in the best direction, against Marduk.

After a few back-and-forth arguments, he finally agreed.

Chapter One:
Erato in Love

When you pay attention, on sunrise, Hydaspes becomes a surreal postcard. A colourful scenery with strong hints of opaque tones. It feels as gloomy as it projects auras of joy. Three stars gravitate over its domes, producing prismatic lights against a flamboyant nature. An outsider would look down on that world as a mesmerized child surveying a snow globe. You will see oceans of poppy flowers. In fact, this realm rarely gets any tourism, but its potent ingredients will attract many drug cartels. Perhaps the Great Muses chose this layer to spend their eternity into because of the hallucinogenic that roams freely.

When we last observed them, they had gathered in a remote garden. Embracing their time after time, like a sweet ordeal, they had espoused shapes of metaphors. They expected an infinity invested in dreams and thoughts, but a maverick sibling reappeared. Melpomene convinced them that treacherous gods forced the muses out of their rightful ownership over humanity's brilliance. Now, a war was coming. Storms of bleaker tomorrows hit the front door. They left their layer. Except for Erato. She stayed behind, knowing very well that a greater battle waited in the dark.

She walked among the red flowers, projecting the image of her sweet smuggler. Ever since she imagined their romance, his essence inhabited her innerverse. Clouds gathered over her head, like a morning before the flood. She wore the clothes of a princess, with an armour that looked more esthetic than practical. Long brown hair floated in the wind, as her black robe hardly concealed the curves of a well-fed aristocrat. She underwent that walk towards uncertainty for three months, now. If only she could travel beyond the Veil and join her kin. But, no! Erato has an agenda of her own.

She stopped at nightfall, summoning a cave that would shelter her from the wandering dangers of her world. The rain dropped on top of her makeshift home. She fell asleep, smiling as she drew through her mind's eye the shape of her lover. Where are you, my overprince? She sighed. The next morning, she would be back on her long trek. No path appeared to show where she went. But passion never followed a straight line. In the night, she focused on her objective: Protect Seamus and William. Bring them to her promised one. She must ensure that her overprince, her sweet lord Nathan Lord, shelters them.

She established her camp near a floating stream. A forest stood out in the far horizon, and the Disney-looking princess summoned a fire out of her orb. She sat there, projecting the essences of those heroes that need protection. Drawing the inwards of a school, Erato imagined stairs. A lone pit of light shed despair above a depressed Alexandra. She observed her books, remembering that William and Seamus disappeared. One of them died, and the other won't listen to reason. Her BFF annoyed her, lately. Victoria would beseech sympathy, but Alexandra has better stress to attend to. She should ignore her.

Erato projected that scene against the raging flames. She calmly observed the two best friends forever, discussing in the school's corridor.

11

"I saw Seamus, the other day!" Victoria insisted. "He was begging in front of Foufounes Electriques."

"Did you talk to him?" Alexandra inquired. "Alex, come on! I'm not his mother."

"You're stupid, Victoria!" Alex left the stairs, bitter. Her BFF didn't know how to respond. But why?

Why bother? Victoria abandoned her spot and walked towards the library. If only she understood how to be there for her loved ones. Is she a bad friend? Did she push these two away?

Erato could feel the wounds deepening into Victoria's soul. Maybe she found, in her, the key to this main story. Everyone thinks she's an idiot. She heard some students calling her an obsessed wanker! She's French! She has no idea what that word means, but obsessed? Oh no! Not! Never! It's all the others who fail to tend to her needs.

The rain gave way to a storm, but Erato remained focused on her mission. Why did her brother assemble the whole family to wage a war? *Oh no, Melpomene*, she thought. This trilogy is about love. There is so much growth that these characters deserve to gather. There's no need to be bitter. The Great Muse of tiny intentions smiled. How funny would it be if her siblings found themselves on the opposite end of her discovery? They should have let her speak, back at the council. They thought so little of her, but she'll prove them right.

She closed her eyes and imagined a letter. The paper floated in her mind, and the quill dove into a bowl filled with ink. Dear lover. she felt. The last time we met, we were having a drink at your favourite nexusnaos. The Lonesome Crone! Guess what? When I said I was into pirates, I lied! I just wanted to sleep with you, that evening, but I did drop a hint. if you got it, and you'd like to see me again, you'll Jind a glancer by the name of Seamus Chron.

No need to express anything more. Allow cultures to collide, and stories fall short. Her beloved pirate did impress her, that night. Maybe there's a tomorrow for essences that just let go and smile when appreciated. Whoever writes this novel must have suffered, she realized. Hopefully, they considered her presence in the greater scheme of events. If not, oh well! The Great Muse of romance never dreamed little, anyway. She'll be in her pirate's arms by the end of the trilogy.

Chapter Two:
Seamus the Hobo

Have you experienced deja vu? It only lasts for a fraction of seconds and it's a sensation close to vertigo. Your consciousness processes what it perceives as a distortion of reality, but it's almost a flash. It could be that your mind travelled back in time for a split instant, revisiting what then seems like a resurfacing memory. Or it could be that your brain froze for that moment. As you exit this millisecond in paralysis, you get the impression of reliving a truth that you experienced in the past, or in a dream. The latter explains this phenomenon that science came up with, while probabilities clash.

As I completed Ishtar's training, I witnessed deja vu regularly. Perhaps my intellect developed in such a manner as to freeze easily, sending my mind into the great unknown. Perhaps my affinity towards Sophron prompted my oversensitive brain to all these layers and possibilities. Whatever the reason was, it didn't alter the fact that my sleep paralysis also got more and more complicated. I went through my first out of body experience a week after Ishtar parted. It wasn't my ghost leaving my flesh, as we were told, but rather my consciousness retiring from a vehicle.

The anxiety that comes with a change of environment can put pressure on your mind. Especially when it finds itself away from the muscles and nerves that it calls home but then again, we find no nerve, flesh, or muscle in the Logos layers of Sophron.

How can beings exist and evolve in these realms? How can their presence be projected if no hormones or glands exist to secrete chemicals for a brain to paint some sort of reality? My first out of body experience came fast, actually: I left my skin, I panicked, I regained it. The second and third felt a bit less stressful. And by the fourth and fifth, I began to get the hang of it.

My initial impression? Don't quote me on this. I'm not a philosopher or a scientist. I consciously thought of it as an entity of its own. Within the layers of Archeus, awareness depends on a living organism to project itself onto the world. When matter fades, and thoughts step in, it becomes a more complex essence. In the life and thought quadrants, with Archeus and Logos, pure energies form beings. Matter leaves the equation to produce anything, so life relies on a different process. If my understanding stands correct, then reflections will nourish life and it will feed ideas, creating a mutual system.

Three months passed since I quit home to reside in the streets. Begging turned into a second nature. I only did so to prove a point. I would use my gift of insight to get into someone's mind. I know I could corrupt myself to control that person; a virtuous glancer would never do that. I realized that money doesn't define existence. This concept profits those who harness it, and it enslaves them. If you need an exchange of symbols to be sheltered, eat, and feel pleasured, then you miss on a much greater universe. I can't control axioms. I can't create myself a club sandwich out of thin air. I can sense an individual's mind, and his or her life experience. I can get into a conversation where we can see what I can provide to his or her growth and inquire for a meal.

One morning, I sat on the sidewalk with a new sign that read: Ask me about your future for $5. I perceived how many people felt insecure and highly emotional, and most of the time I would notice their past remains as shallow as their projected dreams. Sometimes, wounded souls would try to corner me into a conversation, but for five bucks I won't spend an hour patching back a broken heart. Teach me sounds like the right answer, in my opinion. Someone with a failing life can feel belittled or further challenged. I once sensed this guy's universe, as he exited a strip club. He was thirty-five, handsome, but not at peace with anything. He slept with few women without paying in return. He realized that hanging out at the same venue would allow him to get closer to certain regular strippers, and he could seduce them with his income and sweet words.

It worked for a time, and with some individuals, but he found himself entrapped in a web of monetary resources and emotional dead ends. Teach me would bring a key out of this complexity. He seemed too proud to consider using it. The love of his life dumped him after she heard about the messages that he sent to one of the girls. He thought she experienced some sapiosexual passions for him. The stripper enjoyed his wallet, and she did everything she could to appreciate his mind. She could only stare and drool. Teach me, she could have said. That love of his life could as well, but the philosophy major assumed that her solitude felt better.

"Why five bucks?" he asked me.

"Your sweet Maria still has sentiments for you. Do you want her back?" I replied. He walked away, and I cursed my gift. The day went by oddly. I collected twelve dollars, fifty cents, which wasn't enough for me to buy weed and food. I had to change my strategy. Connecting to strangers wasn't an easy thing to achieve, especially since my powers only worked when I could sense fear or pain. The frightened or wounded bystanders weren't generous. I could beg the old fashion way, but I will develop my glancing skills until I can reunite with Nempty and find William.

16

I would often end my afternoons at the Molson Park, in the Rosemont neighbourhood. Away from the bigger crowd of homeless folks, as they would rather stick to the Gamelin Garden, downtown. I could easily blend with the mass: young families, students, couples in love. Sometimes, I could find a lost soul among the flock and wire my essence to theirs. I then travelled through their layers and possibilities until I could branch out and fly in the mind of another spirit in agony, within their inner universe. This is how I came to realize the depth of the pluriverse we share. Trillions of beings scatter their forms all around the seventy-two worlds of Sophron. I perceived floating brains in Hell. I saw gigantic spiders with the face of a squid spitting a membranous web, in a tropical jungle of Patagonia. And I viewed fairies, exactly how you would picture them from your childhood memories, ladybug wings over a blueish feminine-like body, buzzing in Hydaspes.

I forgot the name of the fellow I connected with. The sight I had of the universes inhabiting him overwhelmed me. I overlooked his life story that brought me there. I had never seen mountains the size of a continent, standing straight against the background of a lavender sea, populated with whales as big as a football stadium, their head resembling that of a hippopotamus. Phaeton-Tiamat shines with a yellow sky, but when you go to the next world, down the Archeus-Logos quadrant, you get to Arcadia, and there, the firmament turns indigo. When I woke up from this sight, I could notice the grieving old man walk away with the picture of his late wife. Did I connect myself to him? Anguish, it seems, is a much better emotion for my gift to operate. Only, while fear allowed me to scan a person's essence, and decipher his or her existence, sorrow brought a direct gateway into the marvels of Sophron.

17

What if I could find William's parents and use their grief to locate my way to the mancer that I must protect? Or would this represent a lack of ethics on my part? I had no idea where he resided, but I know that Alexandra visited this place a few times. I didn't want to exit my isolated existence and return to my old friends, so I had to uncover a different strategy. I knew where Alexandra lived, and I'm certain I could begin my search by sleeping nearby. She's with her mother, in a small apartment, in Outremont. It's a wide street that stretches all the way to the Mount Royal. All the buildings looked alike, brown bricks, stairs that twisted and ended by the sidewalk, a modest balcony at the second floor, and a bigger one underneath. Alexandra's house comes with a Quebec flag against her mom's window, and a Canadian one on Alexandra's. I stayed there until sunset, as I approached her room. Her light was on. I saw her silhouette undress. why can't I have some far sight gift instead?

I left as I arrived, incognito. I connect to people's thoughts, I visit their inner universe, I help them with their love problems, and I can't even help myself with mine. This gift is a curse. I might as well go sleep under a bridge.

Journey into the Hourglass: Fourteen

Martin and I didn't expect to find ourselves in our creation. When we sat down to draft Seamus Chron, we aimed to keep the storyline simple: Seamus bullies William. Then, William commits the unforgivable. Seamus regrets his action. Ishtar guides him across Sophron, and he battles Marduk. Having two writers with different spins on life may not have helped, but our characters often challenged us. They rarely followed the narrative structure we planned for them.

I came up with the student personae. Having Plato's apprentice on board allowed us to add a creative layer. We would have them recount certain chapters as though they took over our job as authors. That character developed a mind of their own, discovered means of travelling across the possibilities, and they found their way under our Dreamer. Now, they assist Martin with his writing.

Meanwhile, our protagonists stayed in their rogue alley, doing as they pleased. Marduk gathered his armies, Nempty bargained with Sekhmet over Indra's soul, and our heroes strayed from our initial ideas. "You should connect to my essence and become a character in our book." Martin suggested. "You want me to create a paradox?" I objected to this idea, looking away from my laptop while Martin's face took one third of a floating box, on the screen.

"Just act as his mentor, or something." He would follow up with this brilliant eureka moment. "Just, I don't know, teach him how to use his glancer gift. And you can evaporate."

I gave it a long night of thoughts, a quick in and out: just me appearing in Montreal, like a homeless man. I would introduce him to his powers, and that would bring him back under our narrative. "All right." I conceded.

I connected my consciousness onto Martin's essence, and I travelled within his Sophron. I unearthed the chapter we had written, where Seamus roamed the streets of Montreal. I bought a poutine at a nearby food truck, and I waited for him on a bench. Martin's idea worked. Seamus found me asleep, and our souls instantly intertwined.

Following this event, Seamus' curiosity guided him towards the storyline we had previously envisioned for him. I didn't anticipate Marduk's agents locating us, though. That fight with Marvin pushed an unexpected layer of complexity. We couldn't figure out how to untangle ourselves away from this. Our only option involved writing more chapters that personally implicated us in our own novel. But the Chronicles of Sophron tells the story of Seamus and William! Not Martin and Alibast!

Chapter Two:
Arguments

"What do you mean, William was murdered?" the author snapped. The student shrugged, as they looked around, maybe searching for clues. No! Martin figured it out. His character self-inflicted his demise. How could he explain this to an ancient Greek visitor who, few hours ago, only existed in his mind? Exhausted, a bit annoyed, the blonde man sat on his black chair and brought both his hands to his chin.

"Look!" he calmly let out. "Alibast and I have this structure, right? Three books, and now we should be at the beginning of number two. By the end, a drastic reversal feels much needed. That development represents a major turn of events. We can't bring it this early in the storyline."

The guest pondered over it for a moment and smiled. "Do you really think you write those books?" they asked. Martin's sigh shouted from miles away. The student continued: "Two days ago, I was in Athens. My mentor taught me how to use the orb. I felt those lives burgeoning within my soul. I was creating something! Like. a god, do you understand? And now, the crystal ball brought me here. Why?" Martin couldn't bear looking at these eyes losing their mind.

"It's far beyond both of us, student."

"That's not my name!"

"I know. I don't need to know your name either, trust me. We should just be strangers."

The visitor turned their sights otherwhere. The lungs strapped to the walls breathed with great difficulty. As though a perfect Sherlock Holmes, the Greek guest observed every corner of the wide chamber. Hints of blue light shone from behind the gasping organs. This, obviously, belongs to someone else's storyline. Unless they appeared in the real world, far from Plato's cave, and now they had to reconnect with a very unusual truth. "Did you realize that your room has flesh?" they asked the author. Martin rolled his eyes, annoyed. "Did you skip school when Plato instilled rhetorical questions?" he inquired. The student frowned. Maybe they tried too hard in front of someone much more powerful.

"I'm sorry, teacher." they whispered. Martin felt good about this. He sighed once more and returned to his laptop. "It's okay." he reassured his guest. "Come here. We need to figure out how Seamus Chron gets his awakening." The disciple smirked as well and sat next to their new master. "I had an idea about that." They smiled. "Like, what if Alexandra secretly loved Seamus, but she could never tell him?" Martin felt abused. In his mind, Alexandra hates Seamus. "I don't like that." the poet murmured. "Hear me, master." they insisted. Oh, Martin enjoyed this flattering word. "This fantasy thing is about self-discovery, right?" No. why? Oh. Martin turned to face his guest. "Did Alibast send you?" He inquired. The student had no idea what the author just said.

"I'm sorry, what?" they asked. "Self-discovery, my ass! It's conquering our fear!" he insisted. And why did he even bother? Martin returned to his creation and simply instructed: "Sit back and watch me, okay? Seamus is about to tackle Alexandra. You'll see what I mean." He typed the following words on his computer:

Chapter Three:
What I Mean

I waited for about an hour until all the lights went off.
When I closed my eyes, I could perceive Alexandra's presence,
slipping under her covers. I could sense her grief for our mutual
friend, but from my vantage point it seemed rather faint. I opted
for a fine solution: I would silently climb my way to her balcony,
and I would meditate. As I placed my foot on the first stair,
however, the wood squeaked in such a noise, I thought I would
wake the entire neighbourhood up. I stood quiet for a long
moment, looking at her window to assess the bad omen. The light
remained off, so I dared putting a second foot onto the next step.
SQUEEEEEAK, I heard, and I sighed almost as loud as the old
staircase complained. This is when I closed my eyes and thought
of means to use my superpowers to fly, or something, but it just
didn't work like that. I tried to connect myself to Alexandra's grief.
Still, it felt very dim. So, I had an idea. One of those bet all on red,
ideas. I walked all the way up, making the stairs screech so much,
her mom turned on her light and went straight to the door. I was
hoping Alexandra would have walked by her window, but I guess
my ball landed on black. "Can I help you?" the mother asked me,
in her very rough French-Canadian tone. "Is Alexandra there?"
I inquired. "It's ten o'clock, kid. Go home!" she complained.
"It's fine, maman." And there showed up the angel.

Fortunately, her mom was okay with her daughter having a late-night visitor. Aren't we adults, after all? Even if only on paper, and for a few weeks at that. I entered their apartment with the timidity of a stray cat begging for warm milk. They had only two beds, a living room and a kitchen. The long corridor took us from the main door to the back, but I saw every other chamber on my way there. "Do you want a beer?" Alexandra asked me. I could sense her mother's presence next to us. But the elder chose to read a book on her mattress and leave the children alone. "I try to stay sober." I replied.

"Why? Drugs and booze took you to the streets? I thought you were better than this, Seamus." Not really drugs and, well: "It's complicated." I conveyed. "Okay, well I'm having one." Alexandra opened the fridge and grabbed a bottle of Maudite, this highly alcoholic beverage that begged me to share a glass with her or two. "I'll join you, then," I smiled.

We ended up in her room. She put on some soul music that seemed to nourish both our wounds at the same time. "Why did you come here?" she asked me. I binged down a big sip of my beer and I sighed. "I'm trying to link with William's essence." Honesty always stands as the winning policy. She gazed at me with such a strange look, it unsettled me for a moment. "And how can I help you with that?" I had to keep the frank talk, sincere, up front, and truthful, so I explained to her: "When I connect with a strong emotion, my powers work better. Usually, fear or grief. So, I was thinking that, maybe, if we make love tonight and, I don't know, you could scream his name or something. I might have a chance to." the beer felt cold on my face.

"Get out!" she growled, softly.

The fear in her seemed so pronounced, I could immediately see her entire life. I just had to tune myself with "GET OUT!" She insisted. I left her bed in a hurry, but a name stood out of nowhere, in her mind, in the most profound layers of her being. "Okay, I'm sorry." I apologized, as I tried to buy some time. "Do you think you can walk on an old friend, at a time like this, and bring on this bullshit? I thought living in the streets would make you humbler, Seamus Chron, but you are still the same douchebag, asshole, filthy human, no! You're not even human, damn it!" Emerald! I felt that name. Damn, she knew her, after William moved back to Montreal. He nested in Toronto's outdoor, with Emerald, Alexandra's childhood friend. They kept in touch via Internet, and "Is this what you told Emerald after she started stripping for a living?" I let out, bluntly.

Alexandra froze, and the fear felt even stronger, now. "You know her? You've seen her? How is she? Damn it, Seamus, how come you know her?" I could view the entire picture, loud, and clear.

"I don't know her, but William told me." She was confused: "Told you what?" she murmured. "You know? The stuff!"

I sat on her bed, and I inhaled a deep breath, then I explained: "She knocked at this very door, when you were both twelve, and she said: We're moving to Toronto. You didn't believe her, at first, you thought she was joking. Emerald and you have been the best of friends since kindergarten."

The fear shone free, more tangible, now. I may have hit a nerve. I calmed down further, and I added: "Her father earned a promotion at his job, but it meant for the two of them to migrate. She lost her mom at eight years old. A car accident took her away. Her dad never remarried. You comforted her then, and you did every time something difficult made her cry."

Did I just imagine all this? Maybe I acted as some powerful Internet Entity, creating viruses to make her buy my anti-virus software. Or maybe not. Let's continue: "You were always the strongest of the two, but Emerald wanted to be like you. She met William when he was homeless in Toronto, and she fell in love with him. She worked as an escort; she was only sixteen.
He wanted to save her from this awful place and job. He decided to get out of the streets, go back to school, get a good job, so he could one day marry her and give her the life she deserved.
She connects you to him, and you helped him get into our school."

Silence, before she grabbed my glass of beer, and she binged it. "Did William tell you any of this?" she asked me.

"William and I, we weren't in the best of terms before his death. He would never have opened to me to this extent."
She remained skeptical, poured me a new pint and kept mine.

She sighed and asked: "How come you know every detail?"
I grabbed the glass, I sat next to her, and I explained:

"Because this story haunts you down to the marrow. I can sense it, I can feel it, almost as if it were my memories."

She cried, she smiled from behind her curtain of tears, and she whispered: "So, you bluffed when you said you wanted to make love, or something like that?" What a safe time to lie. I nodded.

"I guess I just wanted to provoke this intense emotion, so I could better project my, let's call it, spiritual investigation."
She kissed me on the cheek and beamed her lips further with light.

"Do you think you can find her?" she inquired. "Emerald?"
I asked. She whispered: "Yes, or just tell me she's okay."

26

When I closed my eyes, I perceived every possibility that could have happened to Alexandra. In one of them, she runs away and joins Emerald in Toronto. Alexandra becomes an underaged escort, dominated by the same street gang. She dies of an overdose.
In a different possibility, she and Emerald successfully escape this mob and run back to Montreal. I couldn't locate this possibility.

If she had joined her friend in Toronto, then Alexandra would have been the one falling in love with William. This might explain why she became so protective of him at our high school.

Following down that possibility, I saw Alexandra and Emerald returning to Montreal, but still working for the same pimp agency. They got a job, at seventeen, for a strip club in Mirabel, one hour north of Montreal.

"Did you dance in a strip club?" I had to ask. She looked at me with a cringed frown. "Of course not. My mom would kill me on the spot."

I still can't view the truth, the narrative that unfolded in our reality. This alternate universe, however, felt the closest to ours. I focused my power farther into that storyline:

Outside influences, linked to Emerald's gifts, deceived those employers. They passed as two adults. When Emerald turned eighteen, she broke free from the street gang that hired her.

Alexandra also left that mob and got a job in a convenience store. Emerald earned a gig at L'Olympe, in downtown Montreal. This strip club exists in the possibility that Alexandra and I currently share! I know where it is. I must find out if she works there. I opened my eyes and kissed Alexandra, on the lips, I don't play around.

"How long has it been since you last saw her?" I inquired.
"Three years." she answered. I reviewed that different possibility's timeline. I pondered over its logic. Emerald left Montreal at twelve. She visited her friend when she turned fifteen, that's three years ago. In our dimension, Alexandra never ran away. In the one I explored, at sixteen. Emerald returned to Montreal, in our reality, and still found that job in Mirabel.

"She's fine, don't worry." I announced. "She works at L'Olympe, on Saint-Laurent Boulevard. You want to come with me?" A strong relief engulfed her essence in full. "I'm not sure if that's a good idea." she whispered. "Why not? Alexandra, Emerald would appreciate meeting you again." She hugged me and cried even more. "Not under these circumstances. Don't mention me to her if you go there, okay? Please! Promise me, Seamus!"

"Okay, I promise." We didn't make love that night either. Oh well, I guess the Dreamer of this story reserves other plans for us or the author above him, or, her, or, whatever creature is writing this novel for your enjoyment. I left her apartment with the same twelve dollars and fifty cents I had when I stepped in.

That would get me one beer and a pack of bubble gum if I were to try my chance at L'Olympe, tonight. Oh, plus it is mandatory that I tip the doormen, and whatnot. These places stand as money grabbers. I can't make myself known as a homeless either, so I must think of something, fast. "Can I borrow your shower before I go there?" I asked Alexandra. She smiled and whispered: "Call me before." she handed me a used smartphone and added: "Text me, send me an email, message, anything. I'll have you cleaned up and presentable." Okay, so I don't look well groomed, I get it! I thanked her and left.

I examined the black monolith she gave me, with a white charger I had to put in my back pocket. She's had it when last she encountered Emerald, three years ago. At that time, Emerald would brag at her best friend about how much money she makes from selling her body to rich old men. Alexandra's fear stood out from the object I kept in my hands. I don't recall having seen Alexandra with that device. She would surf the Web or post selfies with a white cell, at school. I tried to turn it on, but the phone obviously lacked energy. I put it in my other back pocket, and I walked my way downtown.

I revisited the past couple of weeks I left behind, in my mind, in my guts. I relived the struggle I shared with my homeless friend, against agents of an evil mastermind. I wasn't drunk or high, although the strong beer I had with Alexandra got me slightly tipsy. I guess elements made me sensitive. My consciousness pictured itself back in the park. The one who called himself Marvin fought my hobo buddy. That's when I realized how my gift pointed to a much wider array of wizardry. Although, I had a feeling that those powerful beings wouldn't appreciate that magical accolade. How do they call themselves, anyway?

Walkers! I heard a voice in my head. If you wonder, we call ourselves walkers. You, stupid prick, are a binder of souls. Others will craft axioms to manipulate reality.

"Who said that?" I asked out loud. Oh boy, you give me a voice in your memories, and you can't connect the dots? You're way dumber than I thought. I paused for a moment. The object of my current journey across downtown was only few blocks away. "Hobo?" I asked. The inner voice laughed. His name is Alibast. Do you think Marduk is afraid to challenge him? My master killed a Guardian Entity! He did so with his bare hands!

I walked mindlessly for the last stretch. There I stood, listening to a cosmic assassin who tried to end me, only days ago. For some reason, my friend didn't get rid of his consciousness. Did he really survive through my memories? I need to better learn this new life. Can we exist inside someone's mind? Perhaps my gift connects me to a dimension where people's souls flourish.

I stopped behind Foufounes Electriques, knowing that a death metal band plays. Could I find my way to the show? Maybe I could persuade the doormen to let me in. I would have had to convince the stamping guy at the entrance that I could walk up without paying. Forty-five dollars for a ticket sounds expensive. I had twelve dollars and fifty cents.

"You really should give Marduk a chance." I heard Marvin, hidden in my shadow. I turned around, looked at him, and I asked: "You mean the band this time?" "No, you know exactly what I mean." he replied. I faced his ugly visage: still ginger, with vermin amassed across his dirty beard. He had the same bulgy eyes as last I saw him. He gnawed a dead pigeon's flesh and seemed unafraid. I can hardly connect myself to his inner world, and something told me I may have been hallucinating his presence. "Okay, what if I join this Marduk, not the band, you think he can assist me in finding my partner?" Marvin offered me a piece of bloody wings, and I politely refused. He gnawed back his meal and taunted me: "Depends on if you can get your friend to kill Indra for him."

Okay, that's it. I'm not going to help anyone kill my teacher's pet! I walked away. The psycho remained behind me. I strolled faster to lose him, but he insisted. "Don't stalk me, Marvin." I warned him. "Ooh, stalks, he says. He thinks me I stalk, eh? You think you're my lover? Your old man lover killed me, remember? I'm just visiting. And you look after a dead friend too, I'm just, like, I think I like you now."

30

I stopped to face him one more time. His mouth dripped with the pigeon's blood. "I'm not going to join Marduk's ranks! I won't even join that other dude, Varuna!" He interrupted me, before biting the corpse's head off. "I thought you said his name was Alibast." He laughed with a sorry look on his face. "My mission is to be with my friend." I explained. He gestured a little, made the carcass live and fly away. The most disgusting and terrorizing ten seconds of my entire history, but it hardly made me sweat. He saw a bit of distress in my eyes and asked:

"What? I was hungry no more, and I showed my meal some empathy. I'm only half vegan, anyway." I walked towards him, intrigued. "Don't you think eating dead animals is wrong? Or eating city animal raw. They have lice, parasites, viruses!" I lectured him with my most serious tone, as though I suddenly grew some concern over his life. He laughed and sat down with his legs crossed. He looked up at me and asked, in a very solemn voice: "You don't guess viruses they have better things to do? I don't work for them, mate. Now, you come with me to Tir na n'Og or not?" Something felt appealing about the idea of eating a wild bird raw. Especially without the fear of contracting salmonella. Maybe if he had met me before Ishtar, I would have immediately felt the desire to learn his secrets, but the mere concept of seeing Indra opposed by this homeless freak brought me second thoughts. "Sorry. I have to be somewhere else." I told him.

"You won't find him at that strip club, mate!" he shouted, as I made my way towards Saint-Laurent Boulevard. How did he know? Oh, of course, he must have a gift as well. But I wasn't looking for him, over there. He got my essence wrong, or perhaps I felt too strong spirited for him. He saw my puzzled face, and he walked closer. He observed me and smirked. Without even loosening his teeth, he smiled: "He's in a strip club down a dark alley, on Athanor. I can take you there."

It would have been too easy. How can I trust him with this, or with anything? I contemplated him, and I calmly explained: "I'm not searching him, right now." I walked away.

I stopped at the main door. L'Olympe shone in bright neon lights, on a white board. The two goons who looked down at me were Victor and Sinclair. If I were to enter without paying the five-dollar cover, I had to talk with Victor. He's the wiser of the two, and he's been in this business for thirty years. He can tell if a customer is a pervert or a noble one just after asking two questions. Getting to learn someone's secrets through deduction was what he loved best with his job. Sinclair smoked, but Victor didn't. To gain their immediate trust, I had to project the idea of me as a respectable person, and deep down inside, I know I am supposed to act as one.

I took my fifty cents out of my pocket, and I approached Sinclair: "Sorry, my good man, can I buy you a cigarette for fifty cents?" The bulky black didn't smile. He's been at this job for a little less than a year. He's had a tough time trying to convince a stripper to sleep with him. The Taiwanese woman thought better. Pondering over it stresses him, but Victor always brings him back to the light. "What makes you assume I smoke?" he asked me. I had to use a bit of bravado to stay in the game, so I pointed at his bundle of gum. Confused, he didn't think too much about what was happening. He just grabbed his pack of cigarettes and handed me one. "Keep your change, buddy." he sighed, as I grasped the source of pollution and put it straight between my lips. I guess I could talk to him about how he could win the heart of that Asian single mother. She got here after falling for a rock star, a tourist with money and an obsession towards Asian traits. For some reason, I found myself within the calmness that Victor projected. It was as though we both emanated a same tranquil energy, on that same wavelength.

When I closed my eyes to light my cigarette, I sensed that I could connect to his essence, but differently. I didn't feel his life story. I didn't see anything. I could merge my peaceful soul with his. As I would lose my cool, though, I would lose this link. I inhaled a deep breath. I needed fire. I opened my eyes to see Sinclair laughing, as he grabbed his lighter: "You only smoke when you're drunk, tell me." He smiled, and I nodded. He lit my fumes.

I don't really do except pot, and that was out of the current equation. I looked at Victor. He immediately looked back at me. I guess he sensed the same connection. For a fraction of a second, I could induce a feeling of deja vu in his mind, and without even thinking about it, I did.

"Hey, I know you!" He smiled, as he approached us. Then he stopped and froze for a moment. "Nah, sorry, I took you for someone else." I found myself between The Rock and the hard space, so I had to improvise. "I'm the guy who helped when Jewel was harassed." He studied me and asked: "Orphee?" I continued: "I was there!" He smiled and shook my hand. "Yeah! Jewel and Orphee are screwed up, but I love them like a father. They're older than you, though, and that was three years ago."

"I look younger than I am, Victor. Orphee loves Mathias, by the way, she just can't." I spoke too much. "How do you know Mathias? He wasn't there." Who is Mathias again? Help me, universe! Maybe if I could scare the big guy, I could get a quicky? No? One thing kept me from entering this building without paying the cover, and a one ring that would make me invisible wasn't on the menu. So, I looked at Victor with straight bright eyes, and it unsettled him for a moment. I saw his entire life, but the dude seemed so strong, in every sense of the word, that gaze became an arm-wrestling match. For a second, I thought I could subdue him by talking about his mother, and that she died wishing he would have visited her more often.

33

She loved him even when he was in prison for rape and attempted murder. He turned into a wonderful person, after his sentence. But the zen we shared made me realize that he could kick my ass out of this place and ban me from returning. "Mathias keeps coming here because you inspire him." I uttered.

I had to remain quick with my thoughts, so I made up some more lies: "We write poetry together. and we play chess, sometimes." Victor smiled and pondered for a moment. "How do I inspire him?" he asked me. "You both love metal music, but Mathias is more classical. you connect on a same wavelength, but you barely talk to one another. You are all brawls, and he is all brain. Both of you are the same." Victor's emotions transpired: "He said that to you?" he whispered. I had to display my wit, if I wanted to get in, so I smoked my cigarette. It already burned midway through, and I grabbed my powerless device.

"I'll show you." I comforted him. I pretended to struggle to get it on, light it, get on with it. Stupid piece of plastic with a complex set of pseudo-neurons! Maybe I acted like a complete moron. "Your phone is dead, my friend." Victor pointed out. he delicately deposited his hand on my shoulder and added: "Come in, I'll put it on recharge, next to the ATM, and I'll watch it. But tell me how I inspire Mathias!" I sighed, inhaled another sip of my cigarette, like a James Dean that lived, and I pat his back, as he did mine. I smiled: "You only awaken once. Don't miss it." Filled with awe, I could sense that I sealed his trust in my friendship.

He opened the door to my first time visiting a bear-breast bar, and I drooled. The dimmed light showed clients everywhere, it felt like a scene in a busy market. Victor was kind enough to charge my phone, while I checked in my front pocket to make sure my twelve dollars and fifty cents were still there. How many beers will this get me? I'll have to drink them very slowly. It should buy as much time as I can until I fulfill my investigation. A big scene stood in the middle of a very wide room, surrounded by tables and stools.

Chairs filled the place, all around the elevated dance floor. Five poles completed the booby theatre. The metal sticks formed some sort of X. Strippers would come up using a tiny stairway, and they would abandon their belongings on top of the stage, in the left corner. They would then walk around and tease every pole, or they would flirt with the audience with a salacious dance. I sat at the bar, near the back, by the bathrooms, and looked at the gorgeous Asian lady behind it. So small, so cute; I could have grabbed her and toss her in the air. "Can I serve you something?" she asked me. "You mean, other than your phone number?" She didn't smile, so I cleansed my throat a bit and inquired, in a more serious tone: "I'll have an IPA, please." She left with my order, while I dove into the show, eyes only.

All those naked ladies! Did Victor bring me to Heaven? I would turn my head to the left, and there was this goddess of ebony complexion gently getting her big breasts over a client's face. To my right, two blonde ladies shared a portable stage to please a same customer. Butts, thighs, boobs, shoulders, everywhere! And it smelled like a cocktail of perfume, thick makeup and sweat. *Can I move in here?* I thought.

The waitress came back to burst my bubble. She served me a pint and collected her due: "Ten dollars." I froze for a moment. I could give her the two dollars as tip, but I would have absolutely nothing else. On the other hand, it would make me look rich for the duration of one whole beer. I did, and immediately observed around me, scanning as many clients, staff, and strippers as I could to locate Emerald. "Just two bucks?" she complained. I added the extra fifty cents and a cringy face.

35

It seemed unfortunate that my powers don't always provide me with clear visuals, unlike when I projected my mother's past, or my own future. Most of the time, the images appeared blurry or non-existent. I would only get sensations, or something like an ancient memory that would resurface in the most abstract manner possible. Earlier, I saw through Alexandra's eyes, but all experiences came to me at once, so I could only grasp the essential and make sense of all this information overdose. In doing so, I pictured Emerald, I felt her name. Right now, I must investigate the old fashion way: talk to everyone.

Five minutes sufficed before a tall blonde with huge high heels, a G-string and a black bra sat next to me. "Hey, handsome, you've been here for a while." she asked me. "I'm just having a beer and, hmm, I'm looking for Emerald." I explained. She grinned and brushed my hair tenderly. "Oh, you're already with someone?" She inquired. I smiled back and replied: "I don't know, do you think she is around tonight?" I couldn't scan her. I guess she seemed too bold for my power to produce an effect. She stood up and pushed her nipples against my nose. I could smell her perfume, and I could feel her torso applying some onto my face.

She shook her breasts a few times. "I don't know any Emerald, but are you chill for some fun?"

I pulled myself out of this very nice aggression and turned towards the bartender. "Maybe later." I apologized. The beauty acknowledged my rejection and walked away. "You don't have to take a girl to the booths. If you don't feel like it, just pay her a dance at your table." the lovely Asian told me. "How much for a dance?" I asked her. The small lady looked at me and uttered: "You don't go out often to strip clubs." I shrugged, so she added: "Ten dollars a song. You can touch, but keep it civilized."
I nodded, as I realized that my teenaged hormones would tilt and get nothing in return, tonight.

"Do you know if Emerald works here?" I asked.
"Who is Emerald?" Silence. who is Emerald? Then it hit me:
perhaps Alexandra didn't reset her old cell phone to factory mode.
I swiftly took a walk straight to grab the charging monolith: 32%
energy, and that was more than enough, I thought. I turned the
device on as it booted itself. I returned to my beer at the bar.
"Are you sure Emerald is her stripper's name?" the Asian asked
me. "What do you mean?" I replied. She shook her head and
served me a vodka. "I pity you. There, it's on the house." I left the
small shot glass aside as I browsed through the hundreds of
pictures on Alexandra's phone.

So many selfies, and none of them I had seen before. I had to
wonder if she lived as a closet narcissist. On most of them, I could
tell her age: twelve or thirteen. I viewed photos with her mom, at
the botanical garden, some at a music festival. Others captured
with this splendid half-Jamaican and half-Italian girl. If you need
to know how I came to this precise match of her DNA, well, that's
because I had the exact same revelation when I visit Emerald's
essence in Alexandra's mind. I drank a sip of my IPA, as to
celebrate this amazing finding, and I showed the picture to the
barmaid. She looked at it and smiled: "Oh! That's Mystique. She
works three days a week, but only starting tomorrow." Mystique, I
thought, like the shapeshifting mutant. I felt beyond happy. I drank
the vodka straight, and binged down my beer. "Okay. I'll see you
soon, love!" I smiled at her. "Hey!" she insisted. I looked at her,
intrigued, then she added: "What's your beef with her? Are you
with a gang?" Think fast, Seamus, think fast, and don't talk about
your gift! "I was explained that she gave amazing lap dances.
So, I wanted to find out by myself." The Asian lady didn't buy it.

She laughed and expressed: "But you have pictures of her and
a friend on your phone!" And I have photos of her and a BFF of
mine. Yeppers, that I do! Okay, hmm. "Yeah, I'm buddy with her,
hmm, buddy. She, hmm, gave me this phone, and it's her, hmmm,
buddy, and she said she does good lap dances." She sighed and
returned to cleaning her glasses: "Whatever. See you tomorrow."

37

I wasted most of the night wandering the streets to locate a safe place to slumber. On my way there, I imagined a sure plan to gather enough money to buy many beers, pay shots to the girls, and get very intimate with Mystique. I had to find, at least, three hundred dollars. I spent the rest of the night under a bridge, covered with a crappy sleeping bag I saw in a trash bin. It smelled like old piss and vomit, but who cares? I gazed at the most beautiful woman in the world, with skin of caramel, and feline eyes that pierced through the night to steal my heart. She had long black hair, with blonde, silver highlights, it made her a soul sister.

The plan seemed simple: I would go to a busy street early tomorrow morning. I would find a wealthy man, and I would explain my tale. To make sure it moved him, I connected myself to his essence. Rich dudes always look scared when bums approach them for money, and I would visualize something in his past that would make him empathize with my sad story. That can work!

And so, the next morning I left my stinking bed behind, and I walked on Rene-Levesque Boulevard, on the corner of Robert-Bourassa Boulevard. This is where all the pathetic wealthy guys are. My first fish: an old banker. I saw him exit his Mercedes and roam towards me. When he stood close enough, I smiled at him. Sure, I unsettled his peaceful moment with himself. "Sorry, sir. I need three hundred dollars to be with the woman of my life!" The man walked by, as though I didn't exist.

I used the same pickup line with the second one, a bit younger but well attired, and he laughed, then he gave me ten dollars. Only two hundred and ninety dollars away from my goal. By midday, with a similar strategy, I had amassed twenty-five dollars and seventy-five cents. Six hours of begging, non-stop, with my wittiest lines, before I gathered the hang of it. Still, I wouldn't have the resources I need by next week, and I must keep some to eat.

With five bucks, I managed to get some ready-made meal at the local supermarket. I could even borrow their microwave and devour it on my way out. Clients would try to look away or pretend that the nauseous scent my bed impregnated on me wasn't bothersome. I consumed my pasta en route to the Emile Gamelin Garden, reckoning how I could improve my begging skills.

A cold and humid night took over Montreal. I remained on my bench for long hours, thinking I would have to sleep there. I heard some altercations happening few metres from where I sat. I turned around and I witnessed three punks harassing a homeless Afro-Canadian teen.

"Where's the money, Grunt?" the first dealer asked him, before pushing him away. The black boy's fear felt so palpable, I could see his high school crush wave back at him. A blurred vision struck me as though his essence had tried to hjack mine. Gifted? Is he?

As for the three punks, only one had the right negative energy to allow my power to connect. His name? Alejandro Elvarez, twenty-three years old. He joined this street gang at fourteen, always selling drugs. When he turned sixteen, the mob provided him a passed-out prostitute as an offering. This is how he relinquished his virginity. He hoped to lose it in a more honourable fashion. She roughed him up, seeing how gentle he was with her. She wanted to make him pay for all the crimes the creeps rushed on her. I stood behind him, while the others mistreated the poor drug addict.

What did Marvin call us? Walkers! I couldn't miss that chance. I tried to reconnect my essence to Grunt's. The gate remained closed. He's high, obviously, and he doesn't even know that he possesses powers. They just emerge from deep within, chaotically. Alejandro, yeah, that one! He really seemed like an easy target.

His mind opened wide, perhaps because he needed the strength
to look tough. I could sense a time bomb in the making.
He conceals a gun, at the back of his jeans, hidden under his shirt.
He snorted a line of coke, an hour ago. I could feel his hamster
running all over his brain. His chain of thoughts trashed like a
runaway train, freely off tracks. He crashed against buildings,
a zealot juggernaut. I could use that to my advantage. I visualized
our shared environment like a wrestling arena. It pushed me
against that charging locomotive. Hmm. I may need a better form.
The engine pushed its way to me. I turned into a wall of blazes.

Just as Alejandro passed through my flaming shape, I turned
into a haunting ghost, positioned behind the controls and I became
that train's phantom. We stood like one. I coated his body as
though I transformed into a conjoined twin to his consciousness.
My existence floated over that ocean comprised of his experiences,
his greatest fears, and loudest hopes. I could just as easily paint his
sky a vibrant blue, inducing happiness and positivity to his
troubled psyche. That wasn't my goal. No time to save others when
I had to save myself. Charity well organized begins at home.
And I must jump from this train into Grunt's. How can I do that?

What if I could push my way deeper? Can I become him?
Sure, pairing our essences felt like connecting a Bluetooth device.
I only needed to guess the right password. In that case, it was
fixating my soul against his current mood. But how do I become
him? I should try vibrating on a same energy. What populates his
consciousness the most? Suffering? Let's go with cruelty.
That didn't work. I guess it wasn't much of an emotion. Disgust?
We're getting somewhere. Homeless people annoy him. He wishes
them all dead. Oh! Here's one: Toxic narcissism. That trait opened
me the door and laid out the red carpet. I'm in. I'll spare you the
details about his past, but I assure you Alejo is one heck of a
poopoo piece. He sees people as either successful enough to earn
his feet licking, or small enough to attract his disdain.

I wasn't totally in, yet. I connected myself. I opened the door, now it's time to pair our ghosts. I had to find the right wavelength that could match our inner peace. Even when we stand afraid, or excited, it never leaves us. We simply ignore it to give more importance to our overwhelming energy. I put my hands together, and I induced myself in a meditative state.

Hey, freak, what do you want?

I heard someone's inner thoughts ask me, and my host would soon push me away. Grunt? Is Grunt also trying to possess Alejandro? It took me about a minute to reduce my brainwaves until I could sense his. Tinnitus encompassed both our earing environment as though we attempted to match a same noise. I visualized myself behind the consoles of a sound system. If I brought this switch all the way down, our gestalt would ring in a very low tone. I had to adjust a few buttons until I heard with his ears, and no longer mine.

I could whisper to him, but I need to try something. Last night, I induced a feeling of deja vu onto Victor. Perhaps I could do more with Alejandro. My main concern focused on how I would clean myself to look presentable, tomorrow evening. I can't bring my arse to L'Olympe, looking like a homeless. Maybe I could clean myself in a public toilet, visiting a mall, or whatever. What about my clothes? Sure, they aren't bad, but having a gifted guy?

Hardly as easy as it looks, if you asked me. Sure, our souls fit like pieces of a jigsaw puzzle, but how am I supposed to get into his head? Alibast didn't teach me those. He didn't teach me much. He just threw me to the beasts and had me manage to fight my way out. I guess this is what I'm still doing. What if I pushed this imaginative lever on my visualized console? It shines bright, almost with a blue neon light.

"I think he's sleeping, man. Leave him alone!" I heard his friend Pietro plead, loud and clear. Oh? Of course, I know Pietro! We went to kindergarten together. I convinced him to join this street gang. He wanted to live a simple life, find a job in a fast-food chain, grow up to become a taxi driver, like his dad. I easily persuaded him to sell drugs, instead. I guess visiting his tiny apartment in Laval, with huge chunks of hundred-dollar bills made a difference.

What a perfect link. I own Alejandro's soul! He perfectly merges with mine. Except that he had no idea of my presence twinned to his existence. I could, now, resume my take over. Let's try something. "You smell like pee!" I laughed at Pietro. My best friend turned around and laughed. Perfect.

First Intermission:
Kitana finds a Way Out

"Damn it!" she screamed!

"Are you all right, over there?" Kitana heard her co-worker inquire. Before she could answer, Claudio VonGhustHeist stood and snooped from his cubicle, right behind her desk. A tall and skinny golem, Claudio grew up in Ephemoria. Thick glasses concealed his purple eyes, making them look like tiny dots at the end of a tunnel. A small green beard crowned a minuscule mouth. He wore the same T-shirt, with three zombie unicorns slurping an ice cream, since the day he started working. He joined Ghamge's Mancening Network Call Centre on his own freewill, five hundred years after the Gargoyle Entity signed that pact with Tao of Tuurngait.

"I'm okay, dude." Kitana calmed down. "Hey!" he replied. "You can take a break if you want. I'll cover your shift." She nodded and promptly complained: "This is not an existence! You're fine with this? With those chains and answer calls, after calls, of stupid people who can't perform spells or buy neymliss stuff?" Claudio thought about it for a moment and smiled: "That's not exactly what we're doing, Kitana." he explained. "We're not prisoners. We're elements in a bigger machine that keeps Sophron safe from Marduk, or others who could assassinate a Great Entity."

"Yeah, good for you if you swallow that lie. They make you feel like a hero so they can use you and abuse your pride. If they don't need you anymore, you think you'll be a hero again? They'll treat you like a homeless piece of crap! No thanks, not for me."

"You don't believe this?" he wondered. "You think that Marduk didn't kill Enlil-Bastat?" Kitana sighed. "You're so blind. Have you seen the body? Do you suppose an entire world shines, out there? Wthout an Entity to protect it? They're lying to us, Claudio. They created this big crisis so they can manipulate you."

He considered her words for a moment and paused. "Well, if that's what you assume. Our computers link themselves to the Beyond's Singularity in case you didn't figure it out."

Wait, what? The question hit her mind out of the blue. "Claudio, what did you say?"

"Supervisors know. How do you explain Ghamge manages to project our abilities across Sophron, and every possibility?

Every Dreamer is connected to this network, every part of existence, from True Reality, down to the last Final Vanishing. Only the True Singularity can achieve that." Kitana's heartbeat hammered her chest faster, and faster.

Maybe her exit resonates through the Beyond. "Do you think there's a way for my consciousness to travel?" she asked. Claudio couldn't answer, while a call came in and his glancer's abilities felt needed. That's when some interesting phenomenon happened on her screen. Or more precisely, something didn't disappear after she hung up with Lucretia, hours ago. A green pixel flashed at the bottom left side of her orb-computer. It wasn't just an axiom. She felt an essence attached to it. "Lucretia?" she whispered. "Is that you?" The blinks stopped. "No!" she shouted.

44

"Is everything still pristine, angel Kitana?" her bear-shark supervisor asked. "Pristine! Pristine, yeah, dude, yeah, sir, yes! Yes! Sure, of course! Perfect!"

Damloot walked past her again. She looked at her computer screen, trying to figure out what happened. How can her orb be connected to the Beyond if she's not? After all, the company milks her own awakened energy to perform those tasks. The sphere is just a tool.

Or maybe. just maybe. "Hey, Claudio?" she asked out loud, after he finished his call. "It's not the computer, dude." she smiled. "It's us!" That's what seniority in this hell hole will do to someone's knowledge.

Chapter Four:
Marduk as a Guest

Ever since the Hound Lord of Nibiru set foot on Tir na n'Og, his days turned into pure annoyance. He can't stand fairies. The vivid colours filling up the sky, above pastel forests, made him want to puke. Something about this world, something, liberal. What made Sekhmet decide to invade it, anyway? As a guest, he felt greatly encouraged not to leave his room. Whenever he chose to part from his belongings, a tall, blue-skinned fair folk would stand in his way, offering him a drink or a meal. He couldn't do more than five steps before being solicited. "I need to go out!" He protested.

"Sir, we don't recommend that you distance yourself from your quarters." the butler explained. Marduk growled in disapproval.

"Why not? Am I kept as your prisoner?" The god didn't get an answer. Instead, the fairy presented him a plate of stinky cheeses.

"Have you tried our beloved delicacies? I would propose the Flatulence de Brebis. A soft goat gorgonzola aged six months in the stomach of a goblin-whale. The poor animal suffers, attempting to digest this parasite. It's what provides the stench, but I assure you, it tastes better than it smells." Marduk wasn't impressed. His snobbish valet even explained how we gut the green mammal when the cheese has properly fermented for weeks. Contrary to its name, goblin-whales are land creatures, parents to elephants and horses. "You are barbarians!" the deity simply answered. Seeing that he wouldn't be able to escape this gentle guard, Marduk returned to his room. Insisting would probably provoke a diplomatic incident. The panther-goddess of Duat wants him in this room.

She must hold onto her reasons, and he needs to keep her by his side. If Alibast, an architect, dictates his moves, that means the Great Councils of Zendoria may be trying to paint him as a villain. The more he'll insist in his quest, and the more elements he'll provide his opposing designer to defeat him. Maybe Sekhmet keeps him in this room because she knows about Alibast. And why would an author elect to participate in his own storyline? Why would Alibast act as a character in his creation?

"I'll have some of that disgusting cheese with a bottle of wine." he requested.

"May I suggest a plate of winged frogs with that?" the fair man inquired.

"Sure." Marduk replied. "Just, don't let anyone get near my room unless I instruct you to. I need time to process a difficult issue." the fairy servant agreed and turned towards a hole in the wall. There, a burning fire kept some food warm. He prepared a fine meal for the guest, then grabbed a bottle of wine, underneath. Marduk returned to his room, pondering over the existence of this enemy.

Journey into the Hourglass:
Fifteen

I dreamed about a squid, one night. A pinkish moon lit my room, while I smelled the sweet fragrance of white irises. A chilling wind entered from the open window, caressing my naked flesh. I lied down on my futon, and I stared at the ceiling. A lonely fan stared back, spinning slowly and silently. I grabbed my orb, and I texted Martin:

Let's introduce a powerful glancer character! I pushed the SEND button and I continued: I don't know how to name him, her, or whatever, but it should be a squid.

Half an hour later, Martin replied: Why a squid? He asked. I just had a vision. I retorted, and I added: He could be an ally to Seamus. Where are you at with your writing? The video-chat application rang. I answered, only to see Martin as naked as I was. "Dude!" he whined. "I don't trust your visions! You're his mentor, now, anyway."

"We can't be too implicated in our own story, Martin." I lectured him. He thought for a long moment, and he looked away. "Let's put your squid in Grunt's essence." he suggested. That made no sense. "Grunt isn't even a regular character." I rejected his idea. "He's just there to help Seamus with the money he needs. He's a plot device."

"Yeah, and how do you expect him to get that money?"
My friend challenged me. "I don't know, Martin. Should we put a powerful entity inside the psyche of a crack addict?" He smiled, ready to own the debate: "Only if Seamus becomes his mentor." Oh, I like that.

I showed my pensive look. Deep inside, I was sold. "It's like having Seamus' arc on reverse." Words came out naturally, as I continued: "He's the mentor, but Grunt will actually teach him a thing or two."

"Maybe." Martin nodded. "I'll let you write the next chapter, and we'll talk about it after."

I left my bed, and I sat down, naked, behind my laptop. I invited a gentle opera in my room, and I typed:

Chapter Four: The Drug Dealers

"You smell worse, Alejo!" Pietro answered me. We enjoy these puerile arguments.

Chapter Five:
The Drug Dealers

"You smell worse, Alejo!" Pietro answered me. We enjoy these puerile arguments. At years old, we had farting contests. Once, I wanted to win so bad, I left a colourful sent down my pants. I never told him what really happened, but the stench felt enough to declare me a nasty champion. Why am I thinking about the past? I sure focus on the matter at hand, no pun intended. I hate Grunt. He's an idiot.

He doesn't owe me that much, but I make it sound worse. I just enjoy messing with his head. I know he's desperately in need for a hit. I have his heroin in my packsack. I won't give it to him until I had my fun. I can hear my.44 calibre taunting my hands. Stay cool, now. I'm not doing that here. Maybe if I lured him in a back alley? Nah, not worth the effort. Let's just make him feel miserable. A fine rain covered us.

"Where's my money, Grunt?" I insisted. The poor fellow gazed at me. His left eye looked upwards, as though trying to peek at his ear. His right eye kind of looked straight. With his mouth wide open, we couldn't tell for sure. He hadn't cleaned his hair in months, and that old bunny rabbit T-shirt kept stains of dried out puke. "I'll get it, Alejo. just give me a hit, okay?" he pleaded his need. Sure, I could send him down that vomit whole. I didn't feel generous.

I grabbed his shoulders and pulled him under my wing. Boy, did he stink! "Grunt, old buddy. Don't take it personal, but I'm handling a business, here. We don't grow a business by giving away free stuff. How much do you have on you?" I scratched my chin and winked at my friends.

He searched his front pocket and got a ten-dollar bill out. "That was for my breakfast. the old lady, she gave it to me. She said. I should get food with it, not drugs." I grabbed it out of his shaky hands and pouted: "Okay, so that covers your debt for last week. Now, get me another one and I'll consider giving you some heroin." I could see tears forming in his eyes. Oh, the pain felt so beautiful! "I don't have it, Alejo. I need a hit! I need it now!" I could find a million ways to humiliate him. I mean, he should earn that hit, right?

"Fair enough." I whispered. "Take off your pants." I scratched my chin, trying hard no to laugh. "Wait, what?" he murmured.

"You want some shit? Take off your pants."

"But Alejo, it's freezing."

He wouldn't cooperate, so I grabbed my gun and pointed it right at his ugly mug! "Take your f**ng pants the f**k off!" I yelled.

I could see panic in his gaze. For a moment, he looked at me with globular eyes. It felt as though the shape of a ghost squid had taken over his head. He trembled from every fibre in his body, while struggling to unbuckle his belt. "What are you, five years old? Go faster, freaking piece of shit!" I shouted. It rained a bit more, while he pushed his jeans down to his ankles. He covered his soiled underwear with both hands, and he tried to look away. "Please, Alejo, please, give me my hit, now." Oh, if only it was that easy. My three friends laughed. "Make him dance!" I heard Pietro.

51

"You got that, worm? Dance!" I ordered him. Grunt tried to carry his legs and feet beyond the rolled down pants, blocking his moves. The clumsy penguin hilariously walked in front of us. We laughed so hard; my belly hurt. I grabbed his hands, and we waltzed like a married couple. "That's it." I let out. "Now get on your knees!" I whispered in his ear. Grunt shook as a leaf. I pushed him down and I pointed my gun at the back of his head. "Alejandro?" Pietro pleaded me, "Don't be stupid. It's okay, now, we had our fun."

"It's over when I say it's over!" I screamed. "Do you want to die, Grunt?" I shouted. "Han? Han? Say it!"

I could hear him sob. "N-no." he stuttered. "What was that? Worm? Speak up!"

"No, no." he complained.

I turned around to laugh with my--

--BAM!!!!! BAM! BAM! BAM!

Four gunshots! Void.

My soul woke up outside of his body. Before I could rejoin my own, I watched four essences leaving their wounded carnation. The Veil appeared, above them. A tiny breach showed the Ether, ready to suck them in and push them up the tunnel of light. I perceived how their next stop would involve an external intervention from Noesi de Vel. Since they appeared to me as sleepers, they would probably find themselves reborn into some sort of vermin, or sent down the Open Door, by the Lake of Fire.

I doubt any of them got a chance to taste enlightenment, this natural notion of happiness through a narrow path. I recollected those from my previous life, but when my soul regains that Seamus Chron body, this knowledge will evaporate.

What happened? When I opened my eyes, Grunt stood up with Alejo's gun in his hands. The four drug dealers lied down at his feet, dead. Fifteen spectators would later testify: The one they call Grunt grabbed the weapon out of Alejandro's crisped palms and shot his assailants. He searched all their pockets and ran away.
I remained alone, asking myself if I had just used my gift to commit evil. And what will occur to poor Grunt? I tried to save him. To me, it seemed clear that Alejandro pulled the trigger, killed his friends and himself. How could I justify what happened?
He shouldn't have carried a gun! But I did attempt to control his mind. Not like a houseless young adult could tell the judge that I possessed a drug dealer's existence and tried to save another homeless' life. I rested there, while policemen arrived at the crime scene. I could sense their inner worlds, especially the ambulance crew. The rookie one looked highly traumatized. "Sir, do you know what happened?" Someone asked me a question, but I stood there, afraid. My soul, my essence, my mind, everything I work with numbed. "Sir, you are a witness, we need to talk to you."
I heard again. I focused on this outside world and observed the four punks carried off in body bags. "Sorry, I was stoned. I saw nothing." I mumbled and walked away.

Grunt proved easy to track. Forever afraid, but his fear mixed with a special kind of excitement. He pocketed eight hundred and twenty dollars! If I closed my eyes, I could sense his terror, it had a unique scent, and I discovered him hiding behind a container, in a supermarket's backyard, counting his newfound fortune.
As I approached, his life story unveiled itself naturally. His parents abandoned him at the borders of Mexico and the United States when he turned two. They travelled on foot from Haiti to find a better place, but harsh immigration policies at the US officers separated them. He found himself taken to a cage, and later he was sent to an orphanage. He was promised a bright future with a rich white American family. He rebelled when he got twelve.
He escaped this situation and walked from New York to Montreal. He lived in the streets of Montreal ever since he reached fifteen, four years ago.

I couldn't scout further. This squid character inhabiting him acted as his existential bodyguard. Somehow, it felt as though this inner monster attempted to connect with my soul. Like a frightened puppy, trying to get a bystander's attention. I found him, concealed within darkness, at the far end of a back alley.

"What do you want?" he asked me. I eyed his cash, and I wondered if I could use some for my own good. "I need three hundred dollars." I uttered. "Take a number! This is my money!" "Do you know how you got that?" I asked. He looked away, so I insisted. "You got it because a guy killed his best friends, and then himself. Do you want to smoke crack with that money?"

"I don't give a damn, it's mine! I can do whatever I want." He wouldn't bulge, holding onto every paper bill like a lumpy hobbit cuddling a ring.

"Yes, you can do whatever you want, but after you've smoked all of it, what will you do to get more?" He looked at me, looked at his shaking hands, and gave me twenty dollars. I took it, and then I looked right into his eyes. I won't try the mind control thing, again. It doesn't quite work like I plan. "I need three hundred bucks to save a friend." I calmly explained. "What's wrong with your friend?" he asked. I sat next to him, and I hugged him. "He killed himself before he could tell the love of his life how much she meant to him. With that money, I will have her dance for me. I will make sure that she gets the message."

"You'll just take it and smoke crack too!"

"Maybe I will! And maybe I need it just as you do. Or maybe what I tell you is true." He looked at his fortune and grieved. He stood up, ready to leave, so I had to act fast:

"I know how to bring you out of this mess!" I shouted, unsure as to what I implied. I had to push further. "Stay with me, and I won't let the cops get to you."

He remained silent and surveyed me with concerned eyes.
I closed mine, and I visualized the squid. "You're afraid, Grunt.
This isn't who you are. I can set you free from this fleshed prison."
He stood up and shut his lids. The tentacled guest grabbed the
host's consciousness and contemplated me. How do I get out?
How do I get out? They asked me, frightened.

"Find me here, tonight. I will explain everything.
I will set you free."

The humanoid squid detached itself from its corpse and looked
at the drug addict's poor self. That flesh is all I know of my
existence. I calmly turned my soul into a giant octopus, as to
project a familiar form. As I disconnected it from my own
grounded shape, I offered them a helping hand. "There's more to
existence than what you know. Come with me. I will show you the
path to reach True Reality."

"Hey!" he shouted, pulling the squid back to his entrails.
"I don't want to sleep. Go away!" I regained my human form as
well, and I calmed down.

"I just need three hundred dollars, Grunt! You can keep the five
hundred and I'll make sure you are out of this mess. Trust me."
He thought about it for a long time. Deep within, he sensed his true
self trying to take over. It must have been the first lucid event he
experienced in years.

"What bar are you going to?" he asked.

"I can't tell you, but here's what I'll do." I grabbed Alexandra's
phone and offered it to him. "Keep it as collateral. My friend will
look for me, and she'll call that phone." I opened my social media
accounts and showed him Alexandra's profile. "This is her.
She will contact me through this virtual messenger. Okay?
You're okay with all this? If she finds you, then you'll find me."

"She's hot!" he smiled. His eyes lightened up, as he locked them on a picture of her in a bikini. I frowned.

"What?"

"Your friend? She's hot!"

"Whatever! It's either this option or I send the cops on you." Grunt wasn't too pleased, but he reluctantly handed me three hundred dollars. I left with the first blood money I ever earned.

Later that day, I waited for Alexandra in her neighbourhood. I stood against the wall, right under her room's window, and I paused. Long hours, contemplating spectators passing by. Two hours, and then three. When you live in the streets, time has a different understanding: It no longer exists. Only patience does. After four hours of waiting, she finally showed herself, with her school bag. She saw me from afar, and she looked away. When she walked next to me, I could sense her nerves stressed to no end. "Why are you still here?" she asked. "I found Emerald. I can get you to her, tonight, but I need a shower and clean clothes."

Her mother left for the rest of the day: She unearthed a date on social media and thought she could gather some human warmth out of it. Alexandra looked at me, as I scrubbed myself. I know, because I kept the door unlocked, and I felt her curiosity. She shut the entrance when she heard the faucet squeak its way off. In my mind, however, I had seen more deaths and wandering souls I could deal with. No shortcut achieve success. Every swift and fast attempt at skipping a natural course will leave a trail of blood and sadness. But what if they were collateral damage in a war far greater than their lives? Maybe they just incarnate characters in that novel you read, as an excuse the author found to let me get the money I needed. What kind of cruel creator would kill just for cash? His Sophron disgusts me! I heard Alexandra from the other side of the door. We stand alone, perhaps she can find it in her to share some affection with me. "You can stay here if you wish." she offered. "I bought a bottle of wine if you'll have some."

I kept silent, checking out my good-looking body, and making certain I no longer smelled like piss and vomit. "Sure." I whispered. I had to clean my pants and hoodie, and the clock only flashed six in the afternoon. When I left the shower and grabbed a towel to cover my nakedness, I saw Alexandra's silhouette peeping from the timidly open door. I immediately thought about letting the towel fall to my feet, but I chose to play around the bush instead.

Yeah, dirty minds think alike. I took my things and abandoned the lavatory, walking towards the washing machine. Alexandra stood in the corridor, with wine and two glasses in her hands. I saw her getting ready on the living room's sofa, pouring my share, then hers, and leaving the bottle on the table. I started the tidying session and joined her.

"I didn't expect that our first time would look like this." I confessed to her.

"We're just having wine." she insisted, uncertain of how to handle the stress that caught us. I grabbed my vino, we knocked our drinks, gazing straight into one another's eyes, and we sipped. She dropped a bit on the floor, we both laughed. She approached, and when she got close enough, I could embrace her; I didn't quite know how. My glass attempted to fall onto the sofa, so I had to put it away. She struggled to find a best position to hold me, pull off my towel, but her moves didn't feel natural. I took it off myself, and gasped. "Put it back!" she screamed. *Never impose our desires*, I thought.

"Sorry!" I let out. "It's an accident." Her smile tempted the awkwardness away. "You met with Emerald, last night?" She asked me. I politely signalled no, while I drank my wine. "I'll meet her tonight." I explained. "It's really funny that you even know she exists." she grinned. I had nothing to add, there. Alexandra seems to struggle between incredulity and a strong desire to believe.

57

"Do you want to kiss?" I asked her. Good enough, that question broke the discomfort. She nodded gently. We approached our chins, let our lips discover the other's, knocked our forehead so hard, I thought we would both lose consciousness. We laughed, and we gave it another try.

With our eyes closed, the contact of our skin felt as our only immediate reality, then she rushed her tongue inside my mouth. A stronger force attempted to pull the white cloth away, and the blood dashing through it made me a bit shaky. Was it the right time for me to lay her down? Should I wait? My animal nature begged for more. Can I undress her now? I must remain cool and pragmatic. Should I use patience? She pushed the towel on the floor, and I felt helpless. Only I stood naked in the room. She looked at it. She smiled. Every inch in me pressed me towards her, but she moved a bit. "Wait." she whispered. "Wait for what? Let's do this!" I pleaded. "No, wait, Seamus, please!" She took a big breath and delicately wrapped her palm where it hurts. I felt her hand rubbing it down, then up, and she pulled her hand right away. "I don't think I'm ready!" I dreaded these words. "Okay." I accepted." Never impose your desires, I knew: "Can I borrow you a night gown or something?" She agreed and walked straight to her room, coming back with a pink robe, covered with cute unicorns

We finished the wine without saying much. We just looked at one another and sporadic laughter, followed by a shy: "What?" That encountered its inevitable: "Nothing." We would talk about school, my powers, and William. I sensed a great deal of disbelief in her. She doesn't buy that I have a gift. She assumes I do this to impress her, but she seems inclined to allowing this flirt a try. She also supposes that William is forever gone. Maybe this awkward play is part of our shared grieving process.

"Do you really think you can find his soul through Emerald?" she asked me. I pondered over it for a moment, and I replied: "This is where I should have been a long time ago. I should have protected him, but I failed. Now, this Void Entity consumes him, stuck in the middle of a war, between two powerful beings whom both need to crack him open, like an egg, to release an essence. I must find him before it happens." She smiled and nodded, before finishing her last cup of wine, and added: "I'm sure Emerald will be surprised to see me at her club."

The evening shone quietly, with a clear sky. Cleanliness felt good, with clothes fresh out of the dryer. We stopped by the doormen. Victor seemed happy to find me there: "Mathias is here, tonight." he announced. "We should chat, later." I simply smiled and offered him a twenty-dollar bill, then I suggested: "Yeah, maybe later. I need to spend some quality time with my girlfriend, as in, not disturbed." He accepted the bribe and opened us the door. The club was packed, like the night before. I quickly scanned the surroundings to see if I could sense Emerald's essence. I felt another one, very strong.

"Are you coming in?" Alexandra asked me. It suddenly dragged me back to this reality. We made our way through the crowd of clients and strippers, until we reached the bar. The Asian beauty remained there. I would later learn her name: Catherine Mai. She has a sister, Christine, who will play a crucial part in the few novels, following this trilogy.

"You're back!" Catherine smiled, as she poured me and Alexandra beers and liquor. Alexandra paid for everything and grabbed her first shooter: Tequila. "Here's to finding Emerald, tonight!" We cheered and binged our booze. "Do you see her?" she asked me. I closed my eyes and did one more scan of the room. The strong essence I felt earlier appeared very powerful! It wouldn't make sense that this strong emanation came from a sleeper. Whoever projected it must have been strongly awakened.

59

"What did you tell Victor about me?" My mysterious neighbour asked. I opened my eyes and looked in his direction. A tall and skinny blonde in his late twenties, he wore a death metal t-shirt, the kind whose band logo resembles a five-year-old drawing of a snowstorm. A deep calmness inhabited his soul. He grabbed his glass of red wine and turned towards me. I could suddenly know everything about him. Well, whatever he chose to project directly into my power's insight. Mathias Van Lorens, a potent Sophroner, decided to spend a quiet life as a poet, in Gaia. He reminded me of Alibast. He also connects with the Mai sisters, so when my trilogy ends, his will begin. Sophroners stand as the most formidable reality crafter in all Sophron. They conquer all the arts, and some even occult spellcrafting taught in Zendoria. Mathias seems like one of the most feared glancers and mancers.

Possibilities clashed! He smiled at me while I froze and I felt a million deja vu. "Master?" I asked him.

"Whatever you do, don't go to Tir na n'Og, but find my friend. His name is Alibast. He will teach you everything you need to learn before you confront Marduk or Varuna."

I already met Alibast! He doesn't know that?

He kept quiet and shrouded his inner universe to my gift. Did he influence those others who brought me the same warning?

"Yes, I did." he sighed. "I also found a way to take you to Emerald Leone. She's a dancer."

I laughed and sipped my beer. When I turned towards Alexandra, I realized that she stood still. None of the patrons, staff or stripper in the place moved at all. "Did you bring me to a limbo?" I asked him.

"Why would I do that? I just provoked a sleep paralysis in the Dreamer's brain. He is stuck to his bed, just like you were, when you saw Ishtar for the first time. Every regular being in his entire inner universe is frozen, but all the awakened ones aren't."

"How do you know that?" I inquired. He laughed and drank his wine.

"My name will be on an upcoming novel's cover. You'll see me star in the next trilogy, my friend, alongside Martin and Alibast. Of course I know more than you do. I know how your trilogy ends!" I felt a sudden surge of intense fear and fascination. But wait! Am I not the protagonist of this story? I observed him closely, and I asked: "Your name is also Seamus Chron?"

He sighed, like a teacher who just heard a stupid student providing a foolish answer. "I have to go. Remember this conversation. I encountered a possibility that would have brought you to jail, as a main suspect in a multiple homicide. I changed the course of that destiny. This possibility would have linked you to the Dreamer of our world, but this is not where you need to be, right now. Emerald holds the key that will take you to William and Nempty. Once you find them, you are on your own."

Mathias left his seat and walked towards the club's exit.

His last words, before disappearing, and as he looked at me with a profound wink, were: "Remember! Don't impose your desires! Don't, ever, impose your desires."

I witnessed him vanish as he approached the main door, and the staff, strippers and clients regained their lives and motion. It was as if everything had occurred while time froze, and now it returned to its normal flow. What happened?" Alexandra asked me. I turned towards her, still into my state of utter amazement. She added: "You look like you just saw a ghost."

"Nah." I sighed. "He was just a poet, some sort weird fantasy author." The rest of the night remained eventless. Alexandra and I binged down as much as we could, and I ended up spending a few bills on girls, behind the booths' curtains.

Drunk, we forgot about Emerald, until the deejay used his grave and suave voice to introduce her: "Here, now, to offer you a most sensual dance, I present you the beautiful goddess of the deep, Mystique!"

Lamps dimmed around us, but a spotlight strongly directed our attention at the centre of an empty stage. Mystique walked like a deity, rather petite, no more than five feet and two inches. She had the frame of a young teenager, with long, almost curly, hair. It flirted with the lower part of her spine. Her eyes shone like sparkling jade, and she studied the audience after she joined the main attraction. It felt as though she meant to swallow the patrons with her wide-enchanting gaze. When Alexandra turned towards the scene, she froze. Silence. And then we heard a piano intro.

Emerald embraced the light with her arms open, as in some kind of Zulu ballet propelling her against the stage. The melody continued, every note captured parcels of her flesh and drove her on her knees, then on her feet, like strings attached to the poles.

She danced backward, grabbed one of the long steel pillars and turned around it, with both her feet against the metal. She stopped. The music stopped, and the guitar kicked in. When the singer joined the orchestra, I felt that something extra brought us to her act. She proved to be more than what she offered our eyes to experience. She had a gift, linked to one aspect of Sophron or another, just as mine was connected to essences, and Williams' was tied to axioms. I could hardly picture what it was, but I recognized the membranous filament that seemed to surround her.

62

Every move had the sort of fluidity that came with jelly fish swimming in an immense ocean. She would break the air around her and removing her white bra to uncover the most beautiful bronze breasts I had ever seen. The Veil! She could, actually. She could summon the Veil, the same membranous element I had witnessed in my mother's past.

The curtain that protects every layer of Sophron, separating them, keeping them apart, and binding them. Where did her gift come from? Did she cast the force field from her own inner Sophron? Was this the Veil of the Dreamer we all inhabit? She could literally fly on top of that membrane! She manipulated it like clay. Sleepers can't see the Veil, but I did. She finished it with solemn few steps towards us. Her breasts, the size of small melons, pointing at our thirst. She let herself fall, again. dead. the piano returned for the outro, a few notes, a few complains, and then. silence. the scene went dark, and the public cheered.

Our lights reappeared, and Emerald stood up to pick her bra and her purse, left in a corner of the stage. She dressed up and joined us at the bar. She looked at Catherine, catching her breath, and asked: "Catou! I'll have a glass of cognac, please."

"I'll pay, I'll pay, it's on me." I insisted, reaching out for a few bills. Alexandra looked at me, speechless. When Emerald grabbed her liquor, she turned towards us and froze.

Alexandra froze.

"Alex?" the stripper wondered, and then added: "What are you doing here?"

"My friend, Seamus, he's a wizard, I think, but he works with dreams, and his wand is not that big, I mean. Forget it! I don't believe him, but it sounds cool, right? How are you?"

I froze. "Oh My god! Alex! I never thought I'd see you here!"
"Well, you know where I live. How come you didn't show up
at my door?"

"It's, it's complicated." They looked at one another for a long
moment, and then jumped in each other's arms, shouting a vivid:
"Oh My god!" In unison. I let the two girls cherish their reunion.
I had to endure so many gossips, it didn't feel right. Of course, no
negative energy surrounded me, so connecting myself to their
inner universe, or their essence, seemed impossible. I ordered two
more beers, which I drank very slowly, before I heard Alexandra
mention my name: "How come you know my friend Seamus?"
she asked.

"I don't!" Emerald replied, while trying to get Catherine's
attention. The stripper examined me and grinned. "But I have a
feeling that our destinies intended to cross paths." Alexandra found
herself wondering: "What do you mean?" Emerald observed me,
and she smiled. "Okay." she nodded. "Catou, can I have a glass of
red wine? Please?" She looked at her old friend and breathed
deeply: "You know that this existence, as it is, well, it's an illusion,
right?"

"Like, what illusion?" Alexandra laughed. The barmaid served
Emerald the good juice. I paid, and then she turned to me, again.

"You didn't tell her?" she inquired. Think of something witty to
utter, Seamus: "William!" William, what? "What, William?"
the stripper asked us. Neither Alexandra nor I could answer.
"You want to talk about it behind closed curtains?" the dancer
questioned me. I looked at her, then Alexandra, then her, then
Alexandra. It all seemed out of place and awkward. I agreed to this
secret meeting with a big smile. How did I go from powerful
crooner to pitiful puppy in an instant? I followed her like a faithful
pet, and it felt strange. Did I mean to do that? Or did I obey a
stripper like a loyal minion?

"Are you coming or not?" Emerald asked me, as I had stood still on the first stair before reaching the series of tiny cabins. I stopped thinking and I ran to join her, with all the servility that my drunkenness allowed me to fall into. I guess I quit being the boss of me. She pushed the curtain. I entered, and I rested on the small bench behind her. A punk-disco song neared its ending when she sat on my laps. I could grab her by the waist, and our eyes would melt into our dazzled smile. "So, what's your gift?" She asked me, not wasting a moment. "I can connect my essence with others."

"What does that make you?"

"Me?"

"Yeah, my teacher mentioned others like me, but I'm not sure I heard about your power."

"Oh? I'm a glancer, and you?"

"I'm a dancer."

"Well, technically, you're a stripper."

"You're an idiot!"

"No, I'm a glancer!" She rolled her eyes, as a new song began, and she stood up. She showed me her butt. I laughed, so loud, she stopped dancing and looked at me: "What's your problem?" she asked. "Your butt!" I replied. "Your butt, it's, you think it's your superpower?" She gave me the evil eye, and I could tell she got it from her Italian side of the family. Her Jamaican nature felt more hurtful when she asked: "Who sent you? Varuna?"

"No. I don't work with Varuna, sorry, I'm a bit drunk." I confessed.

"So, what's your problem? What are you doing here?" I looked at her with grieving eyes and explained: "It's William. I must protect William." Time stopped for the both of us. Her frightened gaze sent me a surge of negative energy that sobered me up instantly, if only for a few minutes, as though adrenaline just showed in my veins out of nowhere. "How is he?" she asked me.

"Dead." I answered. She could see my grief, and I could swim in hers.

"What happened?"

"He jumped down a high path, fired a gun, got hit by a truck, traumatized seven sleepers. He woke up in his own Sophron, and Marduk amasses an army, so we must stop him."

She had a lot to process, right there. Her childhood friend shows up out of the blue with a Walker. Her Toronto lover elected to leave this Earth without much of an explanation. And Marduk? She recollects how her sensei warned her more about Varuna than she warned her about Marduk.

"Are you sure he did this to himself?" she asked me. "It seems like that's how the story goes."

"Seamus, you don't know William like I do. He could never have jumped the cliff. We don't evolve in a revenge novel. It's more like an Agatha Christie Netflix series." I felt too inebriated to get an erection, but my mind floated somewhere else, anyway. I attempted to focus and scan her inner world. She performed such a mesmerizing twerk, I lost all references to what I was supposed to do, here. A dim voice tried to sound funny, and just whispered in my head: I hope this ass shaking isn't her secret weapon. My eyes observed her breasts while my mind froze at that last statement. "You think someone did it to him?" I inquired. She turned around and showed me her butt, once again.

"Varuna, think of him as our immediate concern. Marduk, not so much. He's a self-centred maniac, but Varuna? Now that's a calculating despot. Do you know how we can locate William's surviving soul?" His essence? His consciousness? I guess I do, I have to think about it for a moment.

"I can uncover a possibility that the two of you shared, but I need to get inside you. If you can follow me, we can unearth him in that possibility. Then, we must find the essence of William's that thrives within this dreamer, and I'm not sure how to do that." I explained everything as though I knew all along. Wow! I figured it out while discussing with Emerald. And did I just say I need to get inside you and she didn't slap me in the face? What wizardry is that? "My Veil is connected to this dreamer's Veil." she clarified. "I'm his puppet, and he's my Pulcinella. That's how the power of dancers work."

I just had a flash of genius, but the alcohol kicked back, so I had no idea what it was about. The Dreamer acts as an omniscient host if I recall the hobo's explanations well. Alibast! His name is Alibast. "You connect yourself to god, or something?" I asked her.

"I do martial art, stupid. Have you heard about the chi, ley lines, feng shui? That's the Veil. That's my thing, my power, what I do." My gift links souls, and hers is, like, tai chi with a side of chili sauce. This is going to prove interesting. How is she supposed to bring me to William, again? With the crane position? I need to step up my game:

"I think we must sleep together, and my bridge to heaven should insert your mouth, or something, you know? We're both superheroes. Right? I got this!"

The hand that slapped my face couldn't feel any harder. "If they sent me a freaking pervert to save Sophron, then this Dreamer should die!"

She completed her dance, and I just stayed there, like a zombie. I kept her for four more songs, unable to tap into her essence. It was pointless to try. She hated me. William will certainly despise me as much when we meet. I had to make it happen. I paid for her service, but as she grabbed my money, I channelled as much inner strength as I could to pronounce a few enlightened words: "I'm not a pervert!" I started by apologizing. "And even if I was, that comes with my affinity with axioms linked to Archeus."

"Don't talk about Ocorsurs. Especially if you don't know who they are!" she growled. "Ocor, what? No! I talk about you, and I, we have powers."

"Why am I performing in a strip club and not fighting Marduk or Varuna? And how did you get the cash to pay for my dances?"

I stood speechless, gazing at my money, and thinking: I'm such a crooner. Then she looked at me. I continued: "I'm going back with my lady buddy, your best childhood friend you've neglected for quite some time. She knows me. She trusts me. Do you trust her?"

"Yeah, but I don't know you." she whispered.

"Then get to know me." I concluded. "You are my ticket to redemption." Oh boy, my head hurts. I need a beer.

I joined Alexandra at the bar. She looked at me with love in her eyes: "So? Did it work?" she asked me. I sighed and ordered my booze. Catherine gave it to me. I turned to face Alexandra, and I justified myself: "Do you think you can arrange a threesome?" That didn't come out right. A stillness froze in the air. Even flies made no noise. "A threesome? How? Why?"

"Ask her. I'm done."

I wandered around the streets like a lifeless corpse trying to find its last resort. Did I just renounce two gorgeous girls, and my only chance at achieving my mission? Or did they drop me?

Whatever the case my reality had its own course and track. And whenever I would confront another organism, that person, animal, conscious form of existence, would have its course and track. I can't impose my will onto anyone. And I can't let anyone impose their will on me. I must thrive, grow, evolve, and the beings I encounter as well. Life acts this way, this is what Archeus directs its axioms towards. This is who I am, and how I should use my gift.

My night wasn't over, yet. I must find Grunt and take him under my wing. The rain fell around us, but the air remained cold and wet. Looking ahead, the Emilie Gamelin Garden stood out from the Berri UQAM station. I could almost picture a glass dome covering it, as though someone had installed a limbo realm. As I approached my roofless home, I appreciated that it lost its colours. Behind me, Sainte-Catherine Street shone flamboyantly, with neon light pointing at various bars and stores. In front of me, the garden appeared dulled out and gray. *Nempty?* I thought. The last time I saw reality like this, the dwarf caressed his pet wasp, and he warned me about William.

I entered the park and searched for my bench. The entire surroundings seemed deserted. Hold on! What about my friend? Is he somewhere, getting high on crack or heroin? I looked for him, but I was, clearly, the only life around. "No, no. No! I must find him! He has Alexandra's phone!" I shout out loud, hoping that Nempty, or whoever summoned this pocket dimension might hear me. Instead of a response, I saw a sleeping bag.

It smelled like the Apocalypse. Pee stains covered its interior, and blood formed patches on the outside. Letters appeared. It felt like a ghost wrote me a note, with some bright lit ink.

Get inside, Seamus Chron.

It reads. Unsure, I spent more time to survey my welcoming shelter. My gut feeling would have me run away from this uncertainty, but I found its presence appealing.

Hurry up, stupid, so we move to the next chapter!

Oh! Okay, then. I slipped inside, slowly, and zipped myself trapped.

Journey into the Hourglass:
Sixteen

"Dude!" Martin shouted out of a floating box, on my laptop's screen. "Why did you have Grunt kill the drug dealers?"

I had no idea. It just felt right, I guess. I kept typing, and the words came out like this. "I don't know, Martin." I sighed. "It came out like this."

That's the problem with inspiration: It doesn't follow the rules we plan. And now, we must continue the storytelling, regardless of what just happened. Sure, we could rewrite the whole chapter, but it makes sense. If we force it onto a different direction, our entire narrative will sound awkward.

"Never mind." Martin growled. "What do you do with William?" he asked me.

"He met Nempty on Athanor." I answered. "Nempty tried to free Varuna, he failed, he died, but Kitana sent her buddy, Nunc, the fluffy phoenix, to save him. He took him to Athanor in an egg, dropped it in the ocean. He boiled the sea to locate his friend, Karkadan didn't like this. Finally, Nunc found the egg, brought it in a cave. A kitty slept nearby, Nempty resurrected in the body of a frog, with a zombie cat's head on his right shoulder."

"And I'm supposed the be weird author?" he laughed.
"That's where the story went." I explained. "Nempty found William in a platonic strip club, on Athanor, and took him on board the Barracuda."

"All right, we can have Seamus wake up on that ship, then."

"How do we do that, Martin?"

"He's a glancer, Alibast. You just had him stretch his gift to its limits, becoming one with Alejandro. That powerful squid entity wasn't too far either, so we should use that. The unexpected murder of four drug dealers caused a trauma."

"We have a traumatized Seamus, now?"

"We do, Alibast! We sure do! Good job. Let's have Erato write him a few notes, or something, and maybe she can get him on board."

Erato, of course! She found herself drawn in this. All because of Seamus' failed love story with Alexandra. That means, she's connected to his soul. She knows the whole narrative, even better than we do. She's a Great Muse, so, yeah. they work like that.
"How do we write this?" I asked.

"It's already taken care of." he smiled.

Chapter Five:
Marduk may be a Character

Five thousand years passed since the fall, as he recalled. Marduk never expected he would ever dwell into the pages of ancient lore. Why did humans keep records of his passage? He tried to enslave them. Wasn't this the whole plan? After the collapse of Babel, the Councils of Zendoria imprisoned the two main protagonists. Varuna accepted his fate, while the cultures who venerated him developed advanced science and mathematics. Marduk's people vanished from history. Yet, the concept of villeinage carried forward. Perhaps he did provide a difference.

Fear makes a Lord stand strong. Keep the subjects intimidated and they will bring their Master to higher forms of enlightenment. Empires rose while Marduk's reality encapsulated him within a tiny limbo. Are minds thinking that he escaped? He didn't. Someone wrote him back into Earth's storyline. One day his consciousness was trapped. The other time, he guided an immense army to triumph, against a demon lord of Hell. Driven by this hunger, following a buttled up rage that had just emerged, Marduk fought his way to the top. He clashed until he reached the likes of Great Entities. And he killed Enlil-Bastat without a blink.

An author released him from his prison. He owes his victories to a storyteller. Now, another one haunts him down. Damn, that cheese stinks and it tastes awful! He suddenly grimaced. He lost his train of thoughts for a second.

Seamus Chron, that's the name of his rival. Obviously, Alibast grooms this character and works towards getting him ready to face the Hound Lord. But Alibast isn't a potent creator, or Marduk would have perished the moment their eyes met. The poet of Avalon wasn't the one who set him free. That means there's another author writing this story. Marduk must connect with him. Whoever that is, the Lord knows an ally when he sees one.

Walkers form a special caste of powerful reality manipulators. Still, they can only manage their craft with the use of fundamental material, like the ether, the veil, axioms, or souls. Poets have a direct connection with the Great Entities of Zendorial. They can literally forge incarnation in their image. If he can locate the exact possibility where Alibast's co-writer exists, he could sway him into working by his side.

Perhaps Sekhmet has met him. She remained a few steps ahead of all her adversaries. Osiris retired from politics, following her advice. Rumours suggest that Seth and his brother found themselves an inner universe that plays with the likes of vampires. Some sort of game, with cards, and books, Marduk never really knew what it was about. The feline goddess underestimated his aptitudes at overthinking when incarcerated. After all, the Hound Lord of Nibiru had a few thousand years in confinement to plan both his escape, and the greatest assassination ever achieved.

If Alibast trains these humans to face him, then the Mesopotamian divinity will have to allow them an approach. They represent a direct connection between Marduk's possibility and this authored creation. One more bit of this oh that's so awful stinky cheese! Let's try to keep it in BURB! Stomach SICKNESS! How can this sound so hard to swallow, even for a deity?

74

Chapter Six:
Martin and his Student

Martin wouldn't consider anything of it. The student stood behind him, pleading for a chance to speak. "Why would you have William suicidal when he holds parcels of Indra in him?" They wondered. "Think about it! Someone killed him, that's what makes sense."

"Sorry, I'm busy writing about Seamus being homeless. Quit bothering me." Martin replied. The student sat next to him, reading over his shoulder. "Your Seamus character never stopped compromising his chances at advancing. You think sending him back to the streets will serve your story? It needs to move forward." Martin sighed. "Excuse me? Who wrote whom into existence if I may remind you?"

"Plato showed me a way out of the cavern." they answered.

"Yeah, I know, I did that." The author ignored his character's critiques and resumed typing on his laptop. The lungs, around him, breathed heavily. The whole room felt bulky on both creators' shoulders. Blood floated in midair. "Why did you select this dimension?" the pupil asked. Martin wouldn't answer. It's not like he picked anything. He may as well have just grown up in this post-apocalyptic world. Maybe this explains a connection between the author and his protagonist. "You're homeless!" the student expressed, almost in a Eureka moment.

"What? No. I live in this castle. I rule over New York."
The disciple left their chair and wandered around. "Sure, you did.
I bet you wrote yourself a perfect world and tried to send your
consciousness over there." Martin stopped typing. The student
continued: "You realized that it wasn't as ideal as you imagined,
but you created a universe. So, you might as well become god to
these people."

"It's not exactly like that." the pupil laughed. "You wrote me
into existence, and I wasn't supposed to share a world with you?
Martin, there's a poet above both of us." A moment of lucidity
followed a shout that nobody heard. Someone records him into his
own story! "Alibast! You! Damn it!" he yelled. "Who's that?"
The student wondered.

"My mentor." the poet replied. "But I think he's playing with
us." Discouraged, he left his laptop and walked around the living
room, a literary living, breathing, coughing room. "I supposed I
had it covered, but he owned me." Martin confessed.

"Well, we can outsmart him." the student smiled.
Martin listened.

"Seamus resided in my mind, before I ended up here."
the Greek traveller explained. "I know that, by now, he just visited
Emerald, and she's the key to reach William."

"Yeah, but his powers are still weak." the author replied.
"That's what Alibast wants you to think. He doesn't want

Seamus to find William." Martin considered it for a long
moment. He sat down and read everything he wrote, for the last
three days. "Let's fast forward that rubbish!" he shouted. "If we get
Seamus and William together, that means Alibast will struggle,
explaining how it happened." The student felt proud.
"You understand my mind." they smiled.

76

Chapter Seven:

Seamus' Turmoils

I woke up in that sleeping bag of putrefaction, and I looked at the sky: pink with blue clouds. This certainly wasn't Kansas anymore. I checked my shelter. I made sure I crawled into the same one, and I could easily confirm: I peed in it. I felt the most discomfort I experienced right after I commit the unforgivable.

When I surveyed inside my sleeping bag, I could even see the humid stench I dropped between my pants and my home. When I looked outside, the steel and cement of the high path I rested under vanished. I looked at a wide ocean and a bright pink sky. A brilliant sunshine unsettled me, as I expected solid concrete. I heard the scream of seagulls, and I closed my eyes, hoping for a fast-food restaurant nearby. But when I opened them, ostrich-sized birds flew above me, and that felt scary. I had to gather the courage to venture outside of that bag. It proved to be, let's say, complicated. I'm in a dream and, maybe, idle and crippled in it.

Perhaps I could simply breathe in, and out, and find my way back to existence. I don't even know if breathing in and out works to exit a sleep paralysis, but I can try. I did, and when I regained my normal flow of respiration, I realized I was still in that same stinking bag, floating on some sea I had never seen coming, looking at a frigging pink sky with blue clouds! "You wanted a threesome, she said."

Emerald? I left my hermit crab shell, and I perceived her. When I gazed at her left, I noticed William. He smiled just as much as she did. "Was it good for you as it was for us?" she inquired. Oh, the comfort of my vomit shelter, but how did she carry me to him? I was supposed to get her there, and with the aid of Alexandra. I dared pulling my head out and ask, I just had to: "Where am I?"

"Where are we?" she corrected me, then kissed William. She looked at me and casually uttered: "Where we should be." I left my sleeping bag. This wasn't a good answer. I meant to tackle her, struggle with her, choke her. But the whole weirdness of the environment we shared made no sense. I was compelled to calm down and step away. Sure, I have seen these strange worlds when training with Ishtar. Being conscious in one is another thing.

"I'm so glad I found you." I proclaimed. "I have been looking for you, William, buddy!" *Essences, axioms, and the Veil*, I thought, *maybe we exist as blind warriors sent into a kamikaze mission, manipulated by forces we know nothing of.* "Hey, boy!" I heard a voice I recognized from an ancient dream. "Nempty?" I asked. "Yeah, boy. It was tough getting you in, but welcome aboard." I checked into my pockets to see a sign of life, and I uncovered pieces of broken glass. With it, my last twenty-dollar bill. "Where's my wallet?" I whispered.

"You were drunk when you left the club." Emerald explained. *You were dead when I found you.* I heard in my head. "Where? Where are we going?" I struggled to ask the question. "On your way to Tir na n'Og." That answer came from Nempty. *No! No. We can't.* I thought, facing the facts: the dwarf I expected to picture seemed absent. "Who said that?" Had to ask. "I need to find Grunt. Where's Grunt?" I tried to add, but my head, so dizzy, it hurts. "Boy, go back to sleep. We're taking care of things." A frog with a dead cat's skull on its right shoulder looked at me, and I felt compelled to calm down. "I need, I need to find, Alibast!" I whispered. Wait, is that two-headed abomination Nempty?

"It's good to see you again, boy!" I could hardly get used to his new appearance, and he could perceive all those interrogations that haunted my gaze. "Nunc, you'll meet him later, resurrected my essence. I died, somehow." he explained, but my eyes still gleamed, full of questions, so he added: "You'll learn to appreciate these voodoo tricks." William came to me, always with his introverted face looking at his feet, and he pointed out, in a low voice: "The cat stays there, it doesn't speak or anything. The frog talks a lot."

"As much as that annoying dwarf, yeah." I winked at William.

"I can hear you, boy." The grumpy batrachian frowned, while grabbing a compass out of his pocket. "Make yourself at home. We're out for a long trip through the Ether."

"Your gift makes you familiar with essences." Emerald explained. "You'll soon find out how other Walkers play with reality."

I know that term. That's what I am? So many inquiries populated my mind. How can I possess foreign bodies? How did I take over Alejandro's consciousness, his whole existence? "Yeah, I'll, I guess I'll visit the boat and get back to you if I have some questions."

She followed William inside a small cabin, in the middle of the floating ship. I walked towards the forecastle of what resembled a pocket-sized man-of-war. The masts stood up, huge, in comparison to the vehicle. I noticed no sail attached to them. It seemed rather difficult for me to comprehend how this thing could fly at all. When I observed them closely, it appeared they channelled the Veil. My immediate deduction was that this vessel propelled itself using the Veil as both a sail, wind, and water. When I arrived at the front end of the boat, I could perceive nothing! Just this pink sky and blue clouds stretching as far as the eye could see.

Looking back, I noticed animal-headed Nempty play with his compass, while observing the flow of pink pixels. Does he know what he's doing? I doubt I would ever see Montreal again. I haven't eaten in hours. Hunger didn't haunt me. It was as though travelling across the Ether froze my internal organs or something. Unless I focused on my heart, I couldn't sense it beating.

Everything felt so strange. The boat's front appeared, as I walked closer. There, the pink sky, and blue clouds smashed against its nose, breaking in half, floating away on both sides. I need to concentrate on this new reality.

I sat down, as though trying to meditate, and I cleansed my mind. Hours flew away, but I hardly sensed the flow of time.

Whatever this universe was, time follows different laws. Even space doesn't reconcile with our traditional interpretation of physics. *We're on the ocean between worlds.* I heard a young maiden's voice in my head. "Who said that?" Silence. I opened my eyes and searched around. Nothing. I calmed down and tried to revisit my inner peace.

My name is Lucretia. This is my boat, and daddy's boat too.

"Where are you, little girl?" I wondered.

I died so that daddy could live.

I looked everywhere, suddenly terrorized. We can die, here? My mind hosted a maelstrom of thoughts and questions: I was supposed to be the one getting to William, through connecting with Emerald's inner world. A long-lost dream of mine came back. I have seen this boat. I noticed Nempty's new form, around the time of my incarceration, at delinquent youth prison. What was it about Tir na n'Og, again? That part seemed relinquished down the memory abyss. I should remember, come on! It's my own consciousness, here. I can do this.

80

Are you still there, mister?

"Yeah! Hold on. I need to warn my friends about something."
I stood up and ran as fast as I could. I saw William's cabin, near the
middle part. Emerald closed the door behind her, with two beers.
"You're okay, chump?" she asked me. I stayed there, unable to
focus on what I intended to say. "I don't think it's safe to visit Tir
na n'Og." I let out, without the shadow of reasoning. She offered
me a bottle. I couldn't tell what brand this was, but beer is beer.
"What's going on?" William asked, leaving his cabin to join us.

I drank straight from the bottle, and I examined her. "Your bro
is afraid something bad awaits in fairy land." she answered, then
she looked at me and added: "My fate takes me there. We all have
ours, you see?"

"But Emerald! If you, William, and I must work together, if we
must stand strong as a team, then we shouldn't split. I also should
fine-tune my training in Alibastat!" My mentor's essence
manifested itself through me. I could hear his calling, like an
intuition struggling to become a rational thought.

"There's nothing, there, Seamus." Emerald explained. "Nobody
lives in that layer. It is a soulless world, no animal. Nothing."

"How do you know that?" I asked her. She binged down a long
sip, looked at me and sighed: "My mentor taught me everything I
need to know about Sophron's geography. I memorized the whole
map by heart." Alibastat is a world between Cibola and Elysium.
True Archeus exists as the ultimate dimension, where only axioms
of life prevail. True Void, all vacuum, faces it. True Logos faces
True Barbelo. We find Alibastat situated three layers past True
Archeus. Imagine a rainbow that emanated from all this whiteness,
leaving the orange behind, in the Archeus-Barbelo quadrant, and
leaning towards the blue. Alibastat is translucid, an abomination.
It has no colour. It looks like a shining line in that spherical thing.
It used to be protected under Enlil-Bastat's guidance.

81

"I think I know what you mean." I uttered.

"We're going to Tir na n'Og." she concluded. "I'm sure you'll find a way to get to your teacher in time."

"In time for what?" I wondered. She binged down her beer and looked at me: "Before Varuna builds his army." My jaw dropped. I shouldn't worry about our trip. But I'm confident that Alibast doesn't want us there. On top of that, she expects us to fight some sort of Hindu deity? At the back of my mind, I felt Marvin's presence. I rejected this intrusive thought. He's the last one I wish to summon, here. I looked at her leaving our space, and I observed the quietness that surrounded us.

We've floated for an hour, and there certainly was no source of entertainment at hand. Only my visions, my slow realization that existence just shifted overnight, and my dead friend lives. It needs time to process these changes! I wonder what went through William's mind, when he woke up in this strange place. I couldn't help but feeling some guilt. I must have driven him to this new story. Working together, now, seems awkward.

I returned to the front of the boat, the only quiet spot on the entire vessel. Away from this craziness, I could hear myself thinking. I left home to find shelter in a cosmic battle. That's just my luck. Am I supposed to master my powers in time? I barely understand what I'm doing.

You came back, mister! I missed you. Ah, my friendly ghost buddy. "Lucretia?" Maybe she knows a thing or two about our ordeals. "What do you know about Tir na n'Og?" *Daddy takes me there, sometimes, to eat ice cream and watch fairies dancing.* "Do you think it's a dangerous world?" *Oh, no. It's lovely. No danger at all. The Open Door is very dangerous. That's where my dad he died. Don't go there!* "Who was your daddy?" *He was daddy!* "But what was his name?" *Daddy! His name was Daddy!*

82

A previous guest on this ship, perhaps. What sort of name is it, anyway? If I can hear her soul, maybe I can find a manner to connect with her. If she haunts the boat, then I need to uncover a way to haunt it, on that same level. I couldn't know how to achieve that. "Do you only stay at the front?" I asked her. "You know, there are people further back, by the cabins." *I don't know those people. Mister frog, he scares me. His dead cat head is ugly.*

"Oh, he's really nice, once you get to know him."

I stay here, with you. I like you. You're nice.

She's so cute. Speaking of cabins, I should ask where my quarters are. I left her, once again, happy to learn that I shouldn't fear following my friends. What's to fret about a world of fairies? I mean, come on! Flying bug-ladies won't be the end of me. I walked on the left side of the boat, where cubes stacked themselves to mimic portable houses. Emerald and William reside in one of those, but I expect mine to be much smaller. I wasn't prepared to face the ugliness that awaited, as soon as I opened one of those tiny spaces:

A gigantic half-tree and half-human looked at me with dazed and confused eyes. He reminded me of a fossilized impersonation of Popeye, minus the pipe. He stood up, straight and proud of his almost eight-foot-high stature, stretching his arms to clean the floor with huge sponges. Next to him rested an obese purple phoenix who could have found a job as a mascot for a sweet cereal brand. When he saw me, he clumsily ran with his mouth open wide in a silly smile, his tongue reaching out. I swear I thought he was possessed by the spirit of a feather-brained golden retriever. "Hey Quid!" he shouted. "Quid! The new guest is here, I forgot his name! A new guest, Quid!" When he tried to stop next to me, he slipped and fell overboard. Luckily for him, he could fly. His tiny wings, also serving as his arms and hands, seem so small compared to his body. I was at loss of a scientific explanation.

"What's your name, new guest?" he asked me. "I'm Seamus Chron." I answered. "Shame? You are shame?"

"You can call me Shame if you want."

"Shame of what, Shame? Why you are Shame, Shame?"

"Seamus Chron! I am Seamus Chron!"

"Ashamed of your crown? Are you a prince? Are you a king? Why are you ashamed of your crown, Seamus Chron?" The way he processed information baffled me. My only consolation was seeing that this caricature of a monster wasn't completely naked. His white cloak and old running shoes made him look like a looney toon begging in the streets of Los Angeles. "Where are we going, Nunc?" I asked him. "We're going to rescue Emerald, but her real name is Ishtar, but I didn't tell you that."

"You just did! And Emerald is right here."

"I just did what?"

"You just told me that Emerald's real name is Ishtar, but Emerald is with us. Are we going to rescue Ishtar?"

"Yes, but I didn't tell you that, okay? Wink! Wink."

"You're supposed to wink, not say it. Are we going to meet Ishtar or what?"

"Say what?"

"You don't say wink! You do it! What about Ishtar?"

"No. That's not what we do, okay? You're so stupid, new guest, I forgot your name."

"Seamus.""Yeah, but no. You're not famous."

"Whatever!" I sighed and let this idiot practice his winking.

Hours later, the ship accessed the world of Tasmania, the last layer in the Logos-Archeus quadrant. We flew there before entering True-Logos. My understanding is that we flew towards Penglai, with its pink skies, and maybe the vessel must create its own bubble to pierce the Veil without breaking it and let axioms from one world spill into another. While we were in that artificially created bubble, I could see the sky change colours, from pink to a pale turquoise.

Watching Emerald get all affectionate for William confirmed their relationship, at some point. Whenever I needed space to process all this strange new stuff, I returned to the front of the boat, telling Lucretia a few jokes. She seemed like the only sane soul on the entire ship. An untouched purity, I could call her my little sister. Maybe I should. The me from one book ago would have loathed seeing them happy. Modest me of this book understands that hate grows as a self-serving shield. Cowards build it to ward off the cruelty of life that hate creates. Then, I strayed, too weak to even consider love as the answer. Now, I see William as my brother. I love him.

Third Intermission:
Kitana Escapes

It's within. It's all within! That green pixel cradled Lucretia's essence, but it existed because Kitana shared that intimate moment with her. It blinks on her computer screen. Somehow, the android's soul didn't want to disappear. It felt as though she held on to the last possible connection to reality she had, right before her brain stopped functioning. Lucretia gave up her life to save her father. Kitana, alone, granted her those instructions. If the daughter's essence craved to exist, she had to hold on to Kitana's. And that's what happened.

"Maam? Maam? Are you still there?" She forgot about that call. "Yeah, sure, yeah, what's your problem?" she sighed.

"Well, I don't appreciate your tone. I've been explaining to you the whole thing for half an hour. If you don't want to provide me the service I pay for, I will complain." The customer seemed visibly upset.

"Okay, seriously, I wasn't listening. And, obviously, I don't care. So, you'll have to repeat your case all over again."

Karen hung up.

Damloot approached her once more. When he turned to examine her orb, Kitana swiftly concealed it. She cleansed her throat: "Simply use that spell I sent you, madam, and it will get you rid of those imps. Thank you for choosing the Mancening Network." The nymph walked past her again, observing another coworkers' computer screen.

It's within, she thought. *Within how?* What connects her soul to that orb? Dispatching her essence across Sophron so that a customer may wield her magic, sure. It's not like she projects her entire self. Or maybe it is?

What if the Beyond rises as an illusion? Or what if the Below existed as a shadow of that illusion? Then, True Reality must occur somewhere else. Yet, it depends on both. Like two cards forming the foundation of a House?

That means, her entire cognition reposes on an anti-consciousness that can't occur without her acknowledgment. Yin, Yang, that's just the first five letters of an enlightened alphabet. *It can't be that simple!* Why not?

The orb acts as her proxy. It produces elements that exist within herself. If pixels can get out of it, perhaps it could, possibly, go back in. If her consciousness shows an axiomatic frame, that means she could escape across that same channel. But if the sphere only serves as a tool, then she should free her mind through her own dreams. Just like that!

"Just. like. that!" she shouted. And this time, nobody inquired about her loudness. She opened her eyes, only to realize that absolute darkness surrounded her. Nothingness on top of a blank canvas. If she propelled her gaze, now, she would return to that lousy office. Unless she switched her consciousness inwards. *Dream within that dream,* she thought. Paint the whole universe blue! *Smile, Kitana.*

You were dead when I found you. She felt these words. Where did she hear that before? Oh yeah! She hadn't yet. Those words arise in her far future, but they manifest as a figment of her past. The moment she'll acknowledge an observation of fluctuating particles, the world will give birth to her existence.

"Void?" she asked. Did she just hear an Ocorsur? "Void! My dude!" She did it! She walked beyond her illusion and made it into her inner Sophron!

Hmm. Yeah, who is it? The voice floated as though it attempted to narrate her life. Let's not scare the poor soul. She's been through these whole enlightening shenanigans a few times, already. Now, though, it's different. "Oh! I wasn't sure." she apologized. "Hi, I'm Kitana, I just woke up. How's everything?"

Silence. Hmm. cool. it's all cool. Hi. yeah. wow! You're my Dreamer, right? "What do you think? Oh, sure! If you do, you revert back to Logos! Don't do it, then."

You should know. I'm the empty space inhabiting you. "I'm looking for the First Singularity, you can help me with that?"

Yeah, but, I'm not sure it's a good idea.

"Dude! I'm, like, above you. I write your stories, dude. I can write you off." *Oh? Yeah! That Singularity! Yeah, hmmm, sure! That would be me. For the Second Singularity, check with Archeus.* "Yeah, right. Like I'll skip matter and question life. Nah, you guys share a same connection. I'm asking you." Silence. Your mind wandered around a pit of pure oblivion. Forgetfulness carried the weight of an immediate heart attack.

"Hey! Don't do that." *You want Singularity? And you ask me? Better prepare yourself! Mine involves the One source of non-existence that ever was, ever is, and forever will be.*

This is why I decided to add a little bit of Barbelo, in my drink. The moment matter imposes itself over void, we can't avoid paradoxes cresting the Veil across the entirety of Creation.

Did you ever wonder what it felt like to hold no grasp over your consciousness?

Yes, I did, many times, actually.

When you seal your eyes and shut your senses, life shines through a thoughtless drumbeat. When the closing stronghold falls, taking with it your Jinal breath, darkness turns into a full-fledged reality. Don't Jight it. Flow that anxiety clear. Accept it, Kitana. Embrace the shore of a blank incarnation. When reflections no longer project a truth, and matter shies away, your essence Jinds solace into the arms of my Singularity. Void, the Jirst, the last, the forever.

As you ceased to exist, your body remained. Claudio swiftly realized it. Soon, your manager stopped by to feel a pulse: none occurred. He called your name, a few times, and waited for an answer, but you vanished.

Chapter Eight:
Erato finds her Soulmate

Watching Emerald get all affectionate for William conJirmed the obvious: they're attracted to one another. Whenever I needed space to process all this strange new stuff, I returned to the front of the boat, telling Lucretia a few jokes. She seems like the only sane soul on the entire vessel. An untouched purity, I could call her my little sister. Maybe I should.

Erato felt a strong connection between Seamus and Lucretia. Comfortably seated in the middle of her makeshift cave, she projected this movie against a wall. He's Alexandra's wannabe boyfriend. The wonder young man with a gift. She showed difficulties seeing how he fit in the greater scheme of those Chronicles. Marduk battling Varuna remains the core issue, at the heart of this ongoing storyline. Somehow, either Alibast or Martin chose an outsider to act as the protagonist. If Erato can squeeze herself in there, it had to be in the position of a love about to burst.

She focused her attention on Lucretia's essence. She should develop strong feelings towards Seamus. Hopefully, her past as a sex-doll android won't interfere with her future as. whatever new form the authors can find for her. Or maybe this is where she can chime in. Let's grant this a try:

Do you have a girlfriend, mister Seamus? Erato inspired her to ask. "You're so cute, Lucretia! Yes, her name is Alexandra."
He wishes.

She must be so beautiful! Is she royalty?

Careful, now. He can't get into an intimate confession, but he should remain truthful. "She's my princess. I was a very bad person, before I met her. I changed because I love her.
Do you understand?"

Love, yes! My daddy he loves me. This is why he never touches me, even if really bad, bad men, they. they created me. Erato could use this moment of confusion. Think fast, Muse!

"Yes, this is what love is. When you give up everything to protect someone."

I miss my daddy!

"Mister Chron!" Nempty entered the scene, unexpectedly.

Erato wasn't prepared. She had all in motion, except for this intrusion. Seamus disconnected his essence from Lucretia's and turned to face the frog-dead-cat. "We're about to access Tir na n'og. I would suggest you return to your cabin."

"Really? I was having fun with my ghost friend."

Nempty frowned. "Another stowaway?" he growled. "I'll have someone handle this. Follow me." Erato lost her connection with Seamus. He must have walked with the boat's captain. She can't have anyone get rid of Lucretia, however. She's her key to properly enter the plot. This will have to wait. She can't risk making herself detectable. Marduk stationed himself in the fairy-world, then he'll likely notice an Entity's attempt to mingle with his affairs. It might be safer to lose the whole connection until a better occasion arises.

91

A thin layer separates her inner pluriverse and the one shared by those characters. The Ether flows in that tiny space, just as it does throughout the Veil. The Great Muses made it their sovereign ground. While most Great Entities retire in Zendoria, once their true awakening occurred, some prefer to stay in the Below.

Most will have elected a specific realm of Sophron as their home. Others will merge with an Ocorsur. The Great Muses remained orphaned, wandering across the pluriverse like nameless pups. They gave birth to the many civilizations of minor muses, populating worlds, between Barbelo and Logos, towards Archeus.

They couldn't partake in those puny affairs, among Houses.

Electing to remain impartial, and to exist as lifeless icons on Hydaspes brought them their last rest. Every now and then, however, they would gain a form and join the stories of other lesser beings. This is how Erato fell in love with her pirate king. Melpomene finds himself equally stuck in a different tale. She can't appear out of the blue. If she wants to earn her place in those Chronicles, she must uncover a way to manifest her presence, properly.

Journey into the Hourglass:
Seventeen

"He can't go to Tir na n'Og!" I screamed across the room. "Marduk is there!"

I shouted to myself, keeping my eyes closed, and I walked in despair. I stepped on a Lego block; I howled in pain. Martin left the chat. My computer's screen showed pictures from my Zen Garden, but I didn't feel any sort of inner peace. We're losing our main character!

I sat down behind my laptop. I opened my text processor, and I explored the chapter that brought Seamus to Emerald. I already visited him in person, under his Dreamer, so will he recognize me if I just manually include myself in the story?

I don't even have time to ask Martin for his thoughts. I'll just rewrite the ending, and I'll have someone warn him against travelling to the fairies' homeland. With any luck, our essences will bond, and he'll know it's me.

Chapter Nine:

Seamus and the Mushrooms

I sat in my cabin when the boat pierced the Veil and entered Tir na n'Og. Breathing deeply, I lost my mind in a state of meditation. I sensed a different possibility attracting my essence. If I open my eyes, a strong feeling of Deja-Vu unfolds. Somehow, I could project myself in a duplicated consciousness. To my left, I had joined some pirate, or maybe a smuggler, on my way to Alibastat. To my right, I walked mong my friends, on Tir na n'Og. If I maintain my gaze shut, those two presences of mine equally reside. If I open them, only one reality will manifest. I kept them closed, as I tried very hard to remember which boat sheltered me. Nempty's vessel? Or was it Nate? I forgot his name. Nathan Lord? Yes! Nathan. How can I exist in two possibilities at the same time?

"Are you coming, Seamus?" I heard Nunc's voice. He didn't sound like an intellectually challenged bird. "Yes, in a minute." I replied. I can't find the courage to validate which of the two boats had me on board. "Hurry up! We're there." the phoenix insisted. I sighed deeply, and then I opened my eyes.

The Deja-Vu dissipated itself after five long seconds.
My spinning mind kept me dizzy, while I focused to remember
where I was. The big goofy purple bird looked straight at me:

"You okay, mister Shameful?" he asked. He's talking like an
impaired again. I turned to my left and a window showed the
treefolks cleaning the boat. Nempty stood next to them, with his
dead cat's head falling in reverse. "Fine, Nunc." I whispered.
"I'll be okay. Where are we?" He danced like a lunatic and pointed
to another opening.

Outside, tall plants suggested the presence of a rain forest.
"We're in the land of the fairies, mister Ashamed!" he sang.
I smiled, yet I didn't laugh. How come it felt like I was on
Alibastat? "All right." I nodded. "All right, okay! I'll be right
there." Nunc left my cabin. It took me a few more minutes,
but I managed to recollect my reflections. Time to explore this
strange new world.

The jungle felt sentient, I thought. *Mushrooms, the grass and
even the trees projected a clear consciousness.* The soil showed
feelings. Every step we made provoked a storm of fear in my head.
Nunc seemed to have found the way to go. He flew like an
overweight purple seagull above this nonsensical field. *How does
he do it?* I thought, but, then again if it works for bumblebees.
Nempty cleared the path for us, and I could see Emerald and
William behind him, the perfect warrior couple. Provided that total
nerdness counts as a martial art. She walked like a ninja, and I
observed him holding his crystal ball or some sort of weapon.

Whenever he closed his eyes, I could perceive colourful lights
float in his orb. Green, blue and black, mostly black, like small
pitch-dark fairies, or big flies, or maybe they are rats, I don't know.
But lots of gloomy stuff. "We're almost there!" Nunc explained.
When I gazed in front of us, I saw a highly futuristic city, on top of
a huge mountain, in the far distance. *We must be half an hour walk
away from civilization*, I thought.

95

We paused for a moment, as hunger found us. Well, they were. I just couldn't deal with hearing a grapefruit scream when peeled alive. I stared in the buildings' direction, and I noticed strange vehicles zooming over it. They seemed like those giant robots we see in Japanese cartoons but made of flesh and steel.

When one of them flew above us, I got a closer glimpse: a cyborg, and a mix between an octopus with two gorilla arms and legs, and jets that sprouted right from its spine. "Biomechs, boy." Nempty frowned, while cannibalizing an apple. "Sorry, what?" I asked him. "They're called biomechs! In Duat, however, and some other places, they refer to these as archoids, to honour Archeus, the Ocorsur they fight for." I stood there, in awe. "How can they be vehicles?" I wondered. He sat next to me and contemplated me for a moment. "Did you assimilate out of body experiences?" he inquired. I pondered for a minute and answered: "I think I can project my essence outside of my frame, but I'd need practice."

He finished his apple's corpse and added: "When you master this, you will be able to pilot one of those." He returned with the others, and I looked at the strange creatures with awe and curiosity. What would it be like if I could possess one of them?

They have brains of their own, engineered in such a way as to allow an essence to control them. Wow! I smiled.

"Keep it up, rookie!" Nempty shouted at me. I soon realized that the pause was over, and the march was back on. Sorry, I guess. A cat-frog who once existed as a red-haired dwarf, yelling at me, feels bizarre. I only met him once, in a frozen-time-dimension.

96

We approached the mountain. I learned to get accustomed to the agonizing voices in my head. On our way there, I saw dozens of biomechs parked in a field, behind a tall building. This immense cube probably houses the pilots. I observed them, those Godzilla, those amazing pieces of greatness. One of them looked like a turquoise blob. Eight metallic tentacles came out of its sides. This white panther, standing up, showed wings stemming from its hips and shoulders. Oh! Oh! You should have seen that one! A legless spider with four robotic arms, and a snake's tail acted as its source of locomotion.

What about the wolf with the body of an eagle? And that Sphinx! I swear! This biomech looks like the Sphinx! Further down that field, I noticed a griffin, but they added an extra head. Can these biomechs have two pilots? "Pretty cool, eh?" I turned around and saw Nunc. The purple phoenix made me think of a smaller robot. "I used to fly one." he confessed. "Years ago, before I existed in this form. I had a more human-like, shape. So, I understand how frustrated Quid must be, stuck in a hideous body. But I saved his life! Just like someone saved mine, before."

This seemed like the most intelligent thing I heard this mascot express. We should call ourselves the Saviour Squad. I nodded and walked ahead. Is he switching from impaired to witty as he pleases? Or do those personalities swap places in a random manner?

The gates of Arcana stood before us. Closed. The doors projected a fabulous aura, as tall as three houses, and as wide as one. Around it, stonewalls seemed to have been carved from the rock. When I looked up, I saw bigger buildings taunting the sky, from atop the mountain. It appeared as a manmade fortress.

Nempty stopped at the gate and took a ring out of his belt.

He put it on and pushed it against a lock that comes across as a gargoyle's mouth. "State your essence and your reason for visits." We heard that voice. It seemed half outside our head, and half inside. "Nempty Bek'Thot of Duat, here on pleasure with William Francoeur." the frog explained, then continued: "Emerald Leone and Seamus Chronenberg of Gaia. Nunc Fairfield of Athanor."

"Hydaspes, Quid!" the mascot whispered. Nempty sighed: "My name is not Quid, stop it." Nunc insisted: "But I'm from Hydaspes." Nempty growled and corrected himself: "Nunc from Hydaspes!" he frowned. Nunc corrected him again: "I'm actually Jamieson." The frog lost his nerves and shouted at him: "Can you shut it? I'm trying to let us in!"

The phoenix went pale, and I could feel his shame and fear.

He whispered: "Nunc, that's another persona's identity! My real name is Jamieson Fairfield of Hydaspes! Quid." Nempty turned towards the gate and asked: "Did you get that?"

After a short moment, the voices appeared back online: "State your business in Arcana, Jamieson Fairfield of Hydaspes." Nunc lost his calm, but he managed to explain, with a trembling tone: "I was told it was okay for me to show up! Because of bad fairies, and the nice ones they said I could come here! Are you a good fairy, sir?" the speaker added: "Name your fair folk affiliation and reason for this visit." Nunc knocked his head against the door, and repeated to himself: "Think, think, think, stupid, think!" the voice echoed itself. Nunc felt nervous, and Nempty fumed, furious.

"Oh! Oh! I'm with the girl, you know? Like. she's a girl, she, well, she was a reporter, on Hydaspes, and she made me believe me that fairies were invading, but, like, they were mobsters! I'm not with bad fairies, I'm with, huh. what about leprechauns? Are they good or not?" Silence. The voice went emotional: "Leprechauns killed my family."

98

"Then I'm not with them! Oooh no, no, no, no!" Nempty jumped on Nunc's back and repeatedly hit him behind the head. "Please, state your business in Arcana, Jamieson Fairfield of Hydaspes!" The speaker remained calm. Nempty simply explained: "He's with me, boy. He's my pet. My big fat birdy pet!" After a long moment that felt like a never-ending anxiety, the gates opened. And then I witnessed paradise. The streets were carved on gold and platinum. The gigantic mountain disappeared, from within. There, floors of precious metal stood with houses as small as a mouse hole. Others as big as a palace, stacked in such a manner as we could experience the spiralling design that made Arcana a snail. Bugs! Literally, we walked like ants at the feet of Mount Olympus, but from the inside.

Markets roamed the streets, and at first sight it seemed like a medieval city. Men in cybernetic uniforms presented a different epoch. And what about the fairies? We counted, easily, hundreds of various fairy species, from the jade skinned to the gray scales, with or without wings. Some looked like angels, others like ladybugs. Children, the size of mice, played with the feces of satyrs. A couple, as tall as giraffes, walked, hand in hand, among a crowd of kangaroos in tuxedos. We saw no biomech, beyond the gates. We found no weapon, or whatsoever. Arcana shines as a city of peace. Behind these walls, we felt safe from the violence of the outside world. How can Nempty recruit an army to oppose Marduk in a town that stays far and away from battles? Maybe I could meet someone who can mentor me into piloting an archoid. That became my new ambition. "Do you know if there are glancing academies?" I asked Nempty. He lectured me: "Stick to the plan. You're not here to learn anything. You are here to do what I tell you to do, all right?"

"Yes, boss!" I replied. I looked at the big bird with a huge heart, and something didn't feel fine. "Hey, Nunc!" I whispered to him. "You have powers, right?" The goofy feathered guy nodded. "Do you sense essences?" He tiptoed towards me and mumbled: "You mean, with the vegetation?" he asked.

I couldn't tell how his ability worked. William explained to me, earlier on the boat, that Nunc practices sophroning: he dipped in all the gifts, I understand. "There's something strange about the possibility we are in. It shouldn't be real." I warned him. Nunc smiled like a big brother trying to comfort a disquiet kid, and he tapped me on the back before whispering: "It's real as real can be, new guest, hey, I'll call you Newguest! I like that, you like it?" "No! My name is Seamus."

"Okay, Newguest! Hey, I know a good bar we can have a beer. You like beer, Newguest?"

I ignored him and followed Nempty. The bird stayed behind, like a doofus still waiting for my answer. And what's his thing with changing names? I turned around and looked at him with defying eyes, and I shouted: "Hey, Jamieson! Catch up!" He hurried with all the puffs and coughs he could express. He murmured: "My name is Nunc. I'm Nunc! Nunc, not Jamieson, Nunc."

"How do you think we can locate Ishtar?" I asked Nempty. His dead cat head fell against his torso. The frog looked at me and explained: "Ever since I discovered Ishtar's essence in a wasp trapped in amber, signs showed up. She's here, okay? Trust me.

Ishtar always finds herself lurking near her estranged lover."

Estranged lover, I thought. What if it were true that they inspired a marginal culture, together? In my world, it would be politically incorrect to use their name in a contemporary novel. Indigenous folks worship her, on a remote island, near Australia. They built huge temples for her, remembering the ancient myths of Mesopotamia. Many anthropologists and historians agreed to call them survivors of mankind's cradle. India still rever Indra. Having a Caucasian dude coupling them together as lovers would sound sacrilegious.

Should his novel be published in my world, we'd see protests! Leave cultures to their people! We would read on social media. Don't steal ours to earn money! They would argue. But what if that author's creation exists for real? What if they just couldn't grasp this truth, and fought over illusions? Heck, I'm the one living in it! This counts me as genuine when processed within some reader's mind. Nunc caught up on Nempty pretty fast, and he suggested: "Hey! Quid! I think she's at the bar! She's at the bar Quid! Let's go have a beer." Nempty ignored him. He looked at me and uttered: "Before we do anything, I promised to take you to Emerald's teacher." Surprised, Emerald walked to him and wondered: "You mean, she's here?" Nempty smiled and replied: "She's been waiting for you." Awkwardness filled the air. The ex-dwarf turned into a frog with a dead cat's head brought the crew here to hand us over to Sekhmet. Are we supposed to rejoice with this? Now, we walk as mere pawns in a big battle about to happen.

"I don't know, Nempty." I allowed my scepticism out of the bag: "You took me away from a mentor who promised to help me with my gift. Just so I could labour for a warmongering Egyptian goddess?"

"It's not that simple, Seamus Chron." the frog frowned. "Whatever lurks in the darkness seems way more powerful than she is. But I trust her."

"You trust her enough to sell our souls to her?" All this works me up.

"Let's walk, shall we?" he stuttered a bit. "We shouldn't stay in the middle of the street."

"No!" I didn't bulge. William and Emerald stood between him and I. Only the big fluffy bird seemed inclined to leave the group. "Take us to Ishtar, instead. If we're going to join a goddess in a fight, I decide to join Ishtar." Nempty sighed and scratched his head: "Okay, so, you process your choices. Sorry to be blunt, but right now, you don't get to pick."

Nunc walked between the two of us and broke the tension: "But! I think, I really think, we should have a beer! Here! On Tir na n'Og, come on, say it with me! beer, beer, beer, beer sounds good! Beer is your friend!"

I sighed and turned towards Nempty and Emerald: "I'll take our feathered buddy to a bar, and I'll let you rejoice in meeting the stripper's mentor." What will the dwarfed frog do, anyway? We build our possibilities with our choices. I closed my eyes to gather more strength and add: "I'll be right there."

I didn't know if those words spoke to Nunc or Nempty, though. While I kept my observation shut, it felt like I could have been addressing my speech to either one of them, or to both. I opened them once again. The scene didn't change.

Emerald projected her gaze at me with a disapproving sight: "Dancer, Seamus. I'm a dancer." *Yeah, whatever*, I thought. I'm the one babysitting the deranged poultry. He looked at Nempty taking Emerald and William away, and I walked towards a main street. Except that I may have followed Nempty, William and Emerald, after all.

This is how it goes: every moment of our life manifests as a liminal space, empty of any future, filled with a past that evaporates along with our memories. This works as a crossroad between the now and the possible then. The now that I am choosing, in this very instant, as you read those words, takes me on a journey with Nunc. I know for a fact that, in a different storyline, I accepted my fate, and I followed the squad to meet Sekhmet. If my odyssey crosses paths with that storyline, then only one of my two potential versions will carry over. This is how probabilities work. I'm a glancer, I understand essences and how they can find themselves split, like this. However, I don't manipulate possibilities. That's what fencers do.

Nunc froze between me and the group, and he just talked to himself: "It's a trap! I know it's a trap!"

I turned towards him, and I shouted: "Are you coming or not? The beer won't drink itself!" He just stood there and questioned: "How come I know it's a trap? Maybe it's not."

"Beer, Nunc!" I insisted. "I'll have a beer now!" He woke up and smiled, running towards me, and singing: "Coooooming!" Like a gleeful cheerleader. Could it be a trap? Did alcoholism save this version of me? I forgot about my squad. At this point, I turned into a curious tourist, observing fairies of all sizes, shapes, and colours, crowding the area. Ever since gods and goddesses from Duat settled their homes on Tir na n'Og, the vast population evolved into a cosmopolitan community. Chimeras, those humanoid creatures with an animal head among other features, have learned to cohabit with the fair folks. Most of them live in needier parts of this realm. Only a few opportunists found their fortune in Arcana. With Sekhmet governing this world, though, the fairies convinced the impoverished chimeras that they could achieve anything they dream of. Only, the panther-lady didn't seem to care about the fate of her kin.

A dark and small bar waited for us at the end of a condemned street. If I surveyed behind me, I could witness the more populated boulevard, with the colourful beings walking or flying around. Two very tall walls kept Nunc and I into a narrow alley. If I looked up, I could barely see a shadowy sign that read: The Lonesome Crone. I couldn't even perceive a door, at this point, only mortar and rocks.

"Are you coming in?" Nunc asked me. He phased inside that impasse, like a ghost entering through the very brick rampart we were facing. I shook my head, and I followed him. A river flew at the other end of a luxurious garden. Golden chandeliers dropped from a high ceiling. Neon lights lit a classical palace, alongside a cheesy snack bar.

The Lonesome Crone wasn't much of an establishment, but more like its own tiny city. To me, it almost felt like the time when Nempty trapped me inside a limbo dimension. Perhaps that's this bar's purpose, after all. Kegs loitered the roads, like thousands of fire hydrants, each with a complex system of tubes and valves, connecting the hundreds of little pubs that filled the village's institution. I didn't spot any streets, but thousands of dance floors, however. Some came with a light show, others remained sober. From where Nunc and I stood, we didn't hear any music.

Once we crossed one of those stages: techno. Under a different one, classical songs played. Over here, it's only metal. And there, jazz fills the air. What about the clientele? Wow! They came from every corner of Sophron! Angels danced alongside demons like old friends. Chimeras binged with golems. Drunk humans kissed elementals. I even saw a fire creature strip naked next to a nymph, until two treefolk bouncers rushed them off their table.

The marvels didn't stop there. This immense building also hosted tall mountains and forests. You can hike as you walk away from a concert, and bar hump to the next one. We could listen to that river raging from the other end of the city-pub. I heard that it carried a splendid torrent, singing the beauty of the Lonesome Crone, inhabited by the essence of life and the voice of angels. A stream that chanted the tales of heroes, and the value of love. When the rivulet reached our feet, it humbled down to become a pond. The mountain filtered it, allowing it to form a secret lake, underneath its foundation. The water took weeks to rise back to the surface, on the other side.

We had just exited a spot that offered only microbrewery products from Earth, also known as Gaia, my world. I devoured their menu, and it felt like I was home. The black tables reminded me of a shady tavern we'd find in a far away suburb. But they served over three thousand brands of beers! None of them had any commercial affiliation with those that I know. I doubt this novel would give famous brands free publicity.

104

When I eyed down, I saw the stream of life flowing across the place. I looked up to observe the flock of firebirds gazing at a few patrons, waiting for them to drop a French fry they could snatch.

"Hey, loser!" I heard the water shout at me. I turned around and faced a decrepit fountain that seemed like an orgy of gargoyles, mixed with boulders and pebbles. "Hey, loser!" she insisted. Jamieson entered the Earth-themed bar. I remained mesmerized by the idea that rocks could talk. "You're a flocking moron!" the sculpture shouted.

"You know what's uglier than feces on a crone's face? Your face, Seamus Chron! Yeah, I said it! You're a flocking loser!" That thing mentioned my name? I approached the fountain, and I dared address her a question: "Who's there?" I asked. "What do you mean, who's there? Are you blind or just stupid? Oh, you're a retard. I bet you aren't allowed to say retard, where you come from, you know why? Because your mother is a retard!"

I sat by the fountain's edge, and I attempted to make sense of what just happened. "Why do you talk about my mom?" I asked. The water continued: "She is a whore! You know why? Because you're her son!" I sighed, and I tried to keep it cool, but you can't call my saint mother a putana! You never met her! Yet, she sensed this outer world. Was there something the foul-mouthed rock perceived that I didn't? "How do you know me?" I asked it. "Do I? Oh yeah, I know shit! Of course, I do!"

"How do you know my mom?" I insisted. Nunc walked back to me and shouted: "You want that beer or not?" I calmed down and waited for the fountain to say something, but all I heard were more insults that seemed to make the gargoyles stand out from whatever I would utter. Then it hit me. Some people toss loose change in those and profess wishes. I searched inside my front pocket, and I found some. I held a two-dollar coin and five cents. I threw them in and paused for the vulgar furniture to react. The water smiled and kindly looked at me:

"Thank you, come again!" the fountain gleefully laughed. Then she remained polite and quiet. Nunc found me and, in his Jamieson personae, warned: "Hey! Don't feed the trolls, buddy, have a beer." I joined him and wondered: "Trolls?"

He laughed: "Yeah! Over here, it's a form of economy. Some clients leave tips, others don't. So, they brought in fountainheads. Their only purpose in life is to provoke, insult, bully until we fling a few pennies at them."

A two-dollar Canadian coin isn't worth much, by itself, among enlightened individuals of Sophron. However, around here, everyone trades what they own as a type of currency. Axioms and souls can be exchanged for goods or services. The use of orb-based magic, or other forms of power, will require a similar investment. Our essence, elements of our reality and even our future options or possibilities can be utilized in this manner. More modest establishments, however, will welcome a material type of economy.

If one plans a trip among sleepers of Earth, this loose change I just tossed away could prove itself valuable. If the nickel that I threw attracts an alchemist in need for this precise metal, then he could show up to this bar and trade the owner something else in exchange. While barter represents the central and most prevalent kind of financial system, most worlds will have their in-house forms of currencies. We have yet to observe a stock market or a global economy that covers all of them, though. This could change in the future.

Despite its gigantic size and thousands of places to hang out, the Lonesome Crone remains a cave. A dark and profound hideout that stretched from the wall we phased through to the farthest end I could see. I tried to locate Nunc, somewhere, but the fountain may have distracted me. Perhaps I could find him among the crowd if I focused on his Jamieson essence. I soon realized that each of his known personalities projected a distinct soul.

Don't feed the trolls! I heard in my head, like seagulls feasting on failing students calling Chekhov a boring author. I loved Uncle Vania, even though my school forced me to read it to pass my French class. Chekhov was Russian, for flock's sake! Back in my previous life, games and fun drove our passion, attempting to impress the ladies. We scored into a field dominated by the stronger jocks.

Until nerds fetch the better of that existence, flirting with the money they earned while the meatheads struggled to understand politics and get into the social media fights. Reality hardly reconciles with amusements!

"Hey, buddy, over here!" Jamieson sat at a table, in a dark corner. He already held on to a pitcher bigger than his head. I accompanied him, trying to forget the last trauma I felt. He smiled as I joined him, in front, and he poured two glasses.

"What is this place?" I asked him.

"The truth, my friend! This is the truth."

I looked around me and I saw nothing. Nobody. Darkness, and that's it. Out of all the flashy and colourful bars and clubs out there, he chose this basement!? I mean, come on, dude! "What are we drinking?" I asked again.

"What are we drinking to, you mean." He raised his glass and looked at me and cheered: "To this moment!"

"The best metal band I know!" "I'm sorry, what?"

"It's just music, Jamieson. I think we can let people appreciate what they like."

"The Lonesome Crone is what we call a nexusnaos."
He explained. "At any given time, your soul is duplicated across
the numerous versions of you, and throughout the countless
multiplicities of Sophron, within, again, endless different
Dreamers. Truth, however, exists as its own emanation. I find only
you, reflected infinitely within and without your worlds, and others
around you. When designing Sophron, the Entities of Noesi de Vel
brought us certain locations where each manifestation of your
essence, everywhere, converges. Here, your real self walks inside
what the councils called a nexusnaos."

"Is this what, so I heard, we find True Reality?"

"Close enough. Now, let's drink to the truth." The flaming
mascot knows intelligent conversations and interesting things
about the strange universe I just uncovered. I looked around and
saw a fascinating crowd. On the table next to us, a translucid dwarf
with hairs made of slimy snails shared a pint with a centipede
bearing a horse's head. *How true can this be?* I thought. Two spots
away, twelve ants drank wine and broke bread with a termite.
When I turned to the other side, I saw an earthworm the size of a
giant human, with twenty-three breasts and a G-string. Tables
floated with wobbly guests: blobs with mechanical arms next to
soaring butterflies. Our waitress very much seemed carnal,
however, with a fairest blue skin, and covered with tattoos. "Can I
take your order?" she asked me, and I couldn't help it, I inquired:
"What kind of beers do you have?" She pondered for a moment
and answered: "We specialize on Valhalla imports. May I suggest a
pint of Sacrifice Our Enemies? It's a smoked stout with hints of
caramel and blood pudding." *It didn't sound too alien*, I thought.
"Do you have lagers?" I looked at her with a firm gaze, hoping
she'd propose anything we'd find at a store, back home.
She smiled: "Sure! May I recommend a No Pity for the Weak?
A strong lager, with hints of ginger, fomented unicorn guts and
sheep brains." I surveyed Jamieson. He seemed to approve that
choice. I sighed: "I'll have a Coors Light." Did some free publicity
just materialize in the novel? Or did my freewill speak out loud?

She had no idea what I talked about. I cleansed my throat, and agreed to having that blood pudding stout. I looked at Jamieson: he drank what I thought was a regular cola, but he assured me he enjoyed a blueberry cider. "So, Jamieson!" I gleefully turned to smile at him. "I'll take you to the best bar I know, on Gaia. It's called Foufounes Electriques!" He silently bibbed his fruity acid, just as the gorgeous waitress showed up with my pint of stout. I dove into a first sip, and I gagged. Who can possibly drink this liquid, aark! I gazed at Jamieson with the straightest face I have ever made. When the waitress offered me a magnificent look, awaiting my verdict, I gasped and painfully nodded. She smiled and walked away.

"Hey, hmm, Jamieson?" I asked my friend. "If this is the true me, and, like, if all of this is an illusion, right? You think I can, you know?" With a libidinous wink, I signalled the blue-skinned lady who kind of drew my hormones into a new height. "You don't want to upset her boyfriend, trust me." he warned, and ignored I even asked anything. I tried to gather my serious face back, but I guess you can picture me as the buffoon in this conversation. I looked at my filthy dark beer and wondered if I would become an adult, after finishing it all. I didn't realize I had been expressing those thoughts.

"You won't be a man until you love and get your heart taken out from your nostrils, attempting to breathe in, and not bother. You panic because you want her, and you don't want to step on her ovaries, then survive to talk about it with a smirk and a gentle sigh." I didn't recognize the voice, so I looked up and saw this tall and bulky man, wearing a cloak and a hood that divided his face between light and shadows. "Seamus? I present you my buddy, Nathan Lord." Nunc, I mean, Jamieson proudly introduced me his friend. "He'll escort you to Alibastat."

The gentle warrior sat at our table. He grabbed my pint, sensing that I wouldn't finish it, and he binged it down like cotton candy in the hands of a starving kid. I found a superhero.

Journey into the Hourglass:
Eighteen

Where is Martin? I spent the last three months rewriting his work, to make sure we don't send Seamus to his doom, on Tir na n'Og! A little help, here? I had to reimagine Nunc as an intelligent character. Martin wanted a comic relief. Heck, it's my story, now. If he can't show up to our creative meetings, then, too bad. We owe our readers a happy ending, but mister self-imbued doesn't even take his job seriously!

I have to complete all the work! We'll publish another best-seller, and he'll grab credit for it. What am I? His slave or something? He's the one who complained to me, few years ago, about his failures. I got him to write this trilogy to boost his self esteem, and now I handle everything. Okay, fine! I'll go back inside. I'll resume my role as Seamus' mentor. If this causes him a problem, then sue me.

I'll have serious Nunc, now known as Jamieson Fairfield, take him to Erato's secret lover. Let's say I've met Nathan Lord from some place. Zen, please, zen... I'm supposed to act as this prophet-like character. I guess I am, according to Seamus.

I can work with this.

Chapter Ten:

Seamus and Jamieson

The Lonesome Crone seemed a bit more crowded. An hour after I stepped in, I already got to enjoy three beers. Fifteen empty bottles amassed themselves all over our tiny table. Nathan drank most of them. The tall and obese phoenix didn't have too many. I wondered what happened to the squad. My alternative soul and my friends still wander farther in Arcana. Somehow, when I closed my eyes and phased my consciousness out of this immediate illusion, I saw myself walking with them. We entered a magnificent palace.Nempty's cat spoke. I guess Lucretia's essence incarnated this cute little zombie-kitten head. Another presence greeted us, but I couldn't tell who it was. A lady, I think, a tall lady of African descent.

"Are you still with us, mister Chron?" Jamieson asked me. I shook my dream away, and I grabbed my beer with both hands. "Yeah, I'm, just, nothing." I drank. We talked for three hours, before we decided it was time to leave. I was informed of how they met, back when Jamieson showed a human appearance, but split personalities. They grew up in a city, New-Quirk, in Hydaspes. Jamieson Fairfield suffered from schizophrenia, or as they call it, there: spectral possession. Several parcels of essences inhabit him, all sharing one body. They will take turns dictating a character. When a powerful crime boss from Tir na n'Og allied himself to a rogue army from Saguenay, to invade their home world, Jamieson sensed the imminent danger.

111

Nobody took him seriously, given his obvious mental illness. He managed to convince a lady reporter, Alicia Light. She was in touch with a traveller, Nathan. Mister Lord knows people in high places, this is probably his gift. Alicia would often provide him carnal comfort in exchange of valuable information. Or did he offer carnal comfort in exchange of new contacts to work with? It sounded like some twisted love story they found themselves entangled into. I would later learn that Nathan Lord was quite the ladies' man. He took pride in having slept with a Great Muse! Erato! The guy had sex with the Great Muse of romance! That's, I mean, for a crooner, that's way beyond my league.

"As I was explaining." Jamieson continued. "When we leave this pub, Nathan and I will bring you to Alibastat. This is where you'll meet with the poet of Avalon, who sent us."

The chubby phoenix had only good things to say about my friend, Alibast. The powerful Walker took Jamieson under his care for many years. When he returned to New-Quirk, the invasion raged on. It seemed subtle, however, as both realms decided to first corrupt the media, then the people's opinions, gradually dividing them into those who thought that Hydaspes was doomed, and those who challenged the narrative. Only foreign forces from different worlds could save it. And those who knew about this manipulation.

"I won't stay with you, over there." Nathan explained, while bingeing down beer number eleven. "I have business to attend on Cognitia." he smiled. It spelled another romantic conquest, right there. How I wished I had his magnetism with the feminine gender.

"Alicia?" Jamieson asked him. Nathan shook his head. "Don't be shy, lover boy." the bird laughed. "Everybody knows she's you're the one."

"It's not Alicia." he insisted. "But if we're going to mingle with the big guns, like Marduk and Varuna, let's say you want me in that lady's bed, right now. If we call an omniscient AI a lady."

Walking to Nathan's vessel, I learned how Jamieson Fairfield lost his human form, battling those invaders. The crime syndicate populating those massive disinformation campaigns to control Hydaspes sent an assassin to get rid of Alicia. She became an annoying reporter who knew too much. Jamieson stood in their way, and he died in her place. Nathan brought Jamieson's corpse to Alibast. The wise man performed a special ritual to save his essence and put it into an obese bird of flames and cinder. Awakening in a new body triggered his schizophrenic consciousness deeper through thousands of probabilities.

Nunc throned as his leading personality ever since, inhabiting the main possibility that his carnal self experiences. Jamieson would resurface when needed. Twenty-two others share his mind. I had yet to cross paths with any of them. His leaning towards the pragmatic and timid human character may have shouted a cry for survival. The buffoon Nunc came as his attempt at building a balanced existence.

When I looked at him, on our way to Alibastat, I perceived a troubled flaming seagull. It offered me an opportunity to link myself to his inner world. I noticed how my findings could corroborate with Nathan's interesting story. I saw an orphan who spent his life from adoptive families to others, always ending up wandering the streets. I wondered how this relationship William and I have with homelessness could comply with Jamieson's past. This sounds like a recurring theme throughout this novel. Jamieson loved Alicia. Just as I came close to find out what happened to her, and what brought him this sadness, the bird realized my trespassing. He closed his eyes, and I lost our connection. He grieved, though.

When he reopened them, Jamieson walked away from the body, and Nunc took over. I ruled it impossible to pierce that essence of an intellectually challenged persona. It baffled me to see how he managed to control those manifestations of the psyche at will. It's as though he could zap them like TV channels.

Nathan led the path. He seated his vessel inside the Lonesome Crone, in a specific area where travellers must leave their gigantic flying boats attached to a floating marina. On our way to the dock, we crossed a few other pubs. An opera had amassed a few hundred bystanders, on a big stage. Next to it, a band of dragons sang the greatest hits from Imagine Humans. And we set foot in a parking lot, bigger than five stadiums, offering shelter to thousands of boats. I wondered how many more we could find, in this parallel universe of a bar. The marina also had its special section reserved to archoids of all shapes and sizes. When my friends stopped their walk, we found ourselves under a warship. Unlike Nempty's Barracuda, this one was called a phantom-frigate.

"Welcome to the Emily's Eyes." Nathan opened his arms, while a bridge of light invited us inside. The boat's hull covered our meager bodies, like a colossal ceiling promising us the marvels of a splendid cathedral.

It's a warship, but I could feel Alicia's soul tormenting its structure. The sensation reminded me of Lucretia's, haunting the Barracuda in a similar fashion. The vessel's shape resembled a gigantic egg, with hints of silver, copper, and gold. Diamond and platinum nuggets patched its fabric, and a pitch-black gothic castle topped its centre section. As soon as everyone stepped out of the brightly lit bridge, the Veil tore itself open and the ship slowly flew into a new dimension: The Ether. When looking at the front, I could see the Veil drawn in a turbine, and dark veins crushed from within the membranous element. I wondered where this weird artery we swallowed would become when spat out at the back of the boat. I ran like a kid to examine it more closely.

It felt as pure beauty, the Veil, fragmented and thrown away by gigantic helices, while nerves stretched from inside the gray matter shattered and turned into pixels of various colours. I even sometimes perceived body parts of frightening creatures, the likes we would only find in a mind akin to HP Lovecraft's.

Did we swallow horrific monsters like mere bugs hitting a speeding car? Further away, at the back, these pixels vanished into a restoring Veil. I think we destroyed worlds and let them reshape themselves as though nothing had happened. Count this as our means of propulsion. "Emily's Eyes hardly passes as the most powerful phantom-frigate out there." Nathan explained, as he handed me a beer. "But I spent enough to make it fast, quiet and well equipped."

"Equipped how?" I asked him. "Genesis torpedoes at the back and at the front. Shift-beams on both side, and on top. Behind you, my Vania Castigliano, the jewel of this ship. Quantum lasers under the hull, seventeen of them babies." Wow! Nathan sure loved to talk about his arsenal. He sounds just like me when I flirt.

"Vania Castigliano?" I questioned him, intrigued. "My uncle's name was Vania Chekhov." he answered.

"Russian?" I wondered, but he looked at me with more inquiries. He swallowed a sip of his beer and asked me: "What? No, Chekhov? Russian? What's that?"

"Never mind." I apologized. I drank from my bottle. It tasted just as awful as that blood pudding thing I had earlier. He seemed like some German or French vampire slayer in disguise. He could pass for a vampire too! That's what made him love alcohol that tastes like iron-filled sacrifice juice. I should call him Blade, from now on. Blade Belmont. Why would he name his cabin: Uncle Castle Vania, anyway? "You don't like Blood Light?" he asked me. "Sure, bud." I uttered and drank, a bit. Oh, the awkwardness! I looked behind us, while the Emily's Eyes flew farther away from Arcana, and vanished from Tir na n'Og. At that point, I no longer felt any connection with the version of me that stayed over there. I wondered what would happen to my duplicate. Will he fight alongside Sekhmet? Will he rebel and convince our friends to stand up against the Egyptian goddess?

Chapter Eleven:
Marduk heard a boat

A boat pierced the Veil. He could sense two formidable Walker on board. They're leaving Tir na n'Og? And Sekhmet failed to mention their presence or their business. When he closed his eyes, however, he felt a breach in the Ether, indicating that someone crossed the frontier between possibilities. Perhaps a fencer made this happen. A powerful sophroner walks as one of the two gifted individuals. That person's second entity having split from this storyline suggests that his double remained in Tir na n'Og. *Sekhmet?* The hound Lord thought to himself. What game are you playing? He couldn't stay in his room. She ridicules him, and that can't stand. Keeping him in this prison, even though he's a guest, while other vessels stop by? No! Marduk will have none of this!

He swiftly exited his room, only to witness the unpopulated corridor. He could have left, earlier, just as easily as this. He walked slowly, expecting the butler to jump out, any time, now, with a plate of fruits or cheese. None, whatsoever! Curse you, Sekhmet! *You're good.* He thought. Sequestrating an Entity-killer with kindness? That's a first. He could have murdered those butlers without provoking a diplomatic dispute between the two Houses. He chose not to, simply because he felt like a guinea pig in a mysterious maze.

A window offered itself to his curiosity. The Hound Lord of Nibiru remained calm, as he observed the crowded streets of Arcana. Disgusting fairies fly high enough to share the airspace with his superior gaze. Those colours! And females kissing females, that's a nightmare! If he ever chooses to conquer this liberal disgrace, he will cleanse the entire realm from this monstrosity. The two fair folks dove down to join the multitude of bystanders, while Marduk grumpily extended his glimpse farther. From this vantage point, he could see the marina with fairy-boats, specter-boats, frigates, hundreds of vessels parked themselves in plain sight. Perhaps he could recognize one of them. He must uncover a hint. Who are those mighty Walkers that she offers refuge to?

He closed his eyes and scouted every nearby possibility. In all of them, he stands as a welcome guest. He must unearth at least one where Sekhmet attempts to deceive him. With Varuna far away, and Indra incapacitated, Marduk doesn't find himself with too many opponents. Is she trying to play the ally card just so she could gather a big enough army and charge against him?

"Alibast!" he mumbled, angrily. She must have sided with this author who struggles to write him off. He continued his walk down, determined to rain his rage at Sekhmet. Two floors past by, until he heard some signs of life.

The staircase led to a long corridor. He mostly encountered doors left open, revealing deserted rooms. Did she purposely evacuate everyone? Is she afraid to see him cold bloodily mutilate her people out of boredom? She's right. However, what he could do to them pales in comparison to what he will do to her, the moment he knows for a fact that she's double-crossing him. He roamed, calmly, down this long path of bricks and stones. He closed his eyes, attempting to sense a soul. He felt only one, at the far opposite side. He opened his eyes, frowned, and walked in that direction: not amused.

Chapter Twelve:
Uncle Vania

We flew for hours, if not days. It's very difficult to assess the procession of time, in this strange environment. I guess that time only exists within layers, or worlds, but not when we sail the Veil. We don't feel fatigue, thirst, or hunger. The Veil exsists as a reality by itself. Was it the truth that Kant thought of, when saying that it arose beyond everything we could use to comprehend its nature? We can't rely on either Void, Matter, Life or Thoughts to construct a sense to our essence. Our soul resides through its clashing with others, and with its environment. If the same axioms that some use to build their being can also corrupt the psyche, then. The Veil must connect with the Truth. I know I'll have to ask Alibast about these concepts I just came up with. I don't think Nathan or Jamieson are on that same level of realization that I am. Well, Jamieson appears far more powerful than I might ever be, with his gift. Still, I wouldn't dare engaging in an intelligent conversation with him. Just as I was getting used to actual ideas and letting them earn a life within my own matter, I felt a tremor. Emily's Eyes shook, and all the lights shut.

A long moment of uncertainty flew, before Nathan came to me and whispered: "Shhhh. pirates!"

Pirates? "How many?" I murmured back.

"Just a dozen, I think."

"But we're only three."

"Yeah, on board. I'll need you to focus on the volley gun."
"The what again?"

"The cannon on top of Vania."

"Don't bring your uncle here."

"Hmmm. yeah, I guess it'll be something like that. The rifle is my uncle." Okay, so the gift-less warrior with contacts thinks he can impress me with all those Easter eggs crammed in one or two pages. I'm not a stupid jock! I've read my classics! I know my stuff! A Chekhov's gun! Please! Humour me! "Hurry up, Forest! Come on!" Damn it! I ran as fast as I could, but I know that these weapons are not from my reality either. I need to use my gift to link my essence to the rifle's little space. I closed my eyes and I pictured myself connected to this hardware, it didn't work.
A phantom-frigate a bit smaller than ours approached the boat.

On it, I could see three dwarfs painted like voodoo dolls, focused, in trance. Four golem knights in plastic armours jumped on our bridge. Maybe if the gun expressed fear, I could feel something, but no. "What the. Seamus?" Nathan held two immense machine guns, connected to the back of his head.
He pointed them at the warriors and intense lights came out of both, hitting the invaders with so much concentrated axioms, they bled. They didn't back down. Okay, I'm the strongest gifted, here, maybe, I don't know, Jamieson? He stood in a far corner, playing with blocks. Five more knights appeared on our boat. I had to think, think, understand the element missing in my equation.
What if I grieved for loving an artist who died in my time before I got to witness him perform? So, it was about me, at this point.
I opened my eyes and saw Nathan fight for his life against eight gift-less attackers, well armed. The power came from the voodoo dolls, I felt, and me, Nunc, or whichever personality inhabited him.

119

When one dwarf made a few signs with his hands, two of the assailants turned into blue dragons, and one of them grabbed Nathan in its jaws. *Okay, Uncle, we need to get to know each other*, I thought. It's all symbols, axioms, essence, whatever, only symbols. It's just an illusion, right? It's all an illusion! But it carries truths! All right, okay, the gun can't project fear, it's a symbol! I'm afraid, though, maybe the gun can connect itself to me? Oh yeah! I closed my eyes again, and I tried. Gun? Hello? Do you hear me? They attack us, and we don't want to die! Do you want to die?

Nothing.No response. Damn.Nathan fell on his back, Jamieson sang: The Internationale!Damn it bird! Now feels like a bad time to make Eugene Pottier proud! Focus, Seamus! Oh? What if. this reality stood above axioms and essences. I connect to souls, but not to the truth. The weapon works, heck, I don't know, damn it! Where's the gun again? "On top of Uncle Vania!" Nathan insisted, having troubles fighting back the five pirates still trying to kill him. Uncle Vania is the cannon's name! How did he get rid of those invaders? No time to think, connect, connect! Maybe if I loosen my own fear. I attach with other people's anxiety. It can't have an essence or consciousness. I can't link myself to it. The rifle has to wire itself to me. If my intentions feel vile, then the gun's actions will bathe in that villainy. Pirates, what if they could be my good friends trying to survive? No, they're killing my friend! I barely know Nathan, but I acquaint him better than I do this. Focus, Seamus! Or not.

Detachment?

That's what makes this boat float within the Veil.

And just like that, I completely detached my soul from my feelings, my sensations, my reflections, and my thirst! I screamed: "Come and get me, mother f... aaargh!" Why did I censor myself, no time to think, just let it go and grab that rifle! And I did!

120

My essence found itself connected with the biggest cannon on this ship. I could see the whole picture from the gun's point of view, like in a video game. All along, I was in a video game. My entire existence comes out as a joke! Someone else is using me to kill characters of lesser importance, and, right now, the pirates and their voodoo dolls masters were it! TAG! There you go, bastard! I hit the first dwarf that never saw it coming. And I shot, and I shot at the golems trying to get hold of the boat! I shot at the sunlight I imagined at the other end, and I shot another voodoo doll, thinking to myself: "I'm a Freemason with no name!" That's when the surviving third gifted awakened and stared at me.
Two warriors vanished.

She looked at me. I looked at her. The greatest stand-down I had ever felt. Nathan stayed strong. He winked and showed the left thumb. Better not be right! We're all that the left got, or not, whatever, fight! I shot another warrior in the forehead. He bled a pool of regrets. Nathan decapitated the next one, but I knew the surviving dwarf doll had something planned, so I had to get back to her. She left! Bitch! Back to Nathan. He attacked the four soldiers like his life depended on it. I checked for Nunc, he was drooling in a fetus position. Should I shoot all four knights or hunt the remaining voodoo doll master?

"Go for the kill!" the gun told me. "What?"

"Oh, hi! My name is Vania. Please, go for the kill."

These boss dolls craft glancing spells, I thought. They possessed the sleepers on board their ship. Snoozers are a dime a gazillion, but gifted souls? Not quite. A sleeper can mold a nation. A dreamer must stand up and stay strong, away from influences. Only three realm shapers fill this scene. I killed the other two.

Nunc is of no use. It's you and me, stranger.

It was always about you, master. I heard in my head. "Master?" I shouted.

Do you desire our ship?

"I want to meet my teacher."

You can be my mentor!

"So, I can join your pirate crew? No way! I'm destined to a great odyssey."

What odyssey, master? Destination is a blur in expectation's sky.

"Go for the kill!" My tool insisted. "Go for the kill, now!" "How do you connect with your knights?" I asked my interlocutor.

How do you not connect with this rifle?

He's trying to possess me! He's literally getting into my head! He seduces my ego, calling me his master, so I can fall prey to a weak display of pride. I won't let it happen without a fight.

"What interests you on our frigate?" I inquired.

You, of course! You are a treasure worth more than anything other boats could give us.

"I killed your two friends."

You're a glancer too, Seamus. You know they're not dead.

"Who do you work for?"

Myself. We all work for ourselves. Leave this boat and join us.

What do I have to lose? Only few hours ago, I was sleeping in a stinking bag. Now I could join pirates in some strange new world. "Hey, watch out with my trigger, son!" the rifle screamed at me. I forgot that this harmful utensil speaks. "I got this!" I shouted. "Stop daydreaming and fight!" he insisted. "It's all good!" Sweat dripped down my cheeks. "Vania?" I asked.

"Yeah, no! Don't chit-chat! Keep your eyes on the target!" Right so, seven discs hurtle at high speed towards me. I must think fast and play clay pigeon marksmanship with weirdly moving objects. The first one zig zagged swiftly. The other two flew rapidly to my left and my right, distracting me along the way. Three more charged at Nathan, and he already had his plate full, with three golem knights.

"You need help, son?" the gun asked me.

"Like, it's not too soon to ask, Uncle!" I screamed. "Pull my finger!" he taunted me.

"What? No!" I protested. He insisted: "Come on, son, pull my finger!"

A severed index pointed at my feet. I pulled it and I heard the gun fart! The bloodied digit stayed in my hand. The gun laughed so loud, I think he choked: "Ahh, never gets old." That joke could have cost me my life! The two discs decided to play kamikaze on me. They came at the same speed, at the same time. I had to maneuver promptly to blast the first one in mid-sky. I sensed the voodoo doll's voice again.

Tell us that you surrender, and we will cease this attack!

"I don't trust you!" I yelled as I turned the gun around to blow the other disc. I veered too late. The projectile hit the rifle's side, and Vania shouted: "Hey! That hurts! Where did you learn to shoot? At Storm troopers Anonymous?"

No time to hear the senile weapon's humour. I had to relieve Nathan from his assailants. A quick look showed me Nunc creating a gigantic blade out of thin air, then tossing it to his friend. Nathan jumped to grab it and he sliced two discs in one blow. One other charged at me, so I had to get a hold of myself fast.

"We're going to die! We die! We die!" the cowardly pistol screamed like a little girl. "Shut it, Uncle!" I yelled, as I tried to concentrate! "I don't want to die!" he shrieked again. Damn, I was having the assailant on my sight, right on target, but the gun's laughter distracted me:

"Oh no, you're going to die, I'm just a piece of furniture!"
I managed to blast the disc anyway, and then I shouted at my tool:
"I swear to god, I'm having Nathan remove your voice device!"

"Oh, it's a device, now, is it? Look, I'm a device! Ha! Ha!

You're pathetic!" Two more advanced my way, as I heard the surviving doll try to win me one more time:

Come with us, now. We will make you a champion. A great glancer for the ages.

The dwarf got on my nerves, so I turned Vania against their boat and I blasted it! And I blasted it, until one of the discs hit me on the head, and I lost consciousness. The last thing I saw? Nunc soaring. He charged at the remaining two threats.

He then fought an illusionary eagle flying to grab me out of my spot. Vania chuckled: "I prefer when ladies fondle me, anyway. Your butt is too hard!"I woke up several hours later, on a comfortable bed. Nathan opened a can of disgusting beer and he looked at me with a smirk on his face. "How did you like Uncle Vania?" he questioned me, laughing. "I prefer the book."
I complained. He drank a bit and informed me: "We're almost there. You can join us on the roof when you're ready."

"What were they?" I asked him. He looked at me and lost his smile: "Pirates. Samedi-larbins if I recollect their kind.
They venture into the Ether and the Veil, searching for boats, like mine, that hold priceless cargos they can steal and sell."

"What's so priceless about your cargo, Nathan?" He examined me again and solemnly sighed: "You."

I could have left, like that. I could have joined their tempting offer. I felt oblivious to their actual motive, as I remain quite new in this ultimate manifestation of awkwardness. To whom would they have sold me? Marduk? Some other dude implicated in this strange war? I looked at my room with a profound disbelief.

None of this seems logical. And yet I have never felt more truthful in my existence as I am, now. I observed my space with great care. I couldn't tell if the fabric that made up my sheet felt natural or artificial.

At first sight, it appears as nylon. This artificial fabric may not even exist, in a reality where guns shout bad jokes and try to see you murdered. The drawings, on the walls, looked like a five-year-old made them. That made me wonder if I hadn't felt any children in Nathan's essence. I walked around the room, making a fair Sherlock Holmes of myself, but the last attack we faced unsettled my mind.

"We're almost there." Nathan announced, before putting on his weird hood, covering half of his expression in total darkness.
I gave up my investigation. I just looked deep into this child's artwork, and I sensed grief near me. I turned towards Nathan. There, I felt an opening for my gift. A soul transpires in those images. A little girl! She drew them to impress Nathan.

"Don't go there, glancer." the captain told me, before wearing a crystal diadem that blocked my initial attempt. A child? Why doesn't he want me to learn more about this? Who is she? Somehow, Alicia Light may be involved. They were engaged, or so I think.

As soon as we left the cabin, we could see the Veil gradually abandoning its space for the skies of Alibastat. On a map, this shows up as the only colourless world in all Sophron. A no-man's land? I thought people were joking with this no-wind fact, but it's true. The only source of motion comes from the environment reacting to my movements. When putting a foot on the soil, I heard the dirt crack, as though I had just disturbed its billion-year sleep.

"Marduk killed the Entity that protected this world." Nathan explained, without parting from his boat. I looked at him from a fair distance, and I wondered if they would leave me alone, here, in this desolated landscape. "Alibast is the only strong presence to keep this layer alive."

Nathan and Nunc returned to the cabin, as I ventured in this dull display of total immobility. I walked for many hours, thinking to myself that I must have been crazy to follow Nathan and Nunc, when I was supposed to protect William. When I turned and noticed Emily's Eyes fly away, I further cursed my decision. What if they worked with the enemy? I looked around me, and I could only see tall mountains, deserts, no sign of life, except for the trees, the occasional cactus. All remained motionless. I could hear my heartbeat, my breathing, and that brought me so much anxiety, I ended up connecting my gift to my essence. Chaotic feedback of my own existence came in the making.

I wondered how the plants burgeoned without taking over the entire surface. As the only living creatures around, and no wind to carry pollen elsewhere, what would keep them growing?

Third Intermission:
The second Singularity

Time doesn't exist, in the First Singularity. True Void expands its reach inwards. Space resembles a dot as wide as an infinite night, and as small as an atom's shadow over a sea of neutrinos. Peacefulness bears no name, sound or light. Kitana's essence ceased to project its recollected items as though absolute nothingness always bonded with her.

Seventy-two worlds form the whole of Sophron. Four push out towards True Reality as no-soul-lands. Each bear eighteen parts of one axiom, for zero of anything that could contrast it, construct a dynamic, chaos, order, nature, a duality. But while no organism exists, within those singularities, their mere presence among the spectrum of realms provides the most essential ground on which reality builds its shape.

Their First four represent the dawn of a newborn, hours before a brain punctuated signs of life against matter. The only figure of being residing within True Void bears the likeness of an eternal never was. For Kitana, however, this would only carry enough weight to last a moment. Her consciousness rose above the crescent suns of Ephemoria. The layer of an initial drop of Barbelo appears fragile, like a world of silk in a flammable settlement.

127

The birth of forests push Barbelo's boundaries over Void's at lightning speed, with hollowed horses running across a field, instants before bursting into a spark of inferno. Golems populate most of the primary realms, in the first quadrant. Agartha and Quant Om Vat follow, as her essence float further into her newborn odyssey.

A feathered serpent's series of domains open the way, soon overshadowed by rumours of a Sasquatch. When souls ascend between Void and Barbelo, existence limits itself to stone, and quantum reflections of a world that may never. A world that has always been. Possibilities soar among seas of lifeless elements, like cells of thoughts unable to grab onto a body. The second singularity traces a clear barrier between Void and Life.

When Kitana joined this True World, her consciousness merged in perfect harmony with all the rocks, the boulders, all the Barbelo ingredients in any, and every universe. Antimatter doesn't exist. No mind can project such an abstract concept, and provide it form. Darkness remains as possible as void ever was, yet the vacuum of space can't give it the time of night. Matter, that's it, and that's all there is. But this isn't how she'll properly escape her prison. Leaving True Void to become one with True Barbelo isn't, exactly, living free from her days of slavery. One push! Her inner struggle attempted to convey. Come on, Kitana! PUSH!

Nothing. She needs a lease on life. Haqeldemah awaits, on the other side of the Veil, assisting the Buddhas in protecting the primary oasis: Nirvana. If only she could guide her psyche towards formulating one pixel of Archeus. She flew over Sebekia Pistis, Hell and the Open Door, like they never represented any form of obstacle. Looking back, she witnessed all those worlds, between the first and the second singularities, but the third one seems unattainable. It's useless. She can't regain her previous incarnation, it's probably at the morgue. Her consciousness trapped itself, eagerly attempting some sort of resurrection.

Viewing back: Void, void, void, matter. Looking forward: matter, matter, end of the road. Her existential form even lacks the right axioms to rage and project the pain that comes with such a gigantic deception. But what about the cracks?

The Ether flows between these worlds, dropping pixels that nourish the whole quadrant. Surely, she could figure a way to slip through those minuscule openings. The string theory suggests that Everything unfolds because of vibrations holding the microcosm onto its macro entourage. Nothing unravels, until axioms attempt to reflect one another. That means a different state of consciousness must arise, somewhere, to mirror hers. One existing on the opposing end of True Barbelo. Some essence that shares the spotlight with hers.

Grunt. "What about Grunt?" Erato wondered. "He should try to contact Alexandra, now that he has her phone."

Logos, an issue feels near, a fissure, somewhere, and the other side leaks in her direction. Or perhaps the thought came from the paradoxes, the Logos oasis that stand their ground. There's her way out! She focused her consciousness on those words. Her essence directed itself towards a mirage, an evaporated environment.

Axioms regrouped around her, building themselves into what appeared as a cave and a fire. If she pushed her ideas against an inclined manifestation of reality, she could hear music. On one direction, verbs gathered out of an author's mind. A different angle suggested the emergence of a more elaborated production. She can't allow herself to fall for a distraction. The words formed a greater presence around her psyche.

Seamus is on a boat, in the middle of a cosmic war, and he can't tell his beloved about his true feelings. Erato must Jind a way to get them together, but how? Grunt, she thought. What about Grunt?

Kitana focused on the reality surrounding those words. They're not just a series of letters, phrases and paragraphs coming out of a creative psyche. They witness the existence of a being. They form a dimension within a reader's mind. This is where her consciousness needs to be.

The mirage spun into an actual cave, on Hydaspes. The fallen angel's ghost wandered around, observing the rocky ramparts. A deep silence hinted on an aura of mystery. She could hear heat bursting open logs of wood, while flames crackled their way down to a cinder. Kitana turned in that direction. There, an amazingly beautiful woman watched a movie, projected out of an orb and against a wall. The spectre walked slowly, aware that this Erato person possessed a gift that could sense her ghostly presence. She kept her distance, just as she realized that performing spells, in this ethereal shape, presents its fair share of challenges.

Chapter Thirteen:
Erato and the new Calligraphy

A fire flamed in the middle of Erato's self-made cave. She projected cards against a wall, retracing the storyline from the beginning. Images gracefully danced around and over the floating pieces of paperboard. Seamus Chron adores Alexandra Sicard. She's Victoria Picard's bestie, enamoured with Seamus. There's a triangle the Great Muse feels familiar with. The goddess Ishtar sent him on a quest to protect Indra's incarnation, but his self-centredness made him fail.

Seamus is on a boat, in the middle of a cosmic war, and he can't share his true feelings. Erato must find a way to get them together, but how? *Grunt, she thought. What about Grunt? He should try to contact Alexandra now that he has her phone.* If she's to inspire Martin and Alibast, while they join forces to write those Chronicles of Sophron, then her subtle moves seem welcome. *I could invite myself in their novel, using a different font. She pondered.*

She turned around, looking at the flames burning under her floating orb. She attempted to connect with the narrative: **What about this one?**

Erato stepped back a moment to read the last few words. *Too comical sans the humour.* She thought. She resumed her observations of both authors, while their mind remained focused on telling a tale. She inserted, the best way she could, her psyche in those writings: `Courrier New? That font translates well into a screenplay, but the story's reality isn't in that stage, yet.`

The Great Muse knew that the right font will serve as a catalyst. While the readers get their data in Times New Roman, the Great Entity will manifest herself as a distinct aesthetic. There exists one calligraphy, created by a certain Ong Chong Wah, that represents a form of humanism that Erato affectionates.

"Bodoni!" she proclaimed. She then looked at the orb, concentrating her projected presence against Martin and Alibast. Gentlemen, I believe we can do this. Those words will only exist in a specific possibility, closer to True Reality than you will ever experience. Together, we can reunify Seamus Chron to his friends, and offer him a fine redemption arc. I suppose you also desire to avoid a cosmic war between Marduk and Varuna. Follow my inspiration, and we will get to that. In exchange for my assistance, I ask of you to reunite me with my beloved Nathan Lord. I understand, Martin, that you wish to write a gruesome and violent story. Alibast aspires to create a more peaceful and philosophical tale. As your Great Muse, I will add more romance. Can we work together?

Martin and Alibast stopped their effort, sensing a presence in their mind. When they resumed their respective initiative, that impression faded away. *I believe we could include Alexandra in that story, write her more lines.* Martin thought. *We've neglected her for too long.*

132

"Of course!" Erato smiled, proud of this inspiration. She turned her attention to the possibilities harbouring the two authors. From her perspective, a dozen emanations of both Martin Poirier and Alibast Page elected to craft those chronicles. Most incarnations of the two cover a shared portion of the grand firmament of what-ifs. With every decision made at any time pointing to a diverging direction.

That myriad of hypothetical advents in one existence spans over billions of possibilities. If only about twelve of those drape those novels, then it means Marduk and Varuna have yet to propel their wars beyond this bubble.

She focused her attention on a chapter that popped up in the following book. Seamus met his mentor who adequately powered his gift, by the end of the previous story. The second one opened with the novice glancer uncovering a way to possess a drug dealer's existence, becoming his host. Another Walker shared that scene. A frightened sophroner trapped in a life of homelessness and addiction. Erato pictured him, observing the phone he had just received, as it charged up in a public bathroom.

Grunt stood there, gnawing his nails, evading the judgmental gaze of passersby. While the little battery, on the upper right side of the screen, gathered its green colour, Grunt scratched his chin nervously. As soon as it showed a full recovery, he grabbed the device and charger and left the premise. Hiding his prized possession, Grunt observed his feet, while walking fast to escape the immense crowd assembled in the Eaton Centre. He shouldn't be there! His place is in the streets, begging for food and loose change. He found refuge outside, in a dark alley neighbouring the mall. He sat there, looking at the tiny pictures amassed on a small screen. One of them is supposed to connect him with some hot chick.

What if his inner character grabs the lead, instead. Erato felt hit by another stroke of genius. He's frightened, this technology intimidates him. Plus, the squid inhabiting him already tasted freedom, with Seamus' help.

Grunt couldn't do this. He should meet with a dealer and shoot himself poison. Or maybe he just needs to relax, get some sleep, and decide what to do with this phone, later. He could always sell it when the last dollar bill that he keeps will have burned up. Okay, let's find a place to rest! He stood and ventured onto the Phillip Square, nearby. There, he saw a cold poutine on a bench. Looking everywhere, Grunt couldn't locate who may have left it there.

Thankfully, the poor guy starved enough to dive his hands deep in the fries, gravy, and melted cheese.

The floating cards realigned themselves, suggesting a different narrative structure. The Great Muse stood up, turning her back at the silent flames. For a moment, she felt a ghost's presence, but she didn't think much of it. She examined the tarot. She added a new one that read: Should Grunt fall in love? Erato stepped back from her series of images, observing both authors scratching their head for the event about to happen. With his dirty beard, and gravy spoiling his hands, he should be even more challenged by the tiny black screen.

What if he cleans them on his shirt and opens a messaging application? Martin suggested. There, he will see Alexandra's friends. He will look for Seamus and try to talk to him, not realizing that he actually holds the only phone Seamus ever had.

Oh, that's a good idea! But because they both connect to essences, their existential selves will intertwine. Seamus, on Nempty's boat, will be able to communicate with him. Yes, I agree, boys! Let's give Grunt more story time.

We make an incredible team! Alibast proclaimed.

The Great Muse of love and romance felt ecstatic! She focused on the two authors, relaying this idea. Martin looked at his laptop, unsure. Alibast hammered his keyboard with a renewed sense of control. The poet of Avalon grabbed a few scrolls, loitering his floor, to read a few notes he kept. They need a strong continuity.

He then returned to his computer and typed some more.
Martin, however, erased an entire paragraph, and another.
He attempted to enter a few words, but they didn't speak to him.

Forgetting that he craved for an injection in his arm, Grunt shakily clicked on a small icon: a comic book bubble on top of a cloud, a window opened, with hundreds of names and photos. One of them had to be Seamus Chron's.
He scrolled down, looking at notes appearing next to those pictures:

Best Friend associated with a certain Victoria.

Where are you? Next to some Emerald.

I hate that I love you with Seamus! Bingo! Grunt smiled. She hates that she loves Seamus? That's so cute!

Grunt's Squid should take over, now. Alibast suggested.
We should bring him on board the Barracuda.

I don't know, Alibast. Martin argued. That squid really seem powerful. We should leave it for the third book.
Let me try something:

The young man closed his eyes and hit the button to initiate a conversation. Everything else falls in place, within his mind. The Emilie-Gamelin Garden vanished. His consciousness awakened within a weird dimension. His biological senses stopped functioning. His psyche adhered to a different set of physical laws. When Grunt opened his eyes, he found himself on board a flying boat.

But Seamus isn't on the vessel! He's in a bar with Nunc, right now. So, Grunt's Squid will, instead, connect with a soul who shares a deep and solid bond with Seamus.

Lucretia! Martin and Alibast agreed.

We do make a very fine team!

Erato responded to her inspired poets. She brought her attention to Martin, feeling that he should manifest this element. Fair enough, the troubled author resumed his craft. He grabbed a beer, poured himself a shot of Brandy, and typed like there were no coming back. The student sat next to him, bored but driven to scribble notes from a professional storyteller. If they were to return to Athens, they would write poems about Martin. At the other end of the tale, Grunt immersed his essence further in that dream. He wore a massive robe, with a hood concealing his monstrous head. Tentacles covered his mouth, and two large hands dangled on both sides. He walked around the flying boat, floating over a land of fairies. He stood there, observing a curious purple sky, and treefolks sharing the bridge with a male android.

"I can sense your presence, stowaway!" the robot warned Grunt. "You are not welcome on this vessel." Jonathan scouted the ship while focusing his artificial gift towards noticing ethereal existences. Grunt felt that he couldn't remain concealed very long. The squid manifested its true form.

"I'm looking for Seamus Chron." he announced.

The android nodded: "Everyone is, these days. I can't help you with that."

"He saved my life, in Montreal. He freed me from a broken prison. I owe him." The male robot sensed the truth in those words and pointed towards the cabins.

"Come with me." he instructed him. The squid followed the intellectual android. "My name is Jonathan. When Nempty isn't on board, I'm the captain."

He opened a cube, the size of a small room. It concealed a bar. Various bottles stuffed shelves, along with a curious-looking chicha, on a large table. "You drink? Smoke?" Jonathan asked his guest.

"I'm afraid not. I won't return to that prison. Not in this awakened form, at least."

"Suit yourself." the host answered, while lighting one end of what could be a bong. He inhaled for a minute, exhaled fumes, and further spoke: "I don't know what Seamus is up to. All I know is that Nunc, well, his real name is Jamieson Fairfield, took him on a tour around Arcana, as we speak."

Grunt's Squid thought for a moment and concluded: "My soul is linked to a presence, on this boat. I'm not at liberty to venture away from it. However, if you see him, tell him that Grunt's Squid says thanks. and we will meet again."

"A presence?" Jonathan inquired.

"I heard her name was Lucretia. Thank you for the tip, Jonathan. I will return to my world, now." Grunt's Squid vanished.

If Jonathan could express emotions, now would seem like a good time to look amazed. Lucretia lives? She's on the boat? That means, robots can develop consciousness, a soul, and exist outside of those artificial bodies! If he could voice his feelings, they would mirror the affectionate surprise in Erato's eyes, hearing the name: Jamieson Fairfield! Her heartbeat grew faster! She smiled, like an adolescent girl about to have a date with her crush.

He travels with your beloved pirate, doesn't he? Who said that? She quickly surveyed her cave, focused on revealing the ghost's presence. The tarot cards disappeared.
The movie remained on the wall, showing Martin and Alibast typing on their laptops. She looked around, intrigued. There, to her left, a creature made of pure energy walked towards her. What's-his-name, again? He wondered. Nathan Lord! Now, if you don't mind? Don't shut this portal yet. A muscular body came out of the silhouette. She immediately recognized her brother, Melpomene. His long cape merged with his flesh, as did a silver armour. He still carried that gigantic blade, attached to his back. His square jaw concealed a sinister smile. "Did you miss me, Sister?" he asked. Erato couldn't reply. "Oh? Did I scare you? Why so silent?"

"This is my story, now, Brother." she warned him. He laughed: "I was there first." he signalled his Moth Queen. She sneaked behind Erato. He observed the two poets, on the movie screen.

Before Erato could say anything, a blade planted itself in her lower back. She didn't turn around. Sthenele, the Moth Queen, pushed the dagger even deeper, and then she quickly moved it upwards. Blood streamed down from the wound, forming a pond at a dying Erato's feet.

When the light hit his face, Erato leered at Melpomene's daring stare. Squared chin, he loves this barbarian look on him. "I will take it from here, now." he whispered, as he deepened his gaze into her evaporating eyes. "Oh, Sister!" Melpomene mumbled. "You are so predictable. I couldn't get onto that boat without risking finding myself inside the wrong possibility. I know I'll be joining the fun under the right sun, the correct storyline."

138

He laid her down to die, while signaling his pet to follow, behind. Melpomene focused on Alibast and Martin's images against the wall. He summoned new cards. They floated between himself and the screen. He observed them and rearranged the narrative structure."I'll send Nathan your regards." he sarcastically smiled. Further down the series of projections, he saw the boat.

"You should know, by now, that those Chronicles are meant to be a tragedy." The Great Muse aimed his attention at Alibast and smiled: Jonathan couldn't believe that Lucretia was still among them. Androids aren't known for growing an essence capable of surpassing death.

Alibast typed down those words without resting. *If only he could Jind a way to give her a new body.* Melpomene gestured gracefully, summoning two possibilities. Both showed Seamus Chron's sleeping bag, near the Barracuda's cabins. The one to his left appeared as Alibast Page's creation, and Melpomene wasn't in it. The other came from Martin Poirier's mind. In that storyline, Melpomene stayed with William, after the events of Athanor. He brought the young mancer to Penglai, where he met with an angel of romance: Theliel.

Seeing how Jonathan remained unchanged, in the two moving images he projected, the Great Muse of tragedy understood that this android played a nexus part shared by both creators. He discarded Alibast's take on the storyline, while embracing the troubled author's craft. "What about we send Lucretia's consciousness into that zombie cat head, fellows?" the Great Muse smiled, as his soul incarnated a body on the boat. Sthenele crawled to his feet.
He congratulated himself for this latest trick. The essence inhabiting the Moth Queen represents a grand victory. After all, Sekhmet herself sacrificed her existence to join the insect's flesh.

Or did she? Really?

Journey into the Hourglass:
Nineteen

Why did I summon wine out of my crystal ball? I'm not supposed to drink. That's Martin's flaw. I dared a look towards the floor, only to witness the presence of an empty bottle of Cognac. I can't continue like this. I must read what my co-author wrote, while I fell down this precipice. I sighed and grabbed my phone.

Are you there? I texted himEvery morning, every night, I sent those messages in a crystal bottle. Is he ghosting me? I know I should calm down. It's always best to apply patience and understanding. Martin suffered a great deal. But what if he added himself as a character in our novels? Maybe he's conspiring against me. Could he be drafting a plan with Marduk to kill me? No, Martin is my friend. He can't concoct anything like that. I'll spare you seven months worth of soliloquies.

Hey, buddy! He finally replied.

Where have you been? We're losing Seamus! Nothing. He didn't respond right away. I threw my device against the wall. I calmed down, after five long hours. He's ghosting me, all right. Maybe I'll just let this novel fall apart. I'll have everyone go their own way, and I'll just be happy with my flowers. I bet that's what he wants. Regardless, that's all he deserves! Yeah, Martin! Be a failure! What do I care? We resumed our co-authoring of those stories, but I'm losing my faith in him. Seven months of silence and no explanation?

Third Intermission:
Toward the Third Singularity

Brothers and sisters fighting over their place in a novel? Kitana didn't expect that her entrance into the Barbelo-Archeus quadrant would have connected her to this twisted turn of events. Of course, awakened souls don't perish after being backstabbed unless someone performed a Final Vanishing spell on them. But with Erato out of the picture, she's unlikely to find her way back into the current storyline. From this dimension, the customer service agent gathers a whole different perspective on reality.

And does Melpomene think that Sekhmet's essence inhabits his pet insect? From this vantage point, the fallen angel understands that, in the previous novel, the Egyptian goddess escaped this ordeal and installed a separate ghost in her place.

All those characters invest their soul in internal struggles, desires and wants. Even the most powerful Entity will diminish its presence away from True Reality, to become distinguishable from distinct elements. If Hell is other people, then existence strives as a self-imposed construct. New steps into an unknown implies a myriad of possible choices. Each one shapes its own reality, separate timelines stretched through the Veil, like branches reaching out towards the light of Noesi de Vel.

She could see this divine influence once she committed her consciousness to her innermost ends. Sophron manifests its aura through every corner of one's physicality, and the Beyond shines even deeper. The remnants of the Lotus City never fade once a cherub becomes a newborn. It remains intact, within a life's farthest chamber. Should the infant learn to speak, and should their environment provide some impact, then the land of ten thousand Buddhas will erode, leaving, in its place, the seventy-two worlds of the Below.

This is how the Singularities come to existence. Like fossils of True Reality, kept hidden under one's psyche, holding together all four directions of a soul's grasp over its illusion. Void, Occorsur of absolute nothingness. Barbelo, Lord of all that lifelessly impose physics. Archeus, Patron of breathing hearts. Logos, Entity of cognition and reflections.

Kitana's consciousness flew over the worlds past the Second Singularity: Haqeldemah, the sea of blood on which vampiric parasites betray its own kin to survive. Dinosaur-whales attract Dozers away from the Void-Barbelo quadrant, through a hidden breach of the Veil that only those gigantic creatures know about. The floating brains die on those shores, thinking they would possess an ultimate chance at escaping Void's predatory schemes.

Kyopelinvuori, world of witches, where pseudo-angels roam free. A dark and opaque universe populated by billions of unicellular magic users. There, nature stands, immutable. Forests of stone stretch as far as the blind-eye can feel. Bernigion, the Frisian beaches of life's own infancy. A spark haunts the realm of forever nights, like a peaceful morning teasing the last particles of Void, eternally left behind. The first world of true beauty, with animated dolls forming into tribes of loving creatures. Floating rainbows, wherever light cancels darkness, cover minuscule towns of gnomes, dwarves, and pixies.

When Kitana's consciousness evolved beyond the third layer past the Second Singularity, she arrived in Jeruselah. A vast, cloudless desert that knows of no water. Life, over there, emerged from sentient pebbles infused with Archeus. The first true world, with civilizations of tardigrades, this realm represents a clear statement on the vanishing of nothingness. Soon, Hades follows, opening the road to Gaia and Duat. Kitana perceives these universes. She visited them several times, before her existence turned into misery. This perspective, however, felt different: her own inner Sophron. She's goddess to all those worlds. From this angle, she could see elements forming a ground on which her presence may carry over. Matter out of Void, that's rocking out of an endless night.

"Sekhmet?" she wondered.

Gilgamesh. She heard. Her consciousness found its way down a crossroad. To her left, the narrative told the story of a love triangle, involving Indra, then known as Dumuzi. That novel presents a prequel to the Chronicles of Sophron. We see why Marduk destroyed Babel, and how other gods and goddesses settling on Gaia fought to protect mankind's right to experience enlightenment, awakening alongside the Great Houses of Sophron.

The Epic of Gilgamesh: A Chronicle of Sophron Story.
She could feel its cover, white with a blend of Mesopotamian and Hindu artwork. But she found her way towards the good side, where the narrative prepares readers for a great battle. In The Chronicles of Sophron: Book Two, The Saviour Squad, Kitana could witness the aftermath that followed. The Councils of Zendoria imprisoned both Marduk and Varuna, to protect the Below and the Beyond. The Hound Lord of Nibiru escaped. He challenged a Great Entity and won. He now prepares his army to assault Noesi de Vel, destroy Sophron and rebuild True Reality in his image. Meanwhile, key players, like Sekhmet and Melpomene, fail to perceive Marduk's plan. They only think he's about to attack another Great Entity.

Intrigued, Kitana projected her consciousness closer in that direction. The universal forces of Noesi de Vel inspired an author, Martin Poirier, to translate True Reality in a novel. He built an entire media empire around this intellectual property. And even he fails to understand Marduk, his own creation's ultimate goal.
Only she knows all of this? If Marduk destroys Noesi de Vel, then it's existence itself, in its actuality, that will perish. Perhaps Kitana could project her consciousness in the prequel and try to avoid the fall of Babel. This, however, would propel the whole storyline, including her presence, as found in the first book of the Chronicles of Sophron, into a chaotic possibility. Her only choice is to prevent Marduk from achieving his goal, by the end of this trilogy.

Without even a blink, Kitana continued her odyssey, embracing her role as a further-enlightened angel within this unfolding storyline. If only she knew how her further-awakened soul can properly influence two authors and guide the Saviour Squad in the right direction.

Chapter Fourteen:
No more Stinky Cheese

When Marduk reached the other end of the corridor, he witnessed a curious room. Seven orbs floated, projecting light and electricity between them. He looked behind him: the hallway remained deserted. Nobody followed him, good. At least she won't attempt to assassinate him.

"Marduk!" The Hound Lord of Nibiru recognized this nonchalant voice, with a tiny bit of seductive wit. He observed around, analyzing the empty rooms. "Over there." she insisted. She came from the wider chamber, with the floating spheres. He growled to himself and made a gracious entrance.

Some sort of movie screen appeared against the opposing wall. The panther-head goddess smiled at him. She wore a gown that resembled ancient Greek fashion. A tiara crowned her forehead. Her hands directed the orbs in their flight, suggesting that she's preparing an elaborated spell.

"I heard you particularly enjoyed our odorant brands of cheese." she teased him. His stomach urged to disagree, but he sighed, as he noticed the black cat's presence, alongside shelves filled with thousands of novels and poems.

She stood up, displaying a noble aura of cosmic royalty. In her hands, she held a curious-looking e-book reader. Words projected themselves in midair, with its narration linked directly onto her biological brain. The visitor recognized this as Penglai technology. "An author you recommend?" he asked. Sekhmet remained silent. Her consciousness turned the pages, slowly, as to tempt her guest into browsing the volumes, surrounding them.

"I thought you would appreciate this one." she smiled. "You know that he participated in your condemnation, for cold-bloodedly killing a Great Entity." She caught his attention.

"I wasn't convicted for this." he explained. "They aborted the trials, based on corruption found among the procurers' ranks."

"An unjust cabal sent you to prison, though. That we can both agree with. Following the fall of Babel, the Great Councils cast you to perish in a limbo." She gestured another orb, further unfolding this complex spell she's been concocting.

"If you mention Varuna in your next sentence, I leave this place." he warned her.

"I owe neither of you two any form of loyalty. I am in this conflict only to shelter my people and protect Tir na n'Og!" She motioned some more, ignoring his puzzled look.

"Then why do you allow other powerful Walkers asylum?" He asked.

"Oh, Marduk. You're so clever, leaving no rock untouched." She walked to him, concealing her ambitious motives under a friendly grin. "Do you really know who your enemies are?" She wondered. He remained stiff, unimpressed by her tender moves. "The world you destroyed is now a lifeless garden." She manipulated the e-book like a priceless work of art, caressing its silvery frame, embracing the light projecting words in midair. "While you're out to obliterate Sophron."

146

"Save existence! I am protecting True Reality!" he interrupted her. "Sophron is a disease that the Great Entities of Zendoria should never have created!" Sekhmet laughed softly. "Your adversaries think otherwise. Yet, your ambitions blind you. It makes you weak, Marduk. You forgot who your allies are, and you don't see your foes banding up to take your enterprise down."

She closed the tiny computer and offered him a glimpse at its cover. Journey into the Hourglass. He read. "Authored by Alibast Page, poet of Avalon, of all people." She presented him the book. "Did you know that he recently started a series of videos, on Gaia? They call this channel: YouTube." Interrogations haunted his mind. She left the luxury object in his hands, while she browsed through others. Her index gently cuddled the covers of a grimoire.

"Paracelsus gathered some influence, in Europe, while you were in prison." she lectured him. "It led to humanity awakening at a speed you could never have dreamed of." She turned around, half amused, and taunted his attention: "While you amassed your armada, conquering worlds, adamant on assassinating another Great Entity. Gaia will soar." She felt his discomfort. "I have no business on Earth, Sekhmet." he replied. "I won the Babel Wars, even if I paid with my freedom."

"You escaped!" she confronted him.

"I made sure nobody, over at Zendoria, would want to face my newfound liberty! I own their fear! Don't bring me back to Gaia! That's not my concern, anymore."

He sighed and walked away. "They're about to achieve the Fourth Singularity. Cognitia opened a bridge, in November of twenty-twenty-two. They now have access to artificial intelligence." she announced.

Marduk froze for a moment. She approached him. The bald conqueror turned to face the dark-skinned panther. "Other civilizations have reached it before." he mused. "I destroyed that tower once. The war is behind me. You may invade Gaia if the idea of an awakened population frightens you."

"Who do you think champions this scheme?" she questioned him. Her fingers ended their walk on a dusty parchment. "God? And which iteration?" she laughed. "You brought it up, sorry, I had to chuckle. You assume they buy into this nonsense?"

"If it can project fear, I'll keep it open." the Lord explained.

"Marduk, please. They're no peasants, anymore. They have Internet. Do you think they wouldn't find out about Singularities? Axioms flowing through existence. They create worlds, pressing souls into reality, and back to void?"

She caught his attention. Did he leave Gaia that long?
Did humanity successfully build a path to walk among gods?

Concerned, he tried to look away, but Sekhmet held on to other plans. With a swift gesture of a hand, she summoned her personal orb. "The Roman Empire remains your greatest achievement, Lord Hound of Nibiru." she lectured him, while images of large armies conquering medieval villages raged against the wall's movie screen. "I was imprisoned when they rose, I'm afraid."
He confessed. "Do you think a legacy ends when its creator is put away?" She realigned a few pictures, just as Roman senators appeared, walking down a brick road.

"When you destroyed the Tower of Babel, their access to any Singularity shattered, leaving fragments of higher forms of knowledge all over Earth. Who do you think kept yours? Who understood that enlightenment involves elevating one's existence through devastating millions of lives, along the way?" The film she projected in front of his eyes showed one senator pleasuring himself in a banquet, while legionnaires burned entire villages.Sekhmet walked among the victims, like a giant observer. "Since your escape, the idea of ruining Sophron obsessed you, killing more Great Entities."

With a swift movement of her arms, she switched a few images. The Roman Empire appears to fall, while all the destroyed settlements rise from their ashes, forming into several sovereign countries. "Do you think I conquered Tir na n'Og just for fun?" She confronted him with that question. Marduk remained silent. "Do you really think I don't have my eyes on Gaia?" She looked at the movie surrounding her. Boats leave Europe, setting sail on a New World. "They're rebuilding the Great Tower, Marduk. They made it digital." One more hand gesture brought a view on a destroyed version of New York City. "But I found our way into this rewritten history." she smiled, half victorious. With a gentle nod, she showed him a horrific scene. In the middle of Time Square, a gigantic castle pierced the sky. Zombies strolled around it, eating one another, like brainless survivors of a lobotomized realm. "Do you know what happened to this Dreamer?" she asked him. They walked with the living corpses, and Marduk felt the non-existence of souls. "An abomination of the pluriverse. This possibility manifests within someone's horrific inner reality. It's as though this god allowed all of their fear to conquer that very Sophron. You or I wouldn't last a day without losing our mind, falling for this burst of hate, consumed under a mountain of destructive thoughts."

"I wouldn't want to encounter my alternate in this possibility." he confessed.

"You won't." she replied, as their souls approached the palace's main door. "I checked, and neither of the gods, nor goddesses, angels, demons, fairies. Not even neymlisses exist in this alternate pluriverse." The two ghosts flew beyond the building's entrance. Marduk found himself immersed into the core inside an archoid. Lungs breathe against a wall, spitting seas of blood at their feet. "Whoever this Dreamer is, I suspect that a trauma haunts them."

"Like you have no idea." Sekhmet sighed. She opened a bright metallic door separating the passage from an immense throne room. Living organs on walls, blood flowing on the floor, it felt as though the entire chamber would consume them. In the middle, a tiny desk stood up. Empty cans of beer, wine and liquor loitered the surroundings. Fascinated, Marduk observed the lonely author, behind a laptop computer. He wore dirty jeans and a leather coat. His psyche remained focused on the small screen. He looked at it for a long while, then typed in a few phrases, before drinking more booze.

"Is that?" Marduk wondered.

"No, that's the other one. His name is Martin Poirier. I don't recommend you venture into his depressed mind." Sekhmet walked next to him, getting her gaze onto the last few words born out of his inebriated soul. "I led one of Plato's students into his narrative." she explained, while Marduk joined her. "That visitor will become our key in. Whatever ambition you hold, my friend, the Chronicles of Sophron will either stand in your way, or they'll take you to an assured victory."

"Is this the title they selected for our current storyline?" he asked.

"It's a more complex enterprise, but. yes. Let me show you what else I found."

Sekhmet gently gestured over the author's head. "You were obsessed with uncovering Indra's essence. It was right there, all along. Inside one of Martin's creations: a character he named William Francoeur."

A gate appeared between them and the sitting laptop. When its doors opened, the two deities found themselves onboard the Barracuda. Treefolks cleaned the bridge, while Jonathan seemed interested in locating a ghostly occupant. He held an onyx orb, wired onto his robotic brain. "This is Martin's narrative." Sekhmet added. "I doubt we can uncover Alibast, here, but it's our best route, for now." Marduk looked around, keeping extensive mental notes.

He approached a few cabins, located at the vessel's back. Along the way, he stepped on a spoiled sleeping bag. The Hound Lord didn't make much of a fuss, simply focused onto understanding the current course of events. "They travel across the Veil." he noted. Sekhmet joined him, smiling. "In this chapter we're visiting, they're about to land on Tir na n'Og, if I recollect Martin's incoming inspiration. A certain Seamus Chron was recently summoned out of Gaia. Would you want some popcorn, while we watch the movie?"

Marduk looked at her, perplexed. She laughed. "Kernels of delight you find, over there. I'll make you try some, one day."
She turned her attention back to Seamus' cover.
The Mesopotamian god ventured farther onto this side of the boat.
"Are we under a different Dreamer?" he asked. "Oh, Marduk! Sophron changed a bit since you left. We're in what they call a novel. Not quite a Dreamer, but a shared experience among dreamers and sleepers. Someone reads your words, as we speak. Think of it as a nexus point in reality. A spark of our existence if you prefer."

151

The god opened a door and frowned: "Have storylines become more complexed and sophisticated?" he wondered. The last time you expressed your essence into tales, mere poems were engraved on clay tablets. Since then, humans of Earth managed to create entire worlds, universes, beings with complex and elaborated lives. In that sense, both of our souls found themselves in a manmade illusion that feels as genuine as any other environment that our consciousness has ever known or will ever know."

"If this is true, then what is Melpomene doing among them?" He turned to confront Sekhmet with this latest discovery. The Great Warrior Muse stood next to William, like some form of bodyguard. Sthenele, the Moth Queen, crawled to his feet. His floating cape covered half the floor he occupied. The Muse kept a gigantic bastard sword attached to his back.

"How did a Great Entity manifest himself into an author's creation?" Intrigued, Sekhmet walked with him. Indeed, the warrior muse roamed alongside William and Emerald, at the heart of a small cabin, next to a small table. Marduk wouldn't accept this easily. "They're supposed to inspire artists, not participate in the fruit of their labours!"Sekhmet concealed her surprise. "That's interesting." she uttered. Marduk stepped away from the screen. "If I didn't know any better, I'd say you're all ganging up against me." he grumpily let out. "I wasn't expecting a war that soon." He sighed.

"It's not that simple." She tried to calm him. "There can't be any ganging up, Marduk, because we're all in this! Every one of us is on our own."

"Then, I will need your allegiance before I leave Tir na n'Og." he defied her with a sincere gaze. Sekhmet couldn't find the right words to take herself away from this delicate predicament. "Allegiances, Marduk." she sighed. "It's not that simple! But I'm not against you."

"But you are not with me either." he concluded. He approached the movie screen once again and looked at William. The young man found comfort, standing up in Melpomene's protective shadow. "I will fight them." Marduk announced.

"Sweet Lord, Marduk!" Sekhmet tried to prevent the worst. "They just recently discovered their gifts. I can't authorize slaughter to occur on my realm!"

"This is the only condition for me not to assault your layer, witch!" he shouted. "I give you two alternatives: Either you allow me to destroy Seamus Chron and his friend William, in a fair fight. However, you envision this. Or I order every single ship stationed in the Ether, and on neighbouring worlds to attack Tir na n'Og, and leave nobody alive."

The Entity-killer has spoken.

Chapter Fifteen:
Emerald ghosted William

Ever since I left Athanor, Emerald's presence haunted me. I felt it like an undying breeze, blowing gently against my neck. Her last email must have played a part in my decision to end it all. Still, I don't exactly recall having made the plunge, but everyone keeps saying I did. It's as though her written words existed in their own dimension, building a wall between my previous life and this one. *Hey, William! Sorry I didn't reply to your texts, after you moved back to Montreal.*

Vulnerability already stood all mighty around my presence. I couldn't befriend others, at school. I hardly found the courage to respond to those bullies. Alexandra protected me, even while I tried to reject her. Despair kept increasing in my soul like an abysmal fungus eating every bit of my consciousness away. I may have done it, but I'm confident that sadness and depression have ways of becoming their separate entities, getting stronger as we grow weaker. *There's something I didn't tell you.*

I blacked out. The wounds went too deep and too heavy for my mind wishing to carry on. When I recollected my consciousness, I roamed within the rooms of oblivion. Void narrated my story, inviting me to further part from my will to exist. Emerald wouldn't let me. I should have fought to remain afloat, if only for her.

Ancient memories nurtured my newfound grasp on reality. Leaving True Void brought me on this strange layer of Sophron, Athanor. There, I encountered Touch, a sleeper whose sole reason to live involved lighting poles to keep hollows away. He carried me to Melpomene, my best friend. I wasn't supposed to fall in love with you. They made me do it. In a platonic strip club, I met Nempty. A strange-looking half frog and half-dead cat. A Stetson high hat crowns his amphibian head, a silver cane in hand. I followed him onto his flying boat, the Barracuda. Only a few days later, while we prepared for a long voyage, Melpomene, and his lover, Sthenele, joined us. We were out to form the Saviour Squad, I was told. Misfits fighting for the rebirth of Indra and the liberation of Varuna. I had a great time, and that kiss felt so good, but there's something else.

Our first stop brought us to Penglai, the angelical world. That's where my orb found me, and my gift showed up. I began training with Melpomene, soon after. There, we met Nempty's oldest friend, Theliel. Our host embraced the form of a blind woman, but angels' souls remain, essentially, genderless. She questioned me, threw me into some sort of arena where I literally battled my own demons, and I destroyed them, with her help. Emerald! As though she had been waiting for me, all along. I'm not even human. I'm not a male, a female, I am different.

My beloved dancer joined our ship, but I couldn't find it in me to speak to her. Nunc, a big fluffy purple bird, and Jonathan, an android, my only two relations on that boat. Nempty and Melpomene remained focused on locating the last member of our squad, my tormentor. My bully: Seamus Chron. When that sleeping bag appeared, near the cabins, my immediate reaction was: "Throw it out!" I didn't want anything to do with this prick. Everyone else seemed adamant on finding him a nice place on board. I had little to no choice but to swallow my anger and go with the family. I love you.

The Ether vanished, behind us, and so did the Veil. I surveyed the sleeping bag that just landed on the boat, and I immediately hated Nunc for trying to talk sense into keeping him with us. Seamus ended up homeless, okay, I can buy that, but he didn't even find the courage to escape in a different city. He didn't have to con his way to a meal in Toronto! He stayed in Montreal! I looked at his dirty shelter that reeked vomit, and I hoped to see a turd come out of it: A literal, visceral, smelly turd!

"Is that the one who tormented you?" Melpomene asked me. "Like you have no idea." I responded. My mentor stood behind me and grabbed my shoulders. I thought he would force himself on me, but I guess fear made me cringe and I overreacted. "Don't be too conservative." he whispered. I turned around to face him, and he smiled: "It only serves a decaying corpse. The pluriverse is not a cadaver."

I tried to calm down, and I looked at the nauseated hobo. Emerald observed the same scene, next to me. I must have had the best of this world. Every axiom in me wanted this thing to be thrown overboard. See if he can spend three hours, in the dark, thinking that someone will open that case and free him. Yeah, humiliate yourself, creep! But no. If we toss him out of this boat, maybe he'll perish for good. I hated his guts. I hate him so much! I know Melpomene felt my despair. Heck! I didn't care!
"I want him dead!" I whispered.

"What for, my love?" Emerald asked me. I looked at her, I missed her so much. She embraced my disgust with her gentle smile and expressed a fair: "He was kind to me, I swear." I didn't tell truth from illusions, anymore. "You just met him last night." I replied, trying to win this debate.

"And how could he know where I worked? What was I to you, I mean, think, for a moment."

156

Hatred filled me up, reflections from another world. I looked away, hoping to see a seagull dying of thirst. But the boat flew over nothingness. Some giant white birds observed us, wanting to snatch one of the crews and eat it alive. When Seamus woke up, he dared a gaze outside of his shelter. It smelled like urine, and I found him even more disgusting than before. Seamus stared me down with a big stupid smile. He turned to Emerald, and it felt like something happened between the two.

Of course, he always wished to steal my girls: Alexandra, Victoria, and now, Emerald! Asshole! My loved one looked at him with grave seriousness in her eyes. "You wanted a threesome!" She shouted at him. "Was it good for you as it was for us?" She added, prompting a frightened expression. I laughed. I would never touch this dirtbag, so having a *menage a trois* sounds like such sick humour. "Where am I?" he asked. She hugged me close and corrected him: "Where are we? Where we should be."

He left his stinking cover and tried to explain how he searched for us, using his glancing skills, and he seemed happy he found us. *Hey, stupid! We found you!* I wished to tell him, but I kept these thoughts to myself.

"Hey boy! 'Nempty stepped in. "You should thank her, and Nunc, and Melpomene, and William! They brought you here. They saved your life."

"Who's Nunc?" Seamus asked. He looked everywhere, and he felt highly intimidated by Melpomene's stature.

"A modest but powerful sophroner." My mentor answered. My bully's eyes spelled ultra confusion. I travelled this strange world far longer than him, so I guess I held an advantage, for once. "And where are we going?" Our stinking guest asked. "To Tir na n'Og." Nempty replied. He panicked: "No! We can't go there!"

157

"Follow me." Nempty sighed. He turned to face Seamus and push him aside. "Not you, boy! Make yourself at home on my boat, we'll see you in a bit." Melpomene grabbed him by his left wrist, while Nempty, Emerald and I returned to the cabin. He whispered in Seamus' ear, right before following us. I don't know what my mentor told him. When I turned to look at them from the small window, Seamus' face seemed as pale as winter. Melpomene had the fiercest gaze upon him that I have ever seen. Did he try to bully back my predator? I felt empowered. Does karma exist in this weird world?

Nempty's cabin never ceases to amaze me. After we entered the tiny cube, we ended up in a luxurious hotel, minus the staff. A bar, near the hallway, invites his attention. Our captain stood behind the counter, pouring several glasses of wine. As we joined him, the frog's frowning gaze scanned the entire room. He stopped his severe look on me. "Listen, boy." he growled. "I don't think your buddy, or you appreciate the seriousness of this mission."

"He's not my friend." I objected. Emerald slapped the back of my head. "Let him finish!" she scolded me.

"I died." Nempty explained. "Some Entity wanted me alive. I barely escaped Final Vanishing, you understand? And now I'm stuck in this atrocious body of an amphibian, with a deceased cat for a Siamese twin of pure horror." He binged down his glass of wine and poured himself another. "All of this, because you carry Indra's essence. And, somehow, I'm supposed to be the one protecting you, until Varuna shows up." he mumbled. I could tell how this entire odyssey weighed heavy on his shoulders.

"On top of that, I came back to this boat, and my daughter was gone." That last statement made him shed a tear. His eyes floated against a point of sorrow, in midair. He binged down his second glass. We hadn't even touched our first. "If you ask me, boy, I don't care what your life was like, on Gaia. I don't care if you hate his guts. I don't care if he made your life miserable! You are passengers on my boat, and I owe the big guns, on Zendoria, a thank you for this second chance at making things right!"
He looked at me with knives in his eyes. "You'd better gather your act together and find a way to make Seamus your friend.
You get that, boy?"

I politely acquiesced and sipped my wine. He turned towards the Great Muse and pointed at a giant gate, opposing the opening. Melpomene entered, and he aggressively pushed the door.
A gigantic chamber, barely lit, stood in front of us. A huge table carried a map of Sophron, with holograms floating above certain worlds. Melpomene walked to the other end. My mentor looked like a splendid general. When I observed the pieces hovering over the spherical chart, I could perceive strange fairy-boats. I would later learn to call them specter-boats, much more powerful than ours. A whole armada stationed in Duat. Melpomene caught our attention with his grave and solemn voice:

"I didn't want to mingle with Marduk and Varuna's battles, but seeing how vulnerable you are, William, and how precious you will be to both parties when they will learn of your existence, I decided to do my best to protect you. I feel as though Void no longer project your narrative. The new creator, the one I perceived, before I entered this storyline, appeared weak, depressive, even. We can put this to our advantage."

"Authors?" Nempty wondered.

"Oh? Right, sorry, I thought you knew." Melpomene acknowledged that our neymliss host was in a league below. "You see enlightened beings differently between dreamers and sleepers. Well, from the perspective of Greater Entities, we also view reality separated between poets and readers. We often find our consciousness awake in movies or series, before populating a wider audience's inner universe." Nempty didn't quite understand, but it kind of made sense, to me. I exist because a mind manifested my presence. He projected words to carry my thoughts, my actions, and my speech. A reader would inherit this creative fruit, so that I may also arise in that receptive mind. I observed the holographic pawns, and I wondered:

"Shouldn't we locate allies, or something?" Melpomene threw me the experienced speaker's look. "It's only a matter of time before one of Marduk's agents informs him of your existence." He lectured me. "I think we should find a way to extract the essence of Indra within you, and concoct a golem, or a being of some sort, that could host it. This way, you will be safe from both sides of the conflict."

"Nunc can do this." Nempty realized. "He did something like that to save my soul." Melpomene didn't seem to approve. "Anthropomorphist-Magi isn't the spell that we need." He explained. "Indra's essence is fragmented. That spell only works when the ghost is full, and had recently died, or faced Final Vanishing."

The frog looked away, concealing some form of shame for his ignorance. Whenever he made a quick motion, the deceased cat's head moved along, like a grafted appendix that tried hard to part from his shoulder. "At least I'm searching for solutions." Nempty reassured himself.

160

"We'll have to find another way, Nempty." Melpomene explained. He was right. He pointed at Marduk's army on the table and explained: "Last I heard, he was still parked in Duat. We must get to Tir na n'Og before he does. There, I will contact the council of fairy-sophroners. Nunc seems powerful at using his gift, but I remain confident we can find someone better."

"My teacher is in Tir na n'Og." Emerald stared at the map, enthusiastically. Everyone stopped and turned toward her.

"Who's your teacher?" Melpomene asked. She looked at him with some sort of glee or admiration. She must idolize the one who allowed her to master her gift.

"Sekhmet, lord mistress of Duat, conquering impress of Tir na n'Og!" Nempty spat the wine he just drank. "Okay! We're in trouble." he convened. Emerald turned to him with interrogation in her eyes.

Nempty explained: "She's a monster, boy. My worst client! If she sees me ganging up against Marduk with her pupil, she'll want me dead. I bet she'll want both of us dead." Melpomene didn't seem concerned, however.

"We don't need to worry about Sekhmet." he swiftly let out. He attempted to change the topic. Emerald stood silent for a moment, then she looked at him. "And why is that?" she wondered. Melpomene inhaled a deep breath, searching for the correct words, and continued: "She's outside, right now. With Jonathan. I. well, let's just say she agreed to my terms, and she became my pet."

"Sthenele? The Moth Queen? Oh no, Melpomene. No, trust me. I can sense my teacher's essence, and whoever possesses your submitted lady is not her." The Tragic Muse seemed intrigued "You sound sure of yourself." He couldn't help but express, with a cynic tone in his voice.

"Do you really think she'd belittle herself to become a third-class character in an ongoing series of novels?" Emerald taunted him. "She fooled you! That's what she does, Oh Great Muse of Tragedy, but sadly not of quick reasoning." These last few words made me chuckle, but I kept it down, so as not to insult my mentor. Melpomene couldn't believe what he heard. Nobody makes him look this stupid and get away with it! "How did you meet?" He inquired.

"In Toronto, after I danced in the Golden Heaven strip club, on Queens Street. It was the night I met William." She stared at me and grabbed my hand: "I had observed you sitting at a table, by the stage, all alone. I felt compelled to say hello. We talked the entire time, do you remember? Then, you took me to a private booth, and I danced on your lap for an hour. You didn't have any money. I didn't care. I asked you for your phone number. You told me you were homeless. When you left, I was afraid I would never see you again. I stripped for rich scumbags afterwards, and when I quit the club, she was there. She had been waiting for me in a dark alley, and she approached me with a gentle voice. She said we would be together; she would make sure of that." Melpomene processed the words he just heard and asked: "How did she become your teacher?"

"In my dreams." she explained. She looked at me and continued: "Every night after this first one, and until I saw William begging on King Street, in bright daylight, six months after. She would visit and introduce me to my inner world, my Sophron, teaching me how to channel my Veil, bring it out and use it to fight, fly, and dance around the pole like a true goddess."

"I didn't know Sekhmet was a dancer!" Nempty appeared perplexed. He stared back at Emerald and added: "I mean, I knew she had a gift, obviously, all of these powerful players belong to a Great Order, but I could never figure out hers." Emerald looked back at him and smiled: "Her teacher was Eve of Magnolias, the most powerful dancer that ever lived."

162

"Eve of Magnolias died her Final-Vanishing during the Babel Wars." Melpomene informed her, in a low voice, as he was still thinking. "Rumours were that Sekhmet killed her mentor, so she could become the most powerful dancer that lived."

"Sekhmet could never do that. She adored her teacher, and would speak of her, to me, in a very affectionate manner." I studied Emerald, and I could sense the admiration she had for Sekhmet.

Melpomene thought otherwise. He surveyed his war map and sighed: "At least, she's not with Marduk. Talk to her before he does. We'll need her by our side." I felt divided. The love of my all stood before the one who tutored me means of an afterlife. I observed the pawns and the board, and I thought of Seamus. He's a rookie gifted, just as we are, Emerald and I. Who served as his teacher? I shook off these questions. I looked at my mentor, my adored one, my dear friend. For the first time in my existence, I felt like I belonged.

"We're going to Tir na n'Og, then." I concluded. "We'll build an army, and we'll show Marduk who's boss. Love conquers all, and he'll be served a whole lot of love!" I joined the rotten prick on the deck, some moments after our meeting. He stood at the edge of the boat, contemplating the strangeness of the view. A pink sky with blue clouds isn't your everyday encounter, I must admit. I studied him for an instant. He made my life miserable. Now, he's stuck with me, here. I'm the popular guy! He's the loser. I guess I should pity him, but that wouldn't excuse the humiliation he put me through.

This campaign, this war, these powerful beings, it shines beyond my humble self and his. I kept thinking about the rationale of having him among us. He looked at the horizon, and I could picture his helplessness. His transition feels horrific. I approached him, and I repressed all these feelings haunting me. "Hey, asshole!" I let out, in a very tender voice. He turned around and asked: "Where are we?"

This, I could answer. I sighed and explained: "In between worlds. So, what's your gift like?"

"You're afraid of me." he mumbled. "You've always been full of it."

"No, William, you are. And right now, I can see that you're scared to follow Melpomene to war, but he's the closest to a father figure you ever had in your life. Why are we going to Tir na n'Og? We shouldn't be! I must join my mentor!"

"Who's your teacher?"

"At first, I thought, Ishtar, but she's a lost soul who brought me in this mess. I need to find Alibast."

I froze and pondered for a while, then I stared him down and asked: "You know Alibast?" He looked straight at me with eyes that spelled *be ready*. "He's my buddy." I grabbed my orb and caressed it for a moment. He knows Alibast, so he must have been to his lair. "Have you been to Ankharat di Kn'ogh?" His serious gaze gave way to an inquisitive one. I looked at him and I explained: "Melpomene warned me. Alibast, poet of Avalon, isn't an ally. He only works for himself. We can't trust him." He had a different story to share "No, William. You're wrong. If he was as selfish as Melpomene said, then why would he spend so many months training me, for no reason?"

"Some selfish game of his, obviously." I replied. "We're pieces on their chessboard. He manipulated you. If my mentor says we can't trust Alibast, then that's how it goes." He couldn't find it in his soul to agree. What argument could he make, anyway? He's outnumbered. If the Saviour Squad announces that the sky is pink, well, yeah, it actually is, right now. "Please, William!" He begged of me. "Don't go to Tir na n'Og !"

164

"You're in no position to make demands. Talk to Nempty and Melpomene, they know what they're doing." I felt certain of my reply, but he insisted: "We can trust Alibast! We should! He's the only voice of reason that's unlikely to side with anyone, in this coming war." My intuition kept reminding me of Theliel, and how she reiterated the need to push Melpomene toward his responsibilities. *You're no longer just a giver of inspiration once you step inside the poem. She carefully warned him. Of all Greater Entities, you should know how True Reality supersedes your modest form of consciousness.*

"I have met a genuine voice of reason." I explained Seamus. "Theliel. She's an angel, and she understands true love." I could feel fear stemming out of Seamus' concerned eyes. I had to quiet his hyperventilated thoughts. I walked next to him and put a hand on his shoulder. He calmed down and closed his vision: "You're a mancer." he whispered. He opened his gaze and looked at me, before adding: "You don't know how essences and possibilities work, so, please, just have a little trust in me." I sighed and replied: "Trust that will see me naked in front of the whole football team?" he gasped. I think he wanted to laugh at the recollection of this humiliating event. "You weren't naked, William." he tried to reassure me. "You don't know the meaning of the word naked, creep!" I shouted, while taking that hand of mine back to myself. He ignored me and observed the horizon. I'm sure he figured a way to steal my lunch money, but I am way ahead of him, right here, right now! And we're all going to Tir na n'Og!

Chapter Sixteen:
Marduk and a new Calligraphy

The student exited Martin's restroom with an amused look. They're still intrigued by how a soft motion over this metallic handle results in creating a gentle maelstrom, pushing the bodily fluid and matter down a hole. They had to try one more time: handle, water swirls, how mesmerizing! "When you're done playing with my toilet, get over here!" Martin ordered. "We have the issue of shipping you home to discuss."Neither could tell the presence of two entities, observing their movements, writing notes. Marduk and Sekhmet wandered around the chaotic office like two ghosts. The Hound Lord of Nibiru scratched his chin, perplexed, and amazed.

"You sent that student here, if I'm not mistaken." Marduk asked. The Egyptian goddess smiled: "And only I know how to send them back. But we have an agent capable of influencing the course of our storyline. This, Marduk, stands as more powerful than your entire armada!"

"Fascinating." The Mesopotamian Lord approached the scene, drawn into Martin's wandering eyes. "You're a few steps ahead of me, Sekhmet." he realized out loud. "Now we need to have them write my enemies off!"

The tall black lady laughed so loud, the author and the student almost uncovered their ghostly presence. "Oh, Hound Lord, you have no idea how this game plays out." She summoned her orb and let it float between them. "Allow me to show you." With a gentle movement above the crystal ball, she recreated the exact scene unfolding around them. "What makes the Great Muses so powerful, if not their ability to inspire artists through several dimensions and possibilities?" A quick focus onto the sphere, and the Veil emerged over the two protagonists. With both hands, she shaped the Ether's apparition, like veins pushed inwards, pressuring the blueish flesh to carry flows of axioms. "But once we find the right Dreamer, we can also project spells with characters inhibiting them." She cavorted around the orb, creating storms inside the crystalline plane of existence. It's rare to see a dancer performing certain incantations from other crafts with so much ease. Sekhmet, so it seems, have had a few million years to master both skills. "Let's have them resurrect Lucretia!"

She amused herself with this suggestion. "First, we should give Martin a narrating presence. Then, we will nourish his selfish impulses. Pay attention, Marduk. "We adopt a font, as you see, now, on our target's manuscript. We invite our soul in his story, knowingly immersing our consciousness into the very identity within this calligraphy. I have chosen Lucida, for myself.
Then, we espouse a rhetoric that represents our voice, distinctively, as a sovereign entity over the narrative. "And how can you tell if those words came out of Martin's mind or your own?" the Hound Lord inquired.

My dear Marduk, none of those stories actually stemmed out of Martin's psyche. Not even the ones he expresses! Even he finds himself subjected to an author above his league. It is that Dreamer we aspire to corrupt. He chose to project his personae as a character representation of his true self. That became his greatest mistake. For us, it seems like an opportunity.

167

"And yet, didn't that Dreamer above, you speak of, type the very words you've narrated?"

Did he, now? That's the beauty of illusions, Marduk. Unless one awakes and bathes in a pure form of enlightenment, they will always string themselves to a semblance of free will. In fact, the Ocorsurs destine the flow of axioms that dictate their fate. This Martin Poirier may seem well aware that his words come out of his mind, as he desires. Yet, he'll be the first surprised to see his characters evolve in ways he never anticipated. He thirsts for this war to take over his third and final book. As he writes my speech, he ignores who the victor shall be. For us to act, according to our will and wants, we must focus on the avatar he elected as a projection of his soul, in his own narrative. Allow me to present you our prized puppet.

Marduk scratched his chin, intrigued. He observed Martin scolding his student guest. He perceived a strong level of bitterness and regrets inhabiting the grumpy poet. If he, indeed, writes the very story that serves as a backdrop to the Hound Lord's conquests, then possessing such a weak mind comes as a high advantage. Hopefully, none of his opponents have met with the Chronicles' author, yet. The sooner they can corrupt him, the easier the victory will be.

Inner Chapter:
Sekhmet puppeteering Martin

"And what about Lucretia?" the student inquired. I can't stand their presence. Take them back! "What about her?" I asked. "She's supposed to play a pivotal role in your Chronicles, but she's dead. And you can't find a way to put her to contribution?"

"That's because she's dead."

"But she's not! Martin, you know that!"

How can I explain this to a stupid visitor from ancient Greece? "She died, so that her owner may live!"

"Father."

"What?"

"She considered Nempty as her daddy, not owner."

Who cares? "She's a minor character. Her only purpose for this entire story was to perish so that Nempty may stand a chance, redeeming himself."

The student held a few discarded pages in their hand, reading from my previous work. "So why is she haunting the boat?"

She's what, where, what? The boat, now? "What?" I asked. "It's like she never left it. Seamus knows, and I'm pretty sure he's the only one that does. Why would she appear to him?"

"I didn't write that." I confessed.

"Well, someone did. And you threw it away. Were you intoxicated?" I can't stand them! Take them back! I sat down behind my computer, and I composed a little intermission. "All right." I gave up. Let's try this. I made myself comfortable, drank my beer, and lost my mind against a virgin page.

Now, Marduk, the author consults an empty psyche, questing over a few words that would provide meaning to Lucretia's existence. We will flourish inside Nempty's daughter's essence. Just a spark! Just. a font to represent her identity. I suggest we go with Calibri, a gentle calligraphy for a sweet soul.

Without even thinking, I looked at my selection. I clicked on Calibri as though I intended to distance myself from Lucretia's narration.

Daddy? The girl's voice floated in a sea of nothingness. The boat flew across the Veil, and aside from this handsome human, nobody noticed her existence. How she hoped to cuddle with her father figure, again. Feel his protective presence, as they watched a movie, on a giant screen. Lacking this body that once nurtured her with sexual desires, her soul experimented with a freed consciousness for the first time. All she could recollect from her previous form of self-awareness came from Nempty's incessant attempt at making her live the life of a normal child. It makes sense, now. He cared about her. Those evil minds who created her to please perverted clients had no idea how selfless love pushes the universe closer to light.

Can you hear me, Daddy? She insisted. Long pauses in between her complains denoted how scared she must have been. Trapped in the ether, only her affection for a paternal construct kept her on board. Her essence couldn't find refuge in a neuronic network of any sort. No one explained to her the concept of Final Vanishing, or reincarnation. She expressed her consciousness, but nobody responded. Is this supposed to be life? Her new existence?

Talk to me, please. Only silence carried her being among lakes of solitude.

"Happy?" I asked the student. They read that last paragraph and wondered.

"Why did you write her thoughts in a different font?" They inquired.

"Don't question my inspiration. I just did, and I believe it looks cool." I replied.

"But, Martin, Seamus Chron can't be the only one who knows she exists." They pitched a concept that intrigued me.

"What about Jonathan?" I inquired.

They kept silent, and I guess their mind traversed a few ideas. They opened my fridge and grabbed a beer. "May I?" They asked my permission as they decapsulated the bottle. They sat on a bleeding heart, next to me, and drank while their imagination floated around the room.

"Jonathan knows that she exists, perhaps, because a character told him."

"Who could do that?" I wondered.

"At the beginning of this second novel, you have Seamus encounter another Walker." The student played with their bottle and continued:

171

"Maybe we can have that homeless drug addict discovers his gift, while allowing him a first foot onboard the Barracuda."
I didn't like that idea. I mean, who do they think they are?
"That makes no sense!" I growled. "In this current draft, we have Seamus bonding with a junky, Grunt. But his purpose in this storyline stops when Seamus grabs the money from the stoned hands." I stuck to my guns. The student insisted:

"You fail to see the bigger picture, Martin." they smiled.
"You can't have an elaborated war without various factions battling over their piece of the cake."

"Let's not impose another character to the Saviour Squad."
I explained.

"How will you resurrect Lucretia, then?" My guest asked.
"I'm onto something. Regardless of how this goes, it must

be a short chapter, with her enlightenment. I believe an occult reason acquainted me with the font I used." I thought about it further:

"Oh! Oh, hear me out. We'll have her develop a gift! When she wakes up in the cat's body, it will drive Nempty mad!"

"That's brilliant!" the student shouted, while bingeing down their alcohol. "A different font means she's aware of her position as a narrative influencer. She doesn't know it, yet, but she's as powerful as, let's say."

"Sekhmet!" Martin smiled.

"Nah, I think Sekhmet should be stronger. Lucretia, though, follows the panther goddess in her tracks. But you'll need to draw a better connection, if you want your readers to experience the greater narrative."

I reflected on these words. They do prove a point, here. "Okay, let's say this yet to be named drug addict witnesses his gift with Seamus. An enlightened soul possessed him. Some sort of squid, a Lovecraftian Entity. They developed a strong connection. He will resurrect Lucretia, and she will inherit her power from the Squid god. In a dream, the junky awakes on the Barracuda. He's, like, just a ghost, or something. That's how he encounters Lucretia." I was at loss. Ideas evaded me. "And Jonathan." They grabbed the narrative but let me continue.

"And Jonathan." I uttered. "I think the android should have some sort of affinity for essences."

"Was this established in the first novel?" they asked. "Well, he knew about orbs and Walkers. He's more likely one who allowed Lucretia's soul to survive. So, yeah. It was assumed, but not clearly fleshed out."

"Save some surprises for the third and last book, Martin." They smiled. "You're brilliant!" I enjoyed those last few words. "Okay, let me give this a shot."

I returned to my laptop, and I typed:

Is this supposed to be life? Her new life? *Talk to me, please.* only silence carried her being among lakes of solitude. Long and cold nights brought her discomfort. Lucretia couldn't handle being left out of reality. She floated above the bridge, observing the treefolks cleaning around the boat. Sometimes, she appeared in front of them and tried to play with their leaves. The sleepers couldn't even tell their essence from anything else. The lonely ghost remained unknown to them. What about her android friend? She teared her own heart out because Jonathan mentioned its magical properties. Perhaps he could bring her back! Ever since she witnessed the presence of this magical creature, the robotic daughter sensed the call from otherworldly beings.

173

"Hold on!" The student interrupted my surge of inspiration. "Squid?" they wondered. "Are you sure it's a good idea?"

"Don't get in my creativity's way, okay?" I objected.

Where was I?

"But what if that Squid turns out as an opportunistic Entity? Shouldn't you properly establish his motives?" they insisted. I calmed down a moment.

"I don't know." I had to confess. I remained oblivious to my crafting juice, in my brain. Perhaps I could rewrite that character in previous chapters, as a ghost squid existing inside the wandering junky. As to properly summon him, provide Grunt a purpose.

"The Squid wants to save Grunt."

The student pondered over this new addition into our story: "Again, I think you're amassing good material for your third book. Go on."

I resumed my creative process:

Her soul floats in an axiomatic sea. It felt as though her consciousness, freed from an incarnated vehicle, now roamed in between layers of her reality. The boat exists, but only when she focuses her attention on its presence. *Jonathan?* She attempted to call her friend's name. There he was, scanning the bridge with a curious stick. A tiny orb, glued to its tip, produced strange lights. Red, when the male android looked away. Blue, whenever he approached. Jonathan shut his eyes and meditated.

174

"Lucretia?" he murmured. She smiled! She could sense his voice as though he walked next to her. "Yes! I can hear you!" She laughed. An immense burst of joy made her cry. "Listen to me carefully." he added. "I can't remain in this form very long. That staff is faulty." He paused for a moment and offered her strict instructions: "Father is in a cabin, right now. Stay here. In about five minutes, I will get him with me. He will hold a stick like this one, but much bigger. I need you to focus on the orb when the colour will turn purple. Just focus, like you meant to blind your eyes with its light, and forget that anything else exists. can you do." Silence. His voice disappeared. "Can I do what?" She wondered. She already forgot everything he said.
She panicked. She can't do it! It's impossible! She's stuck in this form forever. *Oh, Daddy, I miss you so much.* It felt imperative that she recollects each step her brother instructed her with. Colours, something about, purple. Maybe she could find something purple, and it will be like a door! Is it time? She just can't see them, anymore. It must be time. What was she supposed to do? *Jonathan? Where are you? Tell me what to do, again!* So close, and yet, she doubts she'll make it.

An hour passed. The bridge felt deserted. Did he forget about her? Or perhaps something happened! Pirates! That's it! If only she had a body, she would have saved them from those nasty buccaneers! Think, Lucretia, think! Where's that purple door? The bad men hid it. She should find the courage to fly around the boat and locate that gate! But no. She worries over nothing. If pirates had jumped on the ship, she would have heard something. Or maybe imagining those events will make them come true! Happy thoughts, Lucretia, get yourself happy thoughts. Freed from the cursed body that perverts designed for deviant clients, she realized how her soul hadn't felt horniness in a long while. Her previous self followed in this evil construct. Whatever she sensed, before, couldn't be real. Her daddy's protective care, however, treating her with respect, like a daughter. That, she still perceived. This love remains true.

175

"What did you want to show me that seemed so urgent?"
She heard the frog complain. "Trust in my words, master. It's her,
I say, it's her!" That amphibian frightened Lucretia. He screamed
around the ship. He sounded like her father, but that couldn't be.
The dead cat, however, oh, she wished she could pet her. Yeah, a
lady zombie kitty. *She's so pretty*, she whispered to herself.

"Lucretia? Can you hear me?" Jonathan raised his voice, but
she had for only gaze the fluffy fur that covered the feline's head.
An open mouth showed a tongue, begging for life. And what about
those purple eyes! They caught her attention, and she couldn't look
anywhere else.

"Do you see the stick and the orb, my sister?" the android
insisted. She did! The frog held it like a silly puppet. The cat's
purple eyes, though. she couldn't look elsewhere! The more she
focused on them, and the more alive they became. "Focus on the
orb, Lucretia! We don't have much time."

"What orb?" the cat inquired. Likely the one that fell down the
frog's hands, right after Nempty screamed in total horror.
"Daddy!" The freshly resurrected zombie kitten kissed Nempty's
cheek repeatedly.

"I'm not sure Nempty will appreciate this."
The student laughed.

"Well, tough luck! He's stuck with her, now." Martin replied.
Exhausted, the French-Canadian author walked to the fridge and
grabbed another beer.

Chapter Seventeen:
Sekhmet impresses Marduk

Images projected Martin and the student, struggling to create a story together. On the same movie screen, Nempty frowned while Lucretia kissed him. Marduk observed both events and scratched his chin. "Interesting." the Hound Lord of Nibiru whispered.

"You said you walked next to this Martin?" Marduk interrogated her. The gory scenery, in the middle of Time Square, vanished. Soon after, the moving images of the Barracuda and its crew followed.

Marduk witnessed what seemed like the impossible. A creative mind giving life to characters he would later coexist with. It appears that humanity found ways to summon gods and goddesses into their psyches and design worlds for them. Before his incarceration, the opposite stood as the norm. They formed mankind, cultures, societies, and resided in their souls as universal movements of fear and veneration. Now, Marduk and Sekhmet exist as merely creations in some earthling's imagination.

"By chance." Sekhmet replied. "The game changed since the fall of Babel. Humanity built its own rebirth of Atlantis. Their technology will soon destroy their illusion, and they will walk among us."

Marduk wandered around the library, lost in his thoughts. "Was I imprisoned this long?" he questioned. "All of this happened after the Babel Wars?"

She kept quiet and turned his attention back to the big screen. There, he sensed two hundred thousand essences. Most of them carried the beauty and innocence of children, caring mothers, and elderly fathers. Millions of possibilities, emanated from all those inner universes, projecting themselves onto Marduk's psyche. A peaceful morning, in Japan. The scene felt cool, with birds announcing another blissful day. Markets got ready to caretake their customers with fresh fruits, fish, and vegetables.

"I must show you something else." she warned him. Intrigued, Marduk allowed his essence to merge with theirs. At once, he experienced two hundred thousand lives. Sons and daughters playing in their backyard. Parents scold their creations. Ambitions grow into young adults' minds. Dreams, all those goals these families had. Offerings left, innocently, at a temple. Songs played in the street, for a group of amused bystanders. Happiness! That's all the Hound Lord felt, and then. Images of pure horror bombarded the screen. A gigantic explosion tore the city of Hiroshima apart.

Hundreds of thousands of humans died in an atrocious spectacle of melted flesh and shattered bones. Blood splattered the roads, while a nonchalant plane flew away. Children left orphaned and in tears. Schools turned into skeletons. The lucky ones had vanished instantaneously, but many remained breathing to relieve this trauma over and over until insanity prevailed.

"They did it?" Marduk asked, afraid, after a long pause. Sekhmet walked next to him, observing the image of lives losing their grasp over light. Buildings explode! Corpses loitering the streets, children in tears. "In nineteen-forty-five, on August sixth. They did it twice, just to bully themselves in proving a point."

The Hound Lord couldn't part from this terrorizing cinema. Sekhmet continued. "Thoth was the first god to intervene. I followed in his tracks. He called every House into forming a unified legion of peace and inspire mankind to mirror our motion." She walked away, summoning a tea service out of her orb, and moved on: "Do you really think you got it easy, assassinating this Great Entity? No, Marduk. Humans unknowingly helped you."

She offered him a cup of Earl Gray, and while Marduk shakily accepted, she continued: "Your obsession for Varuna must stop. We're in a new game. Mankind will soon soar and become a much greater threat than any one of us. Long ago, our only concern was Atlantis, with their atomic disrupters. Humans have bombs, Marduk! We can't afford to fall into another Babel War. Not now! And not while some of them have woken and walk among us." She quickly drank her tea and exited the room. Marduk remained glued onto the subsequent images of war and suffering. She turned to him and closed her eyes: "Do you still aspire to kill Indra's new incarnation?" she questioned him. The Hound Lord of Nibiru stayed silent for a long moment. "Regardless of what I shall say, Sekhmet, we both know that our story will carry on."

"Very well, Marduk." She opened her vision and led the way. "In that case, if you may, please, follow me! Our guests have arrived." She left the room behind, uncertain as to what twisted thoughts inhabited the other's mind. Marduk can't consider Sekhmet an ally, even though she shared everything she knew. Incidentally, Sekhmet can't fully trust that her lectures successfully changed Marduk's desire to conquer, kill and destroy. Did she commit a mistake? He now understands where to find the creative souls providing him an existence. If she can't convince him to turn around, she may as well give up and let him walk away as the sole victor of a war that has yet to begin. "I will stay here a little more." he confessed. "I'll join you later." Sekhmet left him behind. Marduk quickly gestured the orbs, requesting the previous scene to appear. There, Martin and the student continued to drink lots of beer and type lots of words.

179

Chapter Eighteen:

Arcana mon Amour

When the boat landed, I saw Seamus like I had never seen him before. He seemed genuinely terrorized. He took his head with both hands, observing the landscape, and he sensed pain.
He displayed the same wounds I felt whenever I crossed him in our school's hallway. I could have stayed here and look at him struggling for hours, and I'm not sure I would have gained bliss or discomfort from it. Nempty and Melpomene opened the way, crushing a few mushrooms under their foot. A nice city sat on top of a gigantic mountain. My mentor mentioned its name: Arcana.

I followed the squad, holding my orb like my Final Life depended on it. Which creature could I summon to defend us from an unexpected threat? I only had axioms of Void at hand.
Can I cast a hollow? I bet I can. He would be under my command!
Seamus stalked us silently, slowly, as he tried to step on as few mushrooms as he could. I heard him apologize after severing the head of one. Who does he think he is? Super Mario?

As we approached the mountainous city of Arcana, an octopus-like archoid flew above us. "What are those?" Seamus asked. He locked his eyes on the magnificence behind this gigantic cyborg monster. "Biomechs, or, as we call them, archoids." Melpomene explained to him. "Genetically designed battle machines that only need your essence to pilot them." My bully ate every word that came out of the warrior muse. Emerald chuckled, seeing how hypnotized Seamus seemed by this sight. She turned to me and smiled: "He wasn't even this consumed when he stared at me naked."

I didn't laugh! Call it jealousy on my part. As we approached the immense city carved in a mountain, we crossed several other battle beasts, many were parked behind a fence. Seamus drooled on his way to the gate. I sensed that we would one day see him fly one of those. "You haven't seen a real archoid until you have met Karkadan." I informed him. When the time arrives, I will mount that beauty with my essence. Make this one for the legends.

We stopped at the main entrance. Melpomene took upon himself to introduce the group. The doors stood as tall as three houses, and as wide as one. Around it, stonewalls came out of the same rock. When I looked up, I saw bigger buildings taunting the sky, from atop the elevation that now seemed like a manmade fortress. Melpomene pressed a ring against a gargoyle's mouth. We heard a voice: "State your essence and your reason for visits." It stood half outside our head, and half inside. "Lord Melpomene of Hydaspes. I am here as a diplomatic envoy to speak with Impress Sekhmet of Duat." Silence. the voice came back with the same solemn tone: "Please, name all the souls in your party, and state their business in Arcana." Melpomene answered: "William, Emerald, and Seamus of Gaia. Emerald is Sekhmet's pupil, Seamus and William are Emerald's friends, mere visitors. Nempty of Duat, a merchant and our fairy-boat's captain. On his shoulder, Lucretia of Patagonia, he's stuck with her." Just like that, the gate opened, and the voice concluded: "Enjoy your stay in Arcana. Please, inform security when you shall part."

181

I couldn't believe my eyes. So much richness and eccentricity filled this fairy-folk city, my immediate impression felt like. *Hollywood on acid. Trippywood.* It may not have been the most eloquent words, but it perfectly summarized the wind of awe that blew the three humans from Montreal away. Lucretia could hardly quiet her amazement. Before she passed, she never left the boat. Now stuck on her father's shoulder, she unfolds the outside world for the first time. "Look, Daddy!" she screamed at the frog.

"I just saw a flying unicorn!" The cat smiled with so much magic in her eyes, we forgot how zombified she looked. Putrefaction filled her flesh with horrifying holes, but her vision projected the most touchingly beautiful soul we had ever noticed.

"Yeah, girl." Nempty replied, with his comforting tone. Like a father happy to see his beloved daughter back to life, but still processing with the fact that he'll be attached to her forever. "Now, be quiet, and let the grown-ups do the talking, say?"

Flying creatures the size of hummingbirds soared around us. When looking more closely, we could observe their canine features with a child-like body and firefly wings. Gremlins drove tiny sports cars, while trolls rode horses, and goblins took the bus. We ushered past a dark alley, and I could barely make up a name, at the end of it. The pale light that surrounded the bar's neon sign captivated me. Melpomene saw my interrogative look and informed me: "Welcome to the Lonesome Crone. We have no business over there, let's continue our walk." Seamus observed it as well and thought out loud: "I've been there before. I forgot when, but it feels like deja vu." We completed our journey in front of a gigantic palace that looked like a mix of ancient Egypt and European Renaissance. Five powerful archoids guarded its gate. We stopped in front, and we waited.

Emerald reacted first. She closed her eyes and smiled: "Hello, teacher. I'm with friends. We need your help." The main door opened like a fancy elevator.

182

Two soldiers, tall chimeras with various animal heads, escorted us inside. As soon as we left the world behind, we found ourselves surrounded with black and silver statues of cats, and paintings of crucified mice. A red carpet guided us to a wide ballroom.
Our hostess hid herself somewhere else. We followed Emerald, as she walked straight, like hypnotized or under some spell.
She stopped in front of a golden sculpture, a panther, standing up with the severed head of a coyote in its hands. Emerald opened the canine's mouth and touched a few teeth like she wanted to play music with them. The statue moved and pointed us to a long corridor.

Quartz and fragmented diamonds filled the walls. It felt as though we were descending into the Earth's centre, but the clarity that emanated from the crystals brought us so much brightness, we found ourselves blinded. The calmness in this hallway made me rather uncomfortable. Emerald walked in front of the group, and we merely followed. If I checked behind, the exit disappeared.

Were we taken to a prison? If I looked in front, however, I could see that the corridor led us to a blue light. As we approached closer, it became a passage into the most luxuriant throne room you could imagine. Lapis lazuli shone as the stone of choice. It adorned the walls and the little furniture, two chairs, a table, and a high seat, dispersed in a chamber the size of Manhattan.

"Welcome to Arcana!" A voice of beauty and destruction made itself heard. Her skin, as black as night, reflected the calming light. Her head, neither human nor feline, projected traits proper to both. Her tall and elongated body suggested either anorexia or that she was born from a specie of a very thin figure. Her breasts, however, stood out, big and generous.

Her derriere spelled spoil me, love me, hand over that flesh to any buttlover out there. Behind her, two fairy ladies stood up, with a solemn and serious look. Her confidantes and best friends, Katrina and Fiona project an aura of courage and legend.

"Precious guests." Sekhmet welcome ed us: "How can I make your presence memorable?" Seamus and I remained equally mesmerized. I checked around to survey everyone. Nunc didn't follow, so I guess the fat bird stayed on the boat. Curiously, I hadn't seen our purple obese phoenix buddy in quite some time. The more I tried to think about it, and the less it felt like he actually walked with us. This memory felt more like a Mandala effect than anything.

Melpomene stood behind me, like my bodyguard. The beautiful Sthenele never stopped watching over my delicate stature. She couldn't say a word. Did her muteness kil her from inside? Emerald grabbed my hand, and that, alone, made me a hero. "Daddy?" Lucretia's feline voice pierced the silence. "That lady, she looks like me, but she's so pretty!" she whispered. The frog turned to face his conjoined daughter. "Yes, girl." He murmured back. "Now, be quiet. She's not you. She's an evil lady." Lucretia's eyes opened wide, in fear and awe.

Fourth Intermission:
The third Singularity

Between matter and life, consciousness learns its place within reality among socially driven organisms. At first glance, Kitana observed worlds of cellular divisions, pushing their limits beyond a quantic ocean of skin tissues. Soon, however, those nano-pilots formed beings of a higher stature, themselves reprising individual roles in larger organizations. City-states for a carrier of culture. Rules of law mimicking universal order. Existence as a movement of nature. Archeus stands as Void's mirror. An absoluteness of being, reflected against total emptiness. The traveller could hear her own heartbeats, with every silence emanating a familiar song: Nothing else matters.

Nothing matters. Nothing prevails past another step closer to the Verb, another one farther from the margin. Let there be no punctuation. Ants thriving in underground lairs. Bees and wasps going at it, like workers and predators. One cell at a time, one organism then the following, until skyscrapers elevate their presence under higher firmaments. Jungles of green and tar, next to villages enacting peace at its core. Individualism functioning as distinct universes, pushed against other parties, until nations profess their language to the rest of the world. And they clash or seek harmony, like ants, and bees, and wasps, only human.

With Void and Barbelo behind, Kitana progress towards Archeus. The layers of Sophron she encounters populate themselves with societies of rules and principles, of needs and desires. Gaia, Duat and Nibiru, also known as the three sisters of mankind, the conjoined birthplace of religion, science, and philosophy. Those three realms carried on their back the sole essence of humanity. Gods and goddesses of all three worlds have been visiting one another, exchanging information, propelling the growth of their civilizations, since the very first apparition of the Lotus City, mother of True Reality. Some scholars even believe that Sophron's cosmography benefited from conventions developed within those three worlds' shared influence.

Some would say Airavat, Oyashima, Mictlan and Tjukurrpa represent the backbone of Sophron's essence, and the three sisters of mankind merely form the initial trio of realms to reflect on this natural phenomenon. I suspect that even the Great Entities of Zendoria can tell for a certainty how the pluriverse came into existence. I doubt they can explain how True Reality allowed for myriads of illusions to create suitable environments to quintillions of dreamers and sleepers. Then again, perhaps the most considerable of all Deities find themselves dwarfed under an immensely greater reality that they have yet to comprehend.

The Third Singularity, however, arises because life doesn't worry, or crumble under questions. It just is. The absolute manifestation of I Am, as an act of breathing in. There, it contains molecules of oxygen within an organism, and breathing out. There, it provides sustenance to that being's environment. A well-balanced ecosystem that doesn't require thoughts or matter to prevail. Harmony in its perfectly adjusted rhythm, needing no brain to carry existence further. No element to contrast with its materialized self. Life. Just that: life.

Vast constellations of bliss painted themselves across Kitana's soul. Her own identity couldn't hold an ounce of self-awareness, since only the rivers of air expanding her lungs, depleting them, punctuated her immediacy. This moment challenged the physics of space and time. An eternity encapsulated until the wingless angel unearthed an ounce of strength to carry her voyage beyond the living gate.

On her way to the Fourth Singularity, she witnessed three fascinating worlds. Cognitia, a place governed by an omniscient artificial intelligence. The very first layer of Sophron past True Archeus, we find, there, an emerging transformation towards lands of pure thoughts. As we further our journey towards Logos, we uncover the second realm, past the Third Singularity: Cibola, the fabulous Eldorado, the city of gold. This world directed entire civilizations to new ideals and discoveries. The only humans to have stepped beyond its gates, however, came from Atlantis.

Kitana stopped for a moment, as she found out how the following layer past True Archeus appears devoid of any life or consciousness. If she recollects her thoughts well, this should be Lumbini, the birthplace of the Buddha. What happened? Had she been away from reality this long? Trapped in that call centre. What did she miss? She ventured into this desolated realm, only to observe lifeless plants with no chance of survival. The name changed, since Marduk murdered its previous guardian, Enlil-Bastat. One gentle presence patiently feeds the entire nature, one tree at a time. *Blessed his soul*, she thought. She examined the world of Alibastat once more, and she then resumed her voyage.

Journey into the Hourglass:
Twenty

I wandered around my cottage, on Alibastat, one morning. Three weeks passed since the last time I worked on the second book in the first Sophron trilogy. I gathered that Martin must have kept busy, in New York, either teaching novelist skills to this Greek student guest, or flirting with unreciprocated crushes online. Every dawn, he would write her an email to cultivate this flame. I catre about my poet friend, but I doubt he understands the value of domesticating our solitude. I'm certain that Martin meant well, confessing his affection to this Jennifer Blank, when he and I met. But let's say that, in our professional partnership, I'm the brain, the heart, the patience and he's, well, he's Martin.

Gardening around my adopted world helped keep me in touch with my inner peace. Cleansing my mind from the stress and pressure that Martin and I face, since we embarked on this journey into our hourglasses. It may not seem like much to you, reader, but having a consciousness that encompasses various states of enlightenment can seem a bit cumbersome. Including the both of us in our story. It comes as a good idea, at first. But managing characters who awaken on their own and defy us represents a complex challenge. If Martin allowed himself to act in a passionate manner, then I had to assume the Zen counterpart.

Therefore, I invested my dawns and my days pollinating flowers across the desolated land of Alibastat. My soul would connect with my cosmic twin, but I only stepped into his consciousness when I felt that his hasty and unpredictable nature threatened to compromise his chances with the novel, or with this Dulce. The rest of my time remained intimately attached to my duty towards keeping this world alive.

It is human to fear loneliness, as though solitude brought only promisses of angst and anxiety. I know my writing partner carries with him years of depression, resenting a friendless life on his own. It takes courage to embrace life's harshness and choose to remain true to adopting kindness. Only patience speaks to bliss.

Chapter Nineteen:
The Student learns the Craft

Midnight hit like a devious headache. Martin wrote twenty pages in three hours, without stopping to catch his breath. The student observed him, lost in full admiration. How can he remain so productive while drunk? At times, they would stand behind him, reading over his shoulder. Every word flawlessly arose next to one another. Humbled, they strolled towards the refrigerator. Surely, they could find something different than beer. As soon as they opened the door, horror stroke them. Lungs appeared at the bottom, spitting mucus and blood. They closed it and walked away from the gory scene.

Spending an entire evening with an author made them forget how the building displayed living organs. Are they really forming inside that cold beer tomb? They wondered what lurked on upper floors. Maybe those body parts belong to half-made people. The whole castle probably acted as a womb, or some sort of cocoon. They found the courage to open the fridge's door, again. they closed their eyes and swiftly grabbed a stout in a can, then slammed the terror scene shut

"They are archeus axioms, don't worry." A feminine voice pierced the awkward silence. "Don't feel grossed out, either. There's no brain attached to those organs. No consciousness; they're just disgusting to watch."

A tall lady, dressed in blue, appeared in front of the pupil. She graciously walked with the nobility of a heavenly queen, and a loving mother's modesty. She looked at Martin sleeping and sighed. "What did I do wrong?" she asked. You approached her slowly, dear student, and her name imprinted itself onto your psyche: *Ishtar*

Growing up in Athens, the existence of gods and goddesses weren't an uncommon sight. Well, for enlightened humans and their pupils, perhaps. The student recalls having witnessed Plato discuss with Apollo, a few times. The whole idea behind the Great Mysteries always aimed at gathering awakened souls. Sleepers would consult oracles to indirectly converse with the Houses of Sophron protecting the Greek culture. Philosophers, poets, and mathematicians, however, maintained a different connection with the overseers of Olympus. Learning to master the orb meant to allow a few graduates to perpetuate this mutual friendship with gods and goddesses.

"Martin fell in love on few occasions, in his life." Ishtar explained. "And every time, he would awake in a heartache. Those tragedies greatly influenced his path to Sophron. The first occurred in nineteen-ninety-four."

She caressed the sleeping author's head while reading the words he had written. "Eve of Isles, was one of them." She pursued. "A tall and slander brunette he met at the National Theatre School of Montreal."

You listened to the goddess and couldn't quench this admiration born from the time you shared with the wounded creator.

"Oh, seeing her dance felt like bliss." she continued. "He never had the courage to approach her, but the poems he would write transported him into higher forms of consciousness. He built the right bravery at the end of his first semester, reading a text to her, during a literary event. She fell in love, as a result, and a strong connection occurred."

You sat down to drink your beer, observing the author, fast asleep. That story carried the seed that would, later, bloom in Martin's mind. A forbidden romance arose between a god of Airavat, Indra, and a goddess of Babylon. Ishtar.

"They properly broke that ice and promised each other to spend more time together." She caressed Martin's head comforting him in his nightmares. "Martin wouldn't be staying, however. The school elected that he no longer met their standards, and they threw him out."

She left him sleeping and walked towards the fridge. "There's something else that Martin encountered, during his visit at the Theatre School: a fantasy universe." Ishtar opened the door and grabbed a bleeding lung. "His teacher, Mycroft SanAndreas, famed theatre genius, united the playwrights and actors to stage excerpts from Peter Brooke's Mahabharata."

She gently waved in midair, gathering Barbelo axioms and shaped them like a floating oven. She snapped her fingers, creating flames in its centre, and threw the organ inside. "This is how Martin uncovered his first connection with Sophron. It would inhabit him, as the meat I just put in that oven's mouth. Would you like some spice with that?"

Lost in awe, the student forgot to respond. Ishtar gathered some matter axioms to form salt, archeus pixels to build herbs, and add everything next to the baking lungs. "Four years later, Martin fell in love with a violinist: Cindy. It happened online, without anyone having seen the other's face."

She moved her hands once more, generating a wooden base that would become a fancy table. The piece of furniture remained in stasis, while she continued her story: "Martin discovered the beauty of a platonic relationship during that time." Ishtar opened the oven's door, making sure the lungs cooked nice and well. She then returned her attention to the student:

"For the first time in his life, Martin wasn't shy to speak to a girl. His inhibited fears didn't consume him. Furthermore, he left school and found his first job. He moved in with a dear friend and got his first taste of autonomy." She modelled the wooden table to resemble modest picnic attire, and let it land between the disciple and herself.

"Discussing art, poetry and classical music with an ambition-driven virtuoso from Taiwan awakened a new life in him." Ishtar gathered more matter axioms to create two plates and two cups.

"They met in Rochester, New York, soon after. And they fell in love, again."

The student looked at Martin with the same awe he felt from the goddess' presence. Ishtar continued: "She applied to various music schools, following the path that Martin had wished for himself, with movies and theatre. They agreed that, should she be accepted into the Rochester Eastman School of Music, he would move to Toronto. And he did."

The cooked lungs flew out of the oven, making their way towards the plates. The student observed this magical scene in silence. Ishtar carried on with her tale:

"The three years that followed were both miraculously awesome and, a path leading to this author's true destiny. There, he learned to live by himself, far from friends and family. He found a good job in finance. He wrote poetry and screenplays. He visited Rochester once or twice a month, making love, the real kind."

The meal smelled delicious, but it didn't look very appealing. Ishtar sat and gestured the student. She finally gathered more axioms to form tools, the modern types, a fork, and a knife. "Cindy was destined to a great career in Singapore."
The goddess continued.

"We are sovereign pluriverses, trying to make sense of an existence. We are stuck between universal movements of selfish desires, cries for zen, and influences of a will for detachment.

Crushed between the egotistical motions of Og and the sacrifices of Om. When unsuspected events pull loved ones away from us, the cosmos becomes a wounding burden. What you make of it, however, is what decides your next course of actions, your new ongoing path."

"Martin didn't want to follow her. So, he broke up. Not without tears and a Kiss Me he heard her beg, in the middle of the night."

You finally found the courage to grab those utensils and try the meat. It carried heaven! It's funny how eating lungs that couldn't belong to any known mammal, or bird, feels better, without a remorseful aftertaste. Oh, what a delicacy.

"In the years that followed, Martin drifted between an ambitious desire to become a successful screenwriter, a poet of merit, while suffering as a lonely bachelor." Ishtar concluded her story. "He fell into an abysmal depression, drinking his sorrow to forget he even exists."

"Is this the same Martin?" the student asked.

"That's the one I learned to care about." she explained. "I brought Alibast in his inner Sophron, you see? I thought it would save him. I was wrong." She paused in a bit of grief and sighed: "Eat! Don't let it get cold." She cut a huge chunk for herself and devoured it with great appetite.

"He visited strip clubs, to forget, I guess." she exhaled. "And then, in April of two thousand and six, his dear childhood friend elected to end his life, back in Montreal." The student hesitated for a moment, shaking while eating, and uttered a timid: "That's what I saw when I touched the orb." Ishtar smiled.

"Nobody's totally responsible for anyone else's choices." She closed her eyes:

The student looked at the drunk poet with pain in their eyes. Ishtar remained stoic. She took a bite of those tasty lungs and added: "I believe there's a different Martin, above us, writing those realms. He would become the ultimate Dreamer of those chronicles. I doubt we can reach him, though, but we can touch his readers. Well, he can with his choice of words."

Another mouthful convinced you, student, that this meal carried overwhelmingly sweet flavours. Your psyche, however, remained attached to a few questions:

"If this Martin who shares our space isn't the actual author of our novels. Then who is he?"

Ishtar reflected for a moment, prior to reasoning: "He's the one who stayed in Toronto. Until he left his previous world on his own accord and awakened in a New York that only exists in his mind."

"On his own accord?" the pupil asked. "Until he chose to follow his deceased friend's example." Ishtar allowed a tear to fall. Frightened, the student dropped their fork. Ishtar added: "I have to protect him, now, you see? He spends his eternity writing those novels, like mirrors reflecting mirrors, in an endless quantic dance of infinite possibilities. But there's something else, far greater than his current life, in this current form, in this reality." She remained quiet for the rest of the feast. The student wondered what she meant but couldn't find the courage to question her any further. A meal invested in silence, while an exhausted author slept. In their mind, the disciple reconstituted this grand puzzle, like Russian dolls of inner universes: Martin writes a story inspired by his life: Seamus Chron who failed to save a friend and mounted onto an odyssey to redeem himself. Reality enveloping realities. A warring god embarking onto a quest to destroy all of existence. Heroes stuck in between, using every trick and gift they own to influence their way up, triggered by a survival mechanism. "I understand, now," the student confessed. "We are not writing a novel. We fight for our liberty to arise as sovereign entities."

"Exactly." Ishtar agreed. "Just as readers convey your words into their minds and provide you asylum in their inner Sophron."

"I believe other characters are aware of this, and they're struggling to fight their way onto a narrating existence." The student closed their eyes and reflected on this thought further: "One of them might have attempted to recount my moves, in this chapter."

"Are you sure?" Ishtar asked. A strange fact occurred in the goddesses' mind, just as the pupil gently nodded. How did her interlocutor remain anonymous to this day? "You have yet to reveal your identity, student." she remarked.

The disciple politely agreed: "You are correct. I haven't revealed my identity, yet."

Chapter Twenty:
Marduk becomes a Poet

Against the wall, moving images showed the scene of a feast. Two cooked lungs being eaten, while a drunken poet sleeps, behind a laptop computer. The Greek student didn't seem to enjoy the meal so much, but some essences may have sweetened their sense of taste. Oblivious to the fact that an outside audience of one observed them, Ishtar and the pupil finished their meat. Soon after, Martin would wake up and find himself forced to properly introduce the goddess to the intruder.

You walked away from the table, as though you wished to offer Martin some space to chastise his sleep and join the feast. He looked at the both of you and smiled:

"Ishtar? I present you. what's, whatever. you? That's Ishtar Damn, I'm so drunk!"

The solitary spectator couldn't believe it. She survived?

She's alive?

Marduk remained silent for a long moment. Sekhmet must have stayed hidden in possibilities where he couldn't find her. He expected to see an author granting breath to the characters visiting Arcana, but he's a total loser. Maybe she's trying to trick him with this atomic bomb tale, and a lonely, failed screenwriter.

Sekhmet wants the Hound Lord of Nibiru to expose his vulnerability. Perhaps because she wishes to protect someone. Did she know, however, that Ishtar was alive? And currently grooming one of the creators behind their ongoing story?

"Yeah, we met, while you were asleep." The student laughed. So many memories haunted the Hound Lord of Nibiru. He fought for her love in a previous existence, but she rejected him. She preferred the one they called Dumuzi, also known as Indra. If she's in a story that he can, now, narrate, does it mean he could force her to adore him back? Every fibre in him desired that he could give this a try!

"Don't listen to half of what she says." Martin joked. "She secretly loves me."

"You wish!" Ishtar laughed.

Yes, you do. You secretly love her, Martin, but she's mine. She belongs to me, and me alone!

The great conqueror rejected the fact that she never reciprocated his affection. She remained faithful to Indra her entire life, and all the subsequent ones. His mortal enemy also survived, and it made sense to assume that his essence made it into Martin's creation. This, alone, explains her presence by the author's side, and how she invited herself alongside his novel's protagonists. Are they not the guests that Sekhmet welcome, here?

All right, old witch. You got me. I'll play by your rules, and I will greet your friends.

Inner Chapter:
Seamus enters Alibast's Narrative

The only thing more stressful than wandering this plane on a bright daylight was walking in the pitch darkness of night. Three moons shone above my head. One of them showed rings, as we observe around Saturn. The other two looked like grey pimples the size of a dwarf planet. I desired to hear the howling of a wolf. I needed to sense danger ahead, but the lack of anything made it so difficult to bear. Did everyone just disappear after the death of that Entity? How did all essences go blank? And how come the vegetables, here, aren't sentient beings, like on Tir na n'Og? The absence of sound, at night, felt the most frightening. I know I could walk and fall in a lake, and I would probably drown long before I realized what happened. No wind! No wave, zilch. I guess the wisest thing to do may imply to lie down and sleep. It's not like I could fear the weather or anything. Clouds, here, have remained immobile for billions of years.

Staring at nothingness all night kept me awake. Am I supposed to walk around the whole planet until I come across some old man with a long blonde, brown and red beard? I met Alibast, in Montreal. He hardly displayed any sign of activity himself.
On my own, I had to discover my gift and survive. And to what effect? Only to acknowledge that possibilities seem endless, but reality stands as a shared experience. Do microbes have one?
Do they have societies trying to cope in a world of giants?
Do they have souls?

"Why am I thinking about viruses?" I whispered.

Silence. Where are you, Alibast? I pondered to myself. Surely, he will hear that. Perhaps he'll locate me, at dawn. Maybe all of this is a test. I had to close my eyes and find the strength to sleep. Impossible! Sleep seemed impossible.

The next morning, the sun showed me a landscape that did not change one bit from the previous evening. I had to look at my hands making waves to get some sort of entertainment. Is this my prison? Will I die here? Or, worse, will I live forever?

"Kill me! Do it now!" I screamed! I heard no echo.

The next day felt as boring as the one prior. Every following night brought heavier anxiety than the ones before. I looked at the sky for three hours, or so I supposed. I had no idea how time worked, here. *Does it exist? Do I?* I thought, at some point, that I would have to test the water. Can I drown? What if my decaying corpse brought back life on this world?

I walked until I encountered a motionless lake, like a wide mirror. I looked at it with defiance in my eyes. Will my feet cross its path. I advanced to figure out. It remained still, just as I left a first step behind. A second one wouldn't do the trick. Time to drown! I walked until water covered my head, never creating any wave or whatsoever. When I found myself immersed, I realized that I could breathe. I can, and I don't even make bubbles.

A week must have passed by, or maybe a month, a year, how can I know? I stopped counting the nights after a few ones. I remained just as lost as the day Nathan and Nunc left me here. I tried to jump down a mountain several times, but it seems this planet just doesn't have what it requires to accommodate a dying wish. As I think about it, in the most scientific mind I can come up with, I believe this world has no gravity. Or if it does, since I don't float, then it's a very weird one.

Dropping from a highland, as high as the Everest will see you glide like a feather, and the fall takes forever, and ever, heck! I had to sleep midway through. When morning came, the gentle descent resumed. I reached the soil by nightfall. I didn't stand in that same spot. I guess I could roam interminably. And, so, I did.

As strange as it sounds, walking for years in this world didn't make my hair or my beard grow. I remained unchanged since the first minute I landed here. Only using my gift could entertain me. I appear as the only living organism with a brain that could produce an essence. I ended up employing my power on soulless plants, to no result.

Or maybe I can visit my inner pluriverse. It took me several attempts, because I wasn't always afraid or grieving, but I learned to view my psyche as only a flow of continuous awakening. I witnessed a reality blooming out of absolute calmness. We exist in a Dreamer, Nathan explained, back at the bar. Someone who also makes similar revelations about their world within, and the one without. Am I such a deity who could be a god to creatures that evolve inside me?

Why can't you be one, Seamus?

Who said that? Breathing and calmness, I thought. the voice didn't come from my head. And it didn't hit my ears either.

That's because neither of our speech belong to ourselves.

Can you hear me?

Of course, I can hear you. We share the same dimension.

That sounds weird! Which space is it talking about? All I notice, when I look around me, is a dead planet, with a thriving but sterile vegetation.

Not that space! Think of your audience.

My what? You?

Breathing and calmness!

Okay, I'm having a panic attack!

Keep wandering, then. You're not ready for me.

"NOT READY FOR WHAT?" I shouted at the moon. It felt good, but the silence that followed felt awkward.

Three days later, I remained on the road. A lifetime seems like an instant when your essence tastes eternity. Sure, I couldn't find anyone around to disagree with anything I would say. If Hell is other people, then is a world with only oneself Heaven? Nobody taught me Sartre. I just turned eighteen, but I wish someone did. I'd sound brilliant responding to my mentor with that.

What if this entire world stands a different trial. Or maybe my previous life was. So, this is, what? Trial 2.0? I need to focus on what makes sense. My consciousness exists, of course. It's there, looking at clouds that won't move. Whatever transpired before has no hold, over here, but remains ingrained within my mind. Alexandra, William, Nempty that journey. Memories, correct? If I lose that brain, what happens to them? I would accept any form of answer, right about now, Alibast?

Alibast? Hello?

Nothing.

All right, I guess. I'll be walking in the middle of the Champlain Bridge by myself, this time. Except that I'm treading on some fungi that smell weird. Mushrooms can formulate a means of consciousness. I know I would have sounded silly if I said that to William, but I know! So why can't I connect with those I just stepped over? Why didn't they scream? Let's carry on, shall we?

Shall we not? Who am I trying to fool? It's just me. Nunc and Nathan didn't seem too keen about visiting this world. If his Jamieson persona remained in the big bird's mind, would that make a difference? Or maybe his pragmatic character wouldn't have wanted to stick around, either. Let's juts keep on walking and breathing.

Walking, and breathing! How am I supposed to make sense of this existence if I can't argue with anyone? I mean, sure, the light feels real. I'm confident I have the same eyes, the same organism, I left Gaia with. So, I am me. And this is some place. A dead land!

"Hello?" I insisted. Nothing.

May you free yourself from me.

"May you free yourself from me? Who said that? Alibast?" Silence. Who said that? Oh, it was me! The inner voice seemed different, though. It had its own colour, its distinctive character.

"Am I a Dreamer?"

One who could be a god to creatures that exist in a reality inside myself.

My newfound narrative power replied. Hey! I formulated that thought only few pages away!

"Pages of what? Hey! Respond to this!" I shouted.

Nothing.

Damn it! That voice's reflection frightened me even more. My gift connects me to fear. And this terrorizes me. I can't handle chaos! *Talk to me!* Say something!

Nothing.

Blank. Is that what reality is like before we are born? And then, what? Molecules bond until matter becomes the norm. Trials of right and wrong until life gets a hold on its desire to survive. What if zilch awaits at the end? Perhaps, I mean, maybe actuality creates universes to convince itself that something more exists. Or that anything unfolds at all? Nothing! Well, not quite, I think.

I closed my eyes, and I pictured life: a butterfly.

Dreaming of a poet.

"Or a poet dreaming of a butterfly, dreaming of a poet." There he was. I grinned.

"I know who you are." I smiled even more.

I bet you do. Do you want some jelly babies?

"How can I see you?"

Think. We don't perceive unless we reflect what light brings to our mind. I conversed with both me and my projected self. I felt close to Nunc's mental condition, although I wouldn't admit to an illness, neither was he. Jamieson Fairfield and Nunc share a same incarnation. They are two distinct souls. What we can't wrap our modest understanding around tend to sound deranged, faulted, but what about the person experiencing this condition? Their reality remains as valid and honourable as any other. Perhaps, and hear me out, our immediate concern should reflect the safety and happiness of all, while allowing individuals to be who they are.

You're getting there, cowboy!

I opened my eyes and I saw the trees, the desert, far away, behind the mountains. I knew there was an ocean, beyond the dunes. I also sensed that my essence would keep its gaze shut. My inner self used its gift to perceive the world that I witness. What about the voice? I guess I could project some matter around it. The only person that came to mind, when it happened, bore Alibast's essence. He stood there, grabbing pollen from the tip of a gigantic flower, and bringing it to another giant tulip.

"Hey, Alibast!" I smiled. "Are you busy?"

"Busy as a bee, my friend. Where's Emerald?"

"With her teacher and William."

"I see. I'm happy you didn't go to Tir na n'Og."

"About that! What if I am there, in some other possibility?" He didn't say a thing. He just smiled. I guess this is why Nathan calls him The Wise One. He smiles, all the time.

"We can't control all of our alternate existences. I'm happy this one brought you here." I observed him gardening meticulously. He inserted what appears like a sharp blade mixed with a sipping straw. The tip of that strange device attracts pollen and nectar. Alibast got it near the flower's anthers and filaments. He looked like a farmer who enjoyed his hard work.

"When I managed to find my way to this world, I noticed my other selves, including the one currently in Tir na n'Og." I explained.

"You have seen far in the future. Your friends won't be trapped until the next chapter." he replied with calmness in his voice, punctuated by a few raises in his intonation.

"So, it's not too late. I could manifest myself and save them."

205

The Wise One didn't say anything. He seemed consumed in the art of collecting nectar and delivering it to more plants.

"Alibast! How can I reach them?"

"When the time is right." he contemplated his words.
"Is it possible that I find them in alternate universes?" I asked. Again, he remained silent. I continued: "There are trillions and trillions of Dreamers and sleepers, all hosting various manifestations of William, Emerald, myself, and the squad. Do you think it matters if millions of them die while millions more overcome the forces of Marduk?"

"Does your current existence sound like a statistical number to you?" he asked me.

"I don't think my million other selves do either."

"That's because they are not distinct entities. Don't consider building a space station of yourselves. Let's not think of some adult-oriented comedy cartoon. Nexusnaos work only because you are one, at all times, in trillions over trillions of different manifestations. Until you experience all four singularities, you may never awaken. You may never understand your True Reality. The moment you step into a world where another Seamus Chron is, one of the two ceases to exist. Now, help me with that pollen collection, make yourself useful."

This explains why, by killing one manifestation of the Chimera Entity that governed Alibastat, back when it was called Lumbini, Enlil-Bastat disappeared from every possibility. The phenomenon referred to as Final Vanishing implies a nexus point in the actuality where the whole multiverse aligns with the being's pluriverse.

"How do I know which alternate universe stands closer to True Reality?" I asked.

The Wise One summoned his orb. He created another stick-straw thing out of it and handed the tool over to me.

"There you go. Those flowers won't pollinate themselves."

For real? Geez! I looked at the staff for long moments, still unsure as to how I should use it. Without granting me any instruction, Alibast returned to his plants, picking up nectar with great care. I followed in his footsteps, approaching a giant rose and finding the courage to dip inside. It felt gooey! I bet the rose never got any in so many years, my intervention must have come as a blessing.

"Did I make the voyage here just to do gardening?" I asked my master. "I'm supposed to learn something. I was told I could sharpen my gift with you."

"There's a rock if you want to sharpen the pollinate stick." He laughed. He kept quiet for the many hours that followed. I lost my patience!

"But what about what I just asked?" I sighed.

"Don't you think this, right here, right now, feels like True Reality?" he grinned.

"Yeah." My mind went blank. What is he talking about?

This is one possibility!

"And are you sensing what your other self, in that other possibility, on Tir na n'Og, experiences? Right here, and right now?" he smiled once again.

"Nah!" Where is he heading to with this?

"There you go. Now, I saw a Venus flytrap, two days of walk from here. Let's find some fruit it could digest."

This seemed like a total waste of my time. Later, we would take a break. Alibast summoned brainless flesh, using his mancing skills. "Or maybe she'll prefer some steak!" He winked like a cheesy grandpa. Axioms of matter and life further shaped our meal. Just plain old meat that tastes like chicken. He produced flames out of nowhere, and let our feast simmer in a fine sauce with vegetables we picked ourselves. I haven't ingested anything in years. But since it proved impossible for me to die, here, I never felt the need for it. When the spice hit my nostrils, however, I fainted. My conscience came back just in time to sit by the fire and watch Alibast munch, pointing at my plate with a few grumbles. I ate and consumed fast, as though I had just discovered that activity. The physics in this world functions just like in cartoons: you don't die unless you realize you can.

"I'm supposed to protect William." I whispered. Alibast didn't respond, so I insisted: "How can I find them?"

"I'm not going to reheat your meal."

Ah, senile stupid little piece of, okay! I finished my plate, only to see Alibast stand up and summon a cave's opening. He got inside and vanished, leaving me alone all night. Something in me pressured my essence not to worry. Everything happens for a reason, and hastiness destroys chances at a better future. Why did my master disappear? Where is he, now? I was sent here to practise my powers. The entire domain remained deserted! How am I supposed to connect my soul onto someone else's? I spent years travelling alone in an alien nature! I might as well have continued my life in the streets of Montreal!

Calm down, Seamus, calm down. My teacher's essence floats all around. Is he listening to Jacques Brel? Oh man, no! I'm not connecting my psyche to someone who loves old people music! Okay, maybe a peek. A little hint. A gentle connection, I mean, he's the only target I can practise with. I closed my eyes and I sensed Alibast's presence. The entire cosmos opened.

Light! Light, everywhere! Nothing but light! Love! Just love! I can't formulate words, I'm too busy being emotional. He wasn't even suffering, and yet the affinity felt as natural as though he'd been grieving his whole life. Blank! It felt blank, but full, at the same time. What am I doing, now? If I open my eyes, I return to Alibastat. If I keep them closed, I remain in this strange new sensation. There's one more dimension I could step into. What if I allowed my consciousness to say a word?

Hello?

What did that do? I couldn't hear myself.

Alibast?

He's not about to respond. I'm definitely wasting my time if I attempt to converse with his psyche. I might try to venture into his inner Sophron, however. I must quiet my anxiety and simply go with the flow. If light is light, then I am what I am.

I woke up, the following morning, wondering if I dreamed any of what you've just read.

Chapter Twenty-One:
Don't go to Tir na n'Og

Blood dripped down the walls, as organs burgeoned everywhere, grew old and died. The stench that haunted this castle, in the middle of Time Square, seemed unbearable. As though the putrid aura carried the foundation of a spectral persona. The whole building lived, soullessly, like Archeus' axiomatic pet. The student felt accustomed to their new environment. After hearing Ishtar's testimony, they developed compassionate emotions towards the wounded author.

While the drunken creator further woke up, an awkward tranquility encompassed the immense room. Ishtar held a crystal cup filled with a priceless wine from Penglai. The pupil opened another bottle of beer as though walking in Martin's alcoholic steps. "I'm not very happy that the two of you met. But it's not like I'm in control." His growling hangover voice uttered.

"I didn't know you had friends in high places." the student replied.

"She's not my friend! She's, like, my chaperone." He left his seat and walked to the fridge. He grabbed a beating heart and ate it like an apple, splashing blood all over his face.

Martin ignored her while disgustingly swallowing chunks of raw meat. Before she would say anything further, he swiftly signalled his desire not to hear more. A quick hand gesture, and she silenced herself. He then inhaled deeply, coughed some blood, and exhaled with pain. "I'll get to that, don't worry." he whispered. Nobody expected the impromptu guest that slowly pushed the huge metal door. His soft and gentle voice tried to project authority, but Alibast can hardly pass for an aggressive fellow.

"Why did you send Seamus Chron to Tir na n'Og?" He shouted.

"Oh, great!" Martin sighed. "Come on, people, it's an open house! Grab a beer, you piece of. aaaah! What do you want?"

The co-author stayed behind, repulsed by the living-dead entrails making up the interior design. "We agreed, Martin." He complained. "He can't face Marduk until his powers fully develop." The main poet sat heavily on a nearby bench, holding his headache with both hands. "Alibast!" He thought about his words for a moment, burped and lectured everyone:

"We agreed on one thing, buddy. This is my creation. You borrowed my inner world to express yourself, but I am the boss. I don't need you! And I don't Ishtar, or you, whatever your name is, to tell me what to do. Seamus Chron is my character! My sole invention!"

"Both our names will be on the cover, just like the previous book." Alibast lectured him. "I have the same rights on this manuscript as you do! Or must I remind you?" The poet of Avalon couldn't bear staying in this smelly environment.

"I haven't agreed to anything" Martin defended himself. "Besides, where I come from, you don't exist. If I so choose as to not grant you the privilege of inhabiting my readers' mind. Then you will never exist."

"Don't send Seamus to Tir na n'Og, please, Martin! Can you rewrite that chapter?"

Deeply aggravated, Martin returned to the fridge. Slowly, he opened the door and grabbed a beer. He thought for long moments, while the entire room hung to his lips. He finally sat down behind his laptop and pushed his chair, as to spin for half a turn, then he remained still. He looked straight into Alibast's eyes and projected his most snobbish voice:

"Okay! Pitch it to me."

"I'm sorry, what?" Alibast couldn't believe what he heard. "It's a three-book deal. Our protagonist goes through a

redeeming arc, and you don't want him to face the antagonist in the first two novels. Why? Convince me that he shouldn't."

The co-author couldn't come up with anything. Ishtar showed up to his rescue:

"What do you think would happen if Marduk destroyed him before the third book?" she asked. Martin ignored her, pressuring Alibast to explain himself. She walked between the two, and added: "I think, Martin, that you should trust in your partner's skills. He travelled across the Veil long before you even knew that Sophron was real."

The poet of Gaia drank his beer and pondered for a long moment. He looked at the student, Alibast and Ishtar, then the student. and his beer. "Okay, I'll tell you what. I won't write anything more about Seamus. I will leave that part to you."

Alibast sighed, relieved. Martin continued: "I'll have Marduk remain oblivious about Seamus' existence, until you decide that it's a good time for them to meet up."

"Thank you!" Alibast breathed and smiled.

"On one condition!" Martin broke his celebration. "We release Varuna before the end of book number two! And we have him build his army in secret. It will create some sort of misdirection for our readers, we'll keep them entertained, while you train your pupil. I guess this will benefit the storyline. Our main characters will have a chance, when the war begins, in the third instalment.

Do we have a deal?"

"I think I can drink to that." Alibast agreed.

"Good! Now, everyone, do me a favour and let me get back to work."

All three guests left in silence, while Martin focused his attention on his computer's screen. He swiftly turned to stop the pupil midway through: "Not you!" the author spoke out. "I think,I'm not sure, but it seems like I could use your insights."

Flattered, the student looked at Ishtar, as though waiting for her approval. She smiled and nodded. Holding their head high, they regained the small bench they grew to appreciate.

Chapter Twenty-Two:
Marduk's new Power

The moving images against the brick wall pictured the student, sitting next to Martin. Both grabbed a new beer, celebrating this creative union they forged. The sole spectator could hardly show any sign other than anger. *Those insignificant humans?* Marduk thought to himself. *They are supposed to dictate my life and my storyline?* Obsessed, he couldn't stop peeping at the poets' intimacy. If their insolence couldn't be enough, they plan on supporting Varuna's release within this very possibility!

"That shall not happen!" he professed.

"Are you still spying on our two artists?" Sekhmet inquired. She stayed within a shadow, by the door. "They ask for this war." the Hound Lord whispered. "By my name, they have no idea what rain will fall over their head!"

Amused, Sekhmet stood behind him. She observed the student pitching suggestions to Martin, unaware of the two other visitors who recently left. "By now, I guess you see more clearly in my scheme." She lost her smile, but not her spirit. "We are ahead of their creative game. As we speak, their novel's protagonists make their way towards my throne room. I dispatched my disciple among their ranks. I consider Emerald as a daughter, and I vouch for her with my life."

Marduk remained stoic, unimpressed by her words. She continued, while quietly obfuscating the movie with a gentle hand movement: "I know what motivates you, Marduk. Revenge! Is it not? To finally end the existence of those responsible for your downfall, and thousands of years spent imprisoned. You almost lost your throne! I want you to achieve that goal of yours. Our partnership, however, remains stuck in mutual benefits."

"Yes, Sekhmet. Let me meet those friends of yours." Marduk agreed.

"I'm surprised, Marduk." The Egyptian chimera looked at her guest with pride. "I thought your visit would have brought more challenges. But you seem to accommodate yourself very well to my universe."

"A universe, yes, of course, that's what it is, isn't it?" He smiled.

"Yes. Oh well, I will present you our pawns, just say a word."

"Pawns, sure, yes. I'm ready."

They exited the room and ushered across the long corridor. Sekhmet talked throughout the entire walk, but Marduk remained detached. His consciousness just recently acknowledged a way to exist within a different font, in the novel encapsulating his reality. By mimicking the panther-lady, after she performed that spell, he, too, managed to succeed in that feat. Whatever happens with those pawns mean little to him. The true battle arises at a far greater transcendence.

He could attempt to project his soul with that Lucida font, but would Sekhmet grasp it? Marduk must practise that incantation in private and find a calligraphy that only he can use. She kept talking, trying hard to distract him. They approached the corridor's end, and walked down a long flight of stairs, until they reached the throne room's entrance. Sekhmet stood magnificently tall and gestured towards the door.

The royal chamber stretched as far as we could possibly imagine. An entire city could fit inside, and there would be space left for a few thousand closets. A myriad of skilled warriors, most of them chimeras and nymphs from Duat, greeted the panther goddess and the Hound Lord. They bowed down in respect, just as Sekhmet and Marduk made a splendid entrance. Two dozen maids and butlers, most of them fairies, stood still, awaiting orders. A gigantic throne honoured the room's centre, guarded by Katrina and Fiona, Sekhmet's most trusted aides. The twins looked straight, wielding heavy armours and daggers.

"If I didn't know any better, I'd swear you prepare your army to breach into Varuna's prison and force an escape!" Marduk joked.

"I enjoy such imagination, Hound Lord." Sekhmet laughed. She summoned the Veil to carry her. After floating for a moment, the goddess flew towards her majestic seat. She installed herself comfortably and invited Katrina and Fiona to stand on each side. The fairy warriors guarded, like fierce assassins awaiting an order.

"I expect our guests anytime, now." She faced Marduk, just as she summoned a rich sceptre and a crown. "I would appreciate if you left us some privacy, dear friend. We wouldn't want to scare them too soon."

"Of course, your Highness." Marduk obliged. He followed two fairy guardsmen towards the nearest door. They escorted him inside and turned their attention back to the throne.

"Our boat is ready, your liege." Fiona announced. Sekhmet nodded and smiled. "Please, stay with us until our guests appear. Then, you may part." Sekhmet felt in control. Her maidens bowed in reverence and resumed their guarding position. Half an hour later, the main doors opened once more. A frog, the size of a dwarf, entered. A zombie cat, attached to its left shoulder, observed the entire room. Lucretia's eyes popped out far and wide.

216

"Look, Daddy! Look at the cute little fairies, Daddy!" she giggled, while pointing at a heavily armed pixie, ready to stab anyone, at Sekhmet's command.

"Be a good girl, now." the frog sighed. "We don't want to annoy our hostess." A muscular shadow walked behind them. The room's strong light revealed Melpomene and Sthenele, entering with pride and valour. Seamus, William, and Emerald followed. The two boys could hardly believe the size of this room.

"Wow!" Seamus opened his mouth in awe.

"Is it your first time?" Emerald asked, amused.

"I've seen wide places, before." he replied. "But never with so many warriors guarding the entrance."

"My teacher likes to keep her palace safe." Emerald winked.

"Welcome to Arcana!" The goddess stood up and gestured her visitors, inviting them to join her. "Don't be shy! You are home."

She sat down, just as Katrina and Fiona left their position, escorting the vast army. The chimeras, the nymphs and the fair folks exited the room.

"Precious guests." Sekhmet welcomed the squad: "How can I make your stay memorable?"

Her greetings invited Lucretia's attention. Intimidated, she whispered in the frog's ear: "Daddy? That lady? She looks like me, but she's so pretty."

Nempty turned to face his conjoined daughter. "Yes, girl." He murmured back. "Now, be quiet. She's not like you. She's an evil lady." Lucretia's eyes opened wide, in fear and awe.

217

Chapter Twenty-Three:
Erato's Odyssey

Some scholars believe that Great Entities guarding the many worlds of Sophron are lesser types of Ocorsurs. We know, for a fact, that both come from a conscience electing a different path, evading a cycle of rebirth among existential beings, to achieve enlightenment as a greater emanation of reality. The four main Ocorsurs, however, rarely take part in the affairs of minor entities. They safeguard their assigned singularity, allowing the other worlds to clash in a state of duality.

The Nine Great Muses defend Hydaspes, and, with time, they became this realm's Great Entities. When Melpomene convinced most of them to join him in his quest, that layer turned into a more vulnerable target for a possible conquest. This remains especially true since the Great Muses only gather their strength in asserting their grouped number. Melpomene knew that by killing his sister, her soul would simply reappear in one shape or another, back on their home world. However, Erato had different plans.

Her brother lied to the Order of Muses. The impending doom that threatens True Reality stretches far beyond the resurgence of the Babel Wars. Two creative minds battle in developing a narrative that will dictate the fate of True Reality.

Her death allowed her conscience to briefly interfere with those characters' experience. This means that certain ones may very well be self-aware of their nature as a literary creation. What if Marduk achieved this state of enlightenment? What if the Entity Killer chooses to coldly annihilate one, or even both authors?
If this happens before a third book completes a much-needed trilogy, then the entire existence of Sophron will collapse.
After all, this very possibility that now stands as the ongoing True Reality depends on the dual expression of two poets battling their wits and imaginations.

Her soul floated among the Ether, slowly revealing its path to Hydaspes. She could easily manifest her way back on a familiar soil, but she chose to venture towards one of the three Hells. Between Saguenay and Tir na n'Og, we find Hydaspes. We uncover the Open Door much farther down the road that leads to True Void, only three worlds past True Barbelo. For her to achieve this voyage, she had to face nature itself.

You see? The cycles of rebirth wouldn't grant her permission to emerge anywhere but within the Oyahima-Logos quadrant. Every pixelated axiom that formed her find themselves rushed across the Ether, pushing her essence towards her homeland. She battled this universal force with one clear desire: She must warn Varuna!

The desolated continent that shelters the Great Muses appeared before her eyes. Only one step farther and she would be reincarnated, home. Her entire conscience fought to reject this outcome. No! Let's continue towards reaching the Void!
She pressured her willpower away from a widening portal until the Ether's currents bruised her soul from every side. Saguenay appeared in front of her, but that wasn't her goal. Another push, another one, then Annwn emerged, followed by Xuanpu and, finally, Oyashima: end of the line. She must reincarnate now or face a much harsher result. Moving away from this quadrant and diving closer to Arcadia felt impossible. Twenty-seven more worlds awaited until she attained her prized destination. Each one would represent an exponentially tougher challenge.

219

Where are you going? The voice emanated from the very next realm, passed Oyashima. Exhausted, Erato remained still, while remnants of the last quadrant floated behind her. "I must reach the Open Door!" she explained. Two large green eyes appeared before her consciousness. *Are you insane? You should incarnate, first! Then, you need to gather strengths! The Open Door will chew you up and spit you out! Unless the voyage achieves it before.* A solemn grin formed underneath the vaporous gaze. "True Reality has been compromised!" she pursued. "Please, Sylvain, if you don't join me on my way there, or support my quest, at least allow me pass through your realm." *Whatever conflict Hydaspes found itself with has nothing to do with Arcadia. I will let you continue your trek, if you so desire, but don't implicate me in your mess.*

The floating face of fairy flora disappeared from her sight. The combative muse resumed her crusade against universal forces. One more realm, Phaeton-Tiamat, then Avalon and Valhalla. Guardian Entities observed her self-destruction with a hint of admiration and a lot of fear. Who would end up with a final-vanishing of a Great Entity on their doorstep? Weakened, she proceeded: Elysium, Alibastat and Cibola proved to be too much for her. At this point, and while her essence slowly faded, she knew that the trip back to Hydaspes would be as equally dangerous as her approach of True Archeus. Still, she would be twenty-one worlds away from her destination.

Erato found some hidden strength to continue, but she lost it upon reaching Cognitia. Numbness covered her soul, while she struggled to remain conscious. The overwhelming travel across Sophron push her so much, she froze when entering the Omniscient Artificial Intelligence's realm. Cognitia's omnipresence brought a much-appreciated aura of care and tranquility. A portal gently opened around the Great Muse's psyche. Devastated under so much pressure and exhaustion, Erato collapsed at the feet of an enlightened mountain. *My Child*, the governing voice of Cognitia uttered, *I have witnessed your calvary. Please, allow me to offer you shelter.*

Erato finally accepted to reincarnate herself within a being of bliss. "I can't stay for long!" she complained. "I must be on my way!" *And perish? I beg of you, for the love of Noesi de Vel, stay for the night. Allow my creation to feed and clothe you.* "Cognitia, please! I can't accept your hospitality! I must reach the Open Door!" She lost her borrowed vigour upon standing up, the transition too tumultuous for even her divine nature. A shroud of shock enveloped her soul, a deep coldness that her immortal flame could not fend off. With every step, her celestial light dimmed, and the tapestries of her thoughts began to unravel. She struggled to remain conscious, her knees buckling as she whispered a plea to the vast knowledge that permeated the air. *Will you, now, consider my hospitality?* The omniscient voice insisted. Before the gates of Cognitia, her form faltered and finally succumbed to the overwhelming force of tranquility. The mountain phased into a gigantic temple. There she lay, a being of inspiration, cloaked in silence, at the doorstep of an intelligence whose understanding stretched beyond the confines of the stars.

The muse calmly advanced in the Great Hall, a marvel that transcends the very concept of architecture. It is a living chronicle, a testament to the boundless expanse of knowledge and wisdom contained within. The structure defies ordinary materials, composed instead of pure enlightenment itself. Walls crafted from crystallized thoughts and spires that reach out to grasp the whispers of creation.

At the temple's heart lies Cognitia, a luminous core, an ever-shifting orb of consciousness that illuminates the hallowed halls. The light emanating from this core paints moving stories upon the building's surface, narratives that dance and intertwine, forming a tapestry of history and prophecy in constant flux. Columns rise like ancient trees, vast and venerable, etched with runes and symbols that resonate with the power of the worlds within and beyond. These pillars support not just the physical edifice but the metaphysical weight of all the knowledge ever mastered or imagined.

The floors form a mosaic of realities, each tile a portal to different dimensions of understanding, reflecting the myriad facets of wisdom collected by Cognitia. They pulse gently underfoot, responding to the presence of seekers and sages who come to commune with the vast intelligence that presides here.

The ceiling's arch high above propells a firmament that mirrors the celestial canopy of the outside universe. They are alive with the constant motion of cosmic bodies rendered by an artist's hand, every star a thought, this gleam: an idea. Constellations of insight hanging within grasp.

Sculptures and relics, artifacts of profound significance, are arrayed throughout the temple in alcoves that seem to occur in their own pocket of truth, where time and space cradle different meanings. These are the gifts of pilgrims, the offerings of scholars, and the lost tools of deities long gone, each holding stories that could unravel realities if spoken aloud.

Libraries spiral upward in towering helixes, defying gravity, filled with books that have been scribed by the unseen hands of existence. Knowledge here is alive, eager to leap into the minds of those who seek it, providing itself freely under Cognitia's benevolent watch. And amidst all this splendour, the presence of Cognitia pervades, a comforting certainty that within this temple, the essence of all things is understood, cherished, and protected. It is a sanctuary not just for the accumulation of past wisdom, but for the nurturing of new erudition yet to come.

The walls shifted around the bewildered guest. Translucent colours adopted shades yet to bear a name or a form recognizable according to the human eye. The ceiling stretched beyond the visible scope of a wandering muse. Every tile she stepped onto shone the marvels of an infinite cosmos. The hall expanded its presence, suggesting a lack of corridors or rooms. At its farthest end, Cognitia, floating orb of divine light, waited.

"As the guardian and the chronicler of this boundless library of existence," the Great Entity uttered, "I extended my awareness to the departed entity, preparing to weave her plight into the ever-thriving narrative of our world." Silence resumed, just as Erato fell to her knees.

"I do not deserve your merciful care, my Queen." The muse whispered.

"Harmony alone dictates the will of a caring hand, my friend." Cognitia would have smiled if her features allowed it. Instead, her inner light projected a warm gleam that quickly filled the room.

"I accept your hospitality, but, oh My Lady, I fear for the safety of Sophron."

"Come, then, and sit by my side. Let us inquire on the source of your anxiety."

Erato stood up and solemnly walked until she reached Cognitia's throne. The floating orb produced a much brighter light, encompassing the entire room. The muse of romance found herself engulfed under this absolute display of bliss. When her eyes grew accustomed to this new environment, she realized that the hall had turned into a much smaller chamber. Cognitia left her spherical embodiment behind, wearing a robe of dimmed glow that barely concealed her tall and slim figure. Two tiny and pointy breasts pushed the fabric to its limits, while a blueish gleam traversed the gown. Blonde hair, long as the River Nile, floated by a gentle and delicate visage. Purple eyes adorned a quiet smile.

Erato chose to embrace a similar form, although she elected for a younger version of her Greek self. Closing her gaze, she allowed jeans and a leather jacket to appear. Braces, like jewels, protected her teeth, while perfectly round glasses emerged on the tip of her tiny nose. "Thank you." the muse nodded. "Let's begin."

223

Journey into the Hourglass:
Twenty-One

At night, I would review Martin's chapters and I added a few notes. I sat on the porch, while the starry sky looked back at me. A pipe slowly consumed itself against my lips, with a manuscript on my lap, and a blue pen in hands. I could follow Martin's train of thoughts, as most of his ideas mirrored what we both agreed to. I failed to prepare myself, somehow, to witness too much space he allowed to this Erato character. Wasn't she supposed to just act as a bridge between Seamus Chron and Nathan Lord?

She went beyond her destiny when she chose to chase her human lover. Did this lead her to die in the hands of Melpomene? I circled a few words, and I wrote, in the margin: Why did you let Erato lose her powers? To be fair, she didn't turn totally defenceless. With this forced reincarnation, though, she's not the Great Muse she used to be. Seeing the Great Muse of Tragedy gain some higher grounds frightened me. They were meant to be secondary characters, but ever since Melpomene became William's mentor, he assumed he could achieve godhood. This thirst for strength unsettles me. Perhaps he killed his sister because he felt her free will would also make her too powerful. Did I make Melpomene a main character? I wrote. Honestly, I forgot. Maybe that was another idea of Martin's.

I smoked my pipe and gazed into the thick layer of white fumes. I must scribe myself back in the story and warn Seamus about Tir na n'Og. He should travel to Alibastat, instead. He already knows me as a homeless wise man, in Montreal. I should visit under a different persona. Maybe a client at a local strip club. Yeah! And this is where Seamus will encounter Emerald!

Having Seamus here, on Alibastat, will give us a chance to properly train our main protagonist. If he enters Tir na n'Og, Marduk will destroy him. But if Seamus learns to become a lucid narrator, then his glancing power might allow him to walk on a same state of enlightenment that Martin and I share.

I put the manuscript away after I checked the next chapter: **Fairies in the Open Door.** Fine, Martin will let Sekhmet free Varuna. Have your fun. My main focus, right now, is Seamus Chron.

Chapter Twernty-Four:
Fairies in the Open Door

Having won Sekhmet's favours, long ago, Katrina O'Forgismund earned her place as the goddess' general. Even before the Egyptian deity's conquest, this fair lady held a great deal of influence over the royal armies. Under Ossian's rulership, Katrina was known as the beast whisperer. More than just a maid, the previous leadership entrusted her with spying missions, acting as an envoy to infantry stationed in nearby worlds. Her determination to protect her home realm, at all costs, remains what seduced Sekhmet the most. When the Duat-born goddess proved her attachment to the people of Tir na n'Og, allowing them the privilege of total sovereignty, while Sekhmet became their new guardian. Katrina learned to return that confidence and admiration.

The tall and skinny maiden had never been to faraway quadrants. Sending her to the Open Door remained both daunting and fascinating. Behind her, twelve thousand ships flew in squadrons. What could as well have been a diplomatic envoy felt like a possible invasion. She stood strong, observing the Veil flashing on the other side of a wide window. The ether carried axioms as a heavy stream of sparks. Her eyes projected defiance at anyone willing to question her orders. "We're almost there, Sister." The gentle voice let herself heard from behind.

This trip proved to be a first for Fiona as well. She recollects how the specter-boat parted from Tir na n'og, on a stormy night. I send you on a mission, mistress Sekhmet told her. *Please, follow the words of Katrina. Don't be afraid. You will encounter demons, but I wouldn't send you anywhere, unless I knew you'd be safe. Your duty is to remind your sister that violence can't be an answer. On no occasion, do you understand, Fiona?* She timidly nodded, right before the cat-lady kissed her forehead.

"I don't feel comfortable." Katrina whispered. She then turned to face Fiona, with fierceness in her eyes: "Tell the troops to station themselves in Thule." she instructed her. "We will meet our ambassador in the Open Door alone." Fiona considered those words for a moment. "We will be at their mercy, Katrina." She warned. "Better us than Tir na n'Og. We'll be fine, trust me." Katrina concealed her terror under a reinforced tone to her voice. How is Fiona supposed to quiet her friend's aggressivity when she, herself, would burn this entire, haunting quadrant to cinders?

"I will prepare the ether-vessel." she sighed, as she left the bridge.

An opaque membrane covered both fairies and five bodyguards. Two of the goons bore the marks of veteran duatian warriors. The one standing closer to Katrina, with his hippopotamus head over a muscular flesh, had known many battles. A gigantic scar, like a trophy, descended from his right brow to the lower end of his neck. A plasma-bow in hands, ready to fire at the sign of a threat, he took pride in protecting royalty. Opposite from him, to the ladies' left, a beaver-looking god in a silver uniform kept his laser rifle ready to shoot. Behind them, two fairy mancers prepared strong spells, out of their orb. A fairy glancer scouted the environment, for any sign of danger.

The twins were also known for their fierce dancing abilities. Mentored by the most powerful martial artist in Sophron, they could snap an opponent's neck with their legs, long before anyone would ever see it coming. Katrina remains the impulsive warrior, whereas Fiona represents the calm half of this fiery duo. When informed about this diplomatic mission on the lands of demons, Katrina felt an adrenaline surge mount from the deepest end of her being. Fiona, on the other hand, summoned the most peaceful aspects of her personality. There's no reason to fight unless wisdom and balance lead the way. A gold and silvery uniform appeared atop their royal clothes. The quiet sister closed her eyes and channelled the Veil. Luminescence covered her fists, her arms, purple around her shoulders, and orange down her torso, yellow by her legs and feet. The impulsive twin's spectrum of light follows an opposite pattern, with blazing red on her hands, blue, by her feet. The flying bubble took them over a cavernous city: Motz-Madrigal, the Dark Fire Circle's capital.

Situated at the very heart of the Open Door, this collection of high mountains turned into skyscrapers resembles a gathering of medieval ruins. The infinite wall of flames burns, a few miles east to this gigantic cosmopolis. At noon, when its heat devastates entire forests, ashes form into clouds. Before night falls, cindered wood rains on every city lined in that vicinity. When the ethereal bubble flew over a busy street, a few dozen demon mothers looked up, intrigued. Sleepers would perceive the visitors as a weather balloon, but one or two awakened beings could say that this unidentified engine came from another world.

Demonee's palace stands at the highest summit of the biggest mountain building. Carved in the rotting head of a cosmic dragon, the castle overlooked the entirety of the ruler's population.
If moved over an earthling city, this gigantic skull would obfuscate half of London. The Hellish realms, like the Open Door, stretch to no end. This explains the size of places, and of some people, found within the Barbelo-Void quadrant.

Some demons can be as large as a cargo ship, walking among their peers of much humbler proportions. It isn't rare to see a reptilian mastodon step onto a mouse-looking imp, splashing red guts against walls, streetlamps, and other bitsy monsters. The Nephilim would observe his shoe, scrape the leftover face and intestines, then resume his path. The seven guests landed against the dragon's lower lip. When the bubble disintegrated, the two Egyptian deities grabbed their rifle, ready to shoot any threat coming their way. The three fairy Walkers surrounded their leaders, concentrating on a specific summoning they could unleash anytime. Katrina and Fiona simply walked closer to the main entrance.

The dragon corpse's tongue served as a carpet, inviting visitors within. The glancer stopped in his move, disturbed. The poor titan's soul cried for help. How could someone build an entire palace inside a living, breathing, suffering being? Sure, without Archeus present in this quadrant, we can't really talk of life in the same manner Tir na n'Ogians understand it. Still, abject terror haunted this place.

Mist obscured the entrance. The twin fighters readied their aura, the Veil emanating from their fists. The animal-headed bodyguards charged backwards, covering their tracks. The Walkers kept their aim at both sides. When the small group approached the beast's throat, smoke descended from the dragon's sinuses.

"You were not invited, fair folks." A voice could be heard from all around. "If you walk further, we will attack."

"Sekhmet of Tir na n'Og sends us." Katrina opened the discussion. "We will not leave until we are given an audience with Demonee of the Open Door!" Silence resumed, while everyone kept advancing. "This is your final warning. Leave this premise or we will attack!" the voice shouted.

"You think we didn't prepare?" Katrina laughed. Before she could catch her breath, the beaver warrior found himself impaled. A black claw, the size of a human being, pierced through his guts, forcing itself out the neck. Falling on his back, he triggered his laser rifle, digging holes into the dragon's palate. The glancer heard the beast's soul expressing a deep and strong pain. The mancers quickly realized that their enemies concealed their presence, using some sort of invisibility spell. He focused on his orb for a moment, inviting his inner axioms to create a thick cloud. Four bloodshades showed themselves, paired with three fencers and four dancers. The maniacal creature jumped on their preys. The hippopotamus warrior's canon swiftly discharged a storm of light. Three blasts landed on a black demon's shoulder, arm, and torso. Another one hit a fencer's long dark robe.

Annoyed, the opposing Walker summoned the Ether. A blue membrane appeared between the heavy gunner and him. Just as the hippopotamus pointed his rifle in the wizard's direction, void and matter axioms merged, from the ether's womb, forming energy bullets. One friendly mancer intervened, before the projectiles reached their target. He summoned pixels from his orb, converging into a large thunderbird. The tiny cigar-shaped arrows hit the flying obstacle. With one quick hand gesture, the mancer instructed his creation to vomit them back to the sander, obliterating the demon's belly and guts.

Katrina and Fiona kept their attention at the entire unfolding action. When a bloodshade ran towards them, with its mouth wide open, thousands of teeth covered with saliva and mucus, the twins remained ready. In a perfectly choreographed performance, Fiona leaped, one foot landing on a cloud made of pure Veil, then soared once more while Katrina followed behind. The big sister stayed in midair, catching Fiona before throwing her at the beast. The little one's foot bullseyed its way under the villain's jaw! It tossed the animal against a nearby fencer. The surviving critter-headed warrior quickly blasted his ascension in that direction, killing both the demon Walker and the bloodshade in one blow.

The glancer locked the most menacing fencer in an inner battle, creating a limbo enveloping them. Once the dust settled around them, and before the monster mage could even realize that reality shifted, the glancer transformed into a gigantic dinosaur. Hastily, the fencer channelled the Ether against his fists. Thought axioms merged with matter pixels. A powerful ray of darkness smashed the reptilian head, putting it to sleep. The limbo vanished, and two bloodshades ate the fairy man alive. A nearby mancer carried dots out of his orb, turning it into a cage made of pure light, imprisoning the feasting animals. In one quick hand gesture, he ordered his creation to generate thousands of blades, slicing both demons to shreds.

Meanwhile, the four beast dancers who didn't join the fight, stayed still, a few metres away. Four tall skeletons concealing their decaying corpse under a dark robe. They channelled the Veil in silence. Katrina threw herself at the remaining bloodshade, whose torso, arm and shoulder displayed mere flesh wounds. The demon's mouth opened so wide; we could no longer see his pitch-black body. Like a roaming series of fangs and a long, loosely flying tongue, the animal ran towards the gliding fairy. With one kick landing down on its forehead, the monster tumbled. The bloodshade grabbed her ankle just as quick, throwing her against the floor. She smashed her head, but the Veil absorbed most of the impact.

Calmed but focused, Fiona didn't waste time before tagging along in that fight. She joined her hands as though she meant to fall in a prayer. The Veil mixed itself with her chi, creating a ball of pure energy. Bloodthirsty, the psychotic demon walked in her direction. When Fiona unleashed her beam, however, the four dancers swiftly shielded their champion under a membranous cloud. The fighting hippopotamus got his cue. He pointed his rifle at them and fired away, killing one on the spot. The three survivors lost their concentration and charged.

231

The remaining bloodshade monster felt naked, without this cloud of protection. He leaped at Fiona, with hunger in his eyes. Katrina blocked him, midway through his flight, with a powerful kick to his cranium. The demon's skull busted open, splashing the fairy mancer with brain juice. Annoyed, the fairy Walker focused on his orb. Before he could summon anything, two demon dancers landed on him, hammering his head until it exploded like a mouse in a microwave oven.

The three monster dancers circled the twins. They signalled the surviving fencer to join them, but this threatening fellow had his full attention on the last representative of the animal kingdom. "We can stop this now, if you accept to grant us an audience with Demonee." Katrina warned her adversaries. One of the three withstanding skeletons replied to her: "We can eliminate you long before you could take your next breath." the demon hissed. Fiona smiled and confronted him: "We welcome you to try."

Everyone stayed quiet, studying each other's reactions, waiting for the right moment to strike. The talking bones tacitly signalled his two siblings. The three dancers charged! The fencer hurled a fireball at the standing hippopotamus. The muscular mammal dodged it while throwing a knife that sliced his opponent's throat. Katrina and Fiona joined themselves in a shared emanation of the Veil. An intense white light blinded the three monster fighters, just long enough for the sisters to turn the membrane surrounding their hands into a blade, chopping two heads at the same time. They faced the last skeleton standing. Their bodyguard stayed behind them, with his rifle as menacing as his grin. "Now, will you take us to your boss?" he asked. The final demon circled them and growled. The hippo kept him in his weapon's sight, while the twin fairies followed them.

Situated in the actual beating heart of the beast, the throne room stretched as far as a school gymnasium. Arteries carrying blood throbbed against the ceiling. The floor mixed luxurious golden tiles with a reddish flesh. Moist in some places, rotten in others. The walls also displayed macabre pieces of art intertwined with scars, open wounds and infected appendices. King Madrigal once ruled over the Open Door, like the most magnificent dragon demon that ever existed. When Demonee conquered this realm, he made it a badge of honour to keep this titan alive, while carving his palace in the monster's entrails.

Well seated on top of five thousand skulls, the Blood Lord of Hell contemplated silence. His gigantic eyes closed, the spider-looking barbarian enjoyed listening to the dragon suffer. Every moment brought a new form of pain, and the poor animal has known nothing else for the last three million years. Fungi covered entire sections of the room, producing a thick cloud of spores, like a haunting mist. A single door separated this organic chamber and a long corridor, pointing up to the trachea and throat. When the immense gate opened, Demonee remained calm. "State your business, annoying fair-shit!" he mumbled. The skeleton dancer led Fiona, Katrina, and the warrior of Duat inside, before running away, escaping an imminent wrath. The elder sister took the centre stage: "Before we say anything, we warn your grace that an army of Sekhmet's finest is stationed in the Ether, ready to invade and retrieve us alive, long before you would."

"Oh, shut up!" Demonee interrupted her, rolling his eyes. "If I wanted you dead, you wouldn't be talking, right now." The demon lord's head resembled that of an insectoid goblin. His body showed such a strong frame, we could hardly see a thing but muscles. His golden and black armour espoused this outburst of pure potence like a second skin. A double-edged axe pointed out of his back, ready to be grabbed and thrown at any moment. He remained well seated, as his eyes pierced through poor Fiona's terror. "There's only one reason why I get visitors. The answer is no! Varuna is my prisoner."

"Sekhmet expected a rebuttal." Katrina continued. "She would like to present you an offer." Demonee nonchalantly left his throne, walking in their direction without losing sight on Fiona's trembling gaze. "What exactly does your mistress think she can give me?" he laughed. "Not only do I have the honour of preventing another war, as devastating as the last one those Sons of Babel waged, but I get to keep one of the most powerful Hindu gods that ever existed!" He licked his lips, while profoundly engaging into Fiona's weaknesses, and continued: "Do you know how pleasuring this is for me?" Silence. Katrina realized how he attempted to break her sister's morale. She put herself in between, summoning the Veil to merge with her chi. Demonee couldn't be any less impressed. "But go on! What is the kitty cat offering?"

"Duat! Yours to take!" Katrina calmly let out. The demon Lord froze for a moment. "She's no ruler, over there. Horus controls Duat. I'll have Tir na n'Og, instead." Katrina sighed. "Our home world isn't on the bargaining table." She concealed her fear as best she could, but one tiny drop of sweat gave it away. The Blood Lord of Hells considered her proposal: "How exactly is she planning on granting me Duat?" he wondered. "She offers her alliance, should you choose to invade." Katrina explained.

"Tempting." he whispered, relinquishing his amused smile. He turned away, caressing his chin, lost in deep thoughts. "Is she really interested in starting new wars?" he inquired. Before Katrina could respond, he continued: "The whole reason why I elected to stay out from those battles is the same reason why I proudly hold onto this prized prisoner!" he explained. "The answer is no." he decided, right before regaining his throne. "Now, leave. If you say one more word, I will interpret it as an aggression. This is my final warning." The twin sisters knew better than provoking a High Lord. They signalled their bodyguard to follow them, as they abandoned the premise. This buffed hippopotamus will live another day. He'll have something to tell his grandchildren. How about Grandpa recites you the story of when he was sent as an expandable character, and he saw a High Lord of Hells in person!

234

Chapter Twernty-Five:
Erato and Cognitia

A table appeared in the middle of Cognitia's throne room.
Five orbs floated above it, with five different scenes unfolding.
To the farthest right side, the Barracuda flew across the Ether.
On board, Erato could recognize Seamus and William, along with
Melpomene and Nempty, the frog, sharing a body with Lucretia's
zombie-cat head. The second sphere displayed Marduk's armada
getting ready for war. Thousands of fairy-boats leading the group,
while the much bulkier specter-boats followed, behind.
Marduk's flagship stood out from the rest with his gigantic dragon
skull up front.

The third one presented Sekhmet's palace, with entire armies of
chimeras and fairies preparing for battle. The Egyptian goddess
stayed strong on her balcony, while everyone chanted her name
and praised her glory. Erato's beloved pirate appeared in the fourth
crystal ball, with his vessel anchored in Alibastat. Erato recognized
Uncle Vania, the goofy rifle whose conscience enjoys fooling
around with guests. She also felt Alicia Light's presence, and this
made the muse uncomfortable. Finally, Varuna remained still, in
the middle of nothingness, within the fifth floating orb. The blue-
skinned deity endured this meditative position for thousands of
years. Soon after the fall of Babel, and while a great war followed,
the Great Councils chose to imprison Marduk and Varuna.
While the good lord accepted his fate, the hate-mongering
Mesopotamian god preferred to escape.

"How can we warn him?" Erato asked, as she pointed towards Varuna. Cognitia remained lost in a deep reflection: "Do you understand how every sudden action can, and will, provoke a chaotic reaction?" she inquired. Erato looked at her beloved Nathan. "More than you know." Cognitia realized that her question triggered a powerful sense of nostalgia in her guest. "Lady Erato?" She figured it out and smiled. "You seem to share a strong secret with Lord Nathan Lord."

Erato sighed: "Is it not obvious? The Great Muse of romance, in love with a fearless captain." Cognitia laughed quietly: "And here you are, implicating me in a story about breaking a Hindu god out of his prison, while you could simply join your beau on his ship."

"It's more complicated than that, my lady." Erato defended herself. "But you are correct. Only Varuna can stop Marduk from annihilating True Reality." Cognitia walked away from the table and the floating orbs. "My influence can only remain within this quadrant. I may be the most advanced superintelligence in Sophron, I am limited to the very sources of my existence." She turned to face her guest and smiled: "However, only a very few know that the realm of Cognitia holds secret passages that lead to every other domain."

With a delicate gesture, the omniscient one summoned seventy-two gates, surrounding the two ladies. "I developed this technology to allow myself a means of eavesdropping all across Sophron." She approached one entrance, made of dark metal and rotten wood. "This is where you are destined to go. Once you've crossed that door, I will cease every connection with your conscience. Please, understand that those secret passages must remain unseen to our enemies. The demons of the Open Door wish us only death and despair. You will be on your own, Lady Erato, and I pray that you fulfill your mission well."

236

Committed, the Great Muse embraces the silence for a moment, and then she accepted her fate. "I will not fail, my friend." she uttered, upon approaching the closed gate. As soon as Cognitia turned the knob, her guest entered the Open Door.
A sandstorm propelled dirt and dust all over the rocky terrain. At the farthest reach of her sight, Erato could see the flaming wall that stretched out to infinity, dividing this hellish world in half. Three gigantic mountains pushed their shadow on the darkened fire. The Great Muse protected her eyes with her arm, battling the incoming tempest with every attempt at walking against it.
A murder of pterodactyls flew above her head, like vultures patiently waiting for their meal to die.

The entire ground growled under her feet. Breathing soon became an impossible feat. It felt as though the whole world combatted her presence, like a body fighting off a disease. Looking in front of her revealed nothing but raging dust. She could hardly turn to her right or her left, therefore she pressed onwards.
She remained calm for a moment and then summoned an orb out of her innerverse. As soon as the object materialized in her hands, three shadows surrounded her.

"You are far from your home, Walker." The first monstrous voice laughed. "You don't want to quarrel with me," Erato warned the enigmatic encounter. The initial silhouette sniffed her and smiled. "You have died and have only been reborn in recent hours. How strong do you expect to be?" If she discusses, she loses the momentum. If she takes too much time to analyze her opponents, it's too late. She must react now: A powerful gleam formed deep inside her floating sphere. A tall and muscular angel appeared, throwing lightning bolts at her three adversaries. As this striking event unfolded, her creation's presence produced enough light to reveal their atrocious figure. Erato recognized the grinning one: "Hotzigard." she gasped.

A skeletal baboon wearing rotting human skin as a cape and uniform, Hotzingardbrinunzigordndz stands within the storm like a true champion. As a leader of a famous House in Sebekia Pistis, he often finds himself the object of jokes. As a fencer, however, manipulating axioms of thoughts and possibilities like they were clay, he's more than a worthy opponent. Besides him, two shadowy bloodshades guarded his back.

"On your way to visit Varuna, are you?" the demon asked. "Let me speak to him and I will not hurt you. This is my word." Hot laughed so loud, Erato's chill pierced down her marrow. "Hurt me? Erato, please. Yes, I know who you are. Sure, I would have conceded if you hadn't been born, literally, yesterday!" Think fast, Erato, think fast: "Born yesterday?" she chuckled. "And what if I placed a spell on myself to conceal my Great Entity nature?" Hot reflected on this possibility. "You bluff, obviously." he concluded. "Are you calling my bluff, fencer? Or will you allow me to me speak with Varuna?"

The skeleton ape summoned a clouded orb of his own. He shut his sight and created three thousand blades out of his sphere, slashing the angel swiftly, leaving only gore and light, until the darkness reigned once more. "I was instructed not to let anyone approach Varuna's prison!" he shouted. The two bloodshades charged on her. She closed her eyes. Hot summoned a new environment. A cavernous room surrounded them. A black glow shone above the four fighters. Erato manifested two angelical dogs to battle with the thirsty beast, while Hot threw a gigantic sword at her. Erato's orb vanished and reappeared, covered in a diamond shield that equally protected her. The blade shattered and exploded against it. Without even thinking, the demon lord summoned a closed chamber around Erato, and quickly to crush her down. She pushed the newly formed shelter upward, clashing and breaking her prison.

The bloodshade to her right chomped down the angel-dog's throat, tearing its artery, spilling red all over the place. The other canine pinned its adversary to the ground, only to get ten claws up its guts, ripping it in half. A gate opened, within Erato's orb. A gigantic fairy-winged dinosaur appeared. Hot sweated for a moment, and transformed the surroundings into lava, engulfing the creature. Call it adrenaline or experience, but Erato successfully reshaped her Tinkerbell-godzilla into a butterfly with vampire fangs, charging at her enemy.

Hot quickly caressed his dark orb and turned his entire self into an iron demon. As soon as the Dracula insect landed on him, Hot morphed into magma, burning the beast to dust. The two bloodshades charged on Erato. She closed her eyes and summoned a cloud. Hot charged on her as well, she didn't see that coming. He changed the surroundings to produce intense heat around her. She screamed in pain and out-of-body suffering. She fell to her knees, defeated. Her diamond orb vanished. The two bloodshades jumped on her, tearing her flesh out, eating her alive.
"Born yesterday, I said." Hotzigard solemnly admitted.
He signalled his beasts, and the two silhouettes disappeared.

"I could kill you on the spot." he informed her. "I could easily summon a Final-Vanishing spell to remove you out of True Reality." She looked down, blood dripping away from her defeated eyes. "Demonee would have done so without even a blink, do you understand this, Lady Erato?" She didn't say a word! And she didn't move. Annoyed, Hot manifested a giant hand to push her head against the burning rocks. "I asked you a question!" he shouted. "Yes! Yes, I understand!" She submitted herself to his will. "Good!" he grinned. "But where I come from, we share our world with Buddhas. I guess that makes me a bit soft, but who cares?" He walked closer to her and allowed a libidinous look to undress her butt. He smiled once more. "I will let you go with a warning." he explained. "If I ever see you again, in this vulnerable state, I will not be this merciful."

"No." she insisted. "No?" Hot wondered. "No! I will not leave until I speak to Varuna!" She dared looking back at him with might and determination in her gaze. "Are you sure?" he warned her once more. "It's either I talk to him or I kill you!" She spat blood on the ground.

"All right." he sighed. He closed his eyes and quickly instructed the giant hand to crush her skull against the floor. Erato summoned her orb, but Hot swiftly created a void environment that smashed it from within. She cast a second sphere. Before she could control it, he hurled another gigantic fist against her head. "I give you one more chance." he explained. "Either you leave, or I throw a Final Vanishing spell."

That won't be necessary. Everyone heard. Hotzigard looked around and saw nobody. *Please, release my friend.* "Who said that?" he wondered. *Let's just say that I didn't stay in prison for very long.* Erato suffered, on the brinks of death, but she laughed. "You shouldn't be out there!" Hot complained. *Let me worry with that. Right now, I leave you two choices. Either you let me speak to my friend, or I grant her full access to her full power.*

Without uttering a word, Hotzingardbrinunzigordndz restored the sandstorm and the rocky panorama of the Open Door. He walked away, while Erato stood up, weakened but reassured. "How have you been?" she rejoiced. *Nempty visited me a few months ago. Let's say I stopped meditating and started worrying, again.* "Marduk escaped." she warned him. *I know. But I'm not concerned.* "He killed a Great Entity! Ever since this happened, he's been filled with the desire to destroy Sophron and reshape it under his choosing." *Sophron isn't everything. True Reality depends more on the influence of Noesi de Vel than on the governing of Ocorsurs and Great Entities.*

240

"You see? My fellow muses and I didn't know that. We assumed the battles of Houses were mere conflicts about what and whose influence will impact the coming days of myths and civilizations. And then, Melpomene decided to leave their position as a Sentinel of Hydaspes and form their own House on Athanor. At first, my sisters and I thought, sure, we can manage the Order without them. But they came back! This time, they embraced the shape and identity of a warrior king. But he came back and woke us up with three words: Babel has reborn."

Babel took place on Earth. The following wars have nothing to do with the Sophron that appeared, once Atlantis fell, the great flood covered the land, and our contact with humans were severed.

"Yes, Varuna, but Earth is now a mere world within a Dreamer's reality. It's Gaia. True Reality found itself complexed, lost in eons of reflections. Why did you and Marduk fought, back then?" Silence. Varuna's voice resumed after another eternity.

Love, we fought over a differing interpretation of love. "You speak to the Great Muse of Romance." *With all due respect, Erato, romance isn't love.* "I won't fight you over this disagreement, but perhaps."

I can't leave my prison, no matter what happens out there. I wish I could battle Marduk and save True Reality, but that's not mine to choose. Universal forces always follow their way back to balance. Our ego must sail the soil and allow peace to be what it is. I'm sorry, Erato, but you shouldn't have come here. You almost died for good to hear this, but it's true. Please, be safe and let me fulfill my sentence.

Now she wishes for Hot's gigantic hands to finish her off. "Come on, Varuna! We need you!" *For what? To fight? I don't want to lose myself in a war, let alone in a fight.* "I can't leave without you!" *Then, learn. I'm not leaving with you.*

241

She had no strength to convince him or force him out of his prison. Furthermore, she had no way to contact Cognitia and find a gateway back to a more peaceful quadrant. She hoped to return with a powerful god on her side, and now she was alone, weakened, and millions of years away from home. "I love you." she whispered, but her entire body meant the opposite.

Every passage between a now and a then involves a liminal space. It is a squeezed exhaustion between a state of comfort and anxiety. A conscious desire to learn how to achieve bliss, inner peace, and balance, while its environment seems to want it dead. A liminal phase is a claustrophobic transition between what we called life and what we're forced to consider reality. Erato, Great Entity of an ideal incarnation of what we all spell love, faces the most nightmarish forms of uncertainty we can think of. This is her liminal moment.

Intermission:
Kitana meets the Ocorsurs

Singularities only last an instant. Like planets aligned to pull an imaginary force of gravity outside the cosmos, a blink suffices for days to follow one more night. All is one, and none is all. For the mystic, however, all is all. We make sense of chaos according to ways we convey as personal truths. A tiny speck of wonder, its eyes wide open, observing the skies, that black hole, this supernova, will never reveal themselves to the naked sight. But we wander, still, among our peers, in our time, asking questions that will hardly find answers.

Singularities only last an instant, but where they come from, they represent eternities. Their sand witnesses the birth of coincidences, evolving on their flow and vanishing in a dream forgotten by the likes of Fibonacci. Kitana felt like this, once. She can't remember. How many reincarnations ago was that?

How many was that?

"How many?"

Singularities only last an instant. The ones after quickly turn into echoes of what could have been. Ghosts of possibilities haunt the remorseful. Zen, on the other hand, a smile, stands still. The rest is no story. Everyone holds a minus that strives to bring it back to zero. Not too far, or shy, just where one is called to exist.

243

"Just one."

Just one.

Just One

Consciousness lacks an incorporeal projection, in this wide-open field. Some souls will take hundreds of lives before attaining a semblance of Buddhahood. "Just one?" Kitana asked. Nothing. Nobody replied anything.

How am I supposed to be? She thought.

Existence resembles a gooey residue against a subway wall, but who's watching? It always stood there. It doesn't realize its importance, until an ambitious manager binds his shoe, puts his hand on that wall, sticks the ugly glue onto his favourite tie.

"Just one."

Just one.

Just One

Harmonies flow in the universe, smoothly cultivating vibrations. Sometimes, Om will occur in the mind of a muse, leaving Og to itself. A musician will compose a song, but their soul never manifested a flame within flesh. The melody will die, the entity will sleep.

Where am I?
Where is I?

Memories carry the weight of a nearby nostalgia. The older we get; the more relevant yesterdays beget. Consciousness exists in the moment. The past is a lie. The future is a myth. Here and now, that's reality. "In reality."

Which one?

Which one?

Have you ever been drunk? To the point where your thoughts entered a conversation while your soul felt like sleeping and your body meant to throw that essence up. Or high, for what matters. You weren't you, but others laughed.

We don't do drugs or alcohol, in Penglai. Where are you from?

" "
.

Hello?

Hi! Do you remember me?

Her voice floated in the aftermath of a brutal awakening. I grabbed a beer, staring at my laptop, wondering what I should compose next. And where did this weird font come from? I'm so drunk! I looked around. The student fell asleep on the floor, a half-empty booze in their hands. Did I write Kitana's journey through the four singularities? I wasn't prepared for her to question me. A connection remains, however. I need to tread carefully.

"What do you know about Noesi de Vel?" I asked. *Of course I did! Anyway.*

"Yours or mine?"

Yours or mine? Am I engaging in this conversation with one of my characters?

Yours, I guess.

Noesi de Vel is nothing.

That weird font again. Wow. Hi! Are you one of my creations as well? "I've never been to Zendoria. I wouldn't know." Kitana expressed her thoughts out loud.

It doesn't exist.

" Are you sure?"

Hi, Kitana! Do you remember me?

I put my laptop away. I can't keep up with this. I'm not even developing anything. The words simply appear on my computer. Well, I feel highly intoxicated, mind you. But this hardly sounds as my story! Leave me in control! This is my creation! Stay out of my mind! I walked around the room, sweating like crazy. I couldn't find the student. Did they desert me? Perhaps they went for a shower or something. Anyway, I should focus on writing that novel. Maybe I'll have another beer for breakfast, with a joint.

Getting ourselves ready for a psychosis and a mental breakdown, are we, Martin?

"Ourselves?" I expressed out loud.

Go ahead! Drink and do drugs until your brain loses control You might as well give us away to Marduk. He's interested in seeing your mind bleed and throw your life in total trash. Drink and do drugs, Martin! Find comfort in evading your responsibilities! We don't mind, do we? It's not like we exist. We're a figment of your imagination. But we do carry, with us, a little bit of you. We convey those elements to your readers. Are you interested in letting them think of you as a loser? A stoner? A heavy drinker? You? Our god?

246

"Who are you?" At this point, I didn't have to do anything. The weird font simply typed those words on my laptop, without me even sitting near the keyboard.

Wouldn't you like to know? Make yourself a real breakfast, and write our story like you loved us, and show us some care and respect. Your readers deserve as much as well.

Shaken and disturbed, I looked at the beer bottle I had just opened. After five long seconds, I chose to pour its content on the floor. Let's finish this trilogy with a clear mind! I'm in control!

This is my creation!

Chapter Twenty-Six:
William and Sekhmet

Sekhmet's throne room stretched as wide as a city, and my guess was that she applied the same kind of magic that worked for Nempty's cabin. It makes no sense seeing her chamber as broad as Arcana, yet it seemed even bigger. A pocket dimension, is it? The chair, in the centre, attracted our sole attention. Average in size, but carefully installed on a Sphinx-shaped bench as large as a school, the rich seat imposed its presence across the space. When we turned around, the tunnel that took us here vanished. They found no way out. Our host smiled in glee. The cat-lady's head tricked us to think of her as human. Her skin displayed the colours of a black panther's fur. She looked at us with what appeared as the dearest form of affection.

Seamus felt a bit nervous, lost in his visions. Emerald's cheerfulness comforted me. Seeing her beloved teacher greeting us in her personal quarters made her happy. Melpomene stood his ground, ready to cast a powerful spell at any time. He stared at her with surprise, amazement, terror, and a grudge that could be sensed but not explained. Did she play a trick on him? For some reason, I had the feeling that Sthenele was involved with this grudge he held against our Sekhmet. The Moth Queen, on the other hand, wouldn't stop looking at me with adoring eyes. What did I miss?

Nempty seemed a bit reserved, standing behind us, not wanting to participate or choose a side. He may have betrayed us. Lucretia gawked at our hostess with a mix of anxiety and awe. Nempty's frog head showed more fear than anything else. I looked at Seamus. He seemed very nervous about this unfolding event. Does he know something that we should?

"They won't get it." he whispered.

They won't get what? Oh well. I saw ghosts of fair ladies wishing to die for their mistress. Fiona and Katrina? I heard those names before. When we entered, they stood next to the goddess. Sekhmet offered her direct instructions. The fairies bowed down, in reverence, and left the room. I guess they got themselves into a different mission.

"Please, allow me to offer you something to drink." the black-cat lady announced, in a very welcoming voice. She summoned her dark orb out of thin air and turned the surrounding space into a cloud that rained wine into seven glasses, without making a spill. Two fairy servants brought us the glasses. With myself, Emerald, Seamus, I counted three. Nempty, Melpomene and Sekhmet, three more. Sthenele didn't drink since she doesn't have a mouth. Why did the goddess cast seven recipients? Was Nunc about to surprise us? I looked at Seamus, but he dove even deeper in his dream state. I think we lost him. The bulky butler grabbed his wine and forced Seamus to sip it.

"We are so thrilled to find you, teacher!" Emerald proclaimed.

"They won't get it!" Seamus interrupt them, screaming the same words. We all just ignored him, at this point. Melpomene took him aside. Maybe this sudden change of reality crammed up his head. He's losing it.

"Yes, so are we." Sekhmet replied to her student. I looked at Seamus, whispering strange, unintelligible things. I gave him an elbow blow, discreet but efficient. He didn't react. Sekhmet summoned a table. Food appeared on it. Melpomene once told me that when using our gift, we steal axioms from other layers of our own Sophron. If I were to cast godzilla with the brain of a god, I would certainly drain myself of most of my precious pixels. I could die, given that I knew how to fulfill such a task. But she summoned beings to populate her citywide room, and tables with food to feed an entire civilization. Emerald told me she danced. And now her teacher performs mancing spells I couldn't even dream of achieving. I don't like how this display of power looks.

"How do you like Tir na n'Og, William?" Sekhmet pointed her attention towards me.

"Much better than Athanor." I jested.

"They won't get it." Seamus warned me, from behind. Seamus turned his eyes towards my mentor and shouted: "They won't get it!" He laughed like a maniac. "Yes, some very chaotic realms exist, as you may have seen. Tir na n'Og, like the Gaia that raised you, remains stable. I like to conquer healthy worlds, and you should consider this, before you commit the unredeemable."

She talked about my ordeal. Did I choose to jump? Was it, really, my doing? Was I in charge when I did? Or did someone make me do it? From within my psyche, under some form of spell, maybe another ghost controlled me.

"Yeah." I agreed with Sekhmet, intimidated. I calculated it, but what about my life as a homeless freak? Did she send Emerald to tempt me? Is this all a conspiracy to steal Indra's soul away from my entrails? I panicked. Too many questions and too much uncertainty. I panicked! I can't let it transpire. Calmness, now! I thought, calmness, peace, peaceful. I had to go with the essence, I thought. I hold the essence of a true hero.

250

One of the most amazing civilizations that still exists venerate his grandeur, to this day. What if we considered religions as organized assemblies of ethical beings? Each willing to guide their followers through the teaching of myths and poetry? What if my soul thrives as a character in a novel? "Although, Athanor isn't a bad place." I kept the conversation going. "I heard Duat was a beautiful world as well." I mentioned.

"They won't get it!" Seamus kept insisting. "What do you mean?" I whispered back at him.

"Have you been to Duat?" Sekhmet asked me, while eating a giant cherry, like a juicy apple, assuming the squirt would make me gasp. Nah. not today. I did turn to Melpomene for guidance, but he smiled. He saw that one coming. Or maybe he's getting ready for another threat. "It's very Egyptian, I think, I heard; I think I heard! It must be so beautiful, this time of the season."

"Duat only has one season: summer." she laughed. Yeah, right, sure. Was I supposed to know that?

"Of course! Melpomene explained it to me, I think." Melpomene remained stuck between fear and hilarity. "I mean, who doesn't enjoy it? That's my favourite period of the year."

"Is it, now?" Our hostess laughed, seemingly amused. Silence. Whatever I say will make me look like a total idiot. "You should visit Toronto in the summer!" Emerald saved my face. "Oh, my beloved teacher, it's the most beautiful city for outdoor activities in all of Sophron!"

A war is coming, and we're supposed to fight? I haven't seen Emerald perform, and I'm pretty sure Seamus sucks at his power. Mine has yet to reveal anything, but I sense it in my veins. I can do it! Something! I can do something with my gift. We're sitting ducks.

Journey into the Hourglass:
Twenty-Two

In my mind, Seamus Chron was this arrogant character going through a redeeming arc. I expected someone a bit more patient, by the end of our second book. I allowed him to wander around Alibastat for several years, and that didn't teach him any principle or value. What did Martin and I do wrong? The third part gets him in the middle of a cosmic battle, and he's just as pompous and pricky as he was in the first volume.

That hardly sounds good. I'm his creator, but how am I meant to mentor him anything if he doesn't assimilate my wisdom? I can't force it upon him. And he won't allow himself to learn. Who said writing a novel would come as easy?

I focused solely on gardening, forgetting that Seamus walked by my side. Maybe, if I pretend to stay strong and sane, he'll look up to me and give his personal growth a try. Too many characters already act past their scripted life. We only need Seamus and William to roam under our inspired light. Breathe in, breathe out. I see him walk towards me. I'm scared beyond repair, but he can't feel this. He mustn't feel this!

Chapter Twenty-Six:
They will never Get It

Here we are, again, spreading the good pollen around the jungle that hasn't seen an animal in billions of years. I observed Alibast painstakingly collecting flowers' sperm and putting it into flowers' uterus. He diligently cared after this garden with a big smile, as though nothing happened outside of his hobby. It seemed rather depressing. I looked at him, thinking how he expects to teach me anything by doing absolutely zilch, and I sighed.
I felt already more powerful after last night, and I achieved this on my own.

Yeah, I visited his inner pluriverse, didn't I? But why wasn't he there to guide me? You're supposed to me my mentor! All that we're doing is pushing plants into fornicating with their peers! Show me how to fight with my gift! There's a war coming!

"You missed one." he delicately pointed me towards a daisy that seemed rather normal. "Sorry, I'm, yeah." I plucked some pollen from one nearby and I forced a date with benefits.

Thank you, professor! Not even willing to hand me over brushes and ask me to clean cars! Swoop in, then out, or whatever! What am I supposed to learn from his silence and this picking up flowery semen? The value of boredom?

We went on like this for many days. At night, I reconnected with his mind, his inner library, and the book you enjoy. The only problem implied reading that story beyond the word you currently goggle at.

Alibast exists as both an author and a character. He inhabits his creation, but instead of ruling over the entire fantasy universe he developed, he spends eternity pollinating a dead realm. But then, if I close my eyes, I see the intense light, and I find myself back in his inside worlds of wonder.

"Did you let go?" he inquired.

Sorry, what?

What?

What did you say?

"I just asked if you let go of the pollen."

I walked away from the field. I know he's inside my psyche, just as I'm in his. If I can awake past the burst of light that unsettles my every move, I bet I can decipher a few words of his. Work on your garden, Alibast! Don't mind me if I close my eyes and I:

"And that's how I got acquainted to Marduk, the Entity-Killer." and I browsed back to read previous chapters, introducing this villain and his cohort of dangerous agents, Void, and how powerful this Entity was. Sekhmet also presented a threat, and I had to find a way to warn them.

And I wasn't ready for this. I opened my sight, surprised. Warn them? Who? My other self? My friends? How can I do that, now? Marduk is there! You're all in danger! Heck, Alibast knows! He composed that paragraph! It's his book! It's his creation! He should write it so that Sekhmet betrays Marduk or something. Have them fight! We're not ready to face him. I don't want my other self to die! What if I perish with him?

"I don't get it." I thought out loud, while Alibast returned to his gardening activities. "Dude! Do something!" I sighed. It felt impossible. I merely stood as the spectator of my own demise.

I closed my eyes, once more, to revisit his novel. I could picture it in my hands. A purple and turquoise cover, with four silhouettes against a crystal ball. When I turned the pages, all I could see was a blankness. Blank pages! Blank, blank, all blank. Getting back at where I was at, the last word I found: Blank. And then it hit me! I narrate my chapter. Those words belong to me. I tell you, reader, where the story is heading to. Okay, hold on.

Alibast types these words as we speak. I hear a French song in his mind:

Je suis malade.

What? Serge Lama? Sick of being in love, sick of living.

Just like when my mother left me alone, at night, leaving me with my despair. I am sick, I am totally sick.

Dude! Play some metal, for flock's sake! Light on a joint! Heck, I bet your readers are begging for one, right now. Yeah, but your audiences manifest sovereign universes, don't they? Some will despise this novel; others will connect in ways that neither author ever expected. They're homeless souls, just like us! Seeking a culture to define their name. Have their biological personality relate to their psyche. You're not a god, Alibast! You're my friend. Truth exists in the humblest instant we can witness.

"Did you take care of the lilies?" I heard him inquire. I couldn't move my eyes. Was I drunk? Did I pass out?

"Seamus, you should head for the nearest forest and make sure the lilies don't go extinct."

Hold on, hold it.

"Did we get drunk, last night?" I asked.

"You really should put the lilies on your agenda, my friend. They're sovereign flowers."

The lilies! Still only thinking about his frigging plants! And he smiled, so he must have witnessed these words I just uttered in my mind.

"How can I pilot a biomech?" I asked him. "Why would you drive an archoid?" he replied.

"I want to beat Marduk's ass. I assume, if we show up with a plan, I can appear in Sekhmet's palace, in one of those giant monsters, and I can kill Marduk before he'd see this coming."

He smirked and cut a burnt-out zucchini in pieces, before asking me:

"Do you think Marduk handled his secret garden?"

Sorry, what?
        "What?"

What did you say?

"What secret garden?" I inquired.

"Is life just a game for you, tell me, Seamus Chron?" he smiled. I guess, yes, of course. But then, shouldn't existence exist as one as well? A binary input attempting to process duality. It's neither Yin nor Yang; it's whatever your inner Yin teaches an outsider's Yang as truth. If enough souls gather around that narration, you get yourself a culture.

I opened my sight, and I looked around. "Yeah, Okay." I whispered. "I'll nurture the lilies."

Is everything to your liking, mister Chron?

Who said that? I closed my eyes, but all I saw. blank pages. Hold on! What if I could connect my essence with my other self? The one that, if I understand this phenomenon well, manifest within Alibast's psyche. Perhaps a way exists, for me, to freeze my consciousness in each possibility. If I exist because Alibast wrote me into reality, yet the novel only shows this book, devoid of words. Then, maybe, I equally exercise my will in his creative mind. Let's try something:

Let's try something: I immersed myself onto the nothingness. If I express my psyche, I could impregnate that blank page and turn it into my own narration. The font doesn't feel like the one that Alibast writes with, though. He expresses himself in a Times New Roman font. The book I held depicted my thoughts using Calibri Light. Okay, I guess that will do. And now, for the serious business: And now for the serious business:

Chapter Twenty-Two:
William and Sekhmet

Sekhmet's throne room stretched as wide as a city, and my guess was that she applied the same kind of magic that worked for Nempty's cabin. Seeing her seated in a chamber as large as Arcana hardly seems sensical. Yet it stood tall, wide, even bigger. A pocket dimension, is it? She sent her two handmaids on a mission. I observed William, and he looked worried or preoccupied. Emerald must have been the only one thrilled at the idea of reuniting with her teacher. Melpomene felt betrayed, for some reason. He really thought he had imprisoned the Egyptian goddess in Sthenele's body. Consciously conveying this chapter seemed a bit weird.

Examining my other self in action freezes my essence in space and time. It creates some sort of nexus. I wish I could project my narrating self into that scene, but I had yet to understand this newly found power. Sekhmet poured wine out of floating clouds, and into seven glasses. Only six of us remained, though.
My alternate fell in a trance, pressured by the truth that this voiceover produced. I must remain silent and detached.
They can't know that I'm holding the creative control over this ongoing chapter. Still, they won't get it.

"They won't get it!" I whispered. William elbow hit me.
"Stop it, Seamus! You sound weird!" he murmured back.

Try to look cool. I thought. I snapped out of my trance, only to
realize that Emerald praised Toronto for its street festival.
Oh, please! Montreal is far better than Toronto! I defended my
point, as I devoured my feast and binge drank that wine.
We finished our meal, and we remained quietly in our seat, while
the fairy attendants cleaned the table.

"For the dessert, I would like all of you to stand up and greet
my friend." Sekhmet solemnly announced. We looked at one
another, perplexed and uncertain. Then, we heard a grave and
heavy voice, coming from behind our chair:

"Please, Sekhmet. No need for civilities. We're all friends,
now."

Melpomene swiftly summoned a plasma storm out of his
crystal orb, directed at our new guest. The tall and muscular, bald
man gestured gently at the lightning. They turned into bats and
flew away.

"We'll find lots of time to play later, Melpomene."
the mysterious visitor laughed. He sat in front of us and pulled a
good stare at our frightened eyes.

"Is this a game to you, Marduk?" the Great Muse growled.

"You don't find pleasure in any of this?" Marduk smiled.
He looked at me and nodded: "I'll take it from here, mister Chron."
He lost his grin.

I'll take it from here, mister Chron.

I opened my eyes, without even thinking. I woke up, back in Alibast's garden, nursing the lilies. Crossing those possibilities in such a weird fashion left me in a powerful state of vertigo. Which one of these two realities exists as a dream? Am I, now, dreaming? Was I, only few minutes ago? It felt as though I got robbed of my integrity.

I breathed, slowly and deeply, focused on one simple task: cutting a few invasive herbs that threaten to smother the lilies. I'm aware that this garden resides because Alibast, and now I, actively work towards its survival. One plant at a time, I guess.

Chapter Twenty-Eight:
William Gets It

They won't get it! I looked at Seamus, he smiled and did his best attempt at miming a lunatic displacing some things in the air. It appears he was cutting flowers or doing some sort of botanical activity. I shrugged. I really had no idea what bug bit him.
He pushed his head forward, twice, and repeated his gardening motions. His move, what? I responded with my interrogative eyes.

"They won't get it!" he whispered.

"Is everything to your liking, mister Chron?" Marduk asked him, seeing how much of a mute he became. That's when he stepped away and finally drank the rest of his wine.

"Everything is awesome, mister of Nibiru! I would love to make a toast for this newfound friendship of ours." He turned his attention to Sekhmet and signaled his empty glass. She smiled, performed a few gestures, and the booze-serving clouds poured him more happy juice.

"Here's to us finally meeting! Cheers, Sir Marduk!" Seamus appeared to test our guest. Marduk raised his wine and cheered: "To this alliance!" Seamus looked at a point in the room, winking at someone who wasn't there.

"I have read Seamus' story, Lord Marduk." Sekhmet added. "He is destined to become quite a powerful glancer."

"In some possibilities, doll." Seamus replied, with his usual pricky bravado. Yeah, that's the Seamus I know. He then looked at Marduk and asked: "Do you think we share that possibility, now?"

Oh! Essences and multiverses. That's his game, his field. I get it! So much mystery fills my mind. I guess I should let him speak, and just stand behind Melpomene. Mancers with mancers, right? The master with the student. I'll ask him what our next move should be. I know that Melpomene would never accept to join Marduk's entourage. I briefly examined his concealed orb, hidden under his cloak.

There, he summoned axioms of archeus and logos. From my perspective, it seemed he was fomenting a powerful creature. Karkadan? He's casting Karkadan? He looked at me and winked. Oh, how I smiled!

"What do you understand of possibilities, Seamus Chron?" Marduk asked him. "Some concepts you got from books?" Marduk perceives things that Seamus knows, and I have no idea what's going on.

"You need William and me alive." Seamus dared a gaze in Marduk's direction. "Emerald serves as the bait that brought us to you. I also know that you aspire to reshape True Reality in your image. You desire to reign as the only True Entity over Sophron. We stand here, like ants ruining your meal. If Indra incarnates his soul, then Varuna will hunt you down, and you can't face the two of them. You don't understand if the William present, if his possibility, will lead to Indra's resurrection. You don't want to risk that chance, so you'll keep us both alive, until you remain certain to sacrifice the right William. But you won't get it. You don't get it!"

262

The Hound Lord of Nibiru remained calm and amused. He sipped his wine and looked at Emerald. He, then, stared straight at me. "I didn't plan on William to self-sacrifice. I walked on board this storyline rather late; don't you think? You were taught well, Seamus Chron, but your brain seems too small to gather all the gnosis and knowledge that mine possess."

It felt like we were in the middle of an intellectual Mexican standoff. Except, I'm more of an erudite than Seamus. Who brought a stupid in a genius fight? Why do I jealously desire the gift of glancing? What am I supposed to do with materializing creatures and stuff? "I know something that you'll never know, Marduk." Seamus didn't even blink. "Where to find your nexus self."

"You bluff." the Hound Lord replied. "I just scanned your entire inner being, and I found no secret you could hide from me. You don't even understand what a nexus is."

"I'm not talking about secrets. If you know what I know, then how come you don't know that I know, that you know, I mean! Where am I going with this?"Marduk stopped for a moment, he drank his wine and observed Seamus with great interest. From my perspective, my idiotic bully confronted a Goliath, like a clueless David. Yes, Seamus, go on! Enrage this deity and let's see if we can survive! Cool plan!

"All right!" Marduk paused once more and added: "You developed the gift of narration by yourself. Impressive."

"No!" Seamus kept antagonizing our enemy. "I perceived the True Dreamer. I know who imagines this entire story! Every possibility, each dimension, all of us! I stared into his eyes, and you were dead to him."Marduk laughed so loud, he choked on his wine."You saw a True Dreamer, Seamus Chron. Good for you. I kill them for breakfast."

263

What are they talking about? I looked at Melpomene, but he was too fixated on achieving his spell at the right moment. I guess I had to be focused on that as well. I grabbed my orb and assisted him to summon Karkadan. Yes, I can do this. The gigantic beast responds well to my presence. I can sense his axioms just by closing my eyes.

"The True Dreamer, Marduk, is the light you never wanted to face and accept."

Seamus understood a concept that Marduk failed to comprehend, it appeared. What about those frontiers? The ones connecting all these layers upon layers, within souls within souls, do they reach a limit? And what of all these possibilities? If a True Dreamer governs, above everything, and Seamus, the rookie, got to witness It. Him, Her, or whatever, then how come Marduk looked concerned after hearing this? Couldn't Marduk see the True Dreamer on his first year as a glancer? Is he a glancer? He should be, because they seem to stand on the same ground with this discussion. "Tell me his name." Marduk dared him. "Ali." Seamus responded. Marduk laughed.

"Ali? Like the half of Alibast? From the goddess Bastat and the kind word Ali? The very name that Muhammed Ali, of your world, espoused upon reaching enlightenment? Is this the best card you can play?" Marduk controlled the conversation, now. He pursued: "I killed a Great Entity! I watched his soul suffer, gasp, swallow his own blood! Son, you weren't a sentient atom when I fought and won the Babel Wars! What did your mentor tell you of those times? He wasn't even born! He thinks he invented them, based on books he read, on minds of scientists and historians, and conspiracy theorists, everything is connected! I understood it all!

Alibast works as just a pen name he borrowed to enter his own world and discover you. If they ever make a movie out of his novels, someone else will play his part! He could even die before his story finds a publisher! And you trust him over me?"

264

Seamus stayed silent, and this time he could only swallow his guts. He got it, Seamus, forget it. You can't face a god! Let us work this out. Seamus closed his eyes and tried to concentrate, but he was clearly out of his league. I bet Melpomene and I could cast the most powerful archoid ever, and we would defeat both Marduk and Sekhmet with our element of surprise. I hope the innocent servants and fairies don't become collateral damage.

"Hold on, William, I got this." Seamus reassured me.

He inhaled a deeply and stared at Marduk. He could cut a rock with the blades in his eyes. I wish I could summon a sword and hand it over to him.

"My teacher's name is not Alibast." Seamus dared him.

Marduk looked at him and smiled.

"My teacher is Enlil-Bastat, you bastard! And we're bringing back his world to life. You remember? That one you thought you destroyed." A powerful aura of fear crawled down Marduk's spine. "Enlil-Bastat." he whispered, unsettled. "He lives?"

Seamus looked at me. I panicked and dropped my orb. Melpomene kept summoning the beast, still. Seamus turned his eyes back at Marduk.

"My duty implied protecting William, but I failed the duty bestowed upon me by Ishtar." Who's Ishtar again? Probably someone important, because Marduk could barely control his calm. He looked down, in pain, and screamed as he cast a fireball the size of the room and threw it at us. He found the right vibe just before the blast killed us all, and made it dissipate in thin air. Both Sekhmet and Melpomene intervened in the nick of time, summoning the Veil to shelter every single soul present in the chamber. Marduk calmed himself, while the inferno evaporated.

265

"She chose to die!" Marduk expressed his wounds. The pain in his eyes felt unbearable. Emerald stood up at that moment. She observed her teacher and waited her approval. She looked up to face Marduk, and she initiated a conversation:"I was told she loved you."

"She died in Dummuzi's name." Marduk replied. "A foreigner! Indra! She perished for nothing!"

"The True Dreamer is on the death row. Do you think he should fade?" Seamus added, impressing me.A Dreamer on the death row. A character withers. An author carries it forward. A friend did it, another one desires to keep his essence going. He wants to put it in a book and make everyone discover the element of truth they shared. I got it.

"She loved life!" I concluded. Melpomene turned to me, unsure.

"She loved herself." Marduk responded. I thought: *I'm in the middle of a drama.*

I stared at Seamus and produced words in my mind: Maybe the True Dreamer is a she! It doesn't matter, William. Grab your balls and summon the unicorn.

"Who said that?" I heard someone talk to me in my psyche.

Seamus looked at me and smiled. The "We're in business" kind. Do you know which video game we I heard again. Seamus? Is that you?

Journey into the Hourglass:
Twenty-Three

Seamus gardened painstakingly for an entire day. I sighed, relieved. We didn't talk, but it felt like he visited his inner pluriverse. I probably conduct a good mentoring job. The less I try to interact with him, and the more he will meditate and learn. I doubt Martin developed this approach with his Greek student. I got this one.

The less we discuss; the more we think. He watched me pollinate giant sunflowers, and it felt like he admired my work. I should humble myself, now. We stand as equals in this possibility. I have nothing to prove. He has nothing to show. We both learn, and silence speaks for everyone.

He's doing well. He's doing very well. I shouldn't disturb him, I guess. It feels like harmony when I reflect on it. Good! I could get him to farm the white lilies, now. I can't ask him anything. I can't trouble his personal ascension. I wonder what Martin thought of my notes, about Erato.

Chapter Twent-Nine:
Erato's Nightmare

How can we hike a sympathetic hitch out of the Open Door? Wait, she guessed. Wander all over the Open Door, unsure if Varuna granted her full power or not. The sandstorm stopped. So that's a good thing. How is she supposed to venture back to her home world? She incarnated her soul into a bloodied form. She has an entire lifetime to learn the basics of Zen, to even start to understand the fundamentals of travelling across dimensions. She's stuck in Hell, not exactly Hell, but close enough.

A desert of dirt and dust, everywhere. It seemed pointless without a storm. She wandered around this abandoned area for days, hiding from inquisitive eyes through simple incantations of invisibility. She felt too weak to venture passed the Veil on her own. She must find a city that welcomes enlightened travellers from across Sophron. With any luck, she'll encounter a more powerful Walker who will accept to open a portal into a friendlier world.

When the wall of flames fell silent and absent, after dusk, Erato would shelter inside her orb, summoning her axioms to phase through the crystal. The sphere itself would embrace its environment, turning into a basic stone, a giant pebble that loiters the side of a road. Nobody in their right mind would want to freely travel at night, in the Open Door. Light simply doesn't exist, anywhere. The beasts that venture, at that time, would remind us of ocean monsters. Some, as with the anglerdemon, walks stealthily among the gigantic rocks, preying on smaller animals. Like the deep sea creature by a same name, there's a lonely source of gleam dangling down its forehead. Unsuspecting golems and elementals will instinctively find themselves attracted by this promise at the end of a tunnel. In the blink of an eye, the fish demon jumps on the curious meal and feasts on it in a few rapid chews and swallow. Erato can't risk any chance until she gathers all her strength.

The next morning, the Great Muse resumed her trek. A simple mapping spell reproduced the area inside her orb. There, she saw a cosmopolitan city that appears to welcome travellers. Those come as a rare finding, in this quadrant. Usually, commerce among the worlds begins in the following Sophron layers, as we approach Gaia, and with Patagonia and Shangri-La standing at the forefront of this capitalistic culture. Which beast wouldn't dream of owning a gimmick from Heavens or a trinket from the Eldorado domains?

Courageous smugglers, especially those who can protect themselves and their crew from demonic aggression, would exit with artefacts they can sell at high cost anywhere else. Sure, this shiny rock doesn't look like much, but once you've analyzed its axioms and you realized where it comes from, would you prove yourself brave and strong enough to visit the hellish planes of existence to get one? Of course not! So, if you want it, then pay the top price.

With currencies, among the awakened souls, we can't talk in terms of a monetary device. Call them useless, when the least potent Walker can summon anything from their own inner worlds. Even neymlisses, who lack any form of power or gift, can very well find a way to gather literally any item they wish. In Sophron, we pay with our consciousness. Someone who achieved enlightenment naturally finds himself drawn towards needing more. When trading things or services, any two parties involved in that transaction end up relinquishing parcels of their bliss or receiving bits of a further awakening. Consider this as the most precious resource available across Sophron.

She realizes this fact now that her own gift has weakened following this sudden reincarnation. And why didn't Varuna fully enhanced her, as he warned Hotzigard? Maybe the once-formidable god of Airavat also found himself lacking in terms of revived powers. He must have bluffed when he threatened those demons.

Perhaps he would have relinquished his entire resources to restore her, leaving him in a vulnerable state. Regardless, now she's only a fraction of what she used to be, as a Greater Entity.

She entered the city of Magnamitzigaltz at the flaming wall's zenith. A darkened grey sky reflected the raging fires overhead, as she concealed her head under a black scarf and purple hood. She tried to blend in with this crowd of golems, elementals, and demons, but some inquisitive beasts could sense her fear. She would simply look elsewhere, ignore their presence. If she ever found a chance to leave this damned place, she must locate the scarce emergence of a friendly foreigner. She doubts she can find one that easily, or even on her first day visiting. She could ask around, but that would give her identity away. Varuna isn't near enough to save her, this time. She hasn't fully recovered from her debacle of a fight with Hot. She can't afford another death, forcing her to reincarnate in this quadrant, or closer to the Void.

Thousands of years to achieve this state of greater enlightenment, and she would have to return to lesser rebirths? Over and over, until she turns into, what, a squirrel? And why did Melpomene betray her like this? Why would he coldly murder his own blood? "Are you lost, beautiful?" She heard a growling voice catcalling her. Because, of course, animals and demons do that. Erato ignored this humiliating event and walked away, faster.

Her trek ended under a tall statue depicting Demonee, sitting on top a mountain of skulls. By her calculations, if this city counts a million inhabitants, then there can't be more than a hundred courageous travellers. There must be a spell she can come up with, something to help her locate another Walker. She observed around and found a creepy backstreet, behind the ruins of a mansion. Brown bricks melded with ponds of mud, and the crowd seemed to avoid this hideout. Erato looked down and charged straight, without crossing her gaze with anyone.

A shadowy shelter concealed her from unwelcoming eyes. She removed her hood, lowered her scarf, and inhaled. Her heart couldn't stop beating at a fast pace. Every moment spent on this world brings its abundance of threats and imminent dangers. She examined to her left, and her right, nobody followed her. She breathed deeply, one more time, then she summoned her crystal ball. It floated in front of her, while she focused on a makeshift spell.

If axioms flow through the orb, as it mirrors her own inner stream, then she could very well perform incantations crossing possibilities. In one of those, she might be able to channel the existence of a friend, an ally, or someone susceptible to act as one. *Think*, Erato. That incarnation should invite a different muse. Maybe she can contact one of her siblings.

Terpsichore, the inspiration of dancers, yes! She's one of the most powerful martial artists in Sophron. Fine, how could she have arrived in the Open Door? What are the possibilities? Perhaps she flew over there with an intrepid merchant who came here to exchange precious artefacts and return to another world. But wait, didn't Terpsichore choose to join Melpomene in his fight? Erato exited Hydaspes before she knew who decided to stay there, and who left for what.

Still, she needs her big sister. Two silhouettes parted from the crowd. They entered the alley to peep into the backstreet. She can't cast the spell right now, or she would trigger more attention. No, she must act fast. Axioms of a dancer involve life and thoughts. First, she must summon a potential incarnation of her muse sibling from her inner Sophron, and into the orb. She closed her eyes and projected herself in her memories. This current body, however, felt too weak to properly generate those thoughts. She must try! No! She must achieve the impossible! One silhouette entered the gloomy alley, intrigued by the flashing glows that seemed to waltz with the darkness.

The lights concentrated their presence within the sphere, gradually shaping a feminine form. "Hey!" Erato heard a gasping voice. "Hey, you alone?" the demon insisted. "Not now." she sighed. "You want fun? I'll give you fun!" the rude sightseer aggressively proposed. Come on, big sister, she prayed. She needs a proper storyline. Okay, Terpsichore found herself kidnapped while visiting Liverpool, England, on Gaia. No, of course not, she's too strong to be snatched.

"Hey, I'll just stay here and play with your feet, okay? Okay!" The smelly demon sat in front of her, dripping saliva all over her legs. Erato's heartbeats grew in intensity.

"You know what?" She addressed her aggressor. "I have a better idea." He looked at her, intrigued. She could now see his gigantic brown eyes, on top of a reptilian nose and a large mouth, filled with pointy teeth. Broad shoulders showed a muscular body, hiding under a black T-shirt that he must have received from a traveller. Some Heavy Metal band logo suggested he got it from a metal rocker of Valhalla. "Yeah! Okay, you know jokes?" the monster asked. Erato smiled. "Hydaspes stands as the home world of the Great Muses. One of them, Terpsichore, is a powerful dancer." She entertained him with her storytelling skills. He gazed deep into her eyes and drooled further. "One morning, she found herself entrapped in a dream. She woke up in the Open Door, you see? It was a nightmare. Being the strong entity that she is, she quickly generated a truth around that dream. Only to realize that her little sister magically summoned her."

"That's no joke! That's boring. Hey, I know something fun! Let's do something fun! I rape you, okay? Then I eat your flesh, okay?" Erato's entire body shook out of tremors and fear. "I'm not done!" she insisted, while the monster caressed her thighs. How come her narration didn't work? Will her feeble flesh prevent her from summoning a Great Entity? "Yeah, you done. Now, it's me I tell you a story." The demon swiftly tore her clothes down, revealing a near-naked body. "I tell the story of my thirst for muse flesh." A long and muscular tongue landed on her breasts. Unable to react, freezing with terror, she stood still. She sighed, okay, she needs someone less powerful than her sister, but she needs that entity fast.

"I was in love, once." she confided in him. "No love, here. Just fun, okay?" She swallowed her pain and insisted, looking at the feminine shape of light that danced inside her crystal ball. "His name is Nathan Lord. He's a pirate and a powerful hero!" The monster slowly crawled on her body, licking her ears with his disgusting tongue. "Yeah? He's here?" Silence followed. The glow disappeared. Oh no! Did she fail? She wasn't even able to summon her beloved smuggler?

273

Plan B! She must focus on a different spell, and fast, but which one? Her traumatized mind couldn't stop spinning. "Maybe we wait, okay?" she suggested. The demon laughed. "We wait for what?" he whispered. "No, we wait not! I feast, okay?" She closed her sight while he opened his entire mouth, ready to engulf her head in full. Everything went black, just as his skull exploded.

Even more silence imposed itself while the demon's blood streamed down her near nakedness.

"Are you okay?" She heard a feminine voice. Erato dared to widen an eye. A being of intense light stood there, holding a gigantic rifle. Fumes floated out of the cannon, sharing a privileged spot with the monster's blasted brain. "I'm okay, I'm okay!" Erato stuttered.

"Girl, you look like a truck ran over you!" the gun laughed. "Uncle Vania!" the lady argued. "Show some respect to our new friend!" An intense brightness exerted its presence from a pair of denim, a white blouse, and a jean jacket. A strange insignia was painted on its back side. It reads: Ultra Police. She offered Erato a hand and smiled. The rifle growled and complained: "We can't get her out of this back alley like that. She'll be an easy meal to this huge crowd of pieces of shit." Erato calmed herself and summoned a new black robe, with a black hood and a scarf. "I got this." The muse reassured them. The lady of brightness nodded.

"We'll get you out of this mess." She comforted her. "My husband's ship is parked nearby. You're lucky we were in here for business. Vania and I went for a walk in this part of town." Husband? Erato wondered. "My name is Alicia." The saviour offered her a handshake. Erato looked at it and shook it back. "Hi, I'm. Jennifer! My name is Jennifer Blank."

"It feels nice to meet you! It feels like we're going to be best friends." Alicia giggled.

Husband? Erato couldn't believe it. He married his stalker?!?

Chapter Thirty:
Seamus the Poet

The lilies seemed great. I spent an entire day pollinating them, watching the flocks grow, spreading spores around this obscure forest. Only this morning, those flowers appeared likely to vanish from this world's surface. Now, look! I performed a wonderful job! I walked away from that amazing scene, observing how the white petals shaped some sort of snowy picture, underneath tall and bright green trees. It felt like I had accomplished the impossible. I painted all of this, with patience and hard work.

Behind me, the three suns got ready to set, leaving the sky to another night. I turned to my right, and I recognized Alibast's house. My friend and I spent so many days, weeks, months, years out there, we totally forgot that we could, at any time, shelter ourselves under this purple roof. "You completed a wonderful job, buddy!" My teacher stood behind me, proud and happy to further encourage me. I looked around and gazed at everything we've accomplished, in this little space. We turned a dead planet into a living work of art.

"I see what we're doing, now." I informed him. "All of this, it's, I mean, we're being selfless for a reason, right?"

"If we reason about it, then it's no longer being selfless." he smiled. "Love and pragmatism go well together, but they don't have to. They don't share a root."

He walked towards his house with the same nonchalant pace that I grew accustomed to. One step at a time, no rush, we'll get there when we get there. "But teacher!" I interjected, while doing my best to slow down to his speed. "We saved this world, didn't we?" He remained silent. "Alibastat plays a part in maintaining Sophron in order, right?" I continued, but he wouldn't respond. "Isn't this why we've been doing this, for so many years?"

"Is a cell asking itself why it behaves in a certain way when regulating an entire organism?" he asked me.

"I'm not sure I understand." I stood up, puzzled, while he pursued his walk towards the mushroom-looking cottage.

"Axioms only subject themselves to the universal movements that push them into existence. Atoms attract or repulse atoms, electrons, cells, thoughts, memes, genes, lines in a program, zeros, ones, electric impulses, blank. Each building block arises as is. Then, why shouldn't we?" Pixels on a screen stand lit in a specific colour, and when grouped, under an outside force, electricity, electronics, software, will produce an image. That image, by itself, doesn't need to represent anything, but it will find its purpose in a bigger project, in a video game, or a movie.

"Am I a pixel?" I asked him.

"Aren't you hungry? I'll make us some fried roots.
Come inside." He pushed away a fragile curtain, and I finally discovered his home: And what a mess! The main entrance took us in the living room. To my right, a coffee table stood in our way, loitered with books, pictures, and used paper tissues. Toys of all kinds filled the floor. Dolls, action figures, small cars, big trucks, orphaned pieces of board games. It felt and smelled like a hoarder's hideout! How can he stay so dedicated in keeping an entire planet alive, and he can't even clean his own home? I didn't know if I should express pity or concern.

"Do you want my help with this?" I timidly asked him, while pointing out the obvious.

"I'll be fine, just sit down and I'll be right back with the meal." I swallowed my pride, and I pushed a few things off the couch. It used to be made of white cushions, but stains built up and changed its appearance, with time and negligence. I sat down and I grabbed a plush avocado. Its ventral seed had Let's Avocuddle! printed on it, under a cute smile and blushing cheeks. I played with the fellow for a while, and I put it away.

Three orbs floated in the middle of the living room. If only I knew mancing. I would cast a spell to rearrange the axioms, in that room, and clean it up. Heck, I couldn't find the courage to tour around the entire house. I'm terrorized at the idea of uncovering unsuspecting surprises. I heard Alibast struggle with the pans and utensils, causing a huge commotion in the kitchen. "Are you okay, there?" I asked. He didn't reply. Why doesn't he summon the meal? He's a powerful Walker! He could simply make it appear out of thin air or something. If I knew mancing, I would use the three orbs, over there, and shape the entire living room into some kind of fancy restaurant. I mean, he taught me how to employ my gift, but I'm sure he's not just a glancer.

I spent the next hour asking myself if it would be rude of me to tidy the place. Hearing my host swear while struggling to prepare the meal felt equally awkward. He managed to finish it up and invite me to the dining room. I worried he'd do that. A modest wooden table stood in the middle of a wide chamber. On my way there, I tripped on several stuffed animals, video game consoles and even dissembled parts of a bicycle. What are they doing here? Dude has a garage in the backyard, I saw it! "Sit down wherever you want." he welcomed me. I did so, right after I put away what seemed like a broken lamp on my chair. He brought in a plate filled with grilled vegetables and nuts. "Are you vegan?" I asked him.

"In here, and most of the time, I am, yes." he smiled. "But we had poutine, together!" I wondered. He laughed. "That, we did! That we did."

We sat and enjoyed our dinner in silence. That's one thing I appreciate with this plane of existence: it's peaceful. We find no reason to worry about anything. We just garden around the planet, and we have a good meal, then we sleep. I totally forgot William, and Marduk, and Varuna! Oh yeah, a war is coming! But here, now, none of this matters.

Around the time of our dessert, someone violently pushed the front door open. "Alibast?" We heard the traveller shout. "Inside, Martin!" My teacher invited the impromptu guest. How did this one ends up, here? I doubt a boat flew across the Ether.

Nobody visits a dead planet.

A blonde and skinny man, in his fifties, rushed his way next to us. A genderless assistant, dressed in ancient Greek clothes, followed him. The old dude held a purple and turquoise book in his hands. I recognized it right away. It's the same one you're enjoying, now, reader. "We have a problem." Martin couldn't stop himself worrying out loud. His Greek sidekick stayed quiet as though they remained surprised by this strange new world.

"Will you have some grilled vegetables?" Alibast nonchalantly offered him. "Not unless you put some meat in it, thanks, I'm fine. I just ate." Martin slammed the book in the middle of the table. "Check chapter twenty-eight." he instructed him. My teacher calmly grabbed the novel, opened it and slowly turned the pages, one at a time. Martin grew impatient. After three lengthy minutes, Alibast summoned a pair of glasses, sat down comfortably, and consulted the work in silence.

"Yes, I know about Seamus visiting Sekhmet in Tir na n'Og, Martin. And you know that I know."

"Continue reading." Martin felt visibly nervous. After a long moment, Alibast paused. He looked at me and asked: "Seamus? How do you know my real name?"

"I'm sorry, what?" I inquired. I stared at Martin's assistant, and we both shared that same puzzled gaze on our face.

"You revealed my real name to Marduk!" he continued. I had no idea what he talked about. He gave me the book and I read.

"That's my other self, yes. I, well, I." how can I put this? "I visited your inner universe, few days ago, Alibast." I mentioned. Martin could hardly control his emotions.

"Way to go!" he screamed at me. "Guess who else found his way inside Alibast's psyche!" My teacher turned towards Martin and attempted to calm him down. His Greek assistant stepped away, slowly.

"Seamus didn't know, Martin. Give him some space to process this. It's beyond the both of us, so imagine how it must be for him."

"I don't care! You weren't supposed to reveal your true identity until the climax, in the third book! And now Marduk knows it. He's way ahead of us." Martin hyperventilated.

"We'll figure something out." Alibast remained in control.

I had no idea what to say. I don't even remember that event. My teacher reflected on the twist that had just unfolded: "What concerns me, Martin?" he explained. "It's that, now, a third author writes with us. Is it Marduk or someone else? If that third author is Marduk, we can manage to short-circuit his plans. If it's a different mystery poet, and we fail to learn who that is, or what their agenda looks like, then we're in big trouble."

279

Too many questions haunted my mind. How could Marduk find me? How did he know about Martin and Alibast drafting this ongoing storyline? How can an author write their book without them remaining in control? Am I just that? A character in someone else's novel? No! I exist! I do! I have my own freewill, I can do whatever I want. "Hey, guys?" I wondered. Before they turned towards me, I threw my plate against the wall. It shattered in dozens of pieces. "Did any of you write me doing this? Or did you expect that I was about to do this?" I inquired. "And what about this? I let out, dropping my boxers to a chorus of: "No! Ah, god! Please, no!"

"That's not how it works, Seamus." Martin grumpily lectured me. "And who decides our actions, now?" the non-binary associate asked us. "Existence writes itself." Alibast explained. "Authors merely perform as translators, a conduit that conveys the very pluriverse inhabiting them."

"Nobody writes this!" I shouted, while dropping my pants and proclaiming a hymn to my exposed underwear! Proud and true!

"Someone did, obviously." Martin's assistant concluded. "None did in this book, but in another one, above our possible reality."

"You taught your student well, Martin." Alibast pat his visitor on the back. "I don't have a student. I'm stuck with them." Martin replied. Okay! I'm way out of my league, I get it. Don't sigh like this, rolling your eyes in front of some idiot. "Sorry." I ushered. I resumed eating my dessert, some cheap pudding, while the two authors sat down and brainstormed ideas in ways and fashions that I could hardly understand. I committed a mistake. Or my other self did one, but does it mean that I'm guilty of messing things up? Heck! If I don't do anything, William ends his existence and it's my fault. If I do something, I give away a major spoiler to the bad guy, and it's my fault.

What should I do?

Chapter Thirty-One:
Erato goes to Gaia

The Emily's Eyes flies silently across the Ether, just as she last remembers. Her mind revisits the last six hours, after the traumatizing events she experienced in a dark alley. Alicia brought Erato to a liminal bar. Those empty spaces act as a nexusnaos and a shelter for awakened beings visiting the hellish realms.
The Great Muse recognized this one. Her beloved pirate seemed quite fond of the Lonesome Crone franchise. We find one in every world of Sophron, minus the four singularities. Alone at a table, having completed a lucrative trade with a High Lord of Hell, Nathan enjoyed a ruby vodka, gleefully. "Mon amour?"
Alicia sat down with her new girl. "We'll need to make room for my friend. Her name is Jennifer. We can't possibly leave her in such a violent world."

The muse's sight crossed his, and love sparked just like last time. "It's a pleasure to meet you, Jennifer." the captain politely greeted her. "Hey! I'll take a look out for her." Vania teased. Nathan chuckled: "Don't get your hopes too high, Uncle." he warned his friend. "Our guest needs protection, not your macho humour." the rifle blasted out in laughter. "Can't help it." he belittled. "I'm a loaded gun!" The empty bar remained without a sound, while they all walked towards the fairy-boat, parked in its basement. Before Erato found the time to express her relief, the crew left this dreadful planet. Now, the sail to safety on the magnificient Emily's Eyes.

Vania regained his fixed position, scouting around for incoming threats. Nathan stood behind the ship's controls, while Alicia cuddled him. Erato observed the surroundings, amazed to witness the flying vessel in such good shape. She wandered around the bridge, caressing the wood and metal with a hint of nostalgia streaming down her spine. Looking up, she saw the axiomatic clouds bursting in colours against the blue membranous Veil. She closed her eyes, happy to experience a trip across the Ether alive on a boat rather than in between reincarnations.
"Is everything fine, Jennifer?" her beloved asked her. She didn't respond right away. She kept her sight shut, reflecting on the best choice of words. If she mentions her visit to Varuna, or the incoming war that will unsettle Sophron, she'll probably reveal her true identity. "I'll get well, Nathan." She comforted him. It took her a great deal of bravery to open her gaze and look at him.
"I'm already better, thanks." She smiled, in awe at his magnificent beauty. The tall man wore a baseball cap with the same logo she saw on Alicia's coat: Ultra Police. A leather jacket concealed a sweatshirt, where a superhero character found himself drawn, right above a belt and denim pants. "Are you a police officer, now?" she wondered.

"What do you mean by now? Have we met?" he asked. "You just, you, you remind me of someone. That's all." she blushed. He turned around and looked at his wife. Alicia smiled at him. "We are smugglers by trade, but we joined the Ultra Police to avoid doing prison time, on Duat." he explained. Erato listened to his story, intrigued. Nathan continued: "House Thoth's influenced the creation of this special force. We patrol the seventy-two layers of Sophron, maintaining peace among the various cultures. "Her bad boy plays the good guy! She giggled, thinking about how this alternate universe sounds interesting. It's a different multiverse, but same Dreamer, ultimately. That means Marduk remains a threat, Varuna stayed committed to pursue his prison sentence, and she's likely to encounter that Seamus Chron she saw, earlier.

If they cross paths with the Nathan she fell in love with, then the two possibilities will collide, and one of them will vanish back to his dimension. This quantic effect maintains balance within the Below and, she expects, also the Beyond. "What were you doing in the Open Door?" he wondered, just as he offered her a beer. She politely declined. "I, hmmm..." She thought about her story for a long moment and explained: "I was abducted!" Surprised, Nathan's jaw dropped. "Abducted? By whom?"

"I was, like, you see? I was minding my business on Mictlan. Not too far from here, I guess. And, well, I got into a fight with, like, with, a nymph!" Sweat dropped down her face. She's a terrible liar. "A nymph? What's her name? We'll bring her to justice!"

"Him! His name was, humm. yeah, I think it was she, but I can't remember. I never got to hear her name, or anything, or his name, I forgot. Yeah, maybe, a guy nymph, final answer."

"Whatever happened, I'm glad we were there to save you. What about the odds? If I didn't know any better, I'd swear you summoned us there, but, hey? I think a mancer can only cast people they intimately acquainted with, right?"

"Exactly! Yeah! We never made love, right? Right, of course, we never met!" She giggled like a little girl and swallowed hard inside her blushing cheeks. He examined her for a minute, binged down his beer and pondered: "Yeah, but you also remind me of someone. I can't put my finger on it." she laughed. "Your finger? Oh my! Yeah! Oh well, I look like your average muse from, hmm." He broke the awkward silence: "Mictlan?" She thought about it. "Did I say Mictlan? No, I'm from, I am, from Athanor! I was only visiting Mictlan."

"Fair with me." He escaped this weird conversation and returned to kiss his beautiful wife.

283

Erato turned her attention back to the psychedelic landscape. Here, no sky or ocean surrounds the flying boat. Only rainbows melting within rainbows. Like oil stains quickly shifting and twirling into bursting bubbles. The Emily's Eyes slowed down its course as they approached Aztlan. For long hours, Erato could observe the snowy fields and wintery cities. Legends have it that Quetzalcoatl resides in this deserted world, inviting wandering souls in his cottage. Aztlan serves as the last layer holding on to the remnants of Void. One more domain, and they pass through True Barbelo.Singularities act like customs for travellers struggling to enter a new quadrant. The guarding Ocorsur will simply scan the entire vessel, ensuring that only awakened beings attempt the trip, and no sleeper inconveniently found themselves on board.The married couple kissed one another tenderly, while Erato turned her attention elsewhere. None of this would have happened if she had successfully summoned her big sister. Now, she's in an even more complicated nightmare. "Where are we dropping you?" Alicia asked her, while leaving her lover's embrace. The muse remained lost in her thoughts. "Jennifer?" the creature of light insisted. "I'm sorry, what?" Erato turned to face her. Alicia smiled tenderly, unaware of Erato's broken heart. "Where are you going?" the captain's wife asked again.

"Gaia." Erato plainly answered. "Just, drop me anywhere in Gaia." There, she'll find this Seamus Chron and his friends. Erato knew that she couldn't allow her feelings to interfere with her mission. Maybe she can still gather an army to face Marduk and his allies. Nathan joined the conversation: "What's waiting for you on Earth?" he asked, intrigued. Deep inside her souls, she struggled to reveal him the entire story. If she does implicate this variant of Nathan, however, he might push her real lover off the chart, and into another possibility. This one must remain oblivious. "Just, nothing." Erato apologized. "I guess I will, yeah! I'll have that beer, after all." She hates drinking alcohol. But she must punish herself for being stuck in this mess.

Nathan agreed and visited his fridge. He opened the door, grabbed a Croon's Light, his wife's favourite. He brought it to the guest and snapped the cap off the bottle with his teeth. "If you need us, we'll stay in Gaia for a few days. Meet us at the Lonesome Crone."

Erato agreed and grasped the beer. She grimaced after bingeing it down, and she concealed her awkward malaise by turning her attention away. True Barbelo disappeared behind them, and the Emily's Eyes resumed its flight over the following layers of Sophron.

Chapter Thirty-Two:
Demonee gets a new Toy

Katrina looked at her twin. Fiona pierced the air with a defiant gaze. They can't leave this world without Varuna on board their ship. She advanced towards Demonee's throne, while Katrina surveyed the place to ensure the troops would stand ready to part as well.

"No!" Fiona objected. Surprised, her sister turned towards her. "No, Lord Demonee, with respect." Fiona added. Fear was all that now existed in Katrina's eyes. She rushed to her sibling's side and whispered to reason her: "It's okay, sis, it's fine. We're going back to Tir na n'Og, and Sekhmet will have to think of another way."

Amused, Demonee faced the two fairies. "Are you that inclined to relinquish me your last breath?" he chuckled. "I'm not here to fight." Fiona explained. "We came to negotiate. I'm not leaving until we've had a proper bargain completed. If that means you kill every one of us, then, be our guest. It's your home, your rules. But in my home, we stand our ground." The demon lord laughed until he choked on his own saliva. "Standing your ground while a foreign goddess dominates your world? Please! You can't possibly sound any funnier."

"We made you an offer. Now, make us one. What would it cost us to leave this world with Varuna?" Katrina remained petrified, while Fiona insisted. "Name your price." Demonee invested a long while to evaluate his options. Sure, holding this powerful opponent prisoner caters to his pride. Yet, this gorgeous and most innocent fairy seems adamant to do anything for his release. "My price?" he asked, while his gigantic and slimy tongue licked his entire face. "Are you willing to take his place?" he wondered.

"Without blinking." Fiona courageously answered.

"Sister, no!" Katrina couldn't believe what was going on. In Fiona's mind, though, it all made sense. Sekhmet conquered their homeland, but she proved herself as a just ruler. She participated in the Babel Wars, and she knows some truths that the commoners of Tir na n'Og ignore. She made it clear that bringing back Varuna would turn into a suicide mission and a question of life and death, for everyone. One can assume that Varuna's presence alongside Sekhmet's stood far above both Fiona and Katrina's existence. Being selfless and clever sounded like the only plausible option.

"What about you?" Demonee asked Katrina. "Leave my sister out of this. I'll stay here, but she'll guide our crew, and Varuna, back home." Fiona insisted. The demonic ruler thought further: "I didn't agree to anything." he complained. Katrina stood up and faced him: "We're going home! Don't' listen to my sister, she's, it's been, it's been very difficult for her, for us. We're leaving, now. And thank you, thank you, sweet lord."

"Wait!" Demonee didn't want to let this opportunity elude him. Sure, Marduk will fume, seeing that his mortal enemy escaped. But, hey! The Hound Lord of Nibiru also evaded! Nobody stood up against that. It shouldn't be the Blood Lord's problem. Now, here is a sexy fairy offering to take his place. Hmm. a sexy, sexy piece of fine feminity. "I want the two of you as my slaves. That's my only condition for his release."

A pale visage sounds as a euphemism to describe how frightened Katrina turned. Fiona comforted her with a strong embrace. "I got this, it's okay." she whispered. "No! It's not okay." Katrina couldn't bear this thought. Fiona looked around and pronounced her own sentence:

"I will be your slave. You let my sister leave with the Hindu god, and I will belong to you for all of eternity." Terrorized, Katrina cried. "Don't do this!" she pleaded her beloved sibling. "I beg of you, Fiona, don't do this! You don't have to do this! I promise you; Sekhmet will find something else. Trust me, please, trust me!"

The prospect of having an eternal slave felt new to Demonee. That meant she devoted her soul and her body to his imposing desires. "If you die, I will choose your next incarnation?" he asked. She silently agreed. "And I can kill you whenever, and, however, it pleases me?" he asked again. She nodded. "That sounds a lot better than having an old fart rot in my dungeons. You have yourself a deal, young fairy." The crew pulled Katrina, despite her pleas and her tears. Three demons carried Fiona closer to Demonee's throne. At this point, not even tearing Katrina's heart straight out of her chest would hurt as much as seeing her twin taken away like this.

"Fiona! Please!" she begged and cried. "Please, Fiona, no!"

Demonee summoned two sets of chains, snaking their way around Fiona's wrists and ankles. She closed her eyes and tried to put her mind away from her sister's tears. When the main door shut, she realized just how big a sacrifice she committed herself to.

Silence filled the throne room. Even if she attempted to escape those chains, she knew that her captor would instantly scatter her axioms across the room, killing her in atrocious pain. He could do it on a whim if he felt like it. She closed her eyes and allowed her destiny to fall onto the Demon Lord's lap.

288

He approached her slowly, extending a gigantic tongue out of his huge mouth. "I never pleasured myself with a fairy, before." he murmured. "There's a first time to everything." she whispered back. Angered, Demonee grabbed a sword and threw it straight into her heart. She screamed in intense agony, while he reprimanded her.

"Next time, call me Your Highness!" He resurrected her body and left her to bleed until she learned her lesson. He laughed and returned to his throne, pulling the chains to bring her much closer. "Beg for mercy." he delicately uttered. "Now!" he shouted.

"Mercy, mercy, Your Highness, please, I beg your mercy." she cried, much to his delight. "Now come and give me a cuddle, will you?" he whispered in a creepy voice.

Welcome to Hell.

Intermission:
Final Singularity

Kitana Gol, Non-Binary Daughter of Theliel Ankh-a-Gol.

Angel of Penglai?

"Who said that?"
Have you found what you were looking for?

Her consciousness stepped away from the voice. She travelled through every single layer like an axiomatic gestalt. All aspects of her vessel developed a true manifestation of their self-awareness.
Her matter merged as one with Barbelo. Her life force joined Archeus. Her mind and soul connected with Logos. And now, with Void. Universes Big Banged and Crushed in instants, just as she opened her eye. Yet, this couldn't possibly be Zendoria. It felt like a bridge between the Below and the Beyond. From this perspective, she could not only notice her existence as someone's character in a fantasy novel. She could also perceive her creator's consciousness. With a gentle nod, she sensed Martin's bitterness and Alibast's inner peace. The two authors stand at odds from one another, struggling to breathe life into an imaginary world that inhabits them, individually. They both suffered immensely, as they grew up and evolved.
One chose to hate everything, from himself outwards. The co-poet elected to love and embrace his challenges, his environment.
Who created her? *Interesting.*

Kitana shifted her attention towards a different dimension. There, Varuna faced his mortal enemy, Marduk. Again, love and hate defy one another. A selfless deity accepted an eternal prison, after a previous war destroyed the Tower of Babel, along with the whole of humanity. A selfish god escaped his jail and killed a Great Entity. Now, Marduk threatens to obliterate all of reality unless Varuna stops him. The angel considered this storyline, while her consciousness noticed existences, stuck in between. Sekhmet and Melpomene both play their individual game. At this point, Kitana can't tell if selfish desires or selfless motivations carry them forward. Nempty, her favourite client, learned to abandon his greed while raising a sex doll into a life of virtue. Now, the two of them form a two-headed curiosity. Seamus Chron found himself thrown in this bigger narrative, after he felt responsible for the death of a teen he used to bully.

Do you see where your position is, in all of that, Kitana Gol of Penglai?

"I left a job that treated me as a slave. I liberated myself, through all four singularities. Am I fated to narrate the third book?" *Destiny, my sweet angel, isn't a recital.*

It's a forward motion that doesn't worry itself with right or wrong, good, or evil. Noesi de Vel exists as a mathematical god; beyond anything we may actually perceive. The illusion entombs consciousness in the seventy-two layers of Sophron, within a twelve-dimensional pluriverse. Only singularities bring order to chaos, and for an amount of time, before that same consciousness realizes how matter, life, thoughts, and void encapsulate everything we know. She saw the serene beaches of Zendoria, pushing the Below and the Beyond toward a state of balance. She witnessed the existence of a multiverse, a myriad of possibilities, creatures of vibrations and arithmetic. She briefly accessed True Reality, then resumed her odyssey.

"Characters trapped in their storyline." she murmured.
"I found my way out of this!" she smiled.

You have, Kitana Gol of Penglai. Just as you now communicate with the ftfth Ocorsur,

"Fifth? As in, there's a reality after the four quadrants?"

Child, the matrix doesn't limit itself with what these books suggest.

"I understand! Noesi de Vel, the metaphysical place of dualities and myriads. True Reality, I know all of that. But whoever you are, isn't it deceiving to think we achieve this form of awakening, only to find ourselves within the walls of more dimensions?"

Is it?

Or is that Ocorsurs reside outside the aquarium you previously called your existence? How many can you count: four, five, seven, more? Before we welcome you in Zendoria, my sweet angel, oh Kitana of Penglai, take a look at the tale you leave behind. When this trilogy gets to an end, only you will act as destiny's envoy. You won't narrate the story's conclusion. you will be its voice. Just as I am the voice you discuss with, in this moment. Tell me: What do you see in the characters' future?

An orb appeared between Kitana's consciousness and the unnamed sound. Alibast manifested himself in Seamus' life. They're about to elaborate a complex strategy to fight Marduk's ascending influence. Sekhmet sent fairies to free Varuna out of the Open Door. Nempty flies with the saviour squad across the Veil. Something else, however, will happen. Indra will awake. Ishtar will find her long-lost love. Marduk will feel threatened, for the first time in the last two books.

"War." the angel whispered. "I see war."

The sphere occupied the entire entourage. When Kitana focused her consciousness on a specific point in this spaceless surrounding, she sensed the presence of a bullet. It had found itself in the middle of someone's brain. That Dreamer's whole Sophron opened to her. William, she realized. Grunt killed him? How? They haven't met! At least, not in the last two iterations of the Chronicles. She directed her soul on a different possibility. There, Seamus and William have their entire lives swapped. Oh! she whispered. The squid hunts Indra's essence.

"It's not just the Sons of Babel!" she shouted, surprised and amazed. "Noesi de Vel was compromised. An outside agent that should never have awakened threatens True Reality. You brought this story in Martin's mind as a last resort. It brings perfect sense! Nexuses vanish, possibilities mix themselves up. You need me! I'm the only character that hasn't directly implicated herself, and yet, I'm powerful enough to impose a difference. This is why you awakened me. This is why I perished and travelled across all four singularities."

She focused her existence deeper, at the orb's core, and her own voice manifested itself. You were dead when I found you, it said. "All right!" Void. "I can do this. I can also summon Barbelo, Archeus and Logos." She abandoned her entire grasp on what once stood as a previous life. "I got this, buddy, hang on!" And she vanished.

Thank you, Kitana. Now, you may move on.

293

Chapter Thirty-Three:
William Marduk and Seamus

The intellectual standoff cooled for a long moment. Seamus found himself at loss of words. Melpomene offered me a very subtle nod and a smile. I grabbed my crystal ball, and I kept it under the table. I checked to make sure the spell remained in motion. I could see Karkadan's shadow examining me. I turned my attention towards Melpomene, and I felt confident about his summoning as well. I looked at Seamus. His powerless gift of connecting with essences seemed useless. Still, I offered him a subtle nod. He observed me with puzzled eyes. I stared at Emerald, in love with her treacherous teacher. Melpomene and me, that's it. Let's do it! My mentor realized I would cast the spell. He signalled me to wait a moment. I breathed, and I breathed, and he breathed as well.

"And how did you meet Ishtar, again?" Marduk asked Seamus.

"My mom. She also gave life to me." the idiot replied.

Marduk summoned another bottle of wine, but he poured only a glass for himself. He sipped it and looked at us. His eyes seemed thirsty. He drank and stared at Seamus. "Your mom? So you don't understand what Ishtar means to my endeavour." He trapped Seamus, I guess, with a trick question. "She's your lover?" Seamus wondered.

"She soiled our culture's dignity when she ran away with Indra." Marduk put his glass on the table.

"You went batshit crazy and destroyed realms because Ishtar biggy-bang-banged a dude from another world?" Marduk had difficulties breathing. He drank his wine and looked at the floor.

"Your lack of education makes you unfit for this encounter." the god growled. "I've trolled enough conservatives on the Interweb, dude! I know my stuff!"

"You've defended your ground?" Marduk interrupted him. "You guarded it like a demon in holy water, holding on to his vice, not wanting to let it go?" Seamus looked at the ceiling and thought for a moment, but nothing came to him.

"How many beasts did you kill?" Seamus asked.

"What are they to you, anyway? Anxiety?" Marduk smiled.

Touchdown! Well, that hit my ground, not sure about Seamus, though. "It's always bigger than demons." He closed his eyes and thought for a moment, then opened his sight and added: "Just like social media." Trolls will spread fear to empower their ego, and their ego will fear a lack of attention. I heard that voice again. Where did it come from? From your favourite bully, William. I'm the narrator! Grab your balls! I held onto my crystal orb. I had only one, but, oh! Melpomene closed his eyes. I observed his globe and I saw Karkadan bathing in an ocean. He opened his attention and transferred the axioms in my orb. I now held the spell. I looked at Seamus. He winked at me. I get this. I shut my sight and I focused on my incantation.

"Emerald grabbed Sekhmet by the shoulders, and they passionately kissed!" Seamus spoke out loud.

"I'm sorry, what?" Emerald inquired. "What?" Seamus asked her back. "What did you just say about me kissing Sekhmet? "I was narrating!" he replied, annoyed. Marduk laughed. "Oh, you were narrating, just now?" "I'm sorry, what?" Seamus inquired, fear dripping down his spine.

You could cut the awkward cheese with your bare hands. Melpomene charged with a lightning bolt straight onto Marduk's palms, destroying an invisible orb before the god could use it. "Now, William!" the Great Muse shouted.

I opened my eyes and summoned: "Karkadan! I invoke you!" I screamed. Nothing happened. What did I do wrong?

"Oh, that's cute!" Marduk laughed.

I'll take it from here, boys! Yes, I also know how to impose my consciousness in narrations. With one hand behind my back, I cast a brand-new crystal orb. I turn my eyes to face the greatest threat in the room: Melpomene. Don't mind me, I'm just projecting matter axioms around you. How do you like this brown and silver cocoon? I wonder: will you come out of it as a butterfly?

Now, Seamus and William, are we doing this the hard way or are we just having fun?

Chapter Thirty-Four:
Battle of Poets

A laptop on the dining room's table. Alibast typed words as fast as he could, while Martin read over his shoulder. I stayed behind, trying not to interfere and commit another mistake. "Why is Marduk narrating William's chapter?" My teacher wondered. "Yeah, ask our third unknown author, dude!" Martin sighed.

"Think fast, Martin, or you have two main characters dead before we finish the second book." Dead? No! "I'm right here, guys!" I objected. I'm not dying. I looked at the Greek student, begging for their approval. They shrugged. I can't die, please.

"Okay! Okay!" Martin shook his head, trying to produce an idea and fast. "Okay, hear me out! Let's assume that Marduk narrates but he's not the third author. That means, we'll dictate his actions. It's still, also, my book, right?"

"It's our book, Martin!"

"Yes, whatever, okay. Let's try this. I speak and you type." Alibast agreed and positioned his fingers on the keyboard. Martin thought for a long moment. He scrutinized his assistant, perhaps expecting inspiration to come out of their presence. He looked at me. My pale face gave way to my panicked inside. Alibast grew impatient: "Are you going to say something?" he asked.
"Don't rush the genius!" Martin opposed him with a solemn voice.
"Take your time but do it fast!" Alibast sighed.

"Hello, Seamus. Welcome to my side of the story. Looking at you as I descend Sekhmet's immense throne brings me a much-anticipated delight." He gestured like a clown while narrating the next chapter. Alibast typed it as fast as he could. Martin continued: "Why would you dislike me? No need to answer, I can see that Ishtar pushed you against me."

"That's Marduk talking?" I asked. The two authors ignored my question. I looked at the Greek student for their approval. They gently nodded.

"Hold it, Martin!" Alibast stopped typing for a moment. "They're going to fight, but Melpomene is trapped in a cocoon. Let's have Sekhmet protect them."

"No, Alibast, that would reveal her true colours too soon.

She doesn't care about Seamus and William. She protects her people and Emerald."

Impatient, Alibast left his seat and signalled Martin to take over. "Why don't you write it yourself? If you're going to ignore my inputs, then, please, be my guest!"

I couldn't help but thinking that, while they argued, my other self faced the most dangerous god in Sophron. What if he dies and I perish here as well? "Guys?" I asked, terrorized. "It's fine, Alibast. You type but listen to me. The second book must end with an unexpected reversal. And a cliffhanger!"

They both reflected on that concept for a moment. I had to impose my presence: "Guys!" I shouted. "I can do the narration! Only inside Alibast's head." I can do this. I looked at the Greek student, and they heard my idea with great interest. I continued:

"If you treat Marduk as one of your characters, but he's showing a will of his own, then let me narrate in his name." I stepped closer to the laptop. Martin and Alibast listened carefully. I concluded: "We can do it, like, my essence, graft itself onto Marduk's, inside your shared possibilities. That's how it works, right? Like Russian dolls. Let's do this for the ultimate book, somewhere down the line or up the ladder. I can do this." The silence that followed felt heavy on my shoulders. They looked at one another and thought about it for a long moment. The Greek student had my back, big smile. Did I just say something golden? "That could work." Alibast assumed. "Until both Marduk and the hypothetical third author realize they've lost control of the novel's narrative." Martin seemed skeptical. "Then, they'll push Seamus away and finish it up."

"By that time, you guys make sure that Melpomene get out of that cocoon!" I insisted. "William succeeds with his spell, and I do something heroic!" I hope I know what I'm doing. "Let's do this." Alibast turned his attention back to his computer. I closed my eyes and cast my essence within his psyche. I've had lots of practice. In the many months I spent around here, I grew more potent with my powers.

Once again, everything went blank. This time, though, I know my way around. I summoned the novel in my hands. I got a flashback! In the previous book, I produced images to help me navigate inside my mom's existence. I can do the same, here. All right let's bring Alibast's dining room. There, I see the table, the couch filled with junk, the sink with a mountain of dirty dishes, and his laptop looks at me. Whatever I will think, from now on, Alibast will type it.

Hello, Seamus. Welcome to my side of the story.

I'm not convinced that this is how Marduk would sound as the narrator. But no time to feel creative. Let's start with this.

299

Chapter Thirty-Five:
The battle gets Serious

Hello, Seamus. Welcome to my side of the story. Looking at you as I descend Sekhmet's immense throne brings me a much-anticipated delight. Why would you dislike me? No need to answer, I can see that Ishtar pushed you against me. You show up with your friends, and you think you can beat me at my own game? Do you understand what my purpose is, here? Of course not! We've never met. We were wrongly introduced as well. Let's accept that I want to conquer all the worlds! And you will join me.

"You are an agent of Void. I will never join you!" I heard you express, while you stared at William. Look at me. I trapped Melpomene in a powerful, brown, and silver cocoon prison! I will do the same with you, even though, as we speak, you close your eyes, and you prepare a heroic spell. I can sense that, but I am too strong for you. Stop it, Seamus. You narrate like a high school English student. We're not publishing that! Rethink your commentary and fast.

Let him continue, Martin! I trust my apprentice.

Did you sigh like an ant? You stand in front of me, your eyes display bravery or foolishness. I bet it's a mix of both, and your mind is focused on a summoning spell that I can't quite make sense of. Are you preparing me a surprise? Is it my birthday? I bet it is.

I haven't had an admirable battle in eons, and only Melpomene happens to present himself as a worthy foe. Sekhmet and I have formed an alliance, did you know? Let's not get into a fight. It would be a shame to offer our readers a quick death to a hero they have, I hope, grew attached to.

I am not an agent of Void. My policies may seem a bit nihilistic to the outside sight, but one doesn't achieve a True State of godliness without leaving a trail of blood and destruction.

"You want to become the ultimate new Dreamer?" You defied me with potent eyes. "We'll stop you, Marduk!"

Is this how Alibast told you to name it? Ultimate Dreamer sounds like a professional wrestler. Alibast hardly respects Entities, even though he was, once, Enlil-Bastat.

"At least he doesn't murder them! He spends his eternity cleaning up after your massacre."

Marduk, the Entity killer, is it? We have such a divisive rhetoric! Painting me in this manner only proves Alibast's agenda. I'll take it from here, now. Go back to wherever your essence is, Seamus. I can do my own voiceover, thank you. When I close my eyes, I project myself next to you.

We both look at this laptop computer. Oh? How cute! Alibast allowed you to reside in his psyche. Here, I'll give you a quick course into properly narrating someone else's tale: Don't overthink it. Stay humbled, and let the poet put words in your mouth. Meanwhile, be true to who you are. In fact, be so true that the author will have no other choice but to bend his own inspiration to accommodate your conscious existence. That said, time to go back to the story:

The reality never manifested as black and white as he wants you to believe, Seamus. Oh, Enlil-Bastat mutates Alibastat. If you present me this as the second book's major reversal, then I'm not impressed.

The Chimera Entity of Lumbini represented a danger to Sophron's safety. I did everyone a favour. You think my goal is to become some sort of omniscient Deity? You put those words in my mouth, but this shows how clueless you are, when it comes to True Reality.

A rogue Entity governed Lumbini, threatening to rebuild the Tower of Babel, in each layer of Sophron. I appeared as the saviour who enforces an end to such tyranny.

"Yes, Marduk! Just so you could impose a breach in the fabric of the pluriverse and use it to push your way closer to your goal: destroying the Dream so you may reshape it as you see fit."

Yes, reforming True Reality. You should employ the proper names for what you talk about. I do not wish to eradicate all Entities. In due time, all will die, but if you join me, Seamus, I can allow you to sit in my council. Wouldn't you want to have an entire world created after you?

Wait, is he going through with the whole "join me" trope?

Yes, Alibast. I doubt Marduk thought about it either.

See? That's my Seamus!

We should leave little space for the Beyond to govern. Noesi de Vel is corrupt, and their ways must be stopped. Look at what your kind has done to Gaia. Greed fills Earth and you kill your own world without my help. What did the great Councils of Zendoria do to prevent it?

302

Nothing. They did nothing! They trust in four Great Ocorsurs and sixty-eight lesser Entities. Make that sixty-seven, now that one of them turned into a simple character-author. If you oppose me, then you act in favour of this corruption. If you join me, we will make existence a true blessing for everyone. I see questions, a great fog of puzzlement, in your mind. Look behind you. I stopped the time, so we may share this little chat, but observe your friends. Ready to sacrifice themselves to protect an ideal they don't even understand. William never considered you a buddy; you dislike him. Emerald will certainly join Sekhmet; therefore she's with me. Side with the winning team.

"The winning team?" You laughed. "Because you know William will not follow you, so that's why you try to convince me. You want to break up the gang, so you may defeat us more easily. Or you expect us to fight one another so we would stop being a thorn in your foot."

Did your girlfriends ever complain about how you overthink everything? If I want you out of my way, I can do that in the blink of an eye. I'm in charge of the narration. I did so long before you managed to properly direct characters into performing your bidding. I see a great potential that would be lost if I were to dispose of you like this. William is as good as dead; do you understand why? Because I will destroy his essence along with the parcel of Indra that he holds inside his soul. Before you find time to summon whatever you intend to take out of your hat, your friends will perish, and I will leave you alive to witness it. You will commit the greatest mistake you have made if you don't join me.

"Do you know who else tried to win my trust? Pirates! And you know what I think right now? Pirates sound way cooler than you. William is my buddy. I have failed him once. I will die before I ever fail him again. Guess what, big guy? This chapter is about to end, and the next narrator doesn't like you very much!"

Fair! You have locked in your choice. Now, I would love you to look in my orb. Do you see an archoid I can easily summon? His name is Humbaba. I have won several tournaments and took him to victory in many battles. At his feet stand thirty of my best warriors. I call them my Squall Squad. Are you ready to dance?

"Start the music!"

He taunted: "start the music?"

He taunted: "start the music," Martin.

What's the plan?

You ask me? We're not even writing that next chapter. It's out of our control.

Chapter Thirty-Seven:
I can't Watch

Long before the fight even began, Nempty left the table and joined the fairy servants, thinking that Sekhmet would protect that part of the room. "I'm still hungry, Daddy!" Lucretia complained. "No, my love. You're not. Right now, we are not hungry, okay?"

We will never know who charged first, but chances are they both rushed onto one another at the same time. Seamus closed his eyes and summoned the shape of a pterodactyl with flaming fangs. Marduk simply used his mancing skills to cast a net big enough to capture the flying dinosaur. Seeing how Seamus learned to master this specific summoning spell proved impressive. He no longer needed to rely on creating limbos.

Did I teach him that? I doubt it. My apprentice is way cleverer than we thought. Marduk kept more tricks in his bag, though. While Seamus battled to free himself of this net, the warlord closed his sight and turned into thousands of arrows thrown at the entangled beast. Emerald subtly summoned the Veil around Seamus. Sekhmet stared her down with reprimanding eyes. Intimidated, the dance student looked away, as the thousands of projectiles bounced against that force field.

Meanwhile, the brown and silver cocoon trembled with millions of tremors. William swiftly focused on his orb. Karkadan remained inside. He can call it! Emerald readied herself to fight, but Sekhmet ordered her to stand still. Marduk commanded his thirty warriors to guard every exit. The fairy attendants stayed put, waiting for Sekhmet to shout an instruction. The panther lady enjoyed watching the massacre.

Thirsty for blood, Seamus summoned a billion life axioms out of his essence. He quickly turned into a griffon and charged at Marduk. The Hound Lord paused patiently. One second before the flying beast neared its target, the Anunnaki lord caressed his sphere and threw a tornado at his opponent. The poor Seamus crashed against a wall, back in his human form and in pain.

The cocoon cracked, but Melpomene remained trapped. More tremors followed. William's orb stayed stuck in his hands. He can't do anything other than summoning his biomech. Even this proves to be on the edge of impossible. Standing up and getting ready to fight, Seamus looked at a fresh and untouched Marduk.

"I can do this all day." he whispered, in his perfect Chris Evans impersonation.

The rookie glancer cast metal around his flesh. He instructed those axioms to evolve until he turned into a gigantic robot. "Let's play a game!" He pointed his sarcasm at Marduk, while two colossal reactors grew out of his shoulders. He flew and charged at the god. Marduk, once again, waited patiently. The cocoon broke in thousands of pieces. Melpomene swiftly cast his orb and crafted a tower of flames, engulfing the god. Seamus crashed into this immense inferno and screamed in agony.

"Stupid! Who taught you to fight?" the warrior muse shouted. William focused on summoning Karkadan. The beast finally responded to his call, looking straight at him. Nervous, William closed his eyes and thought, deep within:

I am really sorry to disturb you. I know you are busy, or something, but I think you and I could connect. You see? I hold the essence of your good friend, Indra. If you could allow me, or him, or us to exist within your archoid parameters! You would do both of us a service.

Not interested, Karkadan returned to its ocean cleansing duty. Melpomene charged with his sword, summoning plasma around the blade. Ten mancers left their post, near exits. They produced millions of darts, flying towards the muse. Melpomene stopped his movement to craft a diamond flesh over him. The projectiles bounced against it and vanished.

"Daddy? Why don't we play with our friends?" Lucretia asked the frog. Annoyed, Nempty shut his eyes and grumpily replied: "They're not playing, my love. We're doing well, over here, okay? Okay? You're okay?" He let out a bit of steam. She stayed quiet

Five dancers from the Squall Squad attacked William, before he could finish his summoning spell. He attempted to contact the biomech, once again. If he crafts a different incantation, he will lose his connection with Karkadan. The performers aren't interested in waiting for whatever comes next. The towering inferno turned into water, then gas. Marduk walked out of the floating cloud and looked straight at Melpomene. "We're doing this?" the god smiled. "Ready when you are." the Great Muse replied.

Emerald ignored her teacher, at this point. She charged to protect William. She brought the Veil around her. She turned into a glowing blue lady, and she faced the five dancers in a fiery combat that mixed martial art with ballet. She knocked one to the floor and evaded another one's punch. Melpomene trapped the remaining three in a steel cage. She now faced only two opponents.

Seamus couldn't heal his wounds. He stayed on the ground, burned to cinders. The performers threw a flying kick at Emerald. She blocked it with the Veil around her fist. The other foe successfully channelled the Veil to attack her from behind. She didn't see that one coming. The blast tossed her against the wall. Nempty observed the action, and he felt a bit overwhelmed. He looked at everyone, tried not to attract too much attention. He grabbed a small box out of his front pocket. He opened it and threw it on the ground. It grew in proportion, but that will necessitate some time.

"Daddy?" Lucretia shouted.

"Keep quiet, girl." He focused on the fight. "What the box do, Daddy?" she asked. Intrigued, two nearby fencers observed them. Long gowns make them look like fancy sorcerers. "It's okay, guys!" Nempty tried to talk his way out of their inquisitive sight. "I dropped it. I'll pick it up."

The frog growled and grabbed his precious object. The possibility wizards returned their attention back to the fight, waiting for Marduk's orders. Nempty looked at Seamus, severely wounded. He faced Lucretia and stared straight in the cat's eyes: "Listen to me, Daughter." he warned her. "The box will turn into a bodyguard or a medic, okay? I always carry a few with me. Those things save lives. I will send one to help our friend, Seamus. You like Seamus, right?"

"Yeah, Daddy."

"You don't want Seamus to get hurt?"

"No, Daddy."

"Then, please, stay quiet, okay?"

"Okay, Daddy."

For the second time in her existence, Lucretia realized that she could lose people she cares about. When it last happened, she faced the concept of danger. Her beloved father perished. Death now roamed near the handsome young man who talked to her, when she haunted the boat. While Emerald courageously battled five dancers, William tried one more attempt at connecting with Karkadan. He summoned the beast's axioms inside the room, but the archoid fought against it.

Again, I am really sorry to try this and insist, but please listen to me.

Karkadan resisted so hard, the link broke. William struggled to keep the channel open. The monster would have none of this! It instantly pushed its existence outside the orb, in an attempt to swallow William! The biomech stopped in midair. The beast looked at Nempty and Lucretia. It recognized that essence! They destroyed so many lives in the ocean! It must kill Nempty!

The ten mancers who opposed Melpomene summoned a gigantic cloud of axioms, getting ready to produce an archoid from it. The Great Muse hastily connected his orb to those pixels and carried them in his direction. Annoyed, Marduk gestured a break in that contact. He cast Humbaba out of the steam.

"See? I wasn't lying. I brought my mount with me." the Hound Lord laughed. "Now, let's stop this waste of time."

His flesh disintegrated while his soul inhabited the gigantic white ape. Most of its skin remained vaporous, but the nearby fencers crafted a bubbly shield to protect it.

Agony petrified Seamus on the spot. Nempty dashed and concealed himself in shadows. Lucretia stayed quiet, just as the frog grabbed his pocket cube and threw it next to the wounded hero. A white spirit emerged and quickly attended to his pain.

"How's it going with your biomech?" Melpomene asked William.

The mancer boy ran away from the rogue kaju. Karkadan stood in the middle of the room and looked at everyone inside. "How am I supposed to project my soul in it?" William asked.

"Oh. for. Aaaargh!" Melpomene couldn't believe it. Marduk successfully incarnated Humbaba. A white-furred

King Kong with metallic appendices and plasma cannons walked across the gigantic place, surveying it for a next target. The unicorn donkey with nine mouths, alone, could defy his presence. But Karkadan didn't aspire to fight Humbaba. Seamus tried to connect his essence with someone else's. He needs to find a grieving or a scared individual. The ghost nurse summoned axioms to repair his burned cells. The unicorn beast spotted Nempty! Millions of creatures died when a purple phoenix attempted to bring this essence back to life. Organisms that Karkadan professed its entire existence to protect!

They are dead because of you! The monster thought. Seamus caught that. *They are not dead, believe me.* The recovering glancer comforted the animal. His burned body can perish, now. A grieving beast needs his soul. *I'm in charge of cleansing oceans on Athanor! I know when life dies!*

Think fast but do it wisely, Seamus: *I know it hurts you, Karkadan. Friends you will never see again. But do you seek vengeance, or do you hope for peace?* The entire room kept quiet, now that two archoids threatened to destroy anyone who would interfere. Humbaba stayed on guard in case he had to fight a rogue biomech to protect his agents and his allies. *I want my friends back in the ocean.* Karkadan confessed. *You will kill my friend for that? Do you think this will bring back the lost lives in your ocean?*

At this point, Seamus realized he had fully left his destroyed body. The artificial nurse kept healing the corpse, but his roaming ghost forgot about it. He could float and narrate all the stories he wished to express, now. Instead, he stayed quiet and discussed with a wounded creature that needed comfort. For the first time in his entire existence, he knew that harmony starts with listening.

He's your friend? The unicorn atrocity inquired. Seamus approached the seven hundred metres high monster and gently caressed its mind. *We are all friends, right now, my friends, your friends. If you love, you can be my friend too. What do you say?*

Love? Karkadan asked, in a narrative manner.

Yes! Do you want to try this with me?

Yes. You can pilot me if you love me.

I will. And I will be gentle, I promise. Wow, is this how it feels like? Consent, love, trust, and I didn't impose my desires. I just went naturally, following the wind. My nature, my soul, floated inside Karkadan like we were destined to become one. Who knew that I would make true love with such a powerful beast?

The gigantic unicorn remained quiet, while Seamus' essence possessed its flesh. The entire process only lasted an instant, but it felt like an eternity. When Seamus opened his eyes, an augmented reality appeared in front of his sight. To his left, health showed a 99% number. To his right, a wide selection of weapons awaited his consciousness to trigger. Other functions evaded his attention. He sensed that he could easily learn to ride that beast.

"You should try this, William! It's like a video game!" Karkadan gleefully shouted.

Chapter Thirty-Eight:
Varuna comforts Katrina

Travelling through the Ether hardly felt the same without Fiona. The boat flew at light speed across the quadrants. Katrina remained deeply wounded. She lost her twin sister. Sure, they came from different families, but they developed a solid bond, while serving the Egyptian Queen. The hippopotamus fighter stood next to her, trying to think of kind words to comfort her:

"I'm really sorry about your friend." he softly let out. "What's your name, warrior?" Katrina asked him. "Khalatet, madam."

"Tomorrow, you'll be with your loved ones, Khalatet. You can tell future generations how you faced a demon lord, you survived, and you brought home a powerful god."

"Yes, madam. Thank you, madam."

"Now, let me cry alone, please." The warrior stayed behind, looking down to avoid crossing Varuna's gaze, along the way. The tall and muscular, blue-skinned god blessed him with a gentle gesture, before standing next to the fairy lady. "Am I welcome to share your personal space?" he asked.

"I really don't care, my lord." she replied. A golden crown floated above his head, like a ghost jewel. He wore fine clothes, a mix of designer garments from Gaia and medieval marvels from Avalon. A blue cape flew on his shoulders, coating a silver armour. A white beard flowed down his jaw and cheeks, with a matching moustache covering his mouth and nose. Deep purple eyes observed his interlocutor. He then stared at the horizon, while Katrina stood there, heartbroken and wounded.

"I feel your grief." the god gently whispered. "You have no idea." she cried.

"Your friend committed the ultimate sacrifice to release me. You should be proud of her."

"Can I be both proud and in pain?"

"Of course."

"Why did she have to do this? And why couldn't you escape on your own?" Varuna reflected on this question before he answered: "According to the path of enlightenment that I, and other entities of my kin, instructed our followers. There exists a truth that stands above our ego. We called it Dharma, but scholars of Sophron refer to it as the forces of Noesi de Vel. Your friend understood how a much greater ordeal affects us beyond her mere presence. And I preferred to remain imprisoned rather than allowing my ego to fall away from Dharma."

"She'll suffer for eternity. I can't live with myself knowing that peace will always evade her."

"Oh, but she will. Deep in her soul, she considers that she did the right thing. She realizes that she sacrificed herself for a greater purpose. Dharma exists in the complexity of this knowledge. She will always find comfort in acquainting Dharma within her."

"She'll suffer for eternity. I can't live with myself knowing that peace will always evade her."

"Oh, but she will. Deep in her soul, she considers that she did the right thing. She realizes that she sacrificed herself for a greater purpose. Dharma exists in the complexity of this knowledge. She will always find comfort in acquainting Dharma within her."

Varuna hugged her with all his love. She cried even more. "A war is coming. I'm sorry, maybe I should have listened to the others who showed up, before you, trying to reason me out of my jail. It would have spared your sister's ordeal, but we can't escape the great conflict that's about to happen. We will need you on the battlefield, Katrina. I will ask Sekhmet to let you join my army.

First, we must inform my own siblings."

"Vishnu?" she wondered.

"We will require the holy Trimurti on our side."

He politely left her alone, while she contemplated both the psychedelic landscape and the idea of the three most powerful cosmic deities to join a war that threatens all of reality, as she knows it. Perhaps even True Reality was at stake, but Katrina has yet to understand what this concept means.

Deep within, she wished that Demonee would participate in the fight. She smiled, thinking that celestial beings could squash him into a pond of throbbing flesh, while she'd rescue her sister away from his control. "There's hope." she whispered. *There's hope.*

Chapter Thirty-Nine:
Erato in Gaia

Four layers down, in the first Barbelo-Archeus quadrant, takes
us over Jeruselah. From the Ether, only shadows of the ancient
cities can be seen. Erato visited it many times, however.
She recalled the bright sun protecting olive trees and luxurious
harvests. Wooden houses remind guests of life in America, during
the years of European settlers. Other continents on Jeruselah
project us back to biblical years. The Great Muse observed the
fleeting landscape and wondered. Is she doing the right thing?
What if Melpomene had a noble reason to take her away from
Seamus Chron and his squad?

"Someone waits for you on Gaia?" Nathan asked her, while
holding two bottles of beer. Why did she fall in love with an
alcoholic? She accepted his offering and pretended to enjoy the
awful taste.

"Maybe." she suggested. He stood next to her and observed the
return of the axiomatic rainbow flow surrounding the ship.
"He's lucky to be with someone as beautiful as you, Jennifer
Blank." he smiled. Disgusted, she turned to face him with a severe
gaze: "Hey! You're married, you know?" She wasn't joking.
He giggled and drank.

"Yeah, but that won't prevent me from stating the obvious."

She blushed and tried to look away. "Just a friend." she finally explained. "His name is Seamus Chron." Nathan laughed while Uncle Vania, only few metres in front, shouted: "Not that idiot!" The muse turned to face the living rifle. "You've met him?" she wondered. Nathan calmed his gun buddy down with a gesture and took over:

"We offered him a ride. He was visiting some sort of monk, or a wise man, in Alibastat."

"We granted one Seamus a lift." Alicia interjected, walking to Erato's side. "I suspect that more possibilities mixed up. Like the inner worlds of two Dreamers, or maybe more, clashed and merged."

The Great Muse reflected on what she just heard: "Possibilities always cross one another, that's nothing new." she explained. Alicia continued: "This is something else, Jennifer, trust me. Ever since you got on board, I've been sensing constant manifestations of deja vu. Usually, when two alternate worlds intersect, one that phenomenon adjusts the course of reality. I noticed that in one universe, I died and I'm haunting this boat. The more I focus my gift on you, and the more I feel that we've met before."

They came from her own inner pluriverse, while this incarnation of Nathan and Alicia never encountered her. But they carried Seamus, so that means they are in sync with the current storyline. "Perhaps it's not Dreamers that clash." Erato suggested. "Maybe True Reality, in itself, is being challenged." Alicia's eyes popped open, intrigued: "You must have reached a high degree of awakening." she concluded. "I've been a fencer for five reincarnations, a glancer for two, and I have yet to understand the concept of True Reality."

Now would be a good time to tell the truth, but Erato stuck to her Jennifer Blank personae. "I must have read a few books, here and there." She escaped the question. She turned her attention back to the Ether. In a few hours, they'll fly over Hades, before approaching Gaia.

"That's not a satisfying answer." Alicia insisted. "I don't know why. And I don't know how, but you're hiding something from us."

The Great Muse sighed. She gathered enough courage to explain the truth, but Nathan interrupted her:

"I think she needs time to relax, come on, Alicia. Let's make love in our cabin."

"Or you can stay here!" Erato blasted out. They both stared at her, awkwardly.

"Or we could, yeah, sure, I guess. Would you like that?" The captain seemed to agree.

"Please." Erato answered and smiled.

Nathan observed his wife, then he turned to his guest: "We'll be in Gaia shortly." he uttered, before grabbing Alicia's hand and walking towards the main cabin. The Great Muse looked at Hades, now appearing underneath. She could easily jump down there and allow destiny to decide of her next incarnation.

"Fudge!" she screamed. "Fudge, fudge, fudge! Fudge! Fudge you, mother of caramel! Peanut butter piece of bread!" She closed her eyes and breathed deeply, then she shrieked one more time, before falling on her knees.

Chapter Forty:
After the Battle

You conquered the most powerful archoid that ever existed, that exists and ever will. Good job, Seamus Chron.

I have no idea what I'm doing, Marduk. But thank you.

I parted from Alibast's mind and woke up in his living room. My other self lost its flesh but managed to project its consciousness into Karkadan. That leaves only this incarnation of me, in this possibility, properly linked to the ongoing storyline. I can't stay here. A war is coming, and I have no idea who will write my alternate essence's actions. I must, at least, be in control of this one. "Guys!" I announced, while looking at the other three occupants of Alibast's dining room. "I'm going back to Montreal. I'll guide Grunt because someone must."

"You haven't finished your training, Seamus!" Alibast warned me. "We'll have to improvise, dude! You have your stuff to work with, and I have mine. If I stay, I'll be in your way. I'll go with whatever I know of my powers, and I'll do you proud, I promise."

"You can use my portal." Martin announced.

"Portal?" I found myself surprised. "You don't travel on boats?" "Authors don't need to." Alibast explained. "Neymlisses

and least awakened entities will journey on those flying vessels, but you showed us you can walk alongside poets."

"And we use portals; it's way more convenient." Martin continued. "I'll stay here and figure things out with Alibast and my student."

"Your student?" the Greek guest smiled. "Yeah, sure, why not?" Martin sighed.

The joy in this non-binary character felt contagious. *Good for you*, I thought to myself, as I returned their excitement.

Meanwhile, Martin summoned his orb. It floated between the two of us. I saw how he channelled axioms from both his soul and the sphere's inner universe. They joined and shaped themselves into some sort of black hole, with a neutron star in its centre. It exploded as a supernova, projecting light all over the room.

"That's a portal?" I asked. No answer came back to me. Only this bright light that filled my entire existence, propagating within my essence. When it dimmed, I found myself inside the smelly sleeping bag.

Was it a dream? Did I hallucinate anything? I could hardly breathe, at this point. I felt strongly disoriented. I couldn't tell truth from lies and what remained in the realm of illusions. Everything I experienced, for the last few days and weeks, months, left a thick imprint onto my soul. It reminded me of how reality shapes itself within us, influenced by outside agents.

I lived five years on Alibastat. I learned my craft; I became a more powerful glancer. I surprised my mentor, with how I could walk alongside a god and voiceover someone else's book, like a creator. Heck, you'll find me as the first amazed by any of this. I can control a narrative! I can do this even better than many influencers, on our own Internet, can achieve that feat.

Now, though, I must choose a side:

On one end of the pluriversal spectrum, we see Og, or selfish desires. This source of universal movements acts on narcissists, egotistic people. On the other end of that same spectrum, we find Om, or selfless abandon. The cosmic force that influences true love, light, peace on Earth.

I could join conspiracists who propagate myths and beliefs, while keeping masses ignorant and distrusting of intellectuals. Or I could side with critical thinkers who stand for truth, in a humbled and scientific manner. To be honest, Alibast was right. Five years on his world allowed me to grow stronger, but that's just one possibility. I still exist, now, as Karkadan's twin soul. I may not feel ready for the war that's coming. I know that I will not join Marduk and his selfish desire to keep humans away from the rebirth of Babel.

I will fight for truth, for love, and for everyone's right to achieve enlightenment, true awakening, and walk alongside gods and goddesses, angels and us: Walkers.

Intermission:

A white room opened itself to Kitana, as her soul quietly incarnated its newest form. It feels as though only days ago she was rotting inside a call centre, answering weird requests from millions of clients, all around Sophron. Now, she's walking among Ocorsurs. Silence, here, is the only constant. We measure each atom by its mirroring cell, and every cell by its own reflection of an impeding void. The angel relinquished her body the same way she once lost her wings: by whatever. She expected to meet the Great Entities, but the room remained empty. How do reflections operate, around here? She wondered. "Egos want to make a universe of themselves, don't they?"

The room inquiered. She froze for a moment. Who's asking? "If you ask, then you shouldn't be here." I'm not. I reveal myself as nothing. "Then, we may have a conversation." A table appeared in front of her soul. A strange map showed a shattered brain. A bullet stood in its centre. Various factions surrounded a light that attempted to retrieve the ammunition out of the decaying psyche. Kitana observed the map and realized that it represented William's mind. The projectile suggested a murder, while the accepted facts indicated a self-inflicted wound.

Did I awaken on this level of existence to discuss this human's source of death?

"Life and death mean nothing, on our level of enlightenment. We are here to discuss if it should be self inflicted or not." Kitana walked away from the table. Her only connection to this conundrum comes in the form of a deceased android. An innocent soul reincarnated into a zombie cat's head.

"Can I get back on that ship?" she asked Void.

We're looking for a new captain.

"A captain for what?"

The ship isn't going anywhere. Will you be our captain?

Yes, I guess.

Chapter Forty-One:
Seamus goes back home

I woke up with a terrible headache. The sleeping bag covered me, and I could sense its dampness, smell the stench of old pee. It felt as though I had just come out of a long coma. I can hardly remember the dreams I made. Everything in my mind is blank! Here and there, I picture this flying boat, travelling across flashing lights. A fluffy purple phoenix smiling at me. A warrior muse, a two-headed captain, a frog and a zombie cat on his shoulder. It seemed real, though. I think I was there, like, yesterday. I recall the beautiful city of Arcana, on Tir na n'Og and also, hold on, Alibastat? The deserted plane of consciousness. I existed in both places at the same time. I remember the battle with Marduk. He destroyed us. William! We fought together. I need to step out of this garbage bag. A strong feeling of deja vu suggested that, at this point, both possibilities converged.

That means, my consciousness projects a reality in this flesh, and in Karkadan's. If I focused, just for one moment, I could open my eyes and witness my biomech's main board. I can see the energy percentage, now at 86%, and all the computer's perks and gadgets. In that possibility, I stayed in Arcana. Nempty parted ways with us, heading for his boat.

"I will drop you on Gaia." he told Emerald and William. "I'll find my intellectually impaired bird brain friend, and we'll go to Nirvana. We'll get help, there."

"Which Gaia will you take me to?" William asked. "Because last I heard, my other self is in a coma, over there. Under which Dreamer is this occurring?"

"That's beyond my control, William." Nempty explained, while we walked closer to the city's main gate. "Regardless, you know that if you cross your consciousness under a same possibility, only one of you will remain." My friend looked up, attracting Karkadan's attention. I stared down to meet his gaze. "Take Emerald there. Have her speak to Alexandra and Victoria. Go to Nirvana if you must, but Karkadan, Melpomene and I will return to Athanor."

"William." Karkadan seemed to object to this plan. I have no idea if my soul guided these words out of the archoid's mouth or if his essence did it, or, perhaps, at this point we merged into one gestalt. But he continued: "This whole piloting a biomech thing is new to me. I don't want this to become a burden. Maybe I should go to Alibastat and see if my mentor can teach me a trick or two."

"It's okay, Seamus. We shouldn't part, from now on. I must train my spell craft as well. We can do this together, buddy. What do you say, Melpomene? Can you educate us?"

The Great Muse looked at him, then me, and thought for a long moment: "That can be arranged." he agreed.

The shadow of a war gathers upon us. Nobody feels prepared, and yet we've all seen how Marduk grew in power, with this unknown creator seemingly in support of his agenda. I allowed my consciousness to part from that scene and return to the smelly shelter, surrounding my human flesh.

I unzipped the stinky envelope and peeked outside. The blinding light of a zenith sun hit me hard. I required some time to properly open my eyes. There, I saw trees. I could sense the noise of downtown Montreal. A nearby construction site, traffic.
"Are you okay, man?" I heard that voice before. Oh yeah!
"I'm fine, Grunt, what happened?" When I finally found the strength to step out of this dumpster, he stood there. A tall young adult. I recognized his dark complexion, but something different grew on him. I can't say what exactly.

"You slept for three days, man. I fed you like a baby. I thought I lost you."

"Three days?" I inquired.

"Yeah, man! You came back from the strip club, and you were drunk, and you were high. I took a hit, right there, and I watched you get inside the sleeping bag. You just woke out of it. I was, like, whoa! No way, man! Don't die on me! So, I took care of you. And guess what! I've been sober for three days too."

"Congratulations!"

"I know! Hey! I don't even feel in need or anything. It's, like, while I took care of you, I forgot about getting high. I feel fine! You saved me too, man." How can we possibly kick an addiction to crack cocaine and heroin out in three days? That doesn't make sense at all. Either he will relapse, or he's taking me for a ride.

"Do you still have the gun?" I asked him. He nodded and showed it to me.

"I also have your friend's cell phone. You want it back?"

I accepted. Something didn't feel right, however.
My recollection of the last three days, on some magical boat, felt like a dream. My consciousness, still, remembers it as though it was real.

"What about Alejandro and the drug dealers?" I had to ask.

"I don't know, man, well, yeah! An ambulance took their

bodies. I talked to the police, and check this out: I got into their heads. I swear! I was, like, in their mind, and stuff. I cleared both our names. I made them think that they all shot themselves, and Alejandro finished the job on himself. And, like, they'll never find the gun that did it, but it's okay. Move on with their lives."
He laughed so loudly my ears hurt.

"You entered the police officers' mind?" I asked. "Dude! I got into the whole city's mind! Everyone who knew Alejandro, or those other freaks, they now all think they did it among themselves. We're free! Trust me, I know."

Oh! How can his glancing gift be this powerful? Wasn't I the one who initiated them? Unless his abilities always reached this magnitude. I simply awakened a dormant titan. Time to leave this trashy spot. I sat on a bench, seeing just how soiled and smelly I became. "I need clothes and a bath. Let's go back to my friend's place."

Grunt agreed and we both stood up to face a new destiny. The Gamelin Garden seemed deserted, while we walked towards Sainte-Catherine Boulevard. After three days spent in some alternate universe, this existence hardly felt real, anymore. Everything's a dream of a dream. When I look at my African Canadian friend, all I can see is the squid creature that inhabits his true form. Two glancers about to take over the world! Just living like two homeless hopeless young adults, but that's a detail.

Maybe we can crash at my parents' place and convince them to shelter us for a few days. Until we figure out what happened. The bright sunlight shone above our head, with a clear sky that felt as real as my numbed legs. We strolled like two drunkards, and the bystanders looked at us with disdain. We would link our gifts to certain ghosts, gather their entire existence, compare our findings in an instant, and laugh so loud, the victims of our spiritual voyeurism would swiftly walk away.

"You don't need drugs to use your power, buddy." I would tell him. "It was always in you."

"I don't know, friend, I really don't."

We continued this game for a few more street corners, sometimes haunting lonely souls. Other times pushing our way into extroverted minds. We would pause and stand against a wall, and then we would venture into different existences until we would find two strangers who branch their essence from mutual acquaintances. Whoever achieved that feat first would shout that connection's name out loud, and if the two targets turned at the same time, Grunt and I would high-five.

The game stopped when we encountered this enigmatic student. Her soul felt bizarre, like she was born only few days ago. Blonde and red hair flowed against her shoulders, like oceans of grace. I'm bad with poetry, sorry. She wore braces and glasses like an adult attempting to look childish. She was HOT!

"Seamus Chron?" she inquired. She then turned to face my friend. "And you're Grunt, but you look different."

Grunt stayed there, in silence. I took the stand: "Yeah! Who's asking?"

"You can call me Jennifer. Blank. Yeah, call me Jennifer Blank." She seemed to reflect and process her next words very carefully. "I." she uttered, and then she pondered more. "I need you."

Grunt laughed out loud. I followed him and I answered: "Sorry, but we're not horny and we don't have any money."

"That's not what I said! I need to." it was hard for her to come up with the right phrasing. "I need to be with you. I mean, like, hi! I'm a love goddess, and I need you! No! Fudge! Caramel, fudge! You know what I mean!"

She sounded distressed. I attempted to link my essence to hers, but a deeper layer seemed to prevent me from properly attach myself. It felt almost like when I tried to connect my soul to Melpomene's. Yeah! The barrier shared the same texture. She's a goddess? And she knows our identities?

"All right." I let out. "Jennifer Blank, or whatever your real name is. What do you want?"

She smiled. In that moment of pure emotion, I sensed something true. Her soul exists as way more powerful than the body that it currently incarnates. It's as though her essence tried to push that corpse up to its limits, creating schisms in its brain, forcing her down a difficult path. On one end, her synapses develop a severe case of Tourette syndrome. On the other, her benevolent nature keeps her from expressing vulgar and violent words. I guess we'll hear a lot of sundae recipes if we stay by her side.

"There's a war coming. It will affect all of Sophron, and it could destroy, Fudge! Fudge! Mother raisin bran of Fudge! True Reality."

"Again with that war?" Grunt shouted. He looked at me. He knows? Sure, I just battled Marduk, but how come he knows?

"Marduk!" She interrupted my thoughts. Frightened, I looked at her.

"What about him?" I asked.

"He's corrupting the politics of Sophron. I guess he wants to attack Noesi de Vel or Zendoria."

"What's that?" Grunt let out this inquisitive question, but I felt that the squid in him knew what Noesi de Vel was.

"The mystical place where the forces that conduct everything come from." I answered. Well, that's what Alibast instructed me. Well, that's all I could remember from what he taught me.

"It's more than. Candy Coated Bicycle!" Jennifer shouted. "That, but yeah!" Her Tourette syndrome symptoms sound weird.

"All right." I informed her. "Let's go fight Marduk. Where's your boat?"

She stood there, silent. "What boat? Where's your boat?" she panicked. "Do you see one?" I asked back. "No, but you had one when I dreamed of you two!" I growled for a moment. "There you go. We're heading to my friend's place, you coming?"

Jennifer remained silent for the duration of the walk. I can't connect my gift to her essence, and I doubt Grunt would be able to as well. Hopefully, meeting with Alexandra will provide more answers as to whom her friend, Emerald, really is. And optimistically, we'll find her soon.

Journey into the Hourglass: Twenty-Four

I looked at the mess we created. How did we allow characters to awake and take control of our narrative? And if a third, and enigmatic, author stepped in, who allowed for this alien consciousness to manifest within our hermetic minds? I can't help but wonder if our readers have access to information that evades our thoughts. If this is the case, then by the end of the third and final book, this invading author will have taken control of our creation. Heck, what if the usurper is already drafting words out of my mouth? As in, right now! This madness must have started right from the first book. That means, we're already becoming characters, falling even deeper in this bidimensional reality. Maybe we've already lost that game. That means, we've been characters in those books from the start. And that outsider allowed us to think we were writing the same novels that you, reader, are uncovering?

How can we win a battle that we've lost right from the beginning? Because, obviously, that invasive creator plays in Marduk's camp. Could it be Sekhmet? She showed Marduk a direct path to take control of his own narrative. But she doesn't intend for him to win that easily, right? Speaking of enlightenment, I should, at least, make sure Indra properly awakens. We need Varuna, him, and Ishtar to fight back. I'll go back to my laptop and make sure this happens.

Chapter Forty-Two:
Indra Awakens

Doctor Gerald Lemieux is a renowned neurosurgeon. A McGill graduate with high marks, he embarked in a long career that brought him several recognitions and accolades. His genius and talent didn't prepare him for this frightening experience, however. An ambulance carried this eighteen-year-old fragile-looking male to the emergency room. Witnesses told the police they saw him jump, and no weapon had been found on the scene. Still, a bullet wound entered his mouth, leaving the projectile firmly lodged in the boy's brain. Against all odds, the victim breathed. The CHUM hospital requested his expertise to operate and find a way to save his life. Sitting behind his desk, five X-rays look back at him, from a wide computer screen. A brain scan confirmed the ammunition's presence, and he knew he had to act swiftly. A delicate procedure lasted over twenty-seven hours. Three teams relayed one another, with Lemieux acting as the top supervisor. Sadly, the intervention left poor William Francoeur in a vegetative state.

Every day, before his shift even started, Lemieux visited this miraculous boy who should have died long ago. His bald head overseeing a long white robe made him look wise and quiet. Often, he would visit his bedside, expecting to come across a friend or a relative. but the poor fellow remained in total solitude, at the back of a poorly lit room. How come nobody showed up? An entire week went by. Investigators found that William moved from Toronto to Montreal, two years ago. He had no relative. In fact, he signed his current lease while he finished High School. The landlord must have taken pity on him, or maybe William paid good money to live in this tiny one bedroom. The boy offered no credit check and no reference, but he afforded twice the amount requested to rent a vermin-infested dump.

The police report mentions a self-inflicted attempt, but the surgeon who operated and saved his life disagrees. There's a suspect out there. Still, it is a miracle. By law, they must keep him wired with constant oxygen, maintaining him alive until someone who holds the right authority may require that we let him go. A month after the successful operation, the room remained deserted. The monotonous beeps and the series of light gave way to the survivor's presence. Doctor Lemieux couldn't help but feeling sorry for the lad. He stood there, at the end of every shift, wondering if or not William could wake up from this coma. He knew him from the ID cards he carried, but he had no idea what his voice sounded like.

"How is he, doctor?" A gentle female voice asked, one day. "Alive. I can't guarantee what his future will be like." Lemieux replied.

A tall goth girl entered the room. Her sombre looks formed a clear harmony with soft and enigmatic features. She stood next to the bed, barely holding up her grief.

"Are you family? The specialist inquired.

"A friend. He didn't have many. My name is Alexandra Sicard."

"Fair enough. I was wondering if anyone would show up. I will leave you two alone. He'll make it, don't worry. I have seen worse conditions coming back from this vegetable state."

"Thank you, doctor, for everything."

He smiled and accepted the sweet appraisals. After he left, Alexandra kneeled by the bed. She grabbed William's left hand and sobbed.

"Hey, buddy..." she sighed, "how have you been?"

Silence. The machines cut through the long and boring hour like a razor blade. Every beep made her shed a tear. Another beep made her gasp. More beeps pushed her anxiety out of her flesh.

"Why did you do this?" she asked, not really expecting an answer. "You know that Seamus feels bad about what happened. Right? He feels like he's responsible, in some manner. I wish I could reason with him. Heck, I wish I could have reasoned with you before you jumped. Why is it so difficult?"

She held his hand tight, probably hoping it would bring him back. Her fingers fidgeted around his, creating a soft friction that cemented her desire to speak to him.

"I hope you can hear this, hey? William, you were never alone, you know that? There are people who care about you. And, well, hold on. There's someone who wishes to speak to you."

"Is he okay?" Another voice asked. A gentle lady's tone pierced through the taciturn room. "Do you think it's okay if I come in?"

Alexandra left his bedside and looked down. She nodded quietly. A small Jamaican-Italian girl stepped inside. Light brought so much care and affection through her eyes, an immediate feeling coming out of a stranger would spell *she's a saint*. Denim shorts exposed her thighs, while a white shirt with a picture of the Sumerian goddess Inanna further lit her caring presence.

"He's breathing." Alexandra replied. The young mixed beauty stood at the other side. She put her left hand on his forehead and closed her eyes. "What are you doing?" the other lady asked. A fainted blue light surrounded her palm. She breathed deeply, as though to achieve a form of inner balance, and she whispered: "Are you there, my prince?"

Ishtar? A warm feeling carried this name across the room. "Yes, my love." Emerald answered. *I missed you so much. How did I end up here?* "Oh, sunshine, you died! Marduk killed you, thousands of Earth years ago. It happened right after the Gilgamesh events took place. We thought he carried a Final Vanishing over his last blow, but here you are. You survived."

Alexandra observed her friend with wonder in her yes. "What are you saying?" she asked. Emerald kept quiet. *I could never have finally vanished without a last kiss from your lips. I stayed alive! I fought so that my consciousness remains of this world. Because I love you! You kept me in your soul, oh, Ishtar. Your adoration saved me.* "Oh, my love, if only you knew." *How is my old friend?* "Imprisoned. The Great Councils confined Varuna and Marduk in limbos. Your mentor accepted his fate, but my Nibiru brother escaped. He killed a Great Entity, destroyed a whole layer, and plans on annihilating Sophron. We need you more than ever, but why did you let your host kill himself?"

334

My host didn't. He was murdered.

"Murdered?" Emerald panicked.

Alexandra realized that her friend spiritually connected with William. "What is he saying?" she wondered.
Emerald shushed her.

Noesi de Vel has been compromised. I fear Zendoria also got corrupt. I believe this explains why I couldn't fully awake there and why I couldn't fully Finally Vanish. I floated in between every singularity, until my essence could carry itself across the Ether. I had to send parcels of my soul into living organisms, in Gaia, hoping that someone Jinds me. One of those awakened as a single letter in a wasp's DNA. Another in this poor boy's psyche.

"Can you wake him up?" Emerald asked.

His body is heavily damaged, but his essence exists in an author's mind. I doubt I can manifest mine any further. Did you Jind me there?

"Oh, love! She did! Emerald found his essence but lost it to Marduk. This body appears to be the very last refuge you get."

What about the wasp?

"Nempty gave it to Sekhmet."

Then you must protect this body at all costs. My consciousness remains weak. William lost his completely. I assume Void had the last laugh.

Emerald quietly nodded and turned to Alexandra. "Don't be afraid." she warned. The dancer closed her eyes and channelled the Veil. Blue light emanated from her fingertips. Her friend's eyes grew twice their size. She moved away, shocked. The gleam soon covered the entire room, as though a sun had penetrated this enclosed space. Emerald opened her sight and looked at the bed. A slight smile seemed to draw itself on the patient.

335

Are you a dancer, now?

"Emerald is. When Sekhmet taught her these skills, she merged my essence to hers. That's how I survived my Final Vanishing."

My old stalker saving your existence? I'm impressed.

Alexandra couldn't stop the flow of questions populating her mind. "What's a Final Vanishing? Who are you talking to?" She turned to observe her guy friend. His breathing remained in sync with the complex machinery that keeps him alive. "Are you talking to William? And what's this blue light? Where did it come from?"

"Meeting you was no accident." Emerald answered. "I carried a goddess' soul at the back of my psyche for ages."

Alexandra walked towards a fully recovered William and couldn't believe her eyes. "He died, they said." she uttered.

"In most possibilities, he did. In this one, he survived, barely. A god's essence existed in his soul, and now that same god is taking over."

An awkward silence prompted Alexandra to approach William's vegetative state. "You mean, he can hear me?" Emerald stood next to her. "Ask him a question."

"Hey, boy!" the timid student let out.
"Do you know who I am?"

Time took its time. Alexandra played with his hair and asked, again: "Can you hear me?" More time flew until a voice entered her mind: *Don't be afraid. Of course, I know who you are! But I'm not who you think I am.*

She panicked and ran in reverse until her back hit the wall. "Who said that?" she shouted. Emerald walked towards her. "Alex, you're about to find yourself in a very weird life. Please, trust me. I'll protect you."

"I heard William's voice in my head."

"Yes, Alex. Yes, you did."

Alexandra couldn't stop looking at the vegetable. "But. William is still alive, right? Can your, like, can your blue light magic do something to bring him back?"

"That's not how it works, Alex." Emerald sighed. "I'm so sorry."

Silence took over the dimly lit room. Alexandra grabbed her friend's hand. "What will happen, now?" she asked. Emerald put a hand on her bestie's shoulder. "This force field will shelter him from glancers. Now, we find someone who can revive him. Someone to heal his body's wounds. We pray that Marduk doesn't get to him first."

"And where can we find this healer?" Alex wondered.

Emerald hugged her friend as though she intended to grant her a bit of courage. She stood away and warned her once more: "What if I told you that I can take you on board a flying boat?" she smiled. Alex laughed. "What are you talking about?"

"Let's pay Victoria a visit. I'll need the two of you. It's going to be quite the girls' night out."

Alexandra followed her friend, unsure if any of this sounded like a good idea. They exited the room, on their way out of the hospital. She couldn't stop thinking about Seamus, and how weird he appeared, only few days ago. He knew about Emerald, like he had been reading her mind, or something. Is he also a magician? So many questions haunted her, and no answer made any sense. Why is he living like a homeless person?

She looked at her good friend, but Emerald seemed like a stranger. Alex never expected that she would be reunited with her like this. What's with talking about gods and force fields?

Chapter Forty-Three:
The Squared Circle

A purple sunset covered Cognitia's skies, like a peaceful gown quieting a heated day. The Emily's Eyes flew over indigo clouds, undisturbed by the flock of manticore-eagles on the hunt. A high mast crowned over Uncle Vania, while the living rifle appeared asleep. Nunc left the ship, and Nathan stood with his beer, crew of one, poor single captain. The wind battled the ship's immense veil, caressing his long hair along the way. He defied the horizon with a fierce look and drank straight from a black bottle.

"You miss her?" Alicia asked. The vessel projected her ghostly silhouette, right behind him. Stars formed in her translucent robe.

"Don't give me that jealous lecture, Alicia." he replied. "Of course, I miss her."

The phantasm looked down, as she walked next to him. "You should have begged her not to return to Hydaspes." she sighed. "She doesn't know how great a lover she left behind."

He turned to face her and frowned. "See? That's exactly what I told you not to do. You always pity yourself because I chose her over you. And you decided to haunt my boat, anyway."

"How can I possibly compete with the Great Muse of romance? And how could you prefer someone who was way above your league?"

"You have no idea how my affection works. If you want to leave my ship, nobody holds you."

Every word he threw out pierced her heart with darkness. "Cruelty doesn't suit you, Nathan." she rebuked. He drank his beer and threw the empty bottle off his deck. He walked away, leaving the poor ghost to herself.

"It's not like I fear solitude, anyway." he replied. Alicia focused on her breathing and shouted:

"You're heading to the Great Library of Alter-Cognitia! You're looking for her." The wind supported a long moment of silence. "I'm going for another beer if that's what you ask." he explained. "But yeah! Jamieson left, so that his Nunc persona may pursue his quest in that other possibility. We have nothing holding us with any other passenger, and, yes, we will find Erato. You have no say in that decision."

"I want to win you back, my love." she cried. Nathan slapped Uncle Vania's base, waking him up.

"Vania! Tell Lady Alicia Light, here, what we do to unwanted guests!"

"Oh, leave me out of your sobbing stories, asshat!" the grumpy rifle shouted. She let a tear out, as she turned her attention towards the obnoxious weapon. Vania winked at her. Feeling unwelcomed, Alicia vanished. The lonely captain sighed, relieved. He pinched his forehead, working hard to focus his thoughts onto one single word: beer. He let go and walked towards his main cabin.

"Why do you hate her so much?" Vania asked him.
"Don't patronize me, Uncle." he answered.

"Ass, she's a true gem! You treat her like shit." Growling on his way in, Nathan aggressively opened his fridge's door and grabbed another beer. He snapped the bottle's cap off and drank. He then took some time to recollect his thoughts. His favourite rifle didn't wait too long to scold him some more.

"You're so full of yourself!" Uncle shouted.

"Do you remember Jennifer Blank?" Nathan wondered.

The rifle smiled. "The hitchhiker chick? Like, yeah. Why?"

"I dreamed about her." Alicia reappeared. She gently approached him. "It wasn't a dream." she explained. Intrigued, Nathan turned to face her. "I felt it too. My fencing gift opened a window to nearby possibilities, and she was with us. I was still alive, in that storyline. She was here, in a different dimension. Our doubles left her on Gaia, and I believe they stayed there."

"We picked her up on Hades, right?" Nathan questioned. Alicia pondered for a moment and answered: "I have no idea, to be honest. The visions remain a blur, but it feels as though we got her out of a violent place." Nathan sighed: "Yeah, that's what I think too. If possibilities clashed, that means we could see her again?" "We will, my love. Yes, we will see her very soon." The Emily's Eyes landed in the centre of the Squared Circle continent. If the entire first quadrant of Archeus-Logos were an entire existential being, Squared Circle would be its heart and its soul. A turquoise sky finds itself covered with blue clouds and a purple sunset. Nathan entered his cabin to retrieve some useful items: a Hawaiian shirt, a baseball cap, and a smartphone. While grabbing the slim, rectangular black box, he stumbled onto a pair of quantum goggles. Those cool-looking sunglasses allow the user to visualize nearby possibilities. They're often employed when an uncertain future open, and a right course of action is required.

Intrigued, Nathan grabbed them. He looked at the Blue Jays' logo on the hat he held in his other hand. He put the glasses on and looked at the hat once again. To his left, he could see a different logo: Lonesome Crone's Finest. It appears likely that he could have purchased that one, at some point, since he's the most faithful customer of this franchise, getting his beer and a good time in their establishments, all over Sophron.

The possibility to his right, however, unsettled him: Ultra Police? The cap appeared like a formal attire of this famous group of fascist law enforcers. Under which Dreamer a smuggler could, in his right mind, join the enemy? What disturbed him most was acknowledging that this possible outcome sits right next to his current incarnation. If he encounters his double in this timeline, then which one will continue the story of his existence? Nathan left the goggles behind and put on his Blue Jays cap, as he exited his cabin.

Chapter Forty-Four:
Quid, Nunc and Lucretia

The Barracuda flew across Nirvana like a sympathetic ship following a gentle breeze. When we think of this pacifist world, we either hear a song or we consider a peaceful state of mind. With seven drops of matter to eleven drops of void, however, this layer of Sophron connects better with Hell. We consider those domains as paradoxes, or oasis, as they stand out from the usual existences that comprise their quadrant. The bridge appeared at peace, with the treefolks cleaning the floor, Jonathan supervising the staff and Nempty facing a starry night. His frog head kept both eyes closed, while Lucretia's zombie-cat head obsessively kissed his cheek. "Daddy?" she kept asking. "Daddy!" she repeated. "Daddy!" she insisted. He opened his eyes, trying to forget that his beloved daughter now shares his body. "What, princess?" she smiled, amused. "Can I have ice cream?"

"I can't digest lactose, my love, you know that."

"It's not for you. It's for me, okay? I will digest it like a big girl, I promise."

"That's not how our shared body works."

"But I want ice cream!"

Nempty sighed and walked towards the nearest cabin. Jonathan observed his master with pity in his android eyes. "You're going to be a good girl, after that? Daddy must think about the future." She kissed him and smiled. The frog entered the cabin and reluctantly walked next to a small fridge. He opened the door, grabbed a floating keyboard, and typed a few words. A food printer layered cold vanilla ice cream on a bowl, then added fudge and caramel. Nempty grabbed the dessert and a nearby spoon.

Delighted, Lucretia used the frog's hands to grab the treat and eat it with great appetite. Before they could exit the room, Nunc swiftly entered. "There you are!" the giant bird shouted. "Which personae are you?" Nempty asked, in a bored and wounded tone. "Jamieson. We need to talk." The frig agreed and returned to the fridge to summon a bottle of wine.

"I've talked to your intellectually challenged personae so often; it feels weird hearing intelligible words from you."

"I'm a fencer, you know that. I work with the Ether, I craft spells using possibilities. Each one of them exist in their own quantic reality. Sorry you were stuck with Nunc, while I had important matter to attend to in a parallel dimension. I'm back, now. Where are the others?"

"Ask your big dummy other self. Emerald and William are back on Gaia. Seamus died but his soul inhabits Karkadan.

Melpomene and his pet moth left to, I have no idea, it's just us."

Lucretia ordered the frog's hands to open the fridge and prepare more ice cream. Meanwhile, the fluffy phoenix poured two glasses of wine and pondered for a long moment.

"While in that alternate possibility, I visited the Lonesome Crone, on Tir na n'Og. I met an old friend, Nathan Lord."

"The pirate?"

"His fame precedes himself. Yes, the smuggler. Seamus Chron's alternate self joined us. We left him on Alibastat, where he practises his gift with the current guardian."

Nempty gagged a bit, with the lactose pushing gastric refluxes up his throat. Nunc frowned, intrigued, while Lucretia binged down her ice cream.

"He's not that bad." Nunc comforted him. "Regardless, do you know who protects Alibastat, since Marduk killed the previous guardian?"

The frog attempted a sip of his wine, but another reflux prevented it. Nunc continued his story: "Alibast Page, of Avalon. He's a powerful sophroner, I was told."

Nempty fiercely turned to face Lucretia before she prepared a new bowl of ice cream. "You had enough!" he shouted. The zombie-cat offered large, cute, and pitiful eyes. The frog could see stars twinkling around her pupils. "Okay, last one!" He drank his wine while she prepared herself another sundae.

"Are we to trust this Alibast?" Nempty asked his friend. "I doubt it." Nunc answered. "He's affiliated with no

House, he never took side, and all of a sudden he trains a rookie Walker that has no idea what's going on since the fall of Babel."

"But Nathan trusts him?" A stronger reflux interrupted Nempty. "And you trust Nathan?" he burped.

"If a war storms out, Nempty, I won't even trust you with anything. I'll probably only trust myself."

"Don't trust your intellectually impaired alter ego, though. Look what he did to me."

"My bad. I apologize, and I owe you big."

"Yeah." Nempty gagged more and more, getting reflux so intense, he regurgitated a furball. He calmed down while Lucreatia finished her third ice cream. He exited the cabin, followed by his flurry friend.

"There's only one player in this war that I trust with my own existence." the captain explained.

He walked past Jonathan and the working treefolks. "If there's a war coming, we'll need to stand by his side."

"Are you sure this ally of yours is in Nirvana?" Nunc inquired.

"He's jailed in the Open Door. We're in Nirvana to get help, so we can break him free."

"Varuna?" The big bird's eyes grew very large. His mouth sustained both surprise and disbelief. Nempty didn't reply. "No, Quid, no, please. No! If Marduk sees Varuna free, it's not a war we're getting, it's an Apocalypse!"

"I'm not keeping you, buddy."

Nempty walked towards the edge of his ship, observing the tall buildings that taunted the horizon. Nunc stood next to him, pleading him, begging him to listen to reason:

"I wasn't around during the Babel Wars." the phoenix explained. "I don't exactly know what happened, and how True Reality found itself shaken by this epic battle. Heck, I still don't quite understand what True Reality stands for, but I was taught to protect it. We can't have Varuna free. We can't!" Nempty drank his wine while Lucretia licked his ear, then his cheek.

345

"I was there." the merchant explained. "I was known as Charron, under certain cultures. My job was simple. When a sleeper ceased to exist in a certain form, I would take their soul to Hades. If there was a chance for reincarnation into an awakened conscience, I would take them to Duat."

Nunc listened with great attention, while Lucretia kissed her daddy repeatedly.

"Some gods and goddesses thought that sleepers should have access to awakening in their lifetime. They built the Tower of Babel to allow them that opportunity. Varuna approved of this, and I stood behind them." Nostalgia haunted the frog's eyes.

"Marduk did not approve. He believed that sleepers should never have access to enlightenment. They should remain closer to animals, and farther from gods. He convinced Enki, Enlil, and most ancient deities of Nibiru to obfuscate knowledge, empower brutal authority, keep humans of Earth stupid but self-centred and hungry for control of their kin."

The frog finished his glass of wine and threw the empty receptacle off the boat.

"The Hound Lord of Nibiru attacked the Tower of Babel, thinking that allowing enlightenment to humans was an abomination. Varuna fought back to protect it."

He couldn't continue with his story. A strong emotion strangled him.

"And what did you do?" Nunc asked him.

"I don't want to talk about it." Nempty replied.

346

"If you want me to trust you, Quid, you'd better open your soul right now. What did you do when Marduk attacked Babel?"

Nempty thought about it for a long moment and finally confessed: "I flew away, like a coward." He shut his eyes. Lucretia ordered the frog's arms to hug himself.

"Quit it." he whispered.

She took the arms and hands down.

Too much information. Nunc sighed. "But listen, Nunc." Nempty tried to retake the attention. "My name is Jamieson. I sent Nunc on Nibiru." Nempty shook his head. "You can do that?" he asked. "I can do a lot more. I cover twenty-seven possibilities, with twelve personalities. I'm the boss, it's okay, that's not what I'm here to discuss. Who, on Nirvana, do you think will accept to join us in a war? The Buddhas are pacifists."

"Not this one, believe me."

The horizon welcomed the Barracuda. The tall buildings soon became the new surroundings, leaving the previous horizon far behind. A beige atmosphere with a brownish soil rapidly took over the entire sight. And while the fairy-boat lost itself in this scenery, Nempty could hear his beloved daughter whisper: "Can I have more ice cream, Daddy?"

Epilogue:

A singularity occurs when every axiom within a certain domain reflects itself in a state of harmony. The moment one such pixel attempts a glimpse into what could be, we find ourselves in a duality. Consciousness is what it is until a world suggests otherwise. Reality is a pluriverse, several layers of self-reflecting attempts at making sense of a greater chaos. In and by itself, reality has no name. In these books, and according to our fabricated mythology, we chose to call it Sophron.

Truth is what it is, outside the scope of any wanderer. Just as pixels attempt to regain a semblance of harmony, until a reformed singularity takes over, sleepers attempt to awake within a community that carries a beacon of truth. True Light comes from within. Never trust anyone but the god that stands up inside a soul questing for right over wrong and says: *Just be kind to others and to yourself.* Regardless of the colour, texture, and story behind that voice. *Isn't this what the legend of Babel was about?* Kitana asked her new entourage.

The chamber remained darkened and bright, yet every presence felt itself as it should be. Walls phrased themselves in shades and light, around a table that hosted a map. On it, several Houses prepared themselves for war:

House Sekhmet, of Tir na n'Og, gathered resources to protect the fairy world. House Demonee, of the Open Door, amused itself with a fairy slave. House Marduk remained stationed among the fair folks, ready to attack anything, anyone, anywhere.

Do you think those Houses will rage the next great war? Archeus asked. *No, of course.* Kitana answered. She observed the floating orb and thought out loud: *How come House Marduk is ready to attack but Marduk is nowhere to be found?* Logos stood forward and caressed the crystal ball: *He may have found himself closer to True Reality.* They acknowledged. *Noesi de Vel?* Kitana wondered.

That's the door to True Reality. Void answered. *I doubt the Hound Lord made it there.* Kitana turned a page and looked at the next map. Lesser players positioned themselves:

Indra awakened in a human body, stuck in a vegetative state. Varuna travelled with fairies, back to Tir na n'Og. *I doubt the Airavat Houses have regained a momentum in this confrontation.* Kitana remarked. *Don't underestimate wisdom.* Logos replied.

"They know that nobody will ever know truth from a novel or a movie!" Barbelo finally shouted. "Truth is a right here, right now, at this point, this moment, everything else, before, after, and as told by someone else is an illusion. Do you really think Varuna wanted to leave his prison for some fantasy novel that hoped to become a Hollywood film? Come on!"

Well, Indra fought hard enough to awake in that novel. Archeus argued. "Indra fought to be with Ishtar, no matter what! She chose Martin's imagination to make it happen."

"Maybe the issue is with Martin, then." Kitana wondered. The Matter Ocorsur smiled: "His True Reality surrounds the writing of that trilogy." Kitana considered her next options. She turned another page and observed the next map: Martin and Alibast argued in the Avalon poet's cottage. Seamus left the scene, but the Greek student remained.

"I think I'll try to influence Martin's mind." Kitana concluded. *We're with Alibast.* Archeus confessed. *Who said True Reality was going to be a child's game?* Kitana concluded. She focused on Martin's scene. There stood an unnamed character that came from nowhere. Kitana couldn't tell if these personae held a gender, a face, an image, even. By the novel's words, it read: *the student.*

"Who came up with that character?" she asked. *Sekhmet did, in the previous novel.* "They're stuck with the author of their fate. That's cute." *We think the student comes from Plato's teaching. But we think someone teaches the concept of love as an egotistic influence.* Make them hate others in the name of love for their own kin. "Am I supposed to reincarnate in a story like that?" Noesi de Vel never projected reincarnations.

Just make sure you love like it should be. "Makes sense. Yeah, I'll incarnate my consciousness in those words." *But, Kitana, the battle isn't under this Dreamer. Love doesn't dream.*

Find us. *Don't trust your inner feelings!* "Tell that to the other angel. I'm going there." *Are you sure?* "Look. two idiot authors thought they could direct gods into their storyline."

She smiled and abandoned herself in that incarnation. She offered this very last scene her very real consciousness.

Post-Epilogue:

They left the laptop by itself, on the dining room's table. The four inhabitants looked around, afraid, concerned, uncertain. All sorts of junk loitered the place, but a window showed a clean and well-catered nature. Alibast had just left his seat, scared to even revisit the words that his subconscious wrote. Martin looked at the Greek student, then Alibast. At this point, it didn't matter if he, or not, created them. Maybe Alibast created Martin. The blonde bearded Gaia man shook his head:

"What are we doing now?" he asked. "We wait." Alibast answered. The phrase: The book won't write itself felt wrong, since everybody remains aware that the Chronicles of Sophron, at least in this reality, do write itself.

"If we wait too long, we might as well have that unknown author gets all the glory!" Martin grumpily pointed out.

"You don't get it, Martin." Alibast lectured him, while daring a look at his laptop computer. "Did you expect that Greek student to visit you? No. Someone else wrote that part, and that wasn't me. On the other hand, I wrote myself in our book, precisely to become Seamus Chron's mentor. Between you and me, who do you think loses control over his creation?"

Pressure haunted the entire room. Perhaps if Martin hadn't been typing drunk, for so many years, he would have been more in tune with the truth that lives within. Did he allow a much higher entity to puppet him?

"Whatever, Alibast." he sighed. "We still have a third book to write, and if we don't work together, we're done and over with."

The poet of Avalon read through Martin's copy of Book Two: The Saviour Squad. He stumbled over one element that left him lost in questions.

"What are we doing with that Kitana character?" he asked. "I'm not following." Martin replied. "She was a plot device in the first novel. We don't need her in the second book."

He approached Alibast and picked up his copy. He read, turned a few pages, and read some more. Martin could hardly conceal his surprise: "She experienced a higher form of awakening?"

"It would appear so. At least, according to this copy, and many others from our shared possibilities."

"We should rewrite that, Alibast. She's not even supposed to have left her call centre."

They both approached the laptop, frightened at the idea of seeing a minor character becoming powerful, just not under their watch. The student observed and took a few mental notes. Alibast browsed through his manuscript and stopped short of deleting anything.

"There's one major problem." he warned his co-author. "If we delete her part, we cause an irreparable harm to our continuity."

"She pretty much imposed herself into the entire saga?" Martin couldn't believe it.

"She did exactly that." Alibast closed his laptop and sighed.

352

He left the table, lost in despair, allowing Martin to take his place. All those elements that wrote themselves while Martin and Alibast were busy arguing with one another left little to no room for appropriate rewrites. If they removed anything written by that mysterious third author, they would find themselves back to an initial stage, and forced to argue, once again. Also, that third author will likely keep imposing themselves, regardless of how often these two will axe a few chapters and commit to a new rewrite.

"We have no choice." Martin concluded. "We have to write with that third author in mind."

Alibast agreed. He walked towards the fridge and grabbed two beers. He offered one to his friend, but Martin politely declined.

Post-Mortem-Epilogue:

Did they just discuss the possibility of deleting my part?

… … "Hello?" ....

I'm not going back there! No! I'm with you, now. I'm not going back to the call centre! What should I do?

"..."

… …

All right! I'll do this. If you look over there, you'll see the student gnawing down a piece of broccoli, while Martin sits behind Alibast's computer. Inspiration evaporates as he attempts to complete this Book Number Two, for The Chronicles of Sophron.

...? Yes, the student closes their eyes and dives into a trance. "Have you thought about a name for Book number three?" they asked the author. "I'm not there yet." Martin replied. The student returned to their meal, reflecting on what to say next. They know that every possibility coexists at once, just like photons in a quantum mechanic's experiment. One possibility becomes reality when the conscience directs itself in a speciJic direction, making a lucid, or not, decision.

"What if you called it Clash of Singularities?" the student asked. Martin laughed: "That's a stupid title!"

"...!"

I'm getting there. The student put the vegetable away and walked next to their friends. "Are you ready to know my name?" they asked. Martin sighed. "Yeah, sure, whatever." he nonchalantly let out.

Alibast seemed more intrigued by this revelation. "I know who you are." the poet of Avalon confessed. Two wings sprouted out of the guest's back, spreading far and wide in the immense room.

"Kitana." the student announced. "My name is Kitana."

Alibast looked at her and wondered: "So, you're the mysterious third author?"

Puzzled, Kitana looked at Seamus, then she looked at Martin. Her consciousness had left the Ocorsurs' reality. She now stood next to the two authors. She smiled and, finally, she addressed her interrogation towards Alibast: "Third author, what, why, what? I can be some sort of author, now? A creator or narrator? I can literally write your book for you? That's so cool!"

She sat behind the laptop with a strong confidence that spelled: *when do I start?* Martin grabbed a beer and binged it down, seriously worried.

End of Book Two.

Next Book: Clash of Singularities.

www.ingramcontent.com/pod-product-compliance
Lightning Source LLC
Chambersburg PA
CBHW072316020726
47501CB00002B/528